VICKY closed her eyes against the faint glow of the lamp, wishing only to feel. Her body was responding instinctively, moving beneath his hands, his heated mouth. And she, who had never known a man, wanted him with overpowering intensity. She waited, her heart pounding, as he lifted himself above her.

Afterward she lay still, tears dampening her face, too touched by the beauty of what she had experienced to speak. But Michael left the bed and said with jarring self-reproach, "Vicky, I ought to be horsewhipped." His voice was strangled. "After all I told you. All my promises! Vicky, please forgive me."

"Michael, there's nothing to forgive," she whispered. They were married. This was their right.

"It'll never happen again. I swear. Vicky, you won't walk out on me? You'll come with me to Eden?"

"I'll go with you to Eden," she whispered. But the painful truth smote her. Tonight was an accident. Michael would not allow it to happen again. He was determined to maintain their marriage of convenience.

But in her eyes, she was forever Michael's wife. They had just observed their wedding night.

EDEN

by Julie Ellis

A FAWCETT CREST BOOK

Fawcett Publications, Inc., Greenwich, Connecticut

For Irving

EDEN

THIS BOOK CONTAINS THE COMPLETE TEXT OF THE
ORIGINAL HARDCOVER EDITION.

A Fawcett Crest Book reprinted by arrangement
with Simon and Schuster

Copyright © 1975 by Julie Ellis

Printed in the United States of America

First printing: April 1976

1   2   3   4   5   6   7   8   9   10

1

Victoria Wickersham pushed open the door of the dilapidated low clapboard house and hurried out into the early dusk that swathed the narrow, crooked street. She hated living on Pig Alley. She had hated it at first sight, six months ago, even before she knew this was the most depraved, the most dangerous part of all New York. Even the Metropolitans—the police—traveled about Five Points in pairs. This was the haunt of prostitutes, thieves, and murderers.

Her long dark hair falling softly about her shoulders, her blue eyes wary, Victoria walked as swiftly as her burden would permit. The bag of corn, the pot for cooking, the grate and charcoal precariously balanced in her arms, she hurried along a street deep with filth, lined by ancient tenements and clapboard houses like the one in which she lived with Aunt Mollie and her husband, Jim, and their five stair-step children. A grayness smacking of winter replaced the springlike quality of the afternoon. She tried to adjust her inadequate shawl about her small, slight frame to provide more comfort against the raw chill.

She adroitly dodged a foul-smelling drunk; ignored an obscene invitation; averted her eyes as a girl, no older than she, transacted business with a sailor just off a ship. The girl would take him into her one-room flat, where her mother and sisters would also bring their customers. She saw a young sailor with scrubbed good looks and an air of innocence go down into a cellar, where "lodging houses" without windows, infested with vermin, provided bunks for ten cents a night.

In minutes she would be away from the Points and on crowded Broadway, where she would stand on the corner and sell corn to the passers-by on this late-April evening of 1857.

How much longer could she stay with Aunt Mollie? Her delicately boned face was taut with distress. Aunt Mollie knew, didn't she, how Uncle Jim kept making opportunities to touch her, to pinch her? That was why Aunt Mollie, so warm and smiling on Vicky's arrival, now was sullen. Not that she could blame her, Vicky thought conscientiously. Aunt Mollie just did not know how to handle Uncle Jim.

Too many days, before Uncle Jim went off to work, there were the awful fights—Aunt Mollie shrieking at him, Uncle Jim hitting her. She felt sick, remembering her aunt's swollen eyes, the bruises, sometimes a bleeding mouth. Afterward he would drag her into the kitchen, and Vicky would prod the children out into the filthy street— lest her young cousins hear the raucous sounds of passion from the other room. Jim would emerge smug and grinning; Mollie, sheepishly happy. Until the next battle. And too often, Vicky realized unhappily, she was responsible for Aunt Mollie's bursts of temper.

The nightmare had begun two and a half years ago, when both Papa and Edward, only eighteen then, had gone off to the Crimean War, leaving Vicky, motherless since the age of two, in the care of an elderly spinster in the small English village where they had lived. Then Edward had died in Balaklava in late October, 1845, and Papa at Sevastopol scarcely eleven months later. For a year Vicky had stayed on in the village on money Papa had saved for such an emergency, but there was not much, since the Army always paid its men poorly. Soldiers were supposed to feel honored to serve the Queen— though what honor there was in dying in foreign mud Vicky did not know.

When the money that Papa had left her was gone, she

had written to Aunt Mollie, who invited her to come and
live with them in New York. Mollie had written little
about the family except that Uncle Jim was a musician.
She had not said that he played the piano in a brothel.

In any case, there was no other relative except Aunt
Mollie, who had faithfully sent them a Christmas letter
each year. Papa's folks didn't count. They had disinher-
ited him when he married Mama, who had sung in a
London music hall.

On her thirteenth birthday Papa had taken her down to
London for the first time. Her eyes grew wistful in recall.
They had spent the day walking about the city, and in the
evening they had gone to Covent Garden to hear Giulia
Grisi sing in Bellini's *I Puritani*. How excited she had
been! And then, while they had waited for the curtain to
rise on the opera she had turned to Papa, to see his face
pale and distraught. She had followed his gaze to a woman—austere, haughty, beautifully gowned in white satin
—who sat in one of the fine boxes close to the stage. The
woman finally had turned her eyes in their direction,
stared hard, then determinedly swung away from them,
her head high in rejection, her mouth pursed grimly.

"Your grandmother, Vicky," Papa said bitterly. "We
won't bother to stop by to pay our respects." He had
never talked about her again.

Vicky walked swiftly, impatient to put Five Points behind her. She passed the dozen or more grogshops that
sold liquor to whoever had the money to pay, including
children. In a little while the back rooms of those shops
would become "dance houses," catering to sailors, prostitutes, and thieves. On the corners were the groceries, the
secondhand stores, the pawnbrokers, and the Five Points
Mission, which fought a losing battle to rescue the more
depraved from a life of degradation.

At eighteen she was old to be selling corn. This was
usually the job for the younger girls. But Vicky refused to
work in the grogshops of the Points, or in the sailors'
dives along the East River or on Water Street. Aunt Mollie urged her to try for a job as a maid in one of the fine

brownstones where so many of the newly arrived Irish girls found jobs, but Vicky had a headstrong independence that made her balk at becoming a domestic. Selling corn on her specific corner of Broadway—hers by the law of the street—she was her own boss. Nobody could order her about: Do this, do that—"quickly, girl!"

Uncle Jim, tilting the bottle too much, talked ugly to her.

"Think you're too good to be workin' like other girls. Always givin' yourself airs! You even talk funny." He had mimicked her English accent. "You'll end up on the streets, wait and see. Just like the others!"

She had grown up in a tiny house in a cathedral town along the river, not much more than an hour's ride from London, with a small, neat patch of lawn; a gate; and pretty oriel windows. It had always been well kept up, and the motherless little girl had been a pet of just about everyone in the village. It had been a wrench for Vicky to leave.

After the dreadful forty days' passage in a ship that she feared would never sail out of the winter storms, the passengers had landed in New York, huddled uneasily in rough sheds where they were held in quarantine. She recalled those terrifying first hours when rumors were rampant among the landing passengers, and her shoulders tensed as she walked. The old man with the persistent cough, some warned, had a contagious disease and none of them would be permitted to stay. The feverish child carried cholera—or measles—or dread smallpox.

But the rumors had proved false. They were all declared noncontagious. Those who were able-bodied and had funds—Vicky's voice had trembled when she reported seven dollars in cash—were welcomed to America. Aunt Mollie and two of the oldest children had been there to meet her. Her family, she thought with relief. She was not alone.

She had struggled valiantly not to reveal her shock when Aunt Mollie took her to the two small rooms where now eight must live. The woman had been so proud of the old piano, dragged home from Uncle Jim's place of work, that usurped too much space in the kitchen, and so delighted to discover that Vicky played.

"Musical, like your mama!" Aunt Mollie had chortled.

Eagerly Vicky had waited to hear more about her mother. Papa had spoken only of her beauty, her sweetness, the fact that he had loved her very much. From Aunt Mollie she had learned that the two sisters had been born on a farm in Sussex and had gone to London in search of a more exciting life. Mama had sung in a music hall. Aunt Mollie had come to New York where several years later she had met and married Jim.

A smile touched Vicky's face as she arrived at Broadway, the city suddenly coming alive for her. Each night she marveled at the torrent of people who moved up and down the broad avenue, at the incessant parade of omnibuses, hackney coaches, and private carriages. The brilliant gaslights from the restaurants, bars, and hotels bathed Broadway with an impudent glare. It would still be this way when she left at near-dawn. For a few hours, here, she could forget about Five Points.

On Broadway she traveled up to Barclay Street, settled herself at her usual stand at the corner of the Astor House Hotel, and concentrated on what had to be done before she could sell her wares. Hordes of people charged past her, everybody seemingly in a hurry. How far from the little house where she had lived with Papa and Edward! But around her neck on a ribbon she wore two mementos of that other life. Always she wore them: the cameo Papa had given her on her fourteenth birthday, and the medal awarded to Papa after his death by Queen Victoria.

"Here's your nice hot corn," she called out brightly in her cultured English that so antagonized Uncle Jim. "Smoking hot, just from the pot!" Polite to customers and lookers alike.

Dusk blended speedily into night. Vicky felt herself touched by the convivial mood of the throngs hurrying past, all seemingly pleasure bent. For a little while she thrust from her mind the realization that somehow she must find a way out of the impossibly small flat at Five Points.

"Here's your nice corn, smoking hot, just from the pot—" She stopped dead in astonishment, staring at the little girl threading her way dangerously across Broadway. Melinda, the oldest of Aunt Mollie's children, eager-eyed but fearful of the traffic, was pushing her way determinedly toward Vicky.

"Melinda, what are you doing here?" At eleven, Melinda, unlike many children of the Points, was not allowed beyond the front of her house. "Your mother will kill you for running off this way! You could be knocked down by a carriage!"

"Mama sent me!" Melinda was breathlessly pleased. "You gotta go home. She said for me to stay and sell your corn. Mama says it's easy." But Melinda was simultaneously adventurous and scared. "You just tell me what to say."

"Why do I have to go home?" Alarm tugged at her. "Melinda, what's the matter?"

"It's Papa. Mama says he had too many slugs of Irish whiskey. He's out cold, and Mama says you gotta come straight home."

"But Melinda, what can I do?" Vicky was bewildered.

"You have to go over to the parlor house and play the piano instead of Papa. So he won't lose his job. Hurry, Vicky! Oh, first tell me what I gotta say."

Vicky stared at Melinda in disbelief. Aunt Mollie could not expect her to go over to that awful place and play the piano. Her mind rebelled, even while she coached Melinda in the brief necessities and gave her a handful of pennies for change.

"Just sell your corn, Melinda," Vicky exhorted. "Don't go anywhere with anybody. And when it's all sold, you go straight home."

"All right," Melinda promised, impatient to be on her own.

Vicky waited for an opportunity to cross the street.

The white-topped omnibuses, elegant carriages, the "bulletin wagons"—their sides displaying advertisements—charged in a solid phalanx down the gaslit street, making crossing hazardous.

She walked quickly down Worth Street. How could she play the piano in that awful place? Yet she knew she must. Uncle Jim's job depended on it. Too often he was out of work, and Aunt Mollie left the children to go out and do whatever work she was able to find.

Vicky stared unhappily at a pair of vagrant children, half naked despite the cold of the evening, who were poking around in the gutters with the pigs. She had read in the *Herald* that there were ten thousand such children in New York. Nothing in her life in England had prepared her for the Points, though she had read about such conditions in London, she conceded conscientiously, in books by Charles Dickens.

"Here," she called quickly, feeling sick at the plight of the children. "Here—" She gave each of the children a penny, and they dashed off, chortling with satisfaction.

Aunt Mollie opened the door at her approach.

"You have to go over right away." Her voice was strident. "He's dead to the world."

"Aunt Mollie, I don't play well enough," she protested.

"They won't know the difference," Aunt Mollie said impatiently. "Just make it loud, and they'll be satisfied. Vicky, you've got to do it," she said urgently. "He's supposed to be there in five minutes."

Vicky's eyes clung to her aunt's. Of course she had to do it. Aunt Mollie had taken her in when there was nobody else. It didn't matter what it was like living here. What counted was that Aunt Mollie had opened her heart and home to her when that was desperately needed.

"I'll go right away," she whispered, fighting panic.

"Here—" Aunt Mollie reached for a sheaf of music that sat on the piano. "Take this with you." She hesitated, her eyes worried. "If anybody acts funny, you just tell 'em you're taking your uncle's place because he's sick tonight, you hear?"

"Yes, ma'am."

Firmly clutching the sheets of music, Vicky left the house, running over Aunt Mollie's instructions in her mind. Go to Greene Street. To the house with the lamp out front that had NINA written on it.

Aunt Mollie liked to call the place where Uncle Jim worked a "parlor house," but the real "parlor houses" were farther uptown. Though the surroundings were more luxurious, their offerings were the same.

With distaste Vicky approached Greene Street—the most notorious thoroughfare in the United States: she had heard a pair of tourists refer to it that way while they waited for her to serve them corn. They had gone there with a sense of adventure.

Deserted by day, Greene Street came alive by night, with sight-seers and prospective clients jostling one another as they walked. Her teeth clenched tightly in rejection, she walked past the shabby, low-stooped, red-bricked houses, conscious of the gas lamps, in bowls of tinted glass, that blazed over each front door. Most of them were red, though here and there a less blatant one glowed. The names on the lamps had been painted in clear white. LIZZIE. THE GEM. FLORA. Endless names, with the same procession of girls inside.

Vicky's heart hammered as she read the name on the lamp before which she stood. NINA. This was where Uncle Jim worked. Holding the sheet music conspicuously before her, she opened the door and went inside.

She entered a small parlor with a piano set between a pair of windows draped in a heavy green damask, designed to seclude the clientele in the room from the sight-seers who thronged outside. Atop the piano a cluster of pink paper roses emerged from a tall red vase. Small purple sofas flanked three walls. A mirror hung above each sofa. An imitation Oriental rug, worn bare, centered the room. The gaslight was muted.

A woman in a garish yellow frock, her face heavily painted, moved toward Vicky and inspected her with a sharp eye. Vicky cringed.

"My uncle Jim sent me," she stammered, her face hot.

"He's sick, but I can play the piano." She took a deep breath, gearing herself for this nightmarish evening. "Are you Miss Nina?"

"Yeah." The woman grinned. "I'm Nina. So Jim sent you to tickle the ivories." She seemed indecisive. Truantly, Vicky hoped she would be banished—and immediately felt guilty. She was here to help Aunt Mollie. "Somethin' tells me it's a bad idea, but I got no choice. Sit down at the piano and start playin'. You play till I tell you it's time to go home." Nina laughed boisterously, shaking her head, and beckoned to a tall blonde in a red satin wrapper who came down the hall. "Hey, look what Jim sent over!"

Vicky sat down at the piano and began to play, ignoring the action about her. She played the music Uncle Jim played. All the new songs. "Ellen Bayne." "Jeanie with the Light-Brown Hair." "There's Music in the Air." "Willie, We Have Missed You." Compulsively she kept her eyes fastened to the music sheets, trying to avoid looking at the parade of men who strolled into the parlor to transact their business. But their voices ricocheted in the small room. Some were boisterous; others sounded sullen and defiant.

Nina called the girls two at a time, then promptly sent them off with their clients. Vicky tried not to hear what was being said—the bizarre requests by some of the patrons. Now and then a man caused a commotion, demanding a show of several girls before he made a choice. And everything was conducted against a continuous background of raucous piano music.

The door to the street opened and closed with disconcerting frequency, Nina greeting each new arrival with raw high spirits. Now there were two patrons waiting. The pair spoke in soft, liquid tones and were younger than the others, self-conscious. They called each other Alex and Fred. Listening to them subconsciously, Vicky learned that they went to a school in a town called Princeton. Both seemed uncomfortable in these surroundings. Alex talked about a city called New Orleans.

"We'll go to Charlie Pfaff's for supper," Fred said importantly. "Maybe we'll see Ada Clare there. She's Southern, you know. I wonder if she comes from Virginia."

"Her name is Jane McElheny," Alex said with amusement. "And she's a distant cousin of my grandmother's on my mother's side."

"In New York," Fred shot back, "her name is Ada Clare, and she's 'the queen of Bohemia.' " What was Bohemia? wondered Vicky.

The door opened to admit a fresh client: stocky, swaggering, aggressive. Nina strode forward to greet him with a boisterous welcome. Obviously a regular.

'Don't talk to me about Flora and Lulu," he objected when Nina indicated these two would shortly be available. "You got better girls to offer than them two. I want somebody with class." He pounded on a wall to emphasize his demand. "I pay my money, I get what I want!"

"Now, why don't you set down, Clem, and in a few minutes—" Suddenly Nina's voice trailed off.

"Well, looks like we got somethin' new around this joint," he said, walking clumsily toward the piano. "Pretty baby," he said with relish, leaning over Vicky.

She flinched before his whiskey breath, the weight of his heavy, hairy hand on her shoulder. Eyes stormy, her heart thumping, she stubbornly continued to play.

"Come on, baby," Clem coaxed. "Talk to ol' Clem."

"Go away," she whispered, suddenly aware of a newcomer in the room.

"Alex!" The handsome, dark-haired young man's voice was deep, authoritative. "What the devil are you doing here?"

"What my note said," Alex told him with nervous defiance. "What the hell, Michael?"

"Clem," Nina was wheedling. "Come over here and—"

"Hey, baby, let's go somewhere," Clem coaxed Vicky drunkenly. "Let's me and you go back into one of them li'l rooms."

"Go away!" Vicky pulled her hands away from the piano keys. "Don't touch me!" Fury pushed out fear. *"Go away."*

"Clem, don't you start up," Nina pleaded nervously. "She ain't one of my girls—" But Clem's heavy hands were at Vicky's shoulders. "She's Jim's niece, fillin' in for him tonight—"

"You heard the young lady," the newcomer intervened quietly. "Take your hands off her, Sir."

Clem straightened up and stared contemptuously at the tall new arrival.

"Well, listen to the college boy," he taunted, moving forward menacingly.

"Michael!" Alex yelled a warning, but Michael was already swaying from the impact of the man's fist. "Michael, get back!" Alex charged forward with Fred at his heels, both prepared to defend Michael.

Just as Alex swung at Clem, two men swaggered down the stairs, followed by the girls.

"Get them swells!" one of the men on the stairs yelled. "Give 'em hell!"

In an instant the room was a melee of flailing fists. The girls and Nina shrieked, pulling futilely at the embattled clients. Vicky cowered against the piano, her eyes fastened on her would-be rescuer.

"Stop it!" Nina cried. "You'll bring the Metropolitans down on me! They'll close me up!" Enraged, she searched the room until her eyes closed in on Vicky. "You did this to me, you little bitch!" She charged toward Vicky as Clem collapsed to the floor.

"That's enough of that!" Michael thrust out an arm authoritatively to keep Nina from Vicky. "Stop it!"

"Get her out of here before the old woman kills her," the girl in the red satin wrapper warned nervously while two other girls tried to placate Nina. She pointed toward the hall. "You can go out the back."

"Come on," Michael ordered, an arm about Vicky, pulling her beyond Nina's reach. "Alex, Fred—let's get out of here!"

Blindly obeying his instructions, his arm at her waist, Vicky hurried through the narrow corridor with Michael.

Michael reached for the door, then prodded her out

into the moonless night as they heard the shrill whistles of police already in the parlor. "Let's go down here."

They moved swiftly down the ominously dark alley, a cat meowing in reproach as Vicky inadvertently collided with it. Conscious of running feet behind them, she guessed they would be Michael's friends.

Breathless, they emerged from the alley into a gaslit street. For the first time Vicky had a clear view of the two younger men. The tall, slight one was obviously Michael's brother. The resemblance was striking: the same dark eyes; slightly full, sensuous mouth; clean-cut features. The second man was shorter, heavier, with lighter hair.

"I'll find a carriage and take you home," Michael reassured Vicky quickly.

"I can't go home," Vicky whispered. "Not ever. I've lost my uncle his job." Terror welled within her.

"How could he send you into a place like that?" Michael's eyes were angry.

"He's my aunt's husband," Vicky explained. No blood between them, she was saying with defiance. "I had to go there when she asked me."

"What about your parents?" Michael asked.

"My mother died when I was two. My father was an officer in the British Army." She saw Michael's start of surprise. "He died in Sevastopol. My aunt took me in."

"Where will you go?" His eyes were compassionate, concerned.

"I'll have to think." She struggled for an air of dignity. "I'll be all right," she said unconvincingly.

"We'll have supper and talk about it," Michael said firmly. "Alex, find a carriage for us."

2

Michael leaned back in the carriage, somberly inspecting his brother and Alex's roommate. The girl decorously seated beside him displayed none of the hysterics he would have expected, and for that he was grateful. Impossible to talk frankly with Alex now. The confrontation between them that Alex—registered at the same hotel as he—had been dodging all day must be delayed until morning.

He had not even seen Alex until he had followed up that note under his door, when he had come back from the disturbing conference with Mr. Fleming at the bank. *"We're at Nina's on Greene Street,"* Alex had written. *"See you later."* Playing the prodigal son.

Damn, why did Mama have to insist on his rushing to New York in person after that defiant letter from Alex? The fact that he was a practicing attorney now didn't save him from being Mama's errand boy. What the devil did Alex and his roommate mean, walking out on college and setting themselves up at the St. Nicholas Hotel? Fred's father was one of the richest planters in Virginia. Money-rich—not land- and slave-rich like the Edens.

Alex must go back to Princeton. He had to understand that Mama would not send him another cent unless he was working toward his degree. The school would take them back, he reasoned. Alex and Fred were not the first pair who had taken off for rich living in New York.

He stirred restlessly, remembering his second errand for his mother. If he were not in New York, he would not be forced to meet Ava's ship when it docked sometime this week. It was ten years since Ava had left Eden. Why did she have to return? How could he live under the same roof with her again? He felt sick with distaste.

Mama could not know how shaken he had been this morning when he opened her hastily written letter. *"Michael, I've just heard from your Aunt Ava. She's coming home. Please remain in New York a few days longer until her ship arrives, so she can travel home with you."*

Nothing would be the same at Eden once Ava returned to the house. He remembered her temper tantrums, her imperious demands. And he remembered what he had sworn to forget.

"How are Mama and Papa?" Alex asked, interrupting Michael's thoughts. The boy was furious because his brother had followed them to Nina's, and only Vicky's presence was preventing a row. But twenty-year-old students on Greene Street were asking for trouble, Michael reminded himself, and Alex had suffered his share already.

"Mama and Papa are fine."

"Papa still threatening to try again for the Legislature?" Alex demanded with ironic humor.

"He's finally decided the wheelchair would be a hindrance," Michael said, pretending indulgence. But Alex knew. They lived in a divided house at Eden. To Papa the rest of the world, including his family, was The Enemy. It had been that way since his stroke eight years ago.

"I think about him sometimes," Alex said with deceptive gentleness. "The way some Sundays he would summon every one of the slaves—all three hundred of them—and sit there on the gallery, spouting about how much he was doing for them and what they owed him. How lazy and useless they were. For two hours they had to sit there and listen. And you and I with them."

"That's Papa's way," Michael said sharply. What the

devil was the matter with Alex, talking this way in front of strangers?

"Papa should have been a Hapsburg. Maybe then he would have been happy."

"Ava's coming home," Michael told him abruptly, and Alex stared at him.

"What's bringing the Princess back from Europe?" Alex mocked. Did he remember Ava? Michael wondered. He must. He had been ten when she left, on that two-month visit to cousins in London that had extended into ten years. The visit that Papa had engineered.

"Money," Michael said brusquely. "Mama wrote and told her times were tight. Ava was out of funds."

Did Mama ever feel guilty that Eden had been left to her, entailed to him and Alex, cutting out Ava completely? Of course, it had been understood that Mama would take care of her "little sister," Michael acknowledged. But Ava's demands were colossal.

"Everything's so cold and ugly up here," Alex said somberly. "I'll bet it's different back home." A glint of naked hunger sparked in his eyes. It was a shame Mama had insisted on keeping Alex away at school these past three years, when he had been so reluctant to go.

"Everything's green already," Michael acknowledged slowly. "The fruit trees all in bloom." But when Alex came home for the summer, Mama would drag him off to Baton Rouge—not trusting him at Eden. "Hilda had another litter of pups," Michael continued. "Eight this time." Hilda had been Alex's dog before he was shuttled off to that fancy private school in Virginia, where he had met Fred. "Hilda's the prettiest English setter anybody ever laid eyes on," Michael said to Vicky. "Do you like setters?"

Vicky smiled with dazzling brilliance.

"I love all dogs." Suddenly he visualized her strolling across the front lawns at Eden with the dogs at her heels. "Back home we usually had a dog or two." Her eyes were haunted again.

"How long have you been in New York?" What place was there for a girl like this, alone in a city of half a million people?

"For six months." Her voice was low.

He remembered the accounts in the newspapers about the Crimean War. An ugly, painful business.

"Do you miss England?" Alex asked with the gentleness that their father considered unmanly—though Alex, Michael thought, had well established his manliness.

"I miss my father and my brother. I miss our little house." Her voice was a poignant whisper.

He had noticed right away that she was English. Speaking voices invariably made an impression on him. Hers was lovely—the accent charming, unmistakably labeling her a lady. How horrendous for her to play the piano in a Greene Street brothel!

The carriage was pulling up before the huge white marble St. Nicholas Hotel. The New York hotels astonished Michael. Cities within cities, with their billiard rooms, hair salons, telegraph offices, newspaper and cigar stands, libraries, and florists. And the dining rooms open from 6 A.M. to 3 A.M.

Why was Vicky staring at the hotel with such consternation? Suddenly he understood.

"There's a fine restaurant here," he said casually. "We can have supper and talk."

The four walked into the lobby, elaborately furnished with beveled mirrors, cut glass, marble, and bronze objets d'art. Somebody had told him that the gold brocaded curtains had cost forty-five dollars a yard. The interior, he thought with a flicker of humor, was enough to awe even Alex.

In the restaurant, where supper was served from nine to midnight, they were escorted to a cozy corner table and brought menus.

"Mama still giving all those parties, Michael?" Alex asked softly.

Alex was needling him. Mama wrote Alex in detail about the constant parties, designed to throw the unattached young ladies of the parish into Michael's arms.

When would Mama understand? The too-frequent moodiness that pervaded his life rolled over him again.

"Mama still entertains a great deal," he conceded tightly. He was sick of being pursued by every single female within traveling distance; of being obsequiously courted by every mother in the parish who had nubile daughters. Damn, even law cases were being thrown into his lap that would normally go to more prestigious attorneys, because he was the potential heir to Eden and unmarried.

Why was it necessary for every man over twenty-one to take himself a wife? He had finally come to peace with himself. He could awaken in the morning and not dread the hours before he would sleep again. He had his practice, his few friends in New Orleans who shared his views on the disturbed world in which they lived. How could he get Mama off his back?

"I'm famished." Fred inspected the menu with enthusiasm. "The dining hall at school is nothing like this."

Michael concentrated on ordering. He was faintly intimidated by the high prices in comparison with those in New Orleans, and relieved that Vicky obviously knew how to handle herself in such surroundings. But still she was frowning slightly, excitement overshadowed by anxiety.

"Vicky, we'll ask for a room for you here at the hotel," he said briskly. She seemed on the point of protesting. "Tomorrow," he rushed ahead encouragingly, "I'll talk to Mr. Fleming at the bank about a job for you." But an unorthodox proposal for Vicky's future was forming at the back of his mind. One to serve their mutual needs.

Michael, smiling at her earnestness, ordered unimaginatively for all four of them—ribs of beef, potatoes, hot apple pie for dessert, and coffee—his mind compulsively focused on this truant proposal that hammered at him.

Alex and Fred were talking with fresh enthusiasm—though warily, not sure of Michael's reaction—about a night on the town.

"Nobody comes to New York without visiting the Louvre," Fred said aggressively. "It's the fanciest concert saloon in the city. My treat, Alex," he said grandly—a loaded exchange between them.

"And the most expensive concert saloon in town," Michael warned cynically. Alex didn't have the faintest conception of where the family stood financially, always taking it for granted there was plenty of money available.

They were served with commendable speed. Michael smiled at the way Vicky's eyes widened at the sight of the portions. Fine New York hotels served with plantation generosity.

By the time dessert and coffee arrived, Alex and Fred were restless. They exchanged impatient glances, which Michael intercepted.

"If you want to run, it's all right," Michael said casually. "But Alex, drop by my room before you go downstairs to breakfast. I must talk with you."

"Mama's orders," Alex shot back.

Michael talked about Eden as he and Vicky lingered over coffee. He ordered a fresh pot brought to the table, heartened by Vicky's warm interest in his description of the ten-thousand-acre plantation. She had no real conception of the institution of slavery, he thought uneasily. Slavery had been banned in England in 1807. But never mind that, he told himself. He wasn't asking her to own slaves.

"Vicky, I realize you're concerned about your future," he began slowly. "I have a position in mind. A business position," he emphasized, "though outwardly it will wear a different garb." She listended seriously, with no idea of what he was about to suggest. "For reasons of my own, Vicky, I'm offering you what is known in some circles"—he smiled faintly—"as a marriage of convenience." There, he had rocked her. She wasn't sure she had heard him correctly. "Hear me out, Vicky," he pleaded urgently, leaning across the table so that she could hear him. Obediently Vicky listened, trying to assimilate what he was saying. "You would have your own room at Eden. Everything you would require for comfortable living. But in the eyes of my family and our friends you would be my wife."

"I have read of such things," she whispered. "In novels."

"Vicky it would be a good life for both of us," he said earnestly. Mama and Papa might suspect, he thought with uneasy defiance, but would be able to prove nothing. Vicky would be suitable; neither of them could say she wasn't. The daughter of a British Army officer who had died tragically at Sevastopol. She was a lady, though neither Southern nor rich. Papa had hardly been rich when he married, Michael remembered. The plantation had been called Eden at his father's insistence only since his grandparents' death. For five generations before that, it had been known as Ainsley Acres. "Anytime you decide you've had enough, we can arrange for you to divorce me. I'm a lawyer, Vicky. I know how to handle these things. I'll even give you a legal document to that effect, if you like."

"What would I do?" Vicky was struggling to visualize herself in this unfamiliar existence.

"You would do what all young Louisiana wives do," he said with an effort at humor. "Make yourself beautiful. Go into New Orleans a few times a year to shop and attend the theater. Attend suppers and balls when we're invited out." Mercifully, less frequent once he was no longer an eligible bachelor. "Read."

Her eyes lighted. Michael realized she was beginning to see the advantages. Advantages for both of them, thought Michael. For her a lifeline to security, while he would be rid of his mother's irritating efforts to marry him off. And Vicky would be a buffer between him and Ava.

"We'll stay in New York another few days. I have to find out when my aunt's ship arrives. And I have more business to finish up." Apprehension brushed him. "You'll stay here at the hotel while we're in town." He paused, the magnitude of his proposal finally sweeping over him.

"Your family?" she asked fearfully. "What will they say?"

"I'm twenty-four years old and my own man, Vicky," he said tensely. "I'll tell them I met a delightful young

lady in New York and decided to end my bachelorhood."
His smile was cynical. "My mother has tried valiantly to
do that for four years." His eyes rested questioningly on
her. "You'll have to tell your aunt you're being married.
Married tomorrow," he decided. "I'll ask about a Baptist
minister." He paused, then asked belatedly, "What is your
faith?"

"I believe in God," Vicky said quietly. "Papa always
said that was all that was necessary. I'll be happy to
marry you in a Baptist ceremony," she said with astonishing dignity. "But I must get word to Aunt Mollie." Her
heavily lashed eyes were troubled. "I can't let her go on
worrying about me."

"Write her a letter," Michael instructed. "I'll have a
messenger deliver it first thing in the morning." He hesitated. "If you'd like to have her attend the ceremony—"

"No," said Vicky quickly. "It would be best that I just
write to her. And I'll write her again when we are down
in—" She frowned, searching her mind for the locale. "Is
it Louisiana?"

"Louisiana," he confirmed. "An hour's ride out of New
Orleans. One of the most fabulous cities in the world."

Vicky closed the door on the room that had been assigned to her at the St. Nicholas Hotel.

Tomorrow a Baptist minister would make her the wife
of Michael Eden. Three days later they would take a
coach to New Jersey, where they would board a railroad
train. That would be the beginning of the long trip to
New Orleans, via coach, train, and ship.

She would miss Aunt Mollie and the children, but she
was escaping the wretchedness of Five Points. Some
force, some unseen power—God—had taken a hand in
her future.

Then exhilaration was banked by the assault of logic.
Michael's parents would know, of course, that he had met
her only upon his arrival in New York. What kind of girl,
they would ask themselves, would marry a man on such
short acquaintance? Michael would never tell them,
would he, about how they had met?

And why did Michael wish this marriage? Was there someone he loved—with whom he maintained a relationship but whom he could not marry? Was she to be a blind for that?

No matter, she told herself sternly. She had no choice. She would uphold her duties. She would appear, before his friends and family, as a devoted wife. Color stained her cheeks. Michael Eden was the handsomest man she had ever known.

No, she warned herself, no romantic fantasies. Michael was her employer. Kind, considerate, but impersonal. There could never be anything more between them than existed at this moment.

Michael woke early, as though this were a normal morning back home. Then the unfamiliar city traffic sounds four floors below reminded him where he was. Instantly he was aware of the decision he had arrived at last night with such uncharacteristic impetuosity. By three this afternoon he would have taken himself a wife.

He was not doing Vicky Wickersham a bad turn, he considered. Alone in the world, forced to live under horrendous conditions, surely she was bettering her situation by marrying him.

He reached for his watch and wound it. Michael's orderly mind catalogued what must be accomplished. Alex should be knocking at the door soon. At eleven he was meeting with Mr. Fleming again. Prior to that, after his talk with Alex, he would have breakfast with him and Vicky. Arrange to have a letter delivered to Vicky's aunt. Take Vicky shopping for a proper wardrobe.

He frowned. Damn, the situation sounded odd. What would the aunt think about this? But Vicky was bright. She would handle the matter convincingly. The woman would hardly come running up here with shotgun in hand. At any rate, she was welcome to attend the ceremony.

He was dressed and shaved, trying to arrive at the least painful way to break the news of his marriage to his parents, when a sharp knock intruded.

"Come in," he called, gearing himself for this encounter. He was never entirely comfortable with Alex. In some ways his brother, whose eyes could glow with such secret anguish, seemed years older than he. Because of Mama, he and Alex had never spoken of that painful time three years ago which had ended in Alex's being shipped away to school. Banished from Eden. It would have been better if they had talked. Poor Alex, he thought compassionately.

Alex opened the door and came into the room, his eyes guarded.

"I know what you have to tell me, Michael." Alex smiled cynically. "Mama's furious because I've left school."

"Alex, you have to go back," he said calmly.

"Suppose I don't—" Alex challenged.

"Mama won't send you a penny," Michael said bluntly. He hesitated. "You ought to know, Alex, we're running into tight money. I'm having trouble with the factors. They don't want to advance as much as they usually do. But to keep you in college, Mama will manage."

"She could keep me in New York," Alex said defiantly. "Let her sell a slave or two." He shrugged. "She doesn't need three hundred hands to run Eden."

"Three hundred slaves are not three hundred hands," Michael pointed out. "Some are too old to work. Some are children. Besides, you know Mama won't sell a slave," Michael added impatiently. It was an obsession with her to add to the number of hands.

"So let her sell some stocks," Alex shot back.

"That's another problem," Michael said unhappily. "Papa pulled off one of his stunts. He sold a lot of stock to buy into the railroads. Without consulting Mama."

"Railroad stocks should be fine." Alex shrugged.

"Too much money is being shifted into railroads," Michael said seriously. "It worries me. But don't let's get onto that. I want you to go back to Princeton tomorrow. I'm sure we can arrange for you to be readmitted."

"Why must I go back? I didn't want to go in the first

place." A nerve quivered in one eyelid. What was this air of hopelessness that shone from Alex? "Mama puts us all on strings, like puppets. I ought to pack up and go out West. They're still making gold strikes out there."

But Michael knew he would not go. Alex was twenty and spoiled rotten with luxurious living.

"Alex, you'll go back to college," Michael said tiredly. "Tomorrow."

"I'd rather go home," Alex said stubbornly. "How long do I have to stay in exile?"

"Till you get your degree. But you'll be home soon for the summer," Michael consoled.

"I'll be there three days," Alex predicted bitterly, "and Mama will be dragging me off to Baton Rouge or Biloxi." He inspected Michael with curiosity. "Was Papa ever completely honest with you? About why they keep me away from Eden?"

"Look, so there was something between you and Janine," Michael said. He remembered the beautiful, golden-skinned fourteen-year-old girl who had worked in the kitchen the summer before Alex was so summarily shipped off to school. "You're not the first and you won't be the last to get involved with a slave."

"Papa didn't tell you." Alex glowed with vindictive triumph. "Papa couldn't face it, could he?" Then suddenly Alex seemed drained of emotion. "All right. I'll tell Fred. We'll go back to Princeton."

What couldn't Papa face? Michael asked himself. That he was in a wheelchair, paralyzed from the waist down, while Alex carried on in the Bart Eden tradition? Was there something else?

"Alex, there's one thing more." Michael struggled to pull himself out of the mire of the past. "I'm marrying Vicky Wickersham. This afternoon."

Alex stared in disbelief.

"Michael, have you lost your mind?"

"It's a comfortable arrangement for both of us," Michael said self-consciously. "Vicky and I talked about it at great length last night."

"My brother, the levelheaded attorney," Alex mocked. "Marrying a girl he met last night in a brothel!"

"Alex, shut up!"

"I don't believe it!" Alex continued to stare at him. "You're angry enough at Mama to do this to her?"

"I'm doing nothing to Mama," Michael shot back. "I'm bringing home a bride."

"Michael, you'll never have a moment's peace. Mama won't let you get away with it."

"It'll be a *fait accompli,*" Michael said brusquely. "Mama will have to accept it."

"Michael," Alex wheedled softly, "persuade Mama to let me come home."

"Nobody persuades Mama—you know that." Michael frowned. When Alex took on that silken way of speaking, he could be dangerous.

"You could talk to her." Sparks shot from Alex's eyes. "You could tell her I was getting into trouble up here. Tell her you found me at Nina's."

"Let's go down to breakfast," Michael said abruptly. "I've got a heavy day ahead of me. There's lots to be done."

"That's right," Alex drawled. "You're getting married."

To his astonishment Michael realized he was perspiring, despite the chill in the parlor where the minister was now reading the marriage ceremony. Alex and Fred were standing up with them—a last-minute decision of Alex's. Fred would never come down to Eden to visit, Michael reassured himself. No one would know about last night's unconventional meeting between bride and groom.

"The ring, please." The minister spoke with a flicker of impatience. Michael realized he was saying it for a second time. His brother also had not been paying attention to the ceremony.

Alex moved forward with the simple wedding band they had hastily bought that morning in a small jewelry store recommended by a clerk at the bank. Next to the jewelry store, in a tiny shop selling religious articles, he had picked out a present for his friend Ben Wasserman, which he knew would be received with deep appreciation: a fine silk prayer shawl for the Sabbath services at the Touro Synagogue.

Michael placed the wedding band on Vicky's finger, his voice sounding unfamiliar, strained, as he repeated the words. When the ceremony ended, he kissed her lightly on the cheek, since the minister and his wife seemed to expect it.

Mama would be in a bad state; Papa, amused because Mama was upset. Mama would have to stop pushing Betsy Harris into his arms—strange, sweet Betsy Harris, whose father was the richest man in the state.

The act had been accomplished, he thought with a mixture of defiance, jubilation, and apprehension. He had taken himself a wife.

3

Ava stood on the deck of the Cunard Line steamer in a faint drizzle. In a little while she would go to her cabin to dress for the festive, final dinner on board—sitting at the captain's table, as befitted the beautiful Princess Ava Radzinski, she thought with defiant pride. But tomorrow morning the steamer would arrive at New York, and she must begin the dull, depressing trip back to Eden.

Sara should have sent her money. Their father had expected Sara to share with her, she thought with long-simmering rage. Sara could have sold a few slaves. On that she could have lived well in Paris for two years.

She had exhausted all efforts to marry Rudy, and he refused to help her with money any longer. Why? She was still beautiful: her eyes the same brilliant green; her hair the flaming red that Mama had called unladylike and that Papa had adored; her skin milk-white, unlined.

"Ava, go back to the ancestral plantation," he had drawled, knowing her situation. "You have had enough of Europe." And each time, afterward, he had taken her to bed and it had been glorious and she had thought, Now, surely he'll want me to stay. But he had not.

She could have married a dozen times. Fifty times, she thought with pride. But she had cherished her freedom. Except for Rudy. For almost six years she and her artist had been so close. Loving, fighting, loving again. Except that with success, these past two years, he became someone else. It was no longer enough to paint her. He was greedy for fancy commissions. It was for the social contacts that he was so assiduously courting a daughter of one of the banking Rothschilds.

Ava closed her eyes, with the light drizzle cool on her face, and she remembered that last time with Rudy. She had awakened reluctantly to the gray, dank afternoon. Oh, her head ached. The ball the night before had been one to outdo all others. Her last ball in Paris, she had thought, for only God knew how long. In her mind, she relived with painful intensity that afternoon . . .

With a frown she had opened her eyes. Marie was moving about in the kitchen. Marie wouldn't dare to awaken her, even on this last day of her job. Tomorrow morning Ava must be awake at an infamously early hour, to go aboard the ship that would take her to London, where she would board another ship to transport her to the United States.

Her bedroom door had opened slightly. Marie's vivacious face appeared.

"Madame la Princesse wishes her coffee?" Marie asked in French.

"You know damned well I do," Ava shot back imperiously.

Marie knew that Rudy refused to marry her. Marie was going to continue to be the maid in this house which Rudy was taking from her, presumably to care for her furnishings until she returned and to use, meantime, as a private retreat where he could work. A private bordello, she thought with contempt. Rudy was never satisfied.

She had been so young when she met Rudy. Still hurting from that disastrous marriage which had seemed so glorious. A prince, handsome and rich. She had been too young, too inexperienced in court affairs to know why the Prince's parents had been so anxious to marry him off. On her wedding night she had learned.

Ava stared up at the ceiling, visualizing the splendor of the wedding that had made her Princess Ava Radzinski. Sara was supposed to come, but at the last moment she had suffered a change of heart. She could not bring herself to leave her precious children for so long.

Sara was relieved that she was getting married. Sara had been scared to death her darling sister was going to sleep with her husband. Ava smiled reminiscently. There had been times when she was sure it was going to happen. But Bart was scared of Sara, hot as he was for her. He would not have been the first, she thought with amusement. How old had she been—fourteen?—when Bart had bought that glorious black boy. What was his name? Christopher. He had been terrified when she cornered him in the barn, but never afterward.

Bart had suspected what was going on, but he kept quiet. She knew too much about his own diversions. Brother-in-law and sister-in-law, she thought with sardonic amusement. Both with a taste for black meat.

After the wedding she and Jan had gone to a chateau in the south of France. How many of the wedding guests had known about Jan? How many had laughed?

She had prepared herself with such care for the nuptial bed, she thought with bitter recall. A nightdress that had taken two seamstresses weeks to sew—all sheer white lace, revealing enough of her to turn any man to fire.

But Jan had not been a man. He had been a little boy of eight there between his legs. And he had dared to bring that to her in bed. She had screamed at him, cursed him, ordered him out of the bedroom. And in the morning servants working in the garden had found him with his wrists slit, dead beside a lily pond.

Marie came in with her coffee tray and set it carefully across her lap. Marie couldn't understand why she was leaving Paris, which she professed to adore. With money, Ava did adore Paris. She had just enough left to buy her passage home. Jan's inheritance had quickly evaporated. And Papa had thought he was making life easier for her, allowing Sara to handle everything.

Poor Papa, he had been so sweet. Spoiling her so, against Mama's exhortations. She had been his little darling, taken everywhere with him. Even to the slave auctions at the St. Charles and the St. Louis Hotels. A fascinating sight, though most Southern ladies pretended such a spectacle made them ill.

She was still in bed when Rudy arrived. He came straight into the room, calling to Marie to bring him champagne. It was an affectation of his, she thought, to drink only champagne.

"I'm taking you out to dinner," he said in his usual abrupt fashion. Back at Eden it was supper, Ava thought with amusement. In Paris you had dinner in the evening. "Get out of bed and dress."

She inspected his tall, lean length, his sensuously handsome face.

"We're going out to dinner in Paris at five in the afternoon?" she mocked.

"It takes you hours to dress," he said carelessly. "And first I will make love to you." His eyes were strangely guarded. It would be the last time he would make love to her. "Then we will go out to dinner."

"I don't have to go back to Louisiana," she said. She leaned forward slightly, knowing the effect this always had on Rudy, her breasts so full and white all but spilling out of her nightdress.

"You'll return someday," he murmured.

Marie came into the bedroom with the champagne. Rudy drank alone. Ava thrust aside the covers and lay back against the pillows, knowing she excited him. Still, she thought with inner rage, he could turn this aside for the daughter of a Rothschild.

Rudy drained his champagne glass, then set it carefully on a table. He crossed to the bed and laid a hand on her breast.

"You're going to miss me, Rudy," she warned him.

"What am I going to miss?" he taunted. Playing their little game.

"This." One slim hand darted forward to touch him. She smiled in triumph as she recognized his arousal.

Rudy cleared his throat.

"I'll lock the door," he said, his voice deepening.

"Why bother?" Her hand fondled him. "Marie knows not to come in."

He burrowed his mouth at her breast while his fingers stroked knowingly. Already like a sixteen-year-old she thought with pleasure.

"Ava," he whispered, and bit at her nipple.

"Rudy, across the bed," she ordered. A faint smile crossed his mouth as she prodded him to lie along the width of the bed. Nobody knew how to arouse Rudy the way she did, her hands stroking his thighs as her mouth sought him.

"Ava, this way!" His hands were pulling her roughly at the hips, positioning her, his mouth seeking. Oh Rudy, Rudy! Let the Rothschild girl try to please Rudy the way she did!

The room reverberated with the sounds of their passion, but as they paused briefly before resuming their flight into ultimate satisfaction, her fantasies returned to Eden and her sister's husband.

Bart had turned her down. That had rankled. But she'd had her revenge, she thought with bitter satisfaction. As long as he lived, Bart would remember that. Just as she would remember that Sara had stolen her birthright.

4 ～

The approach to Eden was a half-mile private road, lined with magnolias, pines, palms, live oaks and pecans, which opened onto a carefully tended expanse of bluegrass lawn, dotted here and there with shade trees. The house itself was majestically tall and white, with eight massive two-storied columns across the front gallery. A smaller gallery on the west side of the house looked upon the Mississippi. To the right and left of the house were well-planned groves, perhaps ten acres each, of pecans, magnolias, and cedars, planted in formal avenues.

In an upstairs corner bedroom with a view of the river, Sara Eden was stirring already, though it was barely 6 A.M. and most plantation ladies would hardly consider arising. As on every morning at this hour Nancy, Sara's personal maid, was shuffling her short, thick girth into the large square bedroom where Sara rested against a mound of feather pillows in the huge oak bed that had once been her parents'.

"Mawnin', Missy," Nancy said good-humoredly. "Ah brung yo' coffee."

"Thank you, Nancy." Sara smiled automatically, sniffing the aromatic scent of the strong, freshly ground beans. Juno, after all these years, knew exactly the way she liked it; knew how much this first cup of coffee fortified her for the strenuous day she invariably, compulsively, set for herself.

Sara ran a hand through her thick auburn hair, which Nancy would shortly brush. Her luminous hazel eyes were reflective as Nancy settled the tray across her lap. Tall, imperious, mercurial of temperament, though she made a point of holding herself in check, she was still a beautiful woman at forty-three.

"House don' seem de same wit' Mist' Michael away." Nancy clucked. Sara smiled. Nancy had a way of reading her moods.

"Michael will be home any day now." The house, each day, seemed painfully empty when he was away. She loved him, and Alex, with an intensity she had not thought possible when they were born. But between herself and Michael, she admitted with her customary candor, there was this special feeling. Bart taunted her sometimes with being partial to her firstborn. But it wasn't that at all.

"Ah git fresh water fo' yo' to wash," Nancy crooned when she had opened a pair of windows, bringing into the room the perfume of violets, jasmine, roses, and crabapple blossoms. "Be rat back."

Sipping her coffee, Sara frowned as she re-created last night's scene: a nasty battle again over those stupid railroad stocks Bart had bought behind her back—fantasizing himself in the role of a railroad magnate. Officially he was head of the family. Occasionally he exercised this right.

She hoped Michael was succeeding with the bank in New York. She had not liked the tenor of Fleming's letters. But Michael would know how to handle the situation.

Impatient this morning, she idled less than usual over the one cup of coffee she allowed herself. She would have to go over the figures of the new crop with Jack when he arrived for breakfast, she decided as she pushed away the light covers. She was so tired of these constant financial crises.

Right after her parents died, she knew that Bart would never manage Eden. He loathed business details. The only successful business he had ever completed, she thought with recurrent bitterness, was to marry a seventeen-year-old girl dazzled by his fencing-master splendor. At thirty he had been marvelously handsome. Half the girls in the parish had thrown themselves at him. But that handsomeness, that magnetic personality had long since faded.

She had loved Bart with a passion that had frightened her. Her first love. A love he had methodically killed, as he had discarded or alienated friends. In the early days people had clustered around him, eager to be bathed in his splendor. Quickly she had been smothered by his arrogance, his pernicious way of cutting her down. In those years she had been so vulnerable. There was his excessive drinking; there was his way with the women slaves. And then, as time passed and he was unable to make the world his kingdom, his bitterness, his surliness had spilled over onto her.

She hated Bart for killing her love for him. Dead before the stroke eight years ago. Dead by the time he discovered he was no longer the prize stud he had always prided himself on being.

Nancy pulled forth fresh underclothing from a drawer scattered with verbena and musk-cluster roses and brought them and the new dress just finished by the Misses Gardiner to the bed. Sara washed austerely with cold water; accepted the towel Nancy offered; dressed while Nancy stood by to brush her waist-length hair.

With Nancy in her wake, prattling household gossip, to which she listened with half an ear, Sara headed down the long, curving staircase, down the lower-floor hall past Bart's bedroom, where he would sleep till noon, to the dining room.

As she settled herself at the table, a pair of giggling, pencil-thin twelve-year-olds, incongruously dressed in her cast-off frocks, walked with languid grace to serve the hearty breakfast Juno religiously sent in from the brick kitchen attached to the house. Sara could hear Socrates in the foyer, welcoming Jack Lamartine, her overseer.

"Good morning, Jack." She greeted him with a brisk smile. "How's Claudine this morning?"

"I left her sleeping," he said politely. Did his wife ever

arise with him in the morning? "She had a migraine last night." Meaning, Sara interpreted, that she was on morphine again. "Any news yet from Michael about the factors?"

"There should be something today. Socrates sent Napoleon into New Orleans to pick up the mail."

They settled down, over breakfast, to a serious discussion of plantation matters. This morning part of Sara's mind was delinquent. Traitorously, guiltily, she was considering Jack's unhappy marriage. Claudine, from French Quebec City, loathed living the isolated plantation life. She sought relief from reality in morphine, to which she had been carelessly introduced by a New Orleans physician. Jack was thirty-three and good to look upon, Sara thought compassionately, with a wife who refused him admission to her bed. What did Claudine do on those trips of hers into the city, where she stayed, impervious to neighborhood gossip, at the St. Charles Hotel?

"Mo' biscuits?" Athena, the taller of the twelve-year-old twins, asked, casting a covert glance at Jack. Some of them develop so young, Sara thought in annoyance.

"Yes, tell Juno to send in another plate," she ordered sternly, and the giggling stopped.

In the seven years he had served as her overseer, she and Jack had become good friends. Once—only once, four years ago—had their roles shifted. She had been with him in the slave quarters, inspecting some cabins he felt were in serious need of repair. A summer storm came up suddenly, drenching them. He had taken her to his own house at the edge of the quarters. Claudine had been away in New Orleans on one of her "little trips." Jack brought her brandy to ward off a chill. She had drained the glass too quickly, had become light-headed. Without their expecting it to happen he had touched her, kissed her, taken her to bed.

Afterward both of them knew this must never happen again. But now, sitting across the table from him at breakfast, Sara felt that traitorous stirring within her that reminded her how painfully long it had been since she had been loved. But it would not happen again. Not ever.

Jack glanced outside. Where sunlight had poured through the windows earlier, a grayness now crept into the room.

"We'll have rain for sure," he predicted. "Not bad right at this point."

Though it would be good for the crops, she hated rainy days. They made her passionate. She remembered, then, the good first years with Bart. After the first night, she had not been ashamed to show her passion. She had rejoiced in pleasing him. Like some wanton, she had thought with a blend of defiance and exultation. Of those years Michael and Alex had been born.

Too soon she had ceased to please him. Then he had gone to the slaves. Brought them right into the house before her agonized eyes. She became his whipping boy. All his frustrations lashed against her. The repeated unsuccessful runs for the Legislature. The judgeship that never materialized.

"I think we've covered everything," Jack said finally, an eye on his watch. He was the most conscientious overseer Eden had ever enjoyed. He loved the plantation almost as much as she.

"If there's word from Michael about the factors, I'll send someone to the fields to tell you," Sara promised. She knew he was concerned about their receiving the amount she had requested. Food prices were going up. They had a lot of mouths to feed.

Sara left the dining room and headed for the library to go over the accounts, as she did each morning. The lower floor of the house was still except for the lively morning kitchen sounds. The servants never dared clean much before noon because Bart stayed up till four in the morning —reading the magazines brought up from the city; playing backgammon with Jefferson, who slept in his room in the event Bart required his services in the middle of the night; and undergoing the constant massages provided by his Haitian maid, Odalie, who looked like a small, exquisite ebony doll. Bart expected the house to be silent until he awoke.

As Sara worked over the accounts—the kitchen figures

abominably high, she thought with irritation—her mind wandered uneasily to Alex, her baby. Oh, how she missed him! But in a year he would have his degree; he would be more mature; she wouldn't worry so about his being here.

At least, she had persuaded Bart to sell the girl and her mother. At first Bart had been difficult. He could be so irascible, but she had been persistent. How stupid she had been to allow him to bring Janine into the house!

She focused her attention fully on the paperwork before her, and the morning moved along swiftly. Noiselessly Nancy came into the room around nine to bring a tall cup of coffee and a plate of pralines.

By the time she had finished with the book work, Sara heard the dogs carrying on out front. That probably meant Socrates was coming to the house with the mail. Rising, she strode eagerly from the room and down the long hallway to the foyer, noticing that the clouds had again given way to sunshine.

Socrates was coming toward her with a handful of letters. He paused to pat Sam, the ingratiating springer spaniel who had maneuvered, despite their efforts, to sire Hilda's most recent litter of pups.

"Socrates, hurry." She stood with one hand extended.

"Ah comin', Missy," he soothed with a wide grin. "Ah kin jes' smell dis 'un come f'om Noo Yawk."

The letter on the top, which Socrates had been sure was from Michael, was an advertisement for a cough syrup. She thumbed through the others as she dropped into one of the half-dozen cane-backed rockers that were positioned along the gallery.

Here! Her face lighted. She ripped open the envelope and pulled forth the single sheet of paper.

"As I suspected, business is in a bad way all over the country, and growing worse," Michael had begun. *"I've had two long meetings with Fleming. He finally agreed to allow us seventy percent of what you requested.*

"He's nervous about the crop this year. The almanac predicts too much rain and too much heat this summer, which, of course, could wreck the cotton crop. And he fears, as do many in New York, that we're entering a

*period of overspeculation in railroad securities and in real
estate."*

Rail securities, she thought with annoyance. Bart, the
damn fool, had gone over her head and sunk every dollar
of their reserve cash into railroad stocks. If the crop was
bad this year, they would have a financial crisis on their
hands.

*"I'll meet Ava's ship when it docks this morning, and
we'll leave the next day for home. We should arrive a
week from Wednesday. Can you arrange for somebody to
be at the dock with a carriage?"*

Wednesday. *Tomorrow.* Sara glowed with excitement.
Michael would be home tomorrow. With Ava, her mind
insisted on reminding her.

Only now did she flip through the other letters, frowning slightly as she saw the one from Alex. He must be
writing to say he was furious because she was insisting he
return to Princeton. How could he have thought she
would have sent him monthly checks to live there in the
St. Nicholas Hotel with that wild Fred Fields?

She ripped open the envelope and read the first para-
graph. Suddenly she felt encased in ice. Slowly she reread
the first sentences he had written to prepare her. This was
a nightmare. It couldn't be happening.

Hurrying from the gallery into the house, she ran to
Bart's room, and thrust open the door which she had last
opened eight years ago, when Socrates had found Bart
unconscious on the floor.

Jefferson lay asleep on the pallet beside the bed, his
slender legs drawn up to his chin, looking like a small
black cherub. She dropped to her haunches and shook
him into wakefulness.

"Jefferson! Jefferson!"

The small boy opened his eyes with sudden alarm.

"Yessum?" Instinctively his eyes darted to Bart—fast
asleep, snoring, on the bed.

"Jefferson, I must talk to Mr. Bart. I'll call you when I
want you."

"Yessum." He scrambled to his feet and scurried to the
door, closing it behind him.

Sara walked to the bed, gazing for a moment at her husband's slightly bloated whiskey-flushed face.

"Bart!" She shook him by the shoulders. "Bart, wake up! I have to talk to you."

Slowly, reluctantly, Bart came awake, startled to see her standing beside his bed.

"And to what do I owe the pleasure of your company?" he drawled.

"Bart, I have a letter from Alex." Her voice was unsteady. "He tells me Michael has just been married. To a girl who was playing a piano in a brothel."

"Sara," he reproved with sardonic humor, "girls don't play piano in brothels. That's a man's job."

"This one was!" Her eyes were nearly black with outrage. "Michael in a place like that!"

"Sara, he's got standard male equipment," Bart said with savage amusement. "Where would he take himself in a strange city if he felt in the mood to enjoy himself?"

Sara frowned with distaste.

"Bart, stop being crude." She was fighting against hysteria. "Alex writes that Michael met this girl in a brothel—and the next day he married her. Bart, has he lost his mind?"

"Maybe Alex was drinking too much in one of those fancy saloons," Bart suggested.

"Alex wouldn't joke about something like this! Bart, what do we do about this grotesque marriage?"

"We can't do one damn thing," Bart said with infuriating calm. He was enjoying her agitation, she thought with frustration. "She's Michael's wife. You're a lady, Sara. You won't ever forget that. You'll receive Michael's wife as any Southern lady would, with charm and dignity."

"A girl like that?" Her voice soared perilously. She might have expected this of Alex. Never of Michael. "Bart, I will not!"

"Oh, yes, you will, Sara," Bart insisted maliciously. "Because if you don't, you'll lose Michael altogether."

5 ～

Vicky waited while Michael politely edged his way
through the assemblage of fashionably clothed ladies and
gentlemen, with their innumerable portmanteaus and
trunks, who were disembarking from the Cunard steamer.
His objective, as he had pointed out, was a tall, flamboyantly beautiful woman who was taking affectionate fare-
well of an older male traveler. How young to be Michael's
aunt! She seemed not a day older than he, though he had
said she was already thirty.

For a poignant moment Vicky recalled her own arrival
in New York, the steerage passengers allowed on deck
only after the other passengers had disembarked. Now,
squinting in the spring sunlight, she could see these other
passengers, permitted on deck for only an hour each day
during the crossing, lining up at the rails for their first
view of America. And she, after only six months in this
fine country, was Michael Eden's wife, going to live in a
mansion in Louisiana.

She watched, without hearing, the confrontation between Michael and Ava. Michael seemed so painfully uncomfortable with his aunt. But of course, they had not
seen each other for ten years. Michael had been only
fourteen when his aunt went to England. She forced a
smile as Michael and Ava strode toward her.

"So, this is the bride," Ava said without waiting for an
introduction. "How long have you been married?"

"Four days," Vicky stammered, while Michael flushed darkly. Was he afraid Ava understood this strange marriage?

"How long have you known each other?" Ava turned mockingly to Michael before Vicky could reply. "How long have you been in New York?" Her eyes were too wise.

"I have to return to Eden," Michael hedged defensively. "There was no time for a long courtship."

"Does your mother know?"

"Not yet," Michael said shortly. "We're leaving for New Orleans in the morning. She'll meet Vicky when we arrive."

Ava frowned. "Why must we leave New York almost the moment I arrive?"

"I have a law practice in New Orleans." His eyes avoided Ava's. "And living at a New York hotel is terribly expensive in these times when money is so short."

"Where are we staying?" she demanded imperiously. "I hope you haven't put us up at a hovel?" There was a tension between Ava and Michael that disturbed Vicky.

"We're at the St. Nicholas. It's a magnificent hotel that cost more than a million dollars to build," Michael said. "I'm sure you'll like it." He turned about with a frown and gestured to a pair of burly porters who were struggling to cope with Ava's baggage.

In the carriage en route to the hotel Ava maintained a sullen silence, ignoring the sights that Michael pointed out. He looked so unhappy that Vicky supressed an urge to reach out to comfort him.

At the hotel Ava was shown to her room, on a floor below Vicky's. They remained with her while she grudgingly conceded that the accommodations were adequate.

"We'll meet in the dining room for the midday meal," Michael said with strained calm, but Ava shook her head in rejection.

"After that dreadful crossing I'm going straight to bed. They're civilized enough here to send a tray to my room?" she asked with sarcasm.

"I'm sure that can be arranged." Michael smiled faintly. "Will you join us for supper this evening?"

"I guess so," Ava said languidly. "Knock on my door when you come downstairs." Her eyes rested speculatively on Vicky. "You're going to be quite a surprise for Sara." The thought seemed to give her a sadistic pleasure.

The following morning Vicky, Ava, and Michael, hampered by Ava's copious collection of baggage, traveled by ferry to New Jersey, where they began the first leg of the journey south, via horse-drawn coaches. In Philadelphia they changed from coach to railroad.

Ava was restless, quickly discarding each newspaper Michael offered to break the monotony of the trip. Vicky, intrigued by the train, tried to draw Ava into conversation about the railroad. She flinched before the undisguised hostility in Ava's eyes when she told Vicky she preferred to drowse rather than talk.

Increasingly Vicky was conscious of Michael's brooding handsomeness. When their eyes met, she offered a quick, shy smile. He spoke little, engrossed in private thoughts as the train moved with disconcerting speed beside the winding Delaware river.

In the afternoon they arrived in Baltimore and went through the laborious task of transferring luggage from train to station, where they would have time for a meal before climbing onto another train for the run to Louisville.

At Louisville they boarded a boat which Ava indignantly labeled not worthy of cattle. Michael shared a cabin with another man. Ava and Vicky shared another minute cabin hardly larger than a closet. But they left this boat at the point where the Ohio River met the majestic Mississippi, and even Ava conceded that the *Mississippi Queen* merited her title.

The paddle-wheel steamer, with its double stacks, was a floating castle, Vicky thought, enthralled with the luxury it provided. The cabin assigned to her and Ava could almost match the room she had occupied at the St. Nicholas, and the meals were equal to those served in the

hotel dining room. How different this journey down the
Mississippi from the squalid discomfort, the anguish of
the forty days and nights she had spent on the sailing ves-
sel, crossing the stormy Atlantic! More like the fancy
Cunard line steamer on which Ava had arrived.

They sat down to dinner in a velvet-hung dining salon.

"The food is wonderful," Vicky said with determined
admiration, as course after course was presented to them.

"As good as at any restaurant I've ever dined in, except for Madame Alphand's in New Orleans," Michael
said, with the first sign of pleasure he had shown since
they had met his aunt at the ship.

But Ava didn't hear Michael, Vicky realized. She was
engaged in uncomfortably overt flirtation with a man
across the room. Her Paris gown, cut startlingly low,
brought frowns from some of the plantation ladies
aboard. Some of the women—fast ladies, she had heard
someone term them with delicate disapproval—viewed
Ava with hostility.

After dinner there was card playing and drinking in the
saloons. Music played for dancing in the ballroom. Ava
was in a festive mood and quickly deserted her nephew
and Vicky. Michael was furious, Vicky thought uneasily
as he walked with her about the deck after dinner. Ava
was making a spectacle of herself, but there was nothing
he could do except pretend to ignore the fact.

Each day was like the others—the muddy river placid,
the ship a private castle for those aboard. Vicky sat on
deck with Michael for hours each day. He talked to her
compulsively about Eden, which he loved with a passion.
Yet all the while she sensed that he was upset that Ava
was returning with them.

Recurrently she worried about Michael's not having
written—or telegraphed—his mother about their marriage. What kind of reception would she receive at Eden?
Ava, she thought with her customary honesty, looked
upon her with contempt because she was not a rich young
lady from a plantation. Michael had told Ava that she
worked at Mr. Fleming's bank.

Their final night on board, she and Michael remained in the largest of the saloons—hung with red velvet, ornamented with greens and statuary—far past their normal time. Michael was restless, his smile belied by the moodiness of his eyes.

"We'll have champagne," he said with an air of bravado, and he signaled a waiter. "Have you ever drunk champagne, Vicky?" His voice was faintly teasing.

"No," she acknowledged in a burst of high spirits, "but I'd love to try it!"

The waiter brought them a bottle of champagne and two glasses. Tonight was special, and she gazed at Michael with revealing awareness.

How could she feel such tenderness toward him when she had known him such a little while? Was she in love with Michael? All at once she felt her face grow hot. Yes! She loved Michael. How quickly this had happened.

"Vicky, the first few days at Eden may seem difficult for you," Michael said, pouring champagne, "but everything will work out. I promise you. You'll have a comfortable life."

"I'm sure of that, Michael." This was a job, she reminded herself sternly.

"Vicky, I owe you some explanation." She felt the tension in him. He was driving himself to be candid with her. "I don't want to commit myself to any emotional involvement. I know the life I want for myself. There are many people in the South who realize slavery must go, but only a few of them, so far, will acknowledge it. There'll be those who try to pull Louisiana out of the Union. I'll fight against that. Without the Union Louisiana will be nothing. We're a family of strong convictions, Vicky. We've always fought for what we believed." How earnest he sounded! "My grandfather was a Congressman from Louisiana for years, until he decided he preferred to work within the state, among the people he cherished. He ran for the State Legislature. And on the eve of the election he and my grandmother were murdered, because he was determined to fight for clean government. I was seven years old. Nobody knew I stood there at the head of the stairs at Eden that night when their blood-spattered bodies were carried into the house. I heard what was said, and I remembered." A vein throbbed in his forehead. "I swore I would devote my life to making Louisiana a better place in which to live. For them. But until slavery goes, Louisiana will never come into its own."

"I don't understand slavery," Vicky said with honesty. "It seems to me a terrible wrong."

"The South feels victorious because Buchanan sits in the White House," Michael said somberly. "And because two days after the inauguration the Supreme Court handed down a decision that affirmed that slaves are not human beings but chattels. And that," Michael said unhappily, "switched slavery from a sectional problem to a national one."

Vicky listened, pleased at Michael's talking to her with such frankness. He needed a wife who would mirror his thoughts. Who would not make demands on him. And with a wife, she thought, he would appear more settled. More a man of responsibility.

Abruptly he said, "It's late. Tomorrow we must be up early."

Vicky said good night and went to her cabin. But as she put her hand on the doorknob, she heard low, throaty laughter inside. Ava and a companion. Pulling her hand away in shock, she hurried back up on deck.

Passengers strolled the deck in pairs or groups. She paused at the railing, watching the myriad of lights reflected in the still water of the river, wondering how long Ava's guest would remain in the cabin.

"Vicky!" Michael's voice swung her about from the railing. "I thought you had gone to bed." His eyes were uneasy.

"I went there." Vicky lowered her eyes. She felt herself coloring. "Ava was there. She—she was not alone."

"Damn Ava!" he said angrily. He put his hand at her elbow.

They walked in silence, Vicky shivering slightly in the damp night chill. "You're cold," he said solicitously. He hesitated. "I have champagne in my cabin. Let's go down

there and have a drink. It'll warm you up." There was a
glow in his eyes that set her heart to pounding.

"All right." He was just being concerned for her, she
told herself.

With the door decorously unlocked, Michael poured a
glass of champagne for Vicky, then one for himself. There
was nothing wrong in her being here, Vicky told herself
as she sat in one of the comfortable chairs, Michael in the
other. She and Michael were married. Nobody, except
themselves, knew this was a marriage in name only.

"Drink your champagne," Michael urged gently. "It'll
ward off a cold." His eyes seemed to see her as though for
the first time, with an admiration that was exhilarating.
"I'm sorry about Ava," he apologized. "She's lived a
strange life over there in Europe. I think she enjoys flout-
ing convention, but how dare she expose you to that sort
of thing!"

"Michael, maybe she'll change once she's at Eden,"
Vicky said encouragingly.

"You don't know Ava," he said tensely. "You don't
know the evil in her."

As he reached to take the champagne glass from her
hand, their fingers brushed. Vicky felt a strange excitement. Michael reached to take her hand in his and lifted
it to his mouth.

"Pretty Vicky," he whispered. His eyes were aglow
with something she had never seen there before. "Beautiful Vicky."

"Michael—" She was trembling as he rose from his
chair and crossed to stand before her. He lowered his
mouth to hers.

She lifted her face, her hands reaching to close in about
his shoulders as he gently pulled her to her feet.

Nobody had ever held her this way. His hands were at
her shoulders now, pulling her dress to her waist. Nobody
had ever touched her this way.

Without releasing her, he moved with her toward the
narrow lower bunk.

"You're beautiful," he whispered. "So beautiful."

She closed her eyes against the faint glow of the lamp,

wishing only to feel. Her body was responding instinctively, moving beneath his hands, his heated mouth. And she, who had never known a man, wanted him with overpowering intensity. She waited, her heart pounding, as he lifted himself above her.

Afterward she lay still, tears dampening her face, too touched by the beauty of what she had experienced to speak. But Michael left the bed and said with jarring selfreproach, "Vicky, I ought to be horsewhipped." His voice was strangled. "After all I told you. All my promises! Vicky, please forgive me."

"Michael, there's nothing to forgive," she whispered. They were married. This was their right.

"It'll never happen again. I swear. Vicky, you won't walk out on me? You'll come with me to Eden?"

"I'll go with you to Eden," she whispered. But the painful truth smote her. Tonight was an accident. Michael would not allow it to happen again. He was determined to maintain their "marriage of convenience."

But in her eyes, she was forever Michael's wife. They had just observed their wedding night.

6

The port of New Orleans mesmerized Vicky with its color, its movement, its special flavor of excitement. Her eyes swept along the miles of levee. There were ships bearing the flags of every nation, goods piled high on decks that seemed on the point of going under with the weight of their cargo. And everywhere bales and bales of cotton, loaded in precarious pyramids. Vicky remembered how Michael had talked about the South's devotion to cotton, which he viewed with trepidation.

Michael piloted Vicky and Ava down the gangplank, his eyes searching for the carriage that was to take them to Eden. Vicky stared at the tin-roofed shanties that housed small stores; the endless parade of grogshops, with customers waiting in line; the stands selling oysters, fruits, flowers. Blind men were fiddling for pennies, in competition with enthusiastically jigging children, and black women with colorful kerchiefs walked through the crowds carrying coffeepots in their baskets for prospective customers.

The noise was deafening, Vicky thought. Even worse than Broadway at its peak. Drays rattled down the streets; people shouted at the top of their lungs with a kind of joyousness that made itself felt through even the cursing and swearing, talking in a multitude of tongues.

"There's Seth," Michael said suddenly. He turned Vicky and Ava toward a gleaming black carriage, on whose box sat a white-haired black man, his face unlined and kindly. He was turning the pages of a book. "He likes to pretend he can read that old hymnbook," Michael said indulgently.

Suddenly fresh alarm tugged at Vicky. She fought down an urge to run back to the steamer, to hide in the sanctuary of her cabin.

"Mist' Michael!" Seth hopped down to move toward them. "Lawd amercy, it sho' fine to see yo' back home! Yo' mama pinin' away." His smile broadened. "An' Miss Ava! Welcome home."

"Seth, this is my wife," Michael said. He turned to Vicky. "Seth taught me how to swim, how to fish, how to ride a horse. And he tanned my rear when I got out of hand," Michael teased with affection.

"Welcome to Louisiana, Young Missy," Seth said with dignity, his eyes suddenly guarded.

What was Seth thinking? That Michael's parents were going to be shocked when Michael sprang her on them?

What an awful shock it was going to be, Vicky thought with recurrent discomfort.

"We'll be home in an hour," Michael promised when they were settled in the carriage. He reached for a copy of the *Picayune*. "You'll enjoy the view. Seth will take the river road." He buried himself in the newspaper.

Vicky gazed out the carriage window, seeing nothing, trying to visualize Michael's parents, trying to imagine what it would be like to live surrounded by servants. Ava leaned back in the carriage and sulked.

They traveled higher up the river. The air was fresh and fragrant. Here and there, where wooden garden gates were open in the tall brick walls Vicky caught glimpses of wide-galleried houses with columns, ironwork, dormer windows. And then the houses disappeared as they neared the multiacred plantations.

Even before the horses turned into a long private road-way, Vicky sensed they were arriving at Eden. Michael had discarded the newspaper, which he had read, seem-ingly, from front to back; he held it rolled up tightly, in one hand.

Unconsciously Vicky touched her wedding band with her thumb, as though this were a good-luck talisman. *Oh, let them like her!*

Then they were emerging from the imposing avenue of trees. The house rose before them, and she leaned forward in her seat as the carriage rolled toward it.

"It's as large as Kensington Palace," she said with as-tonishment. "Where Queen Victoria was born."

The carriage pulled up before the house. A small black boy, no more than ten, charged forward with an auda-cious grin to open the carriage door for them.

"I'm going to disappoint you today, Jefferson," Michael apologized. "No mints."

"Yassuh," Jefferson said good-naturedly. His eyes were unexpectedly shy as they dwelt on Vicky and Ava.

"Jefferson, you give Seth a hand with the luggage," Michael ordered, and turned to help Vicky and Ava to the ground. The dogs rushed forward to be petted.

"The house hasn't changed a bit," Ava said dryly.

"Another generation of dogs—" She withdrew in distaste from the dogs' show of affection.

Vicky fondled the silken head of an affectionate springer spaniel Michael called Sam, while Hilda's wet tongue lathered her free hand. Now, Vicky thought with a twinge of panic, she must come face to face with Michael's parents.

The front door opened. A tall black man dressed with faded elegance moved toward them as they walked up the steps, his ageless face alight with a wide smile.

"Mist' Michael! Sho' good to have yo' home, Suh! An' Miss Ava. Li'l Missy!" There were sudden tears in Socrates' eyes. "Yo' done come home."

"You haven't changed a bit, Socrates." Fleetingly Ava displayed her considerable charm. But she wasn't glad to be home, Vicky recognized.

"Socrates, this is my wife." Michael's face was strained despite his smile.

"Welcome to Eden, Young Missy." Socrates was genuinely warm. But his eyes, when they met hers, were veiled.

"Thank you, Socrates."

Why did she feel such terror? Michael was her husband. He wished her here. His parents had no way of knowing this was a "marriage of convenience." With a touch of humor she recalled that many royal marriages were such arrangements. That was why everybody talked about the love match between Victoria and Albert.

"Miss Sara be waitin' fo' yo' in de drawin' room." He was nervous. "Wit Mist' Bart."

Cold despite the warm breeze that came from the Mississippi, a fixed smile on her face, Vicky allowed Michael to propel her through the front door, after Ava, into the high-ceilinged foyer.

"Down this way," Michael instructed as Ava fell into step beside them.

They walked down the wainscoted corridor and through open double doors. A tall, regal woman leaped to her feet and strode toward them, arms extended. Michael's mother, Vicky knew instantly.

"Ava!" She swept her sister into her arms. Vicky saw tears fill her eyes. "You look marvelous." The years had briefly hurtled backward. This was Sara Eden's baby sister, home after an unconscionably long absence. Now she turned to embrace Michael. "Michael, we've missed you." She swept him to her with a display of warmth, then pulled away. "But Michael, what is this Alex writes us?" A faint hysteria underlay her gaiety. "That he stood up with you before a Baptist minister in New York?" *Alex wrote. What did Alex write?* "Michael, how dare you do this to us? Deprive us of a wedding at Eden! Your father and I are so disappointed." Only now did Vicky become aware of the man in the wheelchair.

"Papa." Michael crossed to embrace his father, then straightened up. "Alex wasn't supposed to tell you. I wanted it to be a surprise." His voice was tense, self-conscious. "Mama, Papa, this is Vicky. My wife."

"How lovely," Sara Eden said in her vibrant, faintly imperious voice. As Vicky timidly acknowledged the introduction she sensed her new mother-in-law's reined-in fury.

"We must give a party," Sara Eden said, "to introduce you to all our friends and neighbors. Tell me"—she turned to Michael—"how did you meet Victoria? It is Victoria?" she asked politely.

"She's called Vicky," Michael explained with discomfort. Why all this talk about her name? Vicky asked herself with irritation. "She was working at the bank. Mr. Fleming's bank. She's English. She's only been in this country a few months."

"Michael, it's fairly obvious that she's English." Her raillery was edged with sharpness. "Where in England, Vicky?"

"We lived in a village near London." Vicky's voice was not quite steady.

"Ava lived in London from time to time, you know." Sara's eyes were overbright.

"I've only been to London once," Vicky said softly. "When my father took me to the opera."

"Really?" Suddenly hostility glittered in Sara Eden's

eyes. Ava watched her with an inscrutable smile. "Are you musical, Vicky?"

Vicky felt the color drain from her face.

"I play the piano. A little."

Sara Eden knew where she had played the piano.

"What the devil is everybody standing around for?" Bart demanded impatiently, pushing his wheelchair into the center of the room. "Sit down." His eyes appeared to secretly challenge Ava, who dropped herself into a chair beside him with an air of cool deliberation. Then he directed his steady gaze to Vicky, his eyes seeming to bore holes.

Vicky sat next to Sara Eden on an impressive green-velvet-covered sofa with cabriole legs, drinking in the splendor of the Eden drawing room, which she had been too stricken, moments ago, to notice. Michael, his face tense, sat at one end of the matching sofa directly opposite.

The two sofas flanked a marble-faced fireplace, with cut-glass candelabra on either side of the mantel. Above it hung a magnificent oil painting of Ava at fifteen or sixteen. The walls were a muted green, lighter than the near-olive of the sofas, the upholstered seats of the side chairs, and the pair of wing chairs that sat between two windows. In one corner a fine piano was lit by wall sconces. From the ceiling hung an awesomely beautiful glass-and-ormolu chandelier.

"I don't understand Fleming's pessimism," Bart was saying with impatience. "The price of cotton hasn't dropped. The South is as healthy as it ever was."

"All the bankers are pessimistic," Michael insisted.

"To hell with them," Bart bellowed. "We're not going to have a panic while Buchanan sits in the White House. This is one of the most prosperous periods in American history. Men are still rushing to California to mine gold. We'll soon have railroad lines all the way to the Pacific Ocean—"

"If they don't go broke first," Sara interrupted caustically.

Bart scowled and turned back to Michael.

"I tell you, we're embarking on four good years. And Buchanan's the South's man," he added with satisfaction. "As Pierce was. Not that I approve of everything Pierce did. That bastardly business of protecting all the immigrants!" Sara frowned at his profanity. "That was hogwash! I beg your pardon, Vicky, but not all immigrants to the country should be allowed in." She felt discomfited, recognizing the glint in Bart's eyes, the glint she had seen in the eyes of men lurching from grogshops on the Points. "We're getting the dregs of Europe coming here to take away jobs from the American-born." He turned his attention to Michael as Socrates, followed by two very young slaves bearing small tables, came into the room. Socrates settled a tray with coffee service and a plate of English biscuits on one table placed before Sara Eden and Vicky, while the other table was set up beside Michael and his father. Sara began to pour as Socrates dispensed china and gleaming silver.

"Buchanan appeals to everybody who wants to preserve the Union," Michael acknowledged. "And everybody who wants to avoid the slavery question," he added wryly.

"Michael, enough of this political talk," Sara intervened. "We're having coffee." She turned with strained politeness to Vicky. "How do you take yours, Victoria?"

"Black, thank you. No cream, no sugar." Her face flushed as she became aware, again, of Bart's covert interest in her.

"Michael, I have told Nancy to prepare the blue bedroom for—" She hesitated awkwardly. "For Vicky." Had she expected Michael to object to separate bedrooms? "It has always been our special guest room," she explained.

"I think she'll like that," Michael said. Too quickly. "It has a fine view of the river, Vicky." He smiled with poignant encouragement, knowing she was ill at ease.

"Monique will be her maid," Sara decreed. "Monique is part of a deal I made with Joshua Harris: he needed another gardener and I felt we could use another girl about the house. There's hardly enough to keep Monique busy. She'll have plenty of time to care for Vicky. Odalie will look after you, Ava," she added, then turned again to her new daughter-in-law.

"I'm afraid you're going to find life at Eden quite dull after living in New York." Sara's hand was not quite steady as she lifted her coffee cup to her mouth. It must have been an awful shock, Vicky conceded, for Michael to have marched in with her this way. "There's little to do about the plantation. But of course," she said with a sudden, almost triumphant smile, "we must give a party immediately. To introduce Michael's bride."

"Mama, there's no rush." Michael was disconcerted.

"We would be lacking in good manners if we delayed." She turned to Vicky. "Every unmarried young lady in the parish had her eye on Michael. They'll be eager to meet his bride."

Alex must have written his mother the whole story and Sara Eden expected Vicky to disgrace herself. That was the reason for the party.

"Send out the invitations, Sara," Bart drawled. "We could use some diversion around here."

This was the gauntlet thrown in her face. The first attack. Let Michael's bride, whom he had met in a Greene Street brothel, discredit herself before his friends. Let her run away from Eden in shame. *No.*

"You've had a long trip," Sara said abruptly. "I'll have Monique show Vicky to her room. She can rest until we sit down to dinner."

Sara jiggled the silver bell that sat on a piecrust table behind the sofa, and the young girls, who must have been lingering in the hall, moved into the doorway.

"Artemis, Athena, go find Monique," Sara ordered briskly. "Tell her to come here. Quickly, you hear?"

"Yessum," they said in vigorous chorus, and darted off.

"Seth has already taken your luggage upstairs," Sara said with scrupulous politeness. "Monique will unpack and press for you." Her eyes lingered oddly on the Stewart-bought, Paris-made watered-silk dress Vicky wore, as though speculating that she was hardly accustomed to such finery. Amusement brushed Vicky for a moment.

Indeed she was not accustomed to such finery, but she was more than willing to learn.

Seconds later a girl darted eagerly into the doorway. No more than fifteen, Vicky judged, the slave was golden-skinned and delicately fashioned, with eyes the color of fresh honey.

"Me come, Missy." She gazed, wistfully ingratiating, at Sara Eden.

"Monique, this is Miss Vicky," Sara said sternly. "From now on you will take care of her. When Nancy calls you, if you're not busy, then you'll help in the kitchen."

"Me do, Missy," she promised in a warm voice that was pleasingly musical. What was the accent? Vicky wondered.

"Take Miss Vicky to her room now, and see to it that she naps before dinner." Sara turned to Vicky. "Monique is from the Islands. Her French is better than her English."

"My French is very shaky," Vicky said with an apologetic smile. She saw surprise in Sara Eden that she spoke French at all. What little she knew Papa had taught her.

"You'll find your room pleasant, even on the hottest nights, because of the breeze from the river." Sara Eden was talking compulsively now. "Of course, the really hot weather won't be on us for another week or two, though in the city they're feeling it already. But don't let me keep you from your nap, Vicky." Sara remained scrupulously polite, though the handkerchief in her hand was crumpled in a tight ball. "Monique will show you upstairs."

Feeling as though she were acting a role in a play, Vicky rose to her feet and followed Monique out of the room and down the hall to the wide, curving staircase. Monique smiled over her shoulder, plainly delighted at this new assignment.

At the second door at the top of the stairs Monique paused.

"In heah, Young Missy," she said with a sudden brilliant smile. "Prettee room. So prettee."

Monique opened the door and Vicky walked into the

huge corner room, multiwindowed, with sunlight dancing
across a flowered rug. The walls were a smoky blue; the
bed, a highpost of carved pine, japanned in red, black,
and gold and curtained in exquisite white damask. To one
side of the bed stood a commode with gilt chinoiserie on a
black background, to the other side a marble-topped
washstand, above which hung a gilt-framed oval mirror.
A wing chair sat before the richly carved fireplace frame.
It was without question a special room in a splendid
house.

Monique went swiftly to turn down the bed.

"Missy, her say yo' rest," Monique said with charming
sternness. "Me lay out yo' nightdress." She left the bed to
go to the pair of portmanteaus that held Vicky's new
wardrobe. Vicky stood uncertainly in the center of the
room. A nightdress for a nap? But she would not argue
with Monique. From Monique, she told herself with relief, she would learn the Southern ways.

Monique chattered happily, finding a bond in the fact
that both she and Vicky were new to Eden.

When Vicky finally lay back against the pillows, covered by the finely woven sheet, Monique crossed to the
windows and pulled the draperies snug to filter out the
late-morning sunlight, summer-strong already in early
May.

"Now yo' sleep," Monique crooned. "Me wake yo'
when Juno say her about to put dinnah on de table."

Obediently Vicky closed her eyes, conscious of a tired-
ness now, remembering she had slept hardly at all last
night aboard ship. But her mind was too active for sleep.

Mrs. Eden was determined to present her to the family
friends at a big party. Not a gesture of affection, Vicky
warned herself. The party was to make her realize she did
not belong.

Good manners were the same whether displayed at a
modest tea party at the vicar's house in their little village
in England or at one of Sara Eden's sumptuous affairs.
She would *not* be frightened by a show of elegance.

Michael wanted her here, she reminded herself as she
stirred restlessly beneath the sheet.

Impatiently pushing aside her memory of the previous evening, she got up, crossed to the window and pushed aside the draperies. Michael, with a spaniel at his heels, was sauntering off into a grove of trees beyond the sweep of green grass, moving swiftly, as though impatient to renew his relationship with the beauty of Eden.

She pulled the draperies tight, and settled herself in bed again, conscious of the absurd pounding of her heart. She was in love with Michael. She would not allow Sara Eden to drive her away.

Let them all believe her an opportunist, she told herself rebelliously. She would be exactly what Michael wanted of her. A shield against his family. Against the social life that threatened to inundate him. She had escaped from Five Points. She had herself a fine home. And she would not shame Michael.

She swung over to one side, her dark hair fanned across her face and the pillow, providing a screen against reality. All at once the exhaustion, the towering newness of her life overtook her. In seconds she was sleeping soundly.

Vicky came awake slowly, aware that Monique was moving about the room. A breeze from the Mississippi was blowing through a corner window that Monique had opened against the warmth of the day.

"Missy?" Monique murmured. "Almos' time fo' yo' to go downstaihs to de dinnah table. Juno, her be servin' soon."

"All right, Monique." Vicky smiled as she pulled herself up into a sitting position.

"Fus' me brush yo' haih," Monique said with proprietary interest; "den yo' git into yo' dress. Which yo' gonna weah downstaihs?" She was going to the washstand, atop which she had placed Vicky's comb and brush, bought in Stewart's. For an instant tears threatened Vicky. She remembered the dainty comb-and-brush set that had been her father's last present to her before his company was sent to the Crimea. "Which dress, Missy?" Monique pressed.

"You choose," Vicky ordered with an air of camarade-
rie. In the store the saleslady who had helped them had
talked glibly about visiting dresses, promenade dresses,
party dresses, but it was hard to distinguish which was
which.

With pride at being accorded this honor, Monique
chose a double-skirted blue silk that, Vicky knew, was
flattering. And proper to wear downstairs for the midday
meal. Vicky was pleased with this secret ally.

"Did you sleep, Vicky?" Michael asked politely when
she reached the dining room.

"I did. I hadn't realized how tired I was until I lay
down." Again, Bart Eden was inspecting her intensely.

"We might as well sit down," he said. "Sara will be
along in a minute. There's always some last-minute item
that requires her attention." A faint contempt for such
details showed in his voice.

Vicky hesitated. Where was she supposed to sit? Bart
noticed her confusion and laughed.

"Come over here beside me," he ordered in a spurt of
good humor. "Let me have something pretty to look at
over dinner. I have little enough to amuse me." His
glance swept over Ava, who placed herself silently next to
Michael.

"Athena, tell Juno to send in dinner," Sara ordered out
in the hall. "And bring me a cup of coffee right away. I
have a headache."

Vicky felt increasingly tense as Sara moved to the foot
of the table.

"The glassware in the cabinet there is so beautiful," she
found herself saying calmly.

"Sara collects English and Irish glassware," Bart said
sarcastically. "It's her passion."

"The wineglasses on the top shelf are Waterford." Sara
ignored Bart. "They date back to the beginning of the
century. And the four glasses on the shelf below are Ravenscroft, from the last quarter of the seventeenth century. They were brought here from England by my great-
great-grandmother," she said with pride. "They don't

make glassware like that anymore. The art has deteriorated."

While Sara talked, Athena brought her coffee. Then began the parade of food. A pinkly succulent roast beef, black-eyed peas, yams. A huge salad bowl. A plate piled high with golden biscuits, still hot to the touch.

Sara, playing the charming Southern hostess, asked Vicky her impressions of New York. Vicky spoke admiringly of the wonders of the city, then became uneasy when she encountered Sara's contempt for them. To her mother-in-law New York City was crowded, dirty. Yet Sara Eden, Vicky guessed, would not have seen Five Points on her visits to the city.

"I've read the New York newspapers from time to time," Sara said with distaste. "The increase in crime there is appalling. Hardly a day passes without a murder."

"When you disparage New York, Sara, you don't sweeten New Orleans," Bart said dryly. "That fair city accounts for its share of crime, doesn't it, Ava?"

But his sister-in-law refused to be drawn into the conversation, contenting herself with occasional soft-voiced asides to Michael.

Not until dessert arrived—generous wedges of pecan pie—did Sara again allow herself to personally address Vicky.

"We must arrange to have the Misses Gardiner come over to make a party gown for you. I have some lengths of material that—"

"We shopped in New York, Mama," Michael intervened. "Vicky will show you what we bought." Michael was wary, reserved. Was he disturbed that they had spent so much money at a time when finances were tight at Eden?

"I think, Michael, that we'll say you met Vicky when you were in New York last year on business that March. Then this marriage won't seem so hasty," she said with an air of indulgence. "You know how folks are apt to talk."

"Mama, I'm not truly concerned about how folks talk." Michael's voice was unfamiliarly sharp.

"You have to care, Michael," his mother reproached sharply. "You have your profession to consider. You can't go around antagonizing prospective clients."

"Last March I was still in England," Vicky pointed out self-consciously.

"Vicky, cannot you stretch the truth a bit," Sara protested with an air of amusement that barely concealed her irritation, "when it's for Michael's welfare?"

"Of course," Vicky capitulated softly.

Conversation stopped then, as there was the sound of a carriage pulling up out front.

"Who's calling at this hour?" said Bart.

"Probably Jack," Michael suggested.

"Jack would ride over from the fields, or more likely he'd walk," his mother said.

Socrates was walking with unaccustomed swiftness down the corridor to the front door. Any new arrival in the quiet life of the plantation, Vicky guessed, was of interest.

"It's probably Betsy," Bart suddenly decided. "She's not one to be upset by a clock. If she feels like coming over before calling hours, she's not going to be stopped."

"Betsy Harris is not a formal guest," Sara shot back. "She's the daughter of one of our closest friends and a neighbor—a sweet, lovely girl."

They could hear Socrates welcoming someone at the door. A girl with a light, soft voice.

"Betsy," Michael confirmed. "Betsy and Alex studied together here at the house for years under the same tutor, until Alex went away to school. You'll like her," he promised Vicky, with something akin to relief in his voice. He expected her and Betsy Harris to be friends.

A tall, slim girl with long fair hair, green eyes, and delicate features walked into the dining room.

"I had Cyrus bring me over so I could go down to see Mama LaVerne," she explained after kissing Ava hello. "One of the horses has a skin disorder that the animal doctor can't heal, but Mama LaVerne's salve never fails. Is it all right if I go down to the quarters?" Her request was politely directed to both Bart and Sara.

"Only if you sit down and have coffee and pecan pie with us," Bart stipulated with courtly charm. Once, Vicky thought, he must have been a most impressive man.

"Uncle Bart, I never turn down Juno's cooking," Betsy said, laughing, and walked to the chair beside him. Her eyes rested with friendly curiosity on Vicky.

"Betsy, we've had such a surprise." There was none of the strong-willed chatelaine of Eden about Sara now—rather, the ingratiating plantation mistress who did little beyond entertain and make herself beautiful. "Michael found himself a bride up there in New York. This is Victoria," she said with a gracious gesture, "whom we are to call Vicky. Vicky, this is Betsy Harris. The Harrises are our dearest friends."

"Michael, she's so pretty," Betsy said with such genuine friendliness that Vicky felt a surge of pleasure.

"How's your father?" Sara asked. "Has he got over his cold?"

"He's fine," Betsy said.

"And your mother?" Sara asked.

Betsy sighed.

"Like always, Aunt Sara."

Athena arrived to set a plate of pecan pie before Betsy, Artemis following with a cup of coffee.

"Ulysses has had an open sore on his side for weeks, and the animal doctor has done nothing for him," Betsy said seriously. "Mama LaVerne will give me her salve, and he'll be fine in three days."

"Mama LaVerne is an elderly slave who used to work in the house but now is in charge of the infirmary in the quarters," Michael explained to Vicky. "She has a healing hand."

"She was my sister Ava's nurse when Ava was small; then she cared for Michael and Alex," Sara said. "The slaves have some ridiculous belief that she had healing powers. Some kind of magic in her hands."

"I don't believe in the voodoo and the magic," Betsy acknowledged, "but Mama LaVerne has special skills. Perhaps she brought them with her from Africa. I know only that I tell her what's wrong with an animal and she

gives me one of her medicines, and it works." She turned
with a smile to Michael. "Isn't it nice to have your aunt
back? Doesn't Alex miss being home? I think I would die
if I had to go all the way up North to college."

"He's very lonely sometimes," Michael said somberly.

Sara frowned and pushed away her dessert plate.

"Alex knows it's important for him to get his education."

"Papa says that the Northern colleges are hard on our
Southern boys," Betsy said. "They foster sectional issues.
But of course," Betsy added diplomatically, "Alex won't
be influenced."

"Alex appreciates his heritage," Sara said with pride.
"We've lived in Louisiana for five generations."

Betsy focused on Vicky with a warm smile.

"Do you like animals? Folks around here think I'm
rather queer because I'm so fond of them."

"I like every living animal," Vicky declared with quiet
intensity. "I hate the English habit of hunting for sport."

"It's a Southern habit too," Bart remarked dryly.

"Before you go down to the quarters, Betsy, you must
play for us," Sara intervened. She resented Betsy's over-
tures of friendship to her, Vicky realized with a start. "It's
so seldom that I go down to New Orleans for a concert
these days."

"If you like," Betsy agreed docilely.

They went into the drawing room and settled themselves on the sofas. Betsy, with the air of politely performing a chore, played the popular new *Poet and Peas-
ant* overture.

Finished, she turned around with sweet, unaffected
smile at their applause. She knew that her accomplishment at the piano was meager, but seemed undisturbed by
the fact.

"Vicky is musical also," Sara turned to Vicky with a
tight smile. "Now you must play for us."

"I don't play particularly well." Vicky's voice was low.
She was painfully conscious of the way Michael had stiffened in his chair, and of his aunt's sudden attention.

After a moment's silence, she walked to the piano and

seated herself before the keyboard. Her hands were unsteady as they hovered above the keys. Chopin's Polonaise No. 6, she decided after a moment's hesitation. The vicar's wife, who had taught her to play, had concentrated much on this composition. It was her one real pianistic accomplishment.

She played with verve and zest, for a few minutes caught up in the brilliance of the music. Then she finished and turned around to face the polite applause of the others.

Sara Eden was not applauding. She had not even heard the piano music, Vicky guessed. She was gazing with anguished intensity at Betsy's pleasing profile. Suddenly Vicky understood why Sara recoiled from the prospect of her becoming friends with Betsy Harris. Sara had wished for a marriage between Betsy and Michael.

"You play well, Vicky," Bart said unexpectedly. He shot a triumphant glance at his wife. But instinct warned Vicky that he was no more pleased with this marriage than Sara. At the moment he found vindictive pleasure in his wife's distraught state, so precariously concealed. "You must play whenever we have visitors."

"That is the only composition I play well," Vicky said with candor. "It's the one I've practiced most."

Bart laughed loudly. Sara flinched and swung her gaze to him, chastising him with her eyes. But her voice was gentle when she turned to speak to Betsy.

"It's much too hot today to walk all the way down to the quarters. When you go there, have Cyrus drive you," Sara ordered.

"Perhaps Vicky would like to go with me?" Betsy said shyly.

"Not today," Sara decided briskly. "She's had a long trip. Another time, Betsy."

Vicky felt hot color stain her cheeks. Wasn't that a decision for her to make? But she understood clearly: Sara Eden was determined to keep her and Betsy Harris apart. How did she plan to accomplish that? Would she tell Betsy's parents about the brothel on Greene Street? No! She couldn't humiliate Michael that way. Or could she?

Don't run from the truth, Vicky warned herself sternly. Michael's mother would fight, every way she knew how, to drive her from Eden.

7

Bart propelled his wheelchair closer to the library fireplace. Since supper rain had been pelting the house, lowering the temperature at least twenty degrees. The dank chill in the high-ceilinged room seemed to settle low in his spine. Damn this weather! It always got him in the back.

In the old days he liked to walk out into a storm, feeling himself challenging the elements. Best of all, in bad weather, he liked to throw a pretty piece on her rear. His throat went dry as he remembered.

Socrates rose with a satisfied smile. The log in the grate, which he had been struggling to coax into a blaze, had healthily ignited. Soon the raw cold in the room would disappear.

"Another bourbon, Socrates," Bart said with irritation.

Sara was standing looking out into the murky night, waiting for Socrates to leave them for the servants' house. He inspected Sara with detached curiosity. Sometimes he wondered about Sara and Jack. No, Jack might be interested, with that iceberg for a wife, but Sara wouldn't let him near her.

Too many principles to allow herself to sleep with a

man who wasn't her husband. Maybe she was past the age at which a woman gave a damn about those things.

He stirred restlessly. Michael and the girl were both upstairs in their rooms, and Sara had urged Ava out for a walk. She was impatient to talk with him. Hell, what was there to talk about? The damn fool had married the girl.

"Yo' wan' some ice, Suh?" Socrates asked solicitously. "Dey be some lef' out in de kitchen."

"Socrates, you know I don't want you to water down my drink with ice," he said sharply. "Not before it's ninety-two in the shade." Socrates left them, closing the door behind him, and Sara swung away from the window. Bart watched while she settled herself in the wing chair near the fireplace, knowing she was listening for the sounds that told her Socrates was out in the servants' house.

"Bart, we have to warn Joshua," she said tensely. "He must know."

"Must know what?" Bart questioned leisurely, always enjoying baiting Sara. His husbandly pastime, he thought with sardonic humor.

"About that girl!" Sara said impatiently. "Her background. Betsy's so young and innocent." She sighed heavily. "Why couldn't Michael have married Betsy? They would be so good for each other."

"There are those who consider Betsy strange," he reminded her. Sara looked indignant. "All this carrying on with the animals," he pointed out with distaste. "Betsy's the same age as Alex. Twenty. She ought to be married and raising a family."

"Joshua has always given her too much freedom," Sara said unhappily. "Poor man, he's had enough on his hands with Madeline like that all these years. Losing the two little girls when Betsy was only an infant. It's natural he spoiled her."

"Sara, I'd say Betsy Harris is the most unspoiled girl I ever encountered," Bart contradicted. "It's just that she's got this crazy compulsion to meddle with what is the veterinarian's work."

"Bart, Joshua has to be told about this girl Michael picked up in New York," Sara tried again.

"Well, Sara, considering you're planning a party, the whole damn parish is going to know Michael brought himself a wife back from New York." He chuckled. "That won't settle too well with some fond mamas around who cherished ideas about Michael."

"Bart, you know exactly what I mean," Sara said impatiently. "Joshua has to know her background. I won't have Betsy involved with the likes of her—that sweet, lovely child."

"You don't believe the army-officer-father story?" he mocked. "It could be true."

"Are you forgetting what Alex wrote us? She was playing the piano in a brothel." Her voice recoiled from this knowledge. "Alex didn't lie."

"She didn't play too badly," Bart said offhandedly. "Though personally I prefer lighter stuff."

"I can't understand how Michael allowed himself to get trapped this way. To marry a girl like that, knowing her only a few days." She took a deep breath, her eyes speculative. "Michael's an attorney. He'll know how to handle a divorce. A lot of people think a divorce is a disgrace, but we could live with it."

"Damn, you're supposed to be smart, Sara!" A vein throbbed in his forehead. "You start up with that girl and you'll lose Michael." Unexpectedly, he chuckled. "But I'm mighty sure, Sara, that somewhere along the way you'll figure out how to drive her away. I'd take bets on that."

Sara sprang to her feet. "It's useless to try to talk to you, Bart!"

Bart watched her flounce across the room and disappear into the hall. How long since he had slept with Sara? A solid six years before the stroke. She couldn't understand that a man like him couldn't satisfy himself with one piece of tail. After she walked in on that binge with those two Haitian bitches, she had locked him out of her room. It had been no good with them anyway, by that time. She didn't work him up anymore.

On a sudden impulse he wheeled himself out of the library and down the hall to his bedroom door. Jefferson was sleeping on the pallet at the foot of the bed.

"Jefferson," he called sharply. "You no-good, lazy boy, wake up!" He grinned, watching Jefferson snap to attention. Jefferson was mighty proud of being his boy. Pleased, too, with the treats he tossed his way at regular intervals. Jefferson would be out in the fields this year if he had not picked him, two years ago, to come into the house to be his personal slave.

"Yessuh!" Jefferson scrambled to his feet.

"You run upstairs and you tell Mr. Michael to come down to the library, you hear? And no need to let the rest of the household know what you're about."

"Ah tell him." Jefferson nodded vigorously. "Real quiet-lak."

Bart returned to the library and poured himself another shot of bourbon. Thunder rumbled in the black sky. In the distance there was an ominous crackle. One of the pecans in the grove to the west had been hit, Bart guessed.

What the devil were they going to do about Michael? Michael was his firstborn, but he didn't understand him any more than he understood Alex. Less. He'd picked himself a pretty enough wife. Fire in her, once it was released, but he never could figure out Michael when it came to showing he was a man. Never touched any of the slaves. There was one way the girl could stop Sara, he thought grimly. She could make sure Michael gave her a baby right away.

"Papa?" Michael stood uncertainly in the doorway. "Jefferson said you wanted me."

"That's right." He frowned. "Jefferson out there in the hall?"

"Yessuh, Ah's heah, Mist' Bart," Jefferson said good-humoredly, pushing himself into view.

"You go start a fire in my bedroom, Jefferson. And close the door while you're doing it so the heat stays in. I'll call you when I want you."

Michael walked into the library and settled himself in the wing chair where his mother had sat earlier.

"Michael, what the devil is this all about?" Bart demanded brusquely. "Man to man, tell my why the hell you married that girl? Did you get all overheated, take her to bed, and think you had to marry her?"

"Nothing like that!" Michael frowned in rejection. But he was not offering further information, Bart noted.

"Look, Michael, we know where you met her," Bart said bluntly. "Alex wrote us."

"He had no right!" Michael said furiously. "She was there for one night. Out of a sense of responsibility to her aunt. She came from a sheltered home in England—"

"You believe that hogwash about an army-officer father?"

"I know it's true." Michael was pale. "I married Vicky because I feel she's the perfect wife for me." His jaw was set. Bart knew that expression.

"Michael, a girl you met little more than a week ago? I don't know what's going on in your head, but this won't work. Your mother won't have it, I tell you."

"It's done." Sometimes he could be as stubborn as his mother, Bart thought with frustration. "Vicky is my wife." He took a deep breath. "If you and Mama feel that you don't want Vicky at Eden, then we'll move into New Orleans."

"Don't talk like a fool!" Bart snapped. "This is your home. You'll stay here."

"And Vicky is my wife, Papa," Michael said with studied calm.

"It's not going to be easy for her here," Bart warned after a moment. "You know your mother."

"I'm a married man, Papa." Michael smiled faintly. "Mama will grow to understand that. And Ava should help take up her time. She's not going to settle quietly into plantation life."

"Don't underrate your mother," said Bart. "She'll handle Ava and have time left to concentrate on you. Never forget, everything's got to be her way. I could have made

Eden into a kingdom if she'd let me. She was afraid to gamble. But those first years we set this parish on its ear. Parties, balls! Your mother was a beauty. She had all the ladylike gentility you'd expect with her background, but when we were first married," he said with remembered relish, "she forgot it all under the covers. For a while." Damn, why was Michael looking so embarrassed? They were talking man to man. "Something happened to us, Michael. Your mother gave up carnal activities and began to collect English and Irish glass."

Why was it nothing had happened with them in bed after those first few years? A man couldn't go all the way alone. He needed some help. She had used that business about his bringing a pretty black piece to his bed now and then. Other wives shut their eyes.

He frowned, wanting to wash away the night when he had forced his way into Sara's room, into her bed, and nothing had happened. *Nothing.* He had been the prize stud in the state, and suddenly the thing between his legs was dormant. Limp, shriveled, refusing to show that he was a man. Damn, he hadn't been that old.

Now his mind focused on his son's wife. He'd take any bets she would be hot as a pistol. If he were fifteen years younger, he'd show her what it could be like with a real man.

"You'll talk to Mama about Vicky, won't you?" Michael, his voice anxious, brought him back to the moment.

"I'll talk to her," Bart promised. "But you know nobody makes up her mind for her." He looked speculatively at Michael. "What about Alex? What was he doing in that whorehouse in New York?"

"Preparing to do what a man does in a whorehouse," Michael said. "He and Fred were out to sow some wild oats." He hesitated. "Alex was pretty homesick."

"If he's old enough to go to a whorehouse, he's old enough to stay at college until summer vacation," Bart said dismissingly. Damn, when was Alex going to snap back from that business three years ago? It wasn't natural to feel that way about Janine. He'd sold her where she'd never have to work in the fields. Sold her mother along with her. He'd hand-picked Joe Lockwood. Joe with that fine little town house in New Orleans. Janine and Louise to take care of it, and Janine to take care of Joe when he came home from his business. Old Joe would never marry. Janine was set for life.

"I'm tired." Michael rose to his feet with an air of apology. "It's been a full day."

"Go on to bed, Michael." Querulously Bart gestured to him to leave. Too tired to go to his bride? Did he ever go to her? What crazy kind of marriage had Michael contracted for himself? He gazed quizzically at his oldest son. Did Michael still remember that night he'd been caught with Ava? For a few minutes Bart had gone berserk, said horrendous things. But Michael had gotten over that—hadn't he? He had been only fourteen. "Michael, poke your head in my room." He pushed aside ugly memories. "Tell Jefferson to scout for Andrew. I'm ready to call it a night too."

Bart waited for the evening ritual: Andrew wheeling him into his room, transferring him from chair to bed as though he were a baby. Preparing him for the long night when he lay until dawn reading the collection of newspapers to which he subscribed. Cursing the politicians who had kept him out of the Legislature, kept him from acquiring the judgeship. Damn, if Sara were not so tight with the money—if she had been willing to gamble—he might have been a State Senator!

Andrew—small, wiry, but with the strength to handle him as well as any buck who put in fourteen hours a day in the fields—changed him into nightclothes and sponged him down the way he liked.

"Yo' lak de bourbon bottle heah by de bed, Mist' Bart?" Andrew asked the nightly question, knowing the answer.

"Keep it on hand there, Andrew. I might feel a bit uncomfortable during the night and want something to see me through." He had no real pain, he acknowledged, in a rare mood of candor tonight. Mostly, it was the humiliation of being cared for like a baby.

Methodically Andrew moved from window to window, closing the shutters against the threatening storm, pulling the draperies together to blot out the streaks of lightning.

"Hope yo' has a good night, Suh," Andrew said respectfully, and withdrew.

Bart sat up in bed, the lamp lit, the logs crackling in the grate. The *Picayune* was spread out before him, but he was not seeing the words. Instead he was remembering Vicky's face as she sat at the piano, determined to show up Sara. Spunky little baggage. In his mind he pictured himself in bed with her, feeling himself able to do what he imagined so often.

"Jefferson," he called out softly, and Jefferson rose inquiringly to his feet. "My back is beginning to bother me. It's this damn weather. You go out to the servants' house and you tell Odalie to come to me. Don't wake up everybody else," he warned. "Just tell Odalie to come on up here to give me a massage. And you sleep the rest of the night in her place."

"Yessuh." Jefferson's eyes were downcast. Wise little fellow, Bart thought with dry amusement. He figured there was more than massaging when Odalie came to him. That was more credit than anybody else in this household would give him.

He reached for the bourbon and poured himself another shot. It felt warm going down. He pictured Odalie's doll-like face. Twenty-three years old, but with the body of fourteen. Already, in his mind, he felt excitement, seeing Odalie walk into the room with that languid sway, the large nipples atop the faintly swelling breasts pushing hard against her short shift. She never wore Sara's castoffs, he thought. Juno, Nancy, and the twins inherited those. But he took care of Odalie, because she knew how to take care of him.

He settled tensely against the huge bolster behind him, impatient for Odalie to arrive. Doc Stanton laughed at him. The old man said nothing like that could happen to him in his condition—but Doc Stanton didn't know.

He ran his tongue about the dryness of his lips as he

heard the turn of the doorknob. Nobody on this floor except for Odalie and him. Nobody guessing what happened behind that door Odalie would shut after her—and lock —in a moment. Except perhaps that little devil Jefferson, who could only guess.

The door swung open, Odalie's petite, incredibly narrow body moving with unconscious grace as she came toward him.

"Yo' feelin' po'ly, Mist' Bart?" she crooned with sympathy, her dark eyes aglow. Damn it, nobody could tell him he was dead when she looked at him that way— knowing how it would be with them in a little while.

"Back's acting up, Odalie," he said, playing their little game. "Give it a massage for a while."

"Me brung dat salve Mama LaVerne give me," she murmured. "She tell me hit's good fo' yo'."

"Well, get to work and stop talking about it, Odalie." These Haitian sluts were special. They knew in the cradle what it took to make a man happy.

Outside, the storm was building. Somewhere, a shutter flapped against the house. If Socrates woke up, he would go fasten it.

Bart helped Odalie shift him over on his stomach. She pulled up the nightshirt and spread the sweet-smelling salve across his back. Nothing more than perfume, he thought, but he enjoyed the heavy, pungent scent, the feel of her long, supple fingers on his back.

Tonight he was impatient. Because of that wife of Michael's, who made him remember what a stud he had been thirty years ago. Earlier than usual he interrupted the massage.

"Get me over on my back again, girl," he ordered, his breathing already heavy. She smiled faintly. She knew exactly what was happening in his mind, how he was already imagining how it was going to be in a few minutes. Doc Stanton didn't know anything! Let him talk all he wanted about illusionary feelings. "I've got some stiffness down here, Odalie." His hands prodded his lower pelvic area.

Together they manipulated him onto his back. Odalie

thrust aside the covers, her face impassive as she pulled the nightshirt to his waist, his eyes fastened to the nipples thrusting hard against her dress.

"Take off that thing," he ordered hoarsely. He was feeling something. Already he was feeling something. "It'll be easier for you to climb up and massage."

Her face an exquisite ebony mask, warmed by the firelight, she pulled the cotton shift over her head and dropped it to the floor. For a provocative moment she stretched her arms high above her head. Now, with deliberate slowness, she placed a hand on each flaccid, hairy thigh and separated them. Bart's breathing became labored; his mouth parted. Slowly her hands began to massage.

Doc Stanton had been blunt when Bart had recovered enough from the stroke to consider the future. He had said, with that cold clinical voice, that his screwing days were over. "Anything that happens will be purely in your imagination."

Odalie, positioned on her knees between his thighs, was massaging him vigorously. There was a small frown on her face, an absorption in her eyes that aroused him.

"Come on, Odalie," he complained querulously. "Get me moving."

"Yo' movin', Suh," she said complacently, a glint of excitement in her eyes. "Big and proud."

He had not realized that she had produced an erection —what Doc Stanton callously called an imitation, a spastic reaction.

"Now, Odalie!" His voice was unsteady, his mind excited. Sara looked at him and believed he was a vegetable from the waist down. *She didn't know.* "Mount, Odalie. Mount!"

A groan rose in his throat as she lifted herself above him, then dropped with absolute accuracy. His eyes fastened to her face as she moved up and down, her eyes shut tight, her mouth parted in passion. He was making a woman happy. It didn't matter that for him it was all in his mind.

"Shhh," he ordered automatically when she cried out.

They were alone on the whole lower floor of the house, and the walls were thick. "Now the other way, Odalie. I'll make you crazy, girl!"

It was that pretty piece that Michael married who had set him off tonight. He chuckled with sardonic humor. Wouldn't Sara be furious if she knew!

8

Slowly the morning sunlight pried its way into Vicky's consciousness. She was aware of being overwarm. The quilt that had been so welcome during last night's chill rain was now weighing her down with discomfort.

What time was it? She lifted herself on one elbow and reached out to the commode where she had placed the pendant watch Michael had bought her in New York. So late! But sleep had been elusive last night. She had fallen asleep moments after Monique, with childlike pleasure, had tucked the quilt about her, only to wake up no more than twenty minutes later and then lie restless for hours, falling asleep with the dawn.

She stiffened as the door pushed slightly open. Grinning broadly, Monique sauntered into the room.

"Me bring hot watuh," she said, heading for the washstand. "Den me go back downstaihs to de kitchen an' fetch yo' breakfas'. Anything special yo' feel like dis mawnin', Missy?"

"Anything," Vicky said, the fact registering in her mind that she was supposed to have breakfast in her room.

"Coffee," she stipulated, surprising herself. She had learned to drink coffee only since she had met Michael.

"Don' yo' worry, honey, dat Juno, her fix a fine breakfas' tray. Yo' see."

With the washstand in readiness for Vicky, Monique, kettle in hand, hurried importantly out of the room. Vicky could hear her humming to herself as she moved down the hall to the stairs. Vicky left the bed and viewed the accessories to her toilette with interest: a fine English soap; linens chosen with no qualms about cost.

She washed leisurely, enjoying the warmth of the water on her face, the floral scent of the soap. On impulse she hurried, barefoot, to the window. The flowers looked lush after the night of rain, the grass even more richly green. The dogs, Sam and Hilda, were darting about the lawn. There was no sign of the storm that had lashed at the house last night.

An older black man, with young Jefferson at his heels, was working among the roses. A pair of kittens romped under a live oak, gnarled and twisted, that must be, Vicky guessed, a century old. Then, with a guilty giggle, Vicky darted back to the bed, to wait demurely for her breakfast tray.

When it came, her eyes widened with disbelief as she viewed the feast spread before her: A small bowl of strawberries in sweet cream. Eggs; bacon. A mound of grits crowned with melting butter. A plate of golden-brown, high-peaked biscuits. A pot of coffee.

"Monique, I couldn't begin to eat all this," she gasped.

Monique giggled.

"Yo' eat what yo' want," she said practically. "What yo' don' want, hit sho' ain't goin' to waste."

"Everything looks so good." What richness in this land! "Monique, have one of these," she coaxed, pointing to the biscuits.

"Missy, 'tain right," she protested, but her eyes were huge.

"Go ahead," Vicky ordered with happy defiance. "Who's to know? Take one. What do you call them?" she asked curiously.

"Biscuits," Monique said solemnly. "Honey, wheah yo' come from?"

Vicky laughed. "From England. Across the ocean."

"My mama an' me, us come from island where 'tis warm like summah all de time. Me t'ink her say Martinique." All at once Monique was solemn. "Mama, her die two yeahs ago."

Only now did Monique allow one hand to approach the biscuits, to choose one.

When they had finished breakfast, Monique took the tray downstairs to the kitchen, then came back up again to help Vicky to dress.

"Yo' gonna be home today, Missy?" Monique stood before the open wardrobe.

"Yes, Monique." Where else would she be? A touch of panic brushed her as she considered going downstairs this morning to face Michael's mother and father. "Choose a dress for me," she ordered.

The two of them spent infinite time over Vicky's dressing, Monique brushing her hair until it shone. Was this the way Southern ladies all lived? Vicky wondered restlessly. Pushing each day away with such nonsense as this?

Sara Eden was not the typical Southern lady. Michael said she was up at six, busy much of the day with plantation affairs. Michael's mother was glad for these demands on her, Vicky guessed instinctively. Michael said, with admiration, that his mother thought like a man. But her feelings were entirely feminine.

"Yo' feel lak settin' on de gallery fo' a spell?" Monique asked. "Smells so good out deah on a mawnin' lak dis."

"I'll sit out there and read," Vicky decided.

"Us got lotsa books in de lib'ary," Monique said with pride. "Downstaihs—" She gestured engagingly. "Me close de winduhs now agin' de heat of de day." She peered outside. "Mist' Michael, him goin' into Noo Awleans. Colin's in front wit' de carriage." Monique sighed dramatically. "Dat Colin, him so luckee. Go to de city wit' Mist' Michael t'ree, sometimes fo' times a week."

Vicky squelched an impulse to dart to the window to see her husband. Monique moved about closing the other windows, and then together they left the room, Monique leading the way to the library.

"In heah, Missy." Monique stood before an open door to the left of the stairs.

"Thank you, Monique."

Vicky walked into the large square room, her eyes immediately drawn to the book-lined wall to her right, then stopped dead in confusion. Sara sat at the desk in one corner of the room, frowning over an open ledger, a tall, buxom black woman standing before her with a solemn expression.

"Juno, I don't know where all the sugar goes in this—" Sara spied Vicky as she turned to leave. "Good morning, Vicky," she greeted her with unexpected friendliness. "You were looking for something?"

"Nothing important," Vicky stammered. "Something to read."

"Go help yourself." Instinct told Vicky the warmth was not genuine. Sara Eden had decided that friendship was the best course for her to pursue with her son's wife. "That's all, Juno. Just make sure the sugar chest is locked hereafter. I don't like the way it disappears."

Self-consciously Vicky walked to the bookshelves and inspected, without seeing, the rows of beautifully bound books.

"Michael went into New Orleans," Sara said, oddly speculative.

"I know." Vicky gazed over her shoulder with a quick small smile.

"Do you read Shakespeare, Vicky?" Sara asked with a show of charm.

"No," Vicky said uneasily.

"Coleridge? Milton?" Sara pursued. "When I find it difficult to fall asleep at night, I like to read Coleridge."

"I read Charles Dickens. And just a while ago a book by William Makepeace Thackeray." She groped in her mind for the title. *"Vanity Fair.* I—I thought it was dull."

"If you like to read Dickens, you would hardly appreciate Thackeray," Sara said with a sense of humor. "You might like to read the works of a Southern gentleman."

She was hiding, again, behind her mask of friendship. "Edgar Allan Poe of Virginia. In Europe, my sister Ava wrote, he's most highly respected. He's been recommended by such famous writers as Baudelaire and Mallarmé." She smiled faintly, knowing these names meant nothing to Vicky. "There's a book of poems and a collection of short stories by him. Don't read the short stories before bedtime because you'll never fall asleep!"

"Thank you. I'll look for the poems."

Enjoying the pleasing warmth of the morning, Vicky seated herself in one of the rockers that lined the gallery. Sam and Hilda romped up at first sight of her, mounting the gallery to demand attention.

When the dogs were content with her show of affection, they settled at her feet, allowing her to read. But her eyes scanned the words with little comprehension.

Vicky glanced up at the sound of the front door opening. Sara stood there with a small, fixed smile.

"How would you like to have Seth drive you about the plantation when he returns?" she offered politely. "He could take you along the river. The view is magnificent."

"Thank you." Vicky struggled to sound pleased. Sara Eden was anxious to send her sight-seeing. "I'd like that very much."

"I'll tell Monique to come and let you know when Seth returns."

"Thank you."

Vicky sat back and tried to read again as Sara reentered the house. She felt an odd restlessness, the hours of the day suddenly endlessly long. Vicky wondered how Ava occupied herself. She seemed to be spending an inordinate amount of time in her room. But then, Sara was not much warmer toward her sister than she was toward her daughter-in-law.

"Young Missy—" Monique came breathlessly out onto the gallery. "Seth, him back wit' de carriage. Missy say tell yo' he bring de carriage around out front in a couple minutes."

"Thank you, Monique."

"Me help Juno in de kitchen now. String de beans fo' she—less you' wan' me fo' somethin'?" she added eagerly.

"You go and help Juno," Vicky said approvingly. How happy Monique seemed, she thought with recurrent disbelief. How could she be happy as a slave? Immediately Vicky felt guilty at this involuntary condemnation of an institution so important to the South. "Oh, would you please put this back in the library for me?" She held out the book.

"Mebbe yo' lak in yo' room?" Monique gazed at the title with infinite respect. Monique could not read, Vicky realized suddenly. She had read in the New York *Herald* that the slaves were never taught to read or write. In most Southern states this was against the law. "Prettee." Monique touched the gold lettering with admiration.

"Yes, I can read tonight," said Vicky, stifling an impulse to say she had not wished to make Monique run up the long flight of stairs yet again this morning. She must learn to live the Southern way of life, she ordered herself.

She waited for Seth to pull up before the house with the carriage. Jefferson, who was sitting on the box with him, jumped down to open the carriage door for her.

"Mawnin', Young Missy," Seth said genially.

"Good morning." Vicky smiled and allowed Jefferson to help her into the carriage.

Seth circled around behind the house to drive along the carriage path that flanked the river. Vicky leaned back, watching the progress of a steamer en route to New Orleans. She was conscious of the poignant sweet blossoms of the trees to her right: fruit-bearing trees, she guessed, and she wondered what crop they would bear.

Seth turned away from the river to drive the handsome bays along a narrow road that cut through the fields. Endless acres, it seemed—planted with cotton, she remembered. How large the plantation was, she marveled.

Then just ahead to the right Vicky spied a small white house—immaculate, black-shuttered, surrounded by colorful flowers. The garden plot was enclosed by a neat picket fence. An endearingly modest house, Vicky thought; it reminded her of home.

A woman appeared on the gallery and waved to them. Impulsively Vicky leaned out the carriage window.

"Seth, will you please stop?"

The carriage pulled up before the cottage. Jefferson hopped down to open the carriage door. The woman walked down the gallery steps and along the minute brick path to the gate: a small, painfully thin woman of about thirty, with dark hair and dark eyes. She would have been pretty except for an air of painful discontent, Vicky thought as she moved smilingly toward the woman.

"*Bonjour,* Mademoiselle," the woman said politely. "I am Claudine Lamartine. The wife of the overseer." Her accent was clearly French.

"*Bonjour.*" Vicky hesitated. "I'm Vicky Eden." She stumbled over the unfamiliar surname, feeling herself coloring. "Michael's wife."

"Jack told me that Michael had married." Suddenly Claudine Lamartine smiled, a glint of triumph in her eyes because she had, Vicky suspected, been taking bets with herself that this was Michael's bride. "Please, come in and have tea with me. It is such a pleasure for me to have a guest—" She paused because Vicky's eyes were riveted to the rows of cabins visible through the screen of towering pecan trees. She saw the young black children scampering in the dirt between the houses, nearly naked, fighting good-humoredly. "Those are the slave cabins," Claudine explained, with a flicker of annoyance that they were so close. "But please, come into the house."

Vicky entered a small, neat, colorless sitting room, her mind shaken by the sight of those one-room shanties that reminded her of the shabby houses on the Points.

Claudine moved with quick little steps to a china closet that sat between two small windows and reached inside for an exquisite hand-painted cup and saucer. A matching cup and saucer, teapot, and sugar bowl sat on a small table before a tapestry-covered settee. Claudine must have been about to have her late-morning tea when she had heard the carriage outside.

"You are from New York, are you not?" Claudine gestured to Vicky to join her on the settee.

"Yes." Again, a warning in her mind not to betray the brevity of her residence in New York. "Before that I lived in a village near London."

"I was born in Quebec City," Claudine said with a look of painful nostalgia as she poured from the beautiful teapot that was in such contrast to the drabness of the sitting room. "That is in Canada. The English own it," she said with a wry smile, "but the spirit is French. I miss it very much."

"There are many French in New Orleans, aren't there?" Vicky asked sympathetically, accepting the cup that Claudine extended.

Claudine shrugged.

"What does that mean to me? I go to New Orleans perhaps three times a year, to spend a day or two at the St. Charles. The rest of the time I sit here. Alone. A slave comes into do the housework and the washing. I do my needlework. And I remember the life in Quebec City, where I mixed with people. Here my husband is the overseer. We are seldom invited to the parties," she said with disdain. She gazed quizzically at Vicky. "Your family allowed you to leave New York for this life?"

"My parents are dead," Vicky said softly. "I have only an aunt." She sipped the strangely spiced tea and accepted a small cake from a box Claudine extended.

"Did your aunt not warn you of the isolation you would face here?" Claudine's voice was harsh.

"I love the land. I don't expect to be lonely." Vicky spoke with an air of apology.

"Jack has a fever for the land. To see things grow in this oppressively warm climate. Wait until you have spent a summer in Louisiana. But Jack refuses to go back to Quebec City. Even to leave Eden to find a job in New Orleans, where I could be with people." Her mouth worked agitatedly. Her hand, when she set the fragile teacup on the table, was trembling.

"But it's so beautiful here," Vicky said cajolingly. "And now that I'm here, perhaps we could—"

"Sara Eden does not receive the overseer's wife in her house," Claudine interrupted caustically. "Except on

Christmas and at Easter. And at the Fourth of July party
on the lawn. The South has its own way of life, Vicky.
You look about and see so much that is beautiful, yes.
But I look through the trees and I see the slave quarters.
In Canada no one is a slave. I hate this way of life. It is a
land only for the men. Did you know that there are books
in the library at Eden—at every plantation anywhere in
the South—that are kept under lock and key to be read
only by the master? Pure-minded ladies are not supposed
to set their eyes upon these books which are read in Canada and Europe by aristocracy itself," she said with sarcasm. "They are not supposed to allow their minds to
dwell on certain subjects. But all the time there is such
degradation hidden away behind these beautiful houses."

"I know I have much to learn about the ways of the
South," Vicky confessed uneasily.

"And these fine Southern ladies!" Claudine spoke
compulsively. "These ladies who look down upon unfor-
tunate girls with children and no husband, close their eyes
to the prostitution that goes on under their own fine roofs.
What other name can you give to the habit of the white
Southern males in a household who avail themselves of
any Negro or mulatto woman who takes their fancy?
These men who dare to live in one house with their wives
and their mistresses! And so many ladies," she continued,
"are so quick to tell you who fathered the mulatto children in everyone else's household but their own!"

"I didn't know," Vicky stammered, her face hot with
color.

"There is much you do not know," Claudine warned
tensely. "The South is like a beautiful woman dying of a
terrible disease. It does not yet show on the surface, but
soon it will. You do not know what goes on behind the
walls of that beautiful house which sits so grandly up
there by the river. You do not know the curse that lies
over it. You do not know the ugliness of life at Eden,
which strangers never see. But you *will* see, Vicky. And
you will be sorry you ever became an Eden."

9

With Athena and Artemis industriously brushing away the flies brought out by the increasing heat, Vicky and Bart dined alone at midday. Sara was away on business. Ava still remained secluded in her room. Vicky's appetite had ebbed away with the peak heat of the day.

"After dinner go to your room and nap for a couple of hours," Bart ordered. "This heat can be devastating to folks who aren't used to it. Of course, near the river this way, we usually get some relief in the evenings."

Vicky tried to appear interested as Bart launched into an oration about his unsuccessful runs for the State Legislature, but she was relieved when, at last, he indicated he was finished with his meal and called for Andrew to wheel him out onto the side gallery.

Vicky went up to her room, where Monique had closed all the windows and pulled the draperies shut against the sun. She glanced about for the book by Poe that Monique had brought upstairs for her. There, on the commode. She crossed to pick it up and decided to go and sit on the front gallery and read. There might be a breeze there from the river.

Walking down the stairs, she heard Bart on the side gallery.

"Seth, who's that coming up in the carriage?" he was demanding. "It's not one of ours. Who comes calling in the heat of the day like this?" Then, unexpectedly, he chuckled. "It's Charlie," he said with satisfaction. "Charlie Griswold. Seth, move your tail out to the kitchen and bring out some ice. Charlie's going to want it with his bourbon."

Vicky paused, recoiling from the prospect of meeting one of Bart Eden's friends. She swung about and hurried upstairs to her room again. But the closed-in feeling nagged at her. She crossed to the windows and opened them, one by one, pushing the draperies open just enough to allow a stray breeze to enter the room but not enough to bring in the brilliance of the sun.

The voices from the side gallery reached up to shatter the silence of her room.

"Michael straighten out the kid up there?" Griswold inquired.

"He got Alex back to school, all right. Found him chasing after a piece of tail in the whorehouses," Bart reported with distaste.

"Come on, Bart," Charlie chuckled indulgently. "It's natural enough, a boy of that age. A chip off the old block," he added slyly.

"I don't know what the devil college is going to do for Alex, but Sara insists. He doesn't want to go into law, and he sure as hell won't go into the church. Only futures open to the elite in the South," he mocked, "are in agriculture, the Army, the church, and the law. College won't help him any in agriculture, and that's where he's sure headed. Michael and he will have to take over the plantation someday—and you can be sure there'll be plenty of scrapping between those two." He paused. "Oh, some news for you, Charlie. Michael got married."

"A girl from New York?" Charlie was startled.

"That's right. Brought her back with him."

"Couldn'ta known her long," Charlie guessed cautiously.

"Long enough to stand up in front of a Baptist minister and make her his wife," Bart said caustically. "That's my fancy lawyer son. I don't know how long it's going to last, Charlie. God knows, she's pretty enough. Sets my teeth on edge sometimes. But good God, man, with all the rich young girls in these parts, why did he have to bring home a girl we know nothing about? I wouldn't take any bets on how long she's going to stay around here. Not the way Sara feels. You know how she was throwing every girl around with a decent background at Michael. Of course, Sara would never think any girl was good enough for Michael and Alex—but Michael went pretty far out when he chose."

"What kinda family she come from?" Charlie asked. "Bring any money with her?"

"Charlie, I don't want to tell you where she comes from," he said bluntly, "though she claims her father was a British Army officer. Could be true. Then again, it might be fairy tale."

Vicky's face was hot. Nobody believed her when she talked about Papa. Did Michael?

"Sara on the warpath?"

"What do you think? And you know Sara. She'll manage something to send the girl chasing back where she came from. But not with any help from me," he added with relish. "Michael got himself into this."

"I figure Sara was so hellfire bent on getting him married, after all that happened—" *What had happened?* Suddenly Vicky's heart was pounding. "And she must want some grandchildren about the place."

"Sara had Michael's bride all picked out," Bart shot back, "though she wasn't making any headway. She had it all set up with Joshua Harris, I'd lay any odds. She thinks he's the oracle around here. She never comes to ask my opinion about anything. It's always that straitlaced bastard she runs to."

"Come on, Bart," Charlie scoffed. "Don't tell me Joshua Harris ain't lyin' down with some of the blacks around his place. He sure ain't sleepin' with that crazy wife of his. She never was right, was she, after the two little girls drowned that way."

"Madeline still thinks it's 1837. She keeps expecting those two little girls to come back from the lake. Nobody has called on her for years, except for Sara. Sara with that

damned conscience of hers," he added with contempt.
"Joshua's been hot for her for years."

"Him?" Charlies was skeptical. "All he thinks about is
that almighty plantation of his. That and his money.
God, he's so filthy rich he turns my stomach. Ever see
him in a poker game? Sets himself a limit, and nothin' on
earth will make him go beyond it. No, you're barkin' up
the wrong tree if you think he's hankerin' for Sara."

Vicky started at the slight knock on her door.

"Come in."

The door opened. Monique, bearing a frosted pitcher,
walked into the room.

"How come yo' ain't in bed?" she clucked. "Dis heat
no place fo' a white young lady to be movin' aroun' in.
Now yo' heah?" she crooned. "Me brung some lemonade
in case yo' git thirsty. All de white ladies—even Missy
Sara—nap in de aftuhnoons."

Obediently, remembering her determination to be like
the other plantation ladies, Vicky allowed herself to be
coaxed into bed. Sleep, though, was slow in coming because Bart's words kept racing across her brain. Sara had
been plotting with Betsy's father for a marriage between
Michael and Betsy. She had destroyed their dream.

Two mornings later the Misses Gardiner arrived to
begin work on Vicky's dress for the party. At supper the
night before Ava had exclaimed indignantly over this expenditure when Sara refused to give her money to go into
New Orleans to shop. Ava hated her, Vicky thought uncomfortably, while she heard Sara greeting the Misses
Gardiner in the downstairs foyer. Ava had arrived with
trunks of Paris gowns, but she resented Sara's having a
party dress made for Michael's wife. Sometimes, Vicky
thought uneasily, she suspected that Ava hated Michael,
too.

"Come in, please," she called politely at the brisk
knock on her door.

Sara marshaled into Vicky's room two small, elderly
women who resembled each other so strongly they might
have been twins—slightly stooped, their faces heavily

lined, their hands gnarled. One of them carried a tapestry drawstring bag. In preparation for their arrival Vicky had laid out the lengths of cloth she and Michael had bought at Stewart's in New York.

"I've brought out the material," Vicky said self-consciously when Sara had introduced them. "There." She pointed.

Sara walked across the room to inspect the material, the two old ladies smiling, silent, waiting for her decision. Expecting it, Vicky thought with inner rebellion, to be Sara Eden's decision.

"This one," Sara decided, choosing the white crepe imprinted with tiny flowers. "It's quite ladylike."

The Misses Gardiner went quickly into action. One opened up the drawstring bag and brought forth scissors and a measure. The other went to pick up the material.

"Remember, ladies, the party is scheduled six nights from now," said Sara. "You'll have to forget everything else to concentrate on Vicky's gown."

"Only for you, Miss Sara. We'll have it done in time if we have to work up till the last minute."

One of the sisters came forward to help Vicky remove her dress as Sara left them alone. The other was already spreading the flowered crepe across the bed. Out in the hall, Sara called to a servant.

"Napoleon, you must take the carriage and go immediately to deliver the invitations," she ordered crisply. "Give the box to the lady of the house and ask her kindly to pick out her invitation." Napoleon, Vicky realized, could not read.

"Napoleon, do you know if Mr. Michael went into New Orleans this morning?" Sara added.

"Yessum, he did. Colin brought de carriage around whilst yo' was out in de fields."

"Why did he have to go into the city in this awful heat?" Sara sighed. "Napoleon, go on, now. Get those invitations delivered."

"Rat away, Missy," Napoleon promised earnestly.

Vicky stood still as a statue while the two women worked about her.

Suddenly the door opened again, and Sara hovered in the doorway.

"Vicky, in case I forget to tell you later, come downstairs when you have finished your afternoon nap," Sara ordered imperiously. "The dancing master will be here."

Life at Eden seemed to revolve around the coming party. Every morning Vicky stood, with straining patience in the May heat, while the Misses Gardiner cut and fitted lengths of material. They talked avidly about the latest fashions as decreed by the Empress Eugenie in Paris.

In the afternoon, after her nap, Vicky submitted, loathing every moment, to the dandified ministrations of the French dancing master, intent on instructing her in the rudiments of the polka—an enervating activity under the present weather conditions.

"Ah, the young Madame, she moves so well," the dancing master, gleaming with perspiration, his jacket strained between the shoulder blades, would murmur with deep admiration, time after time. "You will be—how do they say here in America—the 'belle of the ball.' "

At supper each night Vicky spoke little. She was exhausted from the heat, from the hours of standing on her feet, from her efforts to please the dancing master, who reported daily to Sara. Michael remained polite but withdrawn, contributing little to the table conversation. Bart continued bombastic, argumentative, full of current news he found objectionable. Ava either made sarcastic innuendos about the cost of the party or sulked. As early as possible each evening Vicky went up to her room.

This morning Vicky sensed a special urgency in the Misses Gardiner. Tomorrow evening the party was scheduled. By tomorrow morning the gown must be presented, completed, for Sara's approval.

"Do you know, my dear," the elder Miss Gardiner said with pride, "that your crinoline requires sixty yards of wire? And the material that goes into the new fashions, oh la la!" She rolled her eyes expressively. "Why, five years ago I could have dressed a family of six daughters on what went into your gown."

Most of it, Vicky thought wryly, below the waist. She viewed with apprehension the deep décolletage of the tight bodice—her arms, her shoulders conspicuously bare. Too much bosom showing? Would Michael like her this way? Would he look at her with pleasure and pride? She dared to wish that he might.

"Damn, you make enough noise to wake the dead!" Bart bellowed somewhere on the lower floor. "Can't you let a man sleep in the morning?"

For several mornings now the normal quiet of the lower floor had been disrupted by the sounds that accompanied the polishing and painting being done in preparation for the party. An endless parade of slaves moved into and out of rooms usually closed off. There was a constant clatter from the kitchen, from which emanated exotic, pungent aromas.

From the house of the Harrises had come their cook, Elvira, who had been sent into New Orleans years earlier to be trained to prepare food in the French fashion. Juno was faintly injured that she was not trusted alone to prepare the sumptuous banquet her mistress had ordered, but was mollified by a gift of a frock to wear to church.

By ten in the morning Bart was pushing his wheelchair from his room, with small Jefferson nervously at his heels, waiting for orders.

"Sara," Bart yelled sharply, and Vicky made an involuntary sound of protest because the younger of the Misses Gardiner had stuck her with the needle. "Where the devil are you going at this hour of the morning?"

"Where would I be going?" she asked sharply. "Down to the quarters to check on the sick."

"Ah, yes," he drawled. "Dr. Eden, with medical book under her arm. Why can't you leave that to Mama La-Verne?"

"Because I prefer to confer with her," she shot back. "It's my responsibility."

The morning dragged. Vicky's feet ached from standing for the fitting. Her head ached from the heat, from her alarm at facing the guests the following evening. Michael moved about the house, moody and withdrawn.

At noon Monique knocked on the door and came in.

"Young Missy, time yo' come downstaihs to de dinnuh table." Her eyes were faintly defiant before the reproach in the Misses Gardiner's eyes.

"Thank you Monique." She sighed with relief. "I'll be right there." A smile of apology for the Misses Gardiner, who had worked an hour beyond their normal stint this morning.

Every meal in this house, except for breakfasts she took in her room, was an ordeal, Vicky admitted inwardly as she tried to carry on small talk with the family. She was glad when she was able to escape from the table and go to her room for the prescribed afternoon nap.

With the bedroom darkened, she lay beneath the counterpane and decided that rather than try to sleep, she would read.

She opened the collection of poems. Someone had underlined the title of one in ink, she noted with rising interest. She prodded the bolster behind her against the headboard and, half-sitting, began to read.

"It was many and many a year ago, In a kingdom by the sea—"

Caught in the beauty of the poetry, she read to the doleful conclusion of Poe's "Annabel Lee." How sad. Tears blurred her eyes. But, compulsively, she read another poem similarly marked, "Ulalume." And still another, "The Raven," also underlined in ink. Now she turned to the front of the volume to read the brief biography of Poe—about his child bride, Virginia, tragically ill so long. Dead so young. And she understood the poems.

Who had marked them? Not Bart or Sara Eden. Michael, the logical-minded lawyer? Alex, she decided Alex, who had been furious enough at Michael's marrying her, though he had displayed none of this at their wedding, to write his parents about the brothel on Greene Street.

Later, after her dancing lesson, she ran into Jefferson pushing Bart into the house.

"Don't go running up the stairs, Vicky," Bart exhorted. "Stay and talk to me." He smiled, and again Vicky was conscious that once her father-in-law must have been a man of great charm. "This isn't my home anymore with all these goings-on." He flinched at the raucous laughter of a pair of slaves painting in the newly opened second drawing room. "Come play for me," he ordered. "You play a hell of a sight better than Betsy." He began to wheel himself into the drawing room. Vicky could only follow him.

In the drawing room she seated herself at the piano and focused her gaze on the keyboard. Bart leaned forward in his wheelchair, staring unflickeringly at her. Why did he stare that way? Like that awful drunk at Nina's, she thought with revulsion.

She played most of her repertoire before Bart allowed her to stop. Glad of the reprieve, she rose from the piano, prepared to flee; but again Bart detained her.

"We'll have some cold lemonade," he said. "Jefferson, go to the kitchen and tell Juno to send us lemonade." He leaned back in his chair with a frown. "The whole damned house is turned upside down for this party. My wife's got to prove to the whole parish that she's not upset that her son ran off and got married." He squinted keenly at Vicky. "You think she's sorry?"

Vicky compelled herself to meet his gaze.

"I'm sure it was upsetting, the way Michael just walked in with me. He should have prepared her."

Monique came in with a tray of lemonade and pralines. Vicky intercepted the covert glances Bart bestowed on the girl in her limp cotton shift that made no secret of her delicate slenderness—glances that brought color into Vicky's face. Truantly, she remembered what Claudine Lamartine had said about Southern men.

When Monique left, Bart asked abruptly, "Why did Michael marry you?" Not *Why did you marry Michael?*

The color drained from her face. "Because," she said slowly, "it seemed good for both of us." She lifted her head with pride.

Bart stared hard at her, sighed, and shifted direction.

"Those women tomorrow night are going to roast you."

"I'm not afraid of them," Vicky lied with determined nonchalance.

"You'll have one friend. Betsy will be there." His eyes were speculative. He was wondering how she would hold up at the party. She would hate every moment of it, Vicky admitted inwardly, but not one of them would know. She would be Michael's bride, delighted at meeting the family friends. "Betsy took to you right away."

"I like Betsy." But Michael's mother didn't want her and Betsy to be friends.

Both Vicky and Bart became aware of the sounds in the foyer. Someone had just arrived.

"See who it is, Vicky," Bart ordered.

The new arrival was Betsy herself, laden with red roses from the gardens, which she handed over to Artemis at the door before she joined Vicky and Bart.

"Your father coming to the party tomorrow night?" Bart demanded of Betsy.

"Of course he is," Betsy said, gently reproving. "When Aunt Sara specially asks him to come, he wouldn't dream of disappointing her." She turned shyly to Vicky. "Papa and I don't do much socializing. It doesn't seem right, with Mama the way she is. And we don't like most parties, anyhow," she said with honesty. "I can only stay for a few moments. I want to go down to the stables and look at Ulysses before we sit down to supper." She hesitated. "Vicky," she said, "would you like to come over some afternoon after the party? I'll show you our menagerie."

"I'd love it," Vicky said enthusiastically.

Betsy explained, with a glow of pleasure, that she was sewing clothes for several newborn slave babies. Perhaps I could do that, Vicky thought with a flicker of interest. She would feel less restless with something useful to occupy the long hours.

"I promised to bring the clothes down to the quarters tomorrow morning," Betsy explained with a smile. "I'll have to sew all evening."

"You and your father spoil the slaves to death," Bart protested. "Takes four of 'em to do the work of one, if you don't lay down the law regularly. Even Sara, who prides herself on her damn efficiency, never gets a decent day's work out of any of 'em."

Vicky walked with Betsy to the door. After the party she would see more of Betsy, she promised herself. She would not feel this terrifying aloneness with Betsy as a friend.

Walking down the hall to the drawing room, where the family gathered before supper, Vicky heard Sara's voice, unfamiliarly high-pitched.

"They were there in that box on my dresser," she was saying agitatedly. "I know because I took them out of the drawer so I could have Nancy clean them properly for the party."

"Now, slow down, Sara," Bart reproached. "You left your diamond earrings sitting on the dresser?"

"Why not?" Sara demanded as Vicky appeared in the doorway. "I've been doing that for years. You know not a servant in this house would steal as much as a sheet of paper."

"Seems to me you're always complaining about missing sugar," Bart said dryly.

"The servants would not steal something valuable," she insisted. Her eyes suddenly rested on Vicky. Vicky felt hot color flood her face, felt the oppressive tension in the room as Sara's eyes lingered on her. "They're worth two thousand dollars."

"Mama, they may have fallen behind something," Michael said uneasily.

"They were in that box on my dresser," Sara insisted. "I know where I put things."

Vicky, her throat tight with anger, took a deep breath.

"Mrs. Eden, I didn't take your earrings," Vicky said with painful politeness.

"Vicky, Mama didn't mean that!" Michael was shocked. Oh, yes she did, Vicky thought defiantly.

"Of course not, Vicky," Sara backtracked self-consciously.

"We'll have all the servants in here," Bart said belligerently. "We'll find the earrings."

"Wait, Papa," Michael intervened. "Let me go upstairs and look."

"All right, Michael," Sara agreed after a moment of hesitation. "But hurry. Juno's sending in supper in a few moments." Her eyes made a point of avoiding Vicky's. "We might as well go into the dining room."

Vicky sat silently at her place at the table. How dare Sara Eden jump to the conclusion that she had stolen those diamond earrings! She tensed as she heard Michael striding down the hallway, then turned her head anxiously as he walked into the room.

"Your earrings, Mama." He handed them to his mother. "The breeze from the river sent the draperies across the dresser. The earrings fell to the floor."

No one at the table seemed to have much appetite for supper tonight. Perhaps it was this awful heat, Vicky thought—unlike anything she had ever experienced. Even the breeze from the river was hot. And she rankled still from Sara's unspoken accusation.

After supper the family, at Bart's suggestion, went out to the gallery. Bart liked an audience. Only Ava defected.

Sitting on the gallery of this magnificent house with the scent of roses and honeysuckle in the air, Vicky thought wistfully of how beautiful the evening could have been. Then Michael said, "I think I'll go upstairs and read," and her heart fell.

"It's going to be awfully hot in the house," his mother warned.

"It's hot everywhere tonight. There's not a breath of air stirring." Michael's eyes were moody. More than the coming party was bothering him, Vicky decided uneasily.

She would have to stay on the gallery another ten minutes. It would look bad to go running upstairs the moment Michael left.

Sara was talking.

"I'm bringing up some field hands in the afternoon to crank the ice-cream freezers. Napoleon will bring up more ice for the claret punch from New Orleans in the afternoon. Nobody has sent regrets—it'll be the best-attended party we've ever given at Eden." *Because the whole parish wanted to see the girl Michael Eden had brought from New York as his bride.*

"Mama—" Michael strode onto the gallery scowling. "Did you take the book of poems by Edgar Allan Poe up to your room?"

"No, I didn't, Michael." Unexpectedly, Sara smiled. "I rarely have time or the inclination to read poetry these days."

"Then where is it?" he demanded. His eyes were stormy; this was a Michael Vicky had never seen.

"I have it," Vicky said softly. "I've had it for several days," she apologized.

"Then why the devil don't you return it?" he lashed at her. And suddenly he was pale, his eyes revealing his shock that he had spoken to her this way. "Vicky, I'm sorry; it's this rotten heat. It was terrible down in New Orleans today."

"Why do you persist in going into the city every day in this weather?" Sara reproached. "I don't know when we've had a hot spell this early."

"I'm sorry, Vicky," Michael stammered, not hearing his mother. "I had no right to snap at you that way. Please forgive me." He swung about and went back inside the house.

Vicky waited a few minutes, uncomfortable in the heavy silence that engulfed them. Self-consciously she rose to her feet.

"I think I'll go to bed," she said with a forced smile. "Good night, Mrs. Eden, Mr. Eden."

In her room she stood with the poems in her hand, uncertain about the proper action. Take the book to Michael, she ordered herself. His room was right next door. It was not Alex, after all, but Michael who had marked "Annabel Lee" and "Ulalume" and "The Raven."

He responded quickly to her knock.

"I thought you might like this," she said gently, extending the volume of poems. "I'm sorry I kept it so long."

"Thank you, Vicky." His face was strangely anguished.

"Good night, Michael."

She wished he would reach out and touch her. She yearned for him to take her in his arms again.

10 ～

Ava stared with eloquent disgust at the breakfast tray Odalie was placing across her lap.

"Why must I have a farmhand's breakfast sent up to me every morning?" she demanded arrogantly. "Can't Juno understand that all I want is an omelet? A perfect omelet," she emphasized, "and a pot of decent coffee. Not this bilge!"

"Me tell Juno," Odalie said uneasily. "Me tell her ag'in," she soothed.

"You do that!" Ava's eyes flashed. With a sudden gesture she reached for the plate of ham and eggs and sent it crashing to the floor. Odalie stepped back in alarm. "Now get out of here," she ordered. "Come back and clean up when I've gone. Wait!" she countermanded. "Lay out my riding dress. I can't bear another morning lying around this stupid room."

Tonight was the party to introduce Michael's bride. All that money spent for a stupid provincial ball. And Sara cried about how short they were of funds.

Was it legal, she considered recurrently, the way Papa had left everything in Sara's hands? Could she go into court and fight for her share? It hadn't mattered too much up till now, though she had been furious nonetheless. Once she had gone through Jan's fortune, Sara had sent her money regularly. And for a while Rudy had been generous. Damn Rudy, she missed him.

98

She ate a biscuit, drank a cup of black coffee, then left her bed to dress. She'd pick up a horse at the stables and ride through the fields. She used to ride with Rudy when they went to the country house he borrowed from a client now and then.

As she descended the stairs, she frowned at the sound of the clatter on the lower floor. Half the slaves at Eden must have been brought into the house for tonight's party.

Sara stood in the foyer, supervising Napoleon as he positioned endless candles in the chandelier.

"All this for a little girl from rural England," Ava drawled. What would Vicky say if she knew about *her* and Michael? Would she run in horror? No. That one was going to stay here, enjoying Eden, until somebody sent her packing. "All this for Michael's bride?"

Sara bristled.

"For Michael."

"She doesn't belong at Eden." Ava's voice was too low to carry to Napoleon. "Why don't you get rid of her, Sara?"

"How?" Sara retaliated—and then frowned in annoyance that she had reacted.

"You're the smart one in the family. You'll think of something," Ava said sweetly, walking out onto the gallery. Bart glanced up at her with a sardonic smile. He didn't trust her, she thought. He hadn't trusted her since she was fifteen.

"What, you got up at the crack of dawn?" he jibed.

"The noise downstairs. This party for your daughter-in-law." Her eyes were arrogantly amused.

"For the whorehouse pianist," he shot back, and flushed.

Ava's eyes lighted with curiosity. She dropped herself into a rocker beside Bart.

"Bart, tell me," she ordered. "I want to know everything."

Reluctantly Bart told her about Alex's letter.

Ava's eyes widened. "Michael didn't deny it," he said, his eyes telling her he was cursing himself for not having kept his mouth shut.

"Why did he marry her?" Ava probed. "What does she have on him?"

"Maybe he's in love with her," Bart said maliciously.

Ava dismissed this. "He hardly knows she's alive." But someday that girl—that whorehouse pianist—would be the mistress of Eden. "Bart, I told Sara and I'm telling you. Get her out of Michael's life. She'll only pull him down to her level."

"She claims her father was a British Army officer who died at Sevastopol." Bart shrugged.

"You don't believe that." Ava gazed scornfully at him. "I'd give her six months at the most, and then she'll be back where she came from." If Sara didn't get rid of her, *she* would.

Ava pulled herself slowly up from her chair, knowing Bart viewed her with lecherous eyes. Well, when he was able, he had refused.

Ava strolled with practiced seductiveness in the direction of the stables. Sara would have a fit when she saw what she was wearing tonight. It was revealing, even for Paris. Once she walked into the room in that dress, not a man at the party would know Vicky was alive. A low sound of passion escaped her. She wasn't meant to live like a nun.

At the stables she was conscious of the furor she created, though the eyes that sought her out did so furtively. A man was a man, she thought complacently, no matter what color skin he wore.

One of the stablemen chose a horse for her.

"She frisky, but not too frisky," he said good-humoredly. "Yo' hol' her in, she behave."

Ava mounted and rode out through the woods, hearing the sounds of the slaves singing in the distant fields. Nothing had changed.

If she had been treated fairly, half of Eden would belong to her. She could sell a few slaves and return to Paris. Damn Papa for doing this to her. Damn Sara. And most of all, damn that whorehouse pianist.

Ava pulled up at the sound of another horse in the field to the left. She leaned forward to see the rider. A

man. Young. Good to look at, she decided with pleasure.
Her mind searched for an identity. Jack Lamartine, the
overseer. Sara had told her to stay away from his wife—
she was often on drugs. Ava's mouth curved in a wise
smile. A woman on drugs was a dead thing in bed.

She slid down from her horse and slapped her across
the shank with her crop. The horse whinnied in reproach
and galloped away.

"Hello!" Ava called with an authentic air of concern.
"Hello there!"

The man stiffened to attention. His eyes searched the
area until they alighted on her. Quckly he rode to her
side.

"Are you all right?" He noted her riding dress, her lack
of a horse.

"I dismounted for a moment to look at the river, and
the horse took off," Ava said, her eyes candidly admiring.
"You must be Jack Lamartine."

"Yes." He thought she was beautiful, she decided with
satisfaction. "And you're Sara's young sister."

"Not that young," she laughed. "Could you give me a
ride back to the stables?"

"If you don't mind riding double," he said self-consciously.

"The best way," she mocked. "If you'll get off and let
me mount?"

"Of course." He was disconcerted, but he immediately
dismounted.

"I rode bareback in France," she murmured. "In a riding dress such as this." She leaned toward him as she prepared to get on—not sidesaddle, as he had expected, but
astride. In a riding dress. Her body brushed his slightly.
She saw his sharp intake of breath. He needed to be with
a woman, she thought with anticipation.

"Well," she challenged because he seemed incapable of
motion. "Are you riding with me?"

"I'm riding."

Her mouth parted in a smile, she watched while he
drew himself up into the saddle with her, his hands moving about her to take up the reins.

"Don't ride directly back to the house," she ordered. "Go along the river for a bit. That view is the only thing I ever missed about Eden."

They rode in silence, his hands taut on the reins. She aroused him.

"Ride slowly so we can enjoy the view," she murmured, while one hand slid behind her.

"Ava, are you trying to kill us?" His voice was strangled.

"That's not what I have in mind," she reproached, her hand active. There. Hot as a pistol already! A phrase favored by Bart, she recalled. "Just ride, Jack, and let me show you."

She was completely in command, the way she liked. With one swift movement she leaned forward, holding on to the horse's neck, her rump raised invitingly, her hand behind her again. Finding him. Guiding him. Oh, good! Good!

"Ava!" He groaned. "Ava!"

The horse slowed down to a sudden stop, almost throwing them.

Fighting back the sounds of passion that welled in her throat, she buried her face in the horse's mane.

"Let's get off the damn horse," Jack ordered hotly. "Over there, in the bushes."

Ava lay back against the greenery, straightening her riding dress, while Jack stumbled to his feet.

"Ava, stay away from me," he ordered brusquely. "That never should have happened," he said with painful self-reproach.

"It'll happen again," she promised complacently. "Anytime I like."

She was humming when Jack helped her to her feet. He'd have to ride her back to the stables. She refused to walk that far in this heat.

11

Vicky stood in the center of her bedroom, the gown made for her by the Misses Gardiner laid across her bed. Downstairs the chief fiddler, Cyrus from the Harris plantation, was running his fellow musicians through their opening number. Sara's voice rose now and then above the music in some crisp order to the corps of slaves who were on duty. There was no sound from the room next door, Michael's room.

Vicky started at the sound of a carriage rolling up before the house.

"Folks are arriving already," she said with alarm.

"Dat don' mean fo' yo' to go arushin' downstaihs," Monique said complacently. "Missy wants yo', her sen' somebody."

Vicky felt a sudden panic. How was she going to walk down those stairs and face all those strangers?—all of them resenting her because Michael had been expected to marry a girl from Louisiana. But Michael thought she could carry this off. He had married her, hadn't he? she reminded herself with pride. He had too much respect for himself to marry a girl he thought might disgrace him.

Monique pulled the delicate crepe of the dress about her mistress, murmuring delight with her appearance.

"Prettee," she crowed. "Not one o' dem kin tech mah Young Missy."

Now Vicky sat for Monique to do her hair, in the style

upon which they had mutually decided yesterday. Using an illustration in one of the magazines Monique had discovered under a pile of discarded newspapers, she piled the long silken strands high upon Vicky's head.

When she was finished, she stood back to admire her handiwork while Vicky gazed into the hand mirror.

"Monique, you're wonderful." Then on impulse she hurried to the dresser and rummaged until she came up with a length of red velvet ribbon. She foraged for scissors, then cut the ribbon in two.

The cameo Papa had given her, she remembered. Her most treasured possession. With hands that were not quite steady she fastened the cameo to one length of ribbon and tied it about her throat. She lifted the second length of velvet to her hair.

"Me do," Monique said quickly.

Vicky started at the faint knock at the door. Monique hurried to answer, and Michael stood, silent for a moment, in the doorway, his eyes fastened on Vicky. Her heart began to pound. Was her dress cut too low? Was the red ribbon disgraceful?

"You look beautiful," he said softly. "Are you ready to go downstairs?"

"Yes." Her smile was brilliant. Michael would be at her side when she walked down that long flight of stairs to their arriving guests. She would not be alone. "Oh, yes, Michael."

Together they descended the long, curving staircase— the foyer chandelier resplendent with a hundred lighted candles, Cyrus leading his musicians in a rousing polka. Vicky felt the soaring curiosity behind the guests' convivial smiles. Her face hot, she was grateful for Michael's hand at her elbow. She could carry this off. *She could.*

Surprisingly, it was Bart who took his place at Vicky's side in the magnificent drawing room recently opened for the party and which opened onto the huge dining salon reserved for such occasions as this. In the drawing room, rugs had been removed for the dancing; in the dining salon, tables fitted together to make a festive dining board for the dozens of guests who filled the rooms. The aromas of roses, lilies, jasmine were poignantly sweet. The slaves moved about performing their small chores with pleasure at the convivial atmosphere, while a bevy of the children seriously wielded peacock-feather fans, which, Vicky thought with a flicker of humor, did little more than move hot air about the room.

Vicky was gravely attentive as Bart introduced her to guests. She talked with him, determinedly effervescent, conscious of the eyes that focused on her from every side.

"You look beautiful," Bart said with cynical humor. "Every mother here hates you."

"They're all so sweet," Vicky reproached, but her eyes told him she understood.

Michael was moving about the room, being scrupulously polite. At irregular intervals Sara's gaze moved to her—Sara beautiful in yellow satin gown and diamond earrings, radiating Southern charm as she talked with her guests.

Nobody was asking Vicky to dance, which simultaneously pleased and disturbed her. Bart in his wheelchair at her side remained her self-appointed guardian. His eyes were surveying the assemblage.

"Good God!" he muttered with shock. "Does Ava think she's attending some artists' ball in Paris?"

Vicky followed his gaze. Ava had appeared in the doorway of the room. With an imperious smile she paused there, knowing the sensation she was causing in green lace over matching silk, cut so low at the neck that her breasts spilled over to a point just above the nipples. The eyes of every man in the room were fastened on her.

Sara, grim-faced, detached herself from a pair of guests to cross to her sister. Reprimanding her, Vicky guessed. Judge King was gaping, open-mouthed. His wife rapped sharply on his arm with a fan.

"Ava and Sara will have a battle tonight," Bart warned under his breath. "Sara must have told her to go upstairs and change, but Ava never listens to anybody."

The musicians began to play again. Ava was suddenly surrounded by guests, eager to meet the Princess Radzinski. Ava chose to polka with Judge King. He would hear about this tonight, Vicky thought with a touch of humor.

Finally, when Cyrus forsook the polkas for a waltz, Michael excused himself to come to Vicky and ask her to dance.

"I dance like a lout," Michael warned. "But let them see us together at least once this evening."

Vicky, caught up in the excitement of being in Michael's arms, was glad that he preferred to dance in silence. Her mind traitorously visualized the last time Michael had held her in his arms—the time he insisted on forgetting.

When the waltz was over, a newly arrived dowager— massive-bosomed and hennaed, with a daughter in tow— swept determinedly toward Vicky as Michael brought her back to his father. Bart introduced them. Vicky acknowledged the introductions with a deferential smile.

"Sara tells me you're a New Yorker," the woman said with deceptive charm. "How fortunate to live in a city where you could dine regularly at Delmonico's," she murmured nostalgically. Her voice was wistful, but her eyes were demoniacally curious.

"I've never been to Delmonico's," Vicky conceded softly. "Of course, I've heard of it." Who in New York had not heard of Delmonico's, the favorite of the rich?

"Never?" the woman clucked in shock. "What a shame."

"My aunt was not well." Vicky felt herself forced to fabricate, conscious of Bart's annoyance at this discussion. "I spent most of my time caring for her."

"But you left her to come all the way down to Louisiana?" She appeared to be shocked at such crassness.

"My aunt had recently found a new doctor," Vicky continued, determined to see this through. "In fact," she added with a touch of triumph, "she married the doctor and they've returned to England to live. Aunt Mollie much prefers London to New York." There, Bart was pleased. She had managed that well.

Vicky remained beside Bart's chair with fresh confidence, wishing, however, that it were time to go into the dining salon. Her gaze involuntarily followed Michael about the room. No one here realized, she thought compassionately, how he wished this night were over.

A tall, distinguished white-haired man, with a ruddy face that hinted of good living, approached them with a hand extended to Bart.

"How dare you monopolize this beautiful young lady?" he chided.

"Vicky, this is Judge Henry King," Bart said with respect. "Before he was a judge he was a member of the Legislature. Now he's a practicing attorney, but we're too used to calling him Judge to use any other title. Henry, Michael's wife, Victoria," he said with a flourish. His gaze was faintly malicious because he knew Sara was watching them.

"How nice to meet you, Judge King," Vicky said softly.

"Michael's showing fine taste," the Judge said appreciatively. Still with an eye for the ladies, Vicky thought indulgently.

"I run into him in court every now and then." Across the room a woman was beckoning to him impatiently. "Excuse me," he apologized. "My wife is demanding attention."

"Oh-oh," Bart murmured, reaching to touch Vicky's elbow. "Here comes Mary Fremont. You're nobody in this parish," he drawled, "unless Mary approves of you."

A tall, angular, ornately dressed woman with diamonds at her throat and earlobes, fan in hand, was moving toward them with determined strides.

"Bart, how are you feeling tonight?" she asked, ignoring Vicky.

"Not too bad. And yourself, Mary?"

"This weather disagrees with me," Mrs. Fremont complained. "But of course, I wouldn't dream of missing your party." Now she turned her full attention to Vicky, acknowledging the introduction Bart perfunctorily made. "You met Michael in New York, I understand?" She made it sound faintly obscene, Vicky thought.

"Yes, I did."

"English, aren't you?"

"Yes, ma'am, I am."

"What was your maiden name?" Mary Fremont inquired. "I've visited London on several occasions. We met some charming people."

"Wickersham," Vicky said, uneasy because Sara was bearing down on them. "But I've only been to London once. We lived in the country."

"Wickersham?" Mary Fremont straighted up, her eyes bright. "I knew some Wickershams in London. They had a country house in Sussex. Lady Barbara Wickersham," she recalled. "Her husband—what was his name?" She frowned impatiently. "Alfred," she fished triumphantly from her memory. "Lord Alfred Wickersham. Are they related to your family?" Her eyes dared Vicky to confirm this.

Vicky hesitated, unnerved by the grimness of Sara's smile as she joined the group.

"We're distantly related," Vickey said with gentle dignity.

Mary Fremont, startled by Vicky's confirmation, speedily departed. Sara was pale with rage.

"Vicky, how could you?" she whispered heatedly. "To tell Mary Fremont that you are related to Lord Wickersham!"

"It's quite likely," Vicky said with quiet defiance. "We Wickershams are all related." Papa had said this.

"That's a lie and you know it!" Sara's eyes were blazing.

"Sara," Bart said guardedly. "Keep your voice down."

"Papa was a Wickersham," Vicky said, her throat tightening with hostility. "He was not on friendly terms with his family." She took a deep breath. "Because of my mother. But he took me to the opera and we saw my grandmother. She sat in a special box. She was a lady," Vicky insisted.

"I don't want to hear these fairy tales, Vicky. Let's hope Mary Fremont doesn't pursue it," Sara said ominously. "She goes to London every other year. You'll be found out." Now Sara smiled warmly because Jack Lamartine and Claudine had just arrived. Vicky remembered what Claudine had said. *Sara Eden does not receive the overseer's wife, except on Christmas and at Easter.* And the night when Michael's wife was introduced to Louisiana society. Only now did Vicky realize that Michael's friend Ben Wasserman was not among the guests, and she was disappointed.

Finally they all were marshaled into the dining salon. The heat in the room was oppressive, unrelieved by the slight breeze from the river. Occasionally a flash of lightning brightened the outdoors. "Heat lightning," Bart said dismissingly. He was enjoying his role of host, Vicky thought.

She was relieved to find herself seated between Michael and Joshua Harris and near to his daughter, Betsy.

Slaves brought in an endless array of food and wines. Platters of roast beef, ham, turkey, wild duck, Pompano, red snapper. And from Elvira's capable hands came gumbo, jambalaya, bouillabaisse, grillades. Red beans and rice. Daube glacé.

Sara wore a fixed smile. She was still furious, Vicky realized unhappily, and she was barely able to touch the superb meal being served. Vicky tried to catch Betsy's eye. The Harrises had arrived late, and Vicky had found no opportunity to speak with Betsy until now.

Dessert was served—an array of elegant French pastries, side by side with Juno's rich pecan pies, Charlotte russes, and custards. American coffee and New Orleans coffee. Vicky chose the New Orleans variety and was delighted with the strong, chicory-laced black liquid.

Had she been wrong in what she said to Mary Fremont? she wondered nervously as the guests began to leave the table. They were returning to the drawing room, where Cyrus was leading the musicians in another lively polka.

Michael was summoned by his mother to join a discussion; Joshua was commandeered to wheel Bart to a corner of the room, where they began discussing some article in a recent edition of the *Picayune*. Except for a small cluster of guests at the far end of the table, only Vicky and Betsy remained in their seats.

With a conspiratorial smile Betsy moved closer.

"We can stay here for a while," she soothed. "Doesn't Cyrus play well? He's so proud of being called to play at all the parties. Aunt Sara pays him five dollars. Papa lets him keep it, of course. Vicky, I'm so happy Michael married you. We were so afraid he would never marry after—" She paused in consternation.

Vicky leaned forward urgently.

"After what, Betsy? Please tell me."

"I have no right to talk like this," Betsy stammered.

"Betsy, please. We're friends. You're my only only friend here," she said with honesty. "Why were you afraid Michael would never marry? Betsy—" She hesitated, her eyes holding Betsy's. "I love Michael, I want to help him. I have to know what I'm fighting against."

"He was to be married." Betsy's eyes were dark with apology. "To Liliane Carter. But Liliane contracted yellow fever. She died the summer before the wedding. He was—he was distraught. He shut himself off from everyone. Four years ago it was. He was different when he began to see folks again. More reserved. Moody. But you'll be good for him, Vicky. I know you will." Her eyes were troubled as they searched Vicky's face.

"That's why he read the poems by Poe," Vicky whispered, anguished. "That's why he was angry when I took the book from the library."

How could she ever make Michael love her? He was in love with a girl who had been dead four years.

12

Monique jumped from the pallet where she had been dozing. She greeted Vicky with a wide smile.

"Evuh'body go home?" Monique asked, coming forward to help Vicky out of her gown.

"Everybody has gone," Vicky said, trying for an answering smile.

While Vicky changed into a nightdress, the storm that had been threatening all evening broke with demoniacal splendor. Monique shivered at a sudden, sharp crackling.

"Dat be one o' dem pecans in de grove," she predicted. "De yard boys, dem be busy in de mawnin' cleanin' up." Her eyes softened as they rested on Vicky. "Young Missy tired."

"I am, Monique," Vicky admitted, not wanting to talk anymore, hearing, over and over again, Betsy's unhappy voice as she talked about Liliane Carter.

Sensing Vicky's need for silence, Monique helped her into bed, straightened out the netting, and left the room. Vicky turned over and burrowed her face into the pillow, engulfed in despair. Michael still mourned Liliane, who was to have been his bride. Would there ever be a place in his heart for someone else? No one else for her, she taunted herself passionately. Only Michael. Always Michael.

She fell asleep at last when the darkness of the sky had given way to a pink-streaked gray. She slept late into the

humid morning, reluctant to face another day at Eden.
But this was her home, she stubbornly reminded herself
as she lay on her back and gazed painfully at the ceiling.
She must make a place for herself.

The mornings with the Misses Gardiner were a thing of
the past. The dancing master's presence was no longer required. She found ironic amusement in the realization that
she had not once danced the polka last night.

Instead of going down to the midday meal today, she
ate from a tray Monique brought to her room. Vicky
heard her, when she left the room, in muted conversation
with Titus, the field hand who had been brought into the
house to help with the heavy polishing. Vicky smiled as
she ate. Titus, no more than nineteen, was tall, strong,
and strikingly handsome, and Monique had been casting
shy but interested glances in his direction.

Vicky remained in her room much of the afternoon,
her mind assaulted treacherously by the recall of last
night's confrontation with Sara, when Sara had chastised
her so sharply for identifying Lord Wickersham as a distant relative. It could be true, she thought defiantly. And
Mary Fremont had meant only to humiliate her.

Vicky spoke little at supper. Michael seemed tired. He
was withdrawn. Bart carried on a tirade against the pessimism that seemed to be inundating the country.

"It's absurd to talk about a panic," he blustered. "It's
not like in '37, when New Orleans bank notes moved at a
discount of from ten to twenty-five percent. We've got
sound money and sound banking. This hysteria is ridiculous!" Ava was watching him with sulky interest.

"The South should at least be able to feed itself," Michael said, briefly breaking his silence. "But it doesn't."

"Bart, what's happening with Fleming's bank and us
is enough to show that something's dreadfully wrong,"
Sara said with irritation. "We can't stick our heads in the
sand."

"All I know is that the South is less likely to be hurt financially than any other part of the country," Bart shot
back. "You'll see."

"I don't know why you couldn't send me money to stay

in Paris," Ava said, with the rage that seethed constantly within her. She turned accusingly to Sara. "All you had to do was sell a few slaves!"

"Ava, we have been through all that," Sara said tiredly. "I don't want to hear any more."

"There are a lot of things you haven't wanted to hear," Ava said with defiant triumph. The atmosphere at the table was suddenly painfully heavy. Michael gazed at Ava, tensed and guarded; then his eyes swung to his father. What did Ava know that so upset Michael? He was never comfortable in her presence. "Things you should know, Sara," Ava finished arrogantly.

"What things?" Sara frowned in annoyance.

"One of these days you'll know," Ava said carelessly. It was a threat, Vicky thought. A threat that in some fashion involved Michael.

Immediately after supper Sara secluded herself in the library to go over business correspondence. Ava, clutching a bottle of claret, went up to her room. The other three went out to sit on the gallery.

Ava leaned back in the carriage with a smug smile while Napoleon prodded the horses into motion. Sara was livid because she was going into New Orleans; but how could her sister refuse to allow her to go into the city to have the catch of a favorite necklace repaired? A catch she had deliberately broken. And she would make sure the jeweler could not repair it today—hence another trip into New Orleans.

When was Sara going to do something about getting rid of that girl? She seethed every time she thought of Vicky being mistress of Eden someday. How could Papa have treated her this way? He had adored her, though he thought she was wild because she was so fond of parties. Suddenly her eyes were guarded. Don't think about those other things that upset Papa. He just didn't understand.

She would stop by the jeweler's on Chartres Street. Sara said that same little man was there. She'd leave the necklace and tell him she would pick it up next week. And

then she would stop by to see Judge Henry King. He had
been entranced with her at the party. His wife had almost
had a stroke when he was dancing with her, with those
big bright eyes glued to her bosom.

Her mind jumped to contemplation of Jack Lamartine.
He avoided her like the plague. It was a shame he seemed
so afraid of that wife of his.

In less than an hour Napoleon pulled up before the
jeweler's shop.

"Mademoiselle!" the jeweler greeted her ecstatically.
"After all these years!"

"Madame," she corrected him with a smile. "A widow
now. Princess Radzinski," she said carelessly as she
handed him the necklace. He knew it was paste—a copy
of Jan's wedding present. "I've been living in Europe.
Most recently in Paris."

They talked briefly about Paris, and then she went on
to the Judge's offices, creating a sensation before she was
finally seated in his private office.

"You were so very sweet at Sara's party," she said,
wistfully seductive. "that I knew you would advise me on
a delicate problem."

"Of course, Ava," he soothed, leaning forward eagerly.

She hesitated.

"It's difficult to talk about—"

"I'm your attorney, Ava," he reproached. "You can
tell me anything."

"It's about Papa. The way he left Eden to Sara. I was
hurt being cut out that way. You can't imagine, Judge
King."

"Henry," he urged. "Sara always calls me Henry."

"Here I am, destitute. Completely dependent on Sara.
It seems so wrong." She watched him carefully. He was
sympathetic. "I've tried to talk to Sara, but she won't listen. She wouldn't even sell a few slaves so I'd have funds
to remain in Paris."

"Ava, your father was a fine lawyer," Judge King said
cautiously. "His will was entirely legal. Since you're so
much younger than Sara, he must have felt as though he
was leaving you in a mother's care."

"It would be useless to take Sara to court?" she asked with sudden candor.

"You couldn't do a thing, Ava."

"So I'm to be left out?" Her eyes glittered dangerously. "Dependent on Sara's generosity, and later on Michael's and Alex's."

"There's no way to break the will," he reiterated. "This is the way your father wished it. And how is the new bride at Eden?" he asked with an effort at cheerfulness.

"The new bride is fine," Ava said coolly.

"That's what Michael needed," he went on enthusiastically. "A wife to give him an air of responsibility. With the Eden name, he ought to go far in politics."

"I don't think Michael is interested in politics." Her voice was edged with sarcasm. "All Michael cares about is law."

Ava left the Judge's office with a towering sense of frustration and ordered Napoleon to take her to Madame Alphand's for dinner, where she superciliously complained about every course served her. From Madame Alphand's she went to the Hotel St. Charles. Her destination was a sight she had not seen in more than a dozen years. The slave market.

She pushed her way through the elegantly dressed guests who thronged the public rooms until she stood at the edge of the crowd gathered to make their bids. Wearing a faint smile, her head held high lest anyone be so forward as to speak, she watched the slaves being brought to the block.

Ah, there was a black buck that she would have bought, she thought with exhilaration as a handsome black youth no more than seventeen and with bulging muscles, was brought to the block. She felt a surge of excitement as she imagined him being recalcitrant, requiring the whip. She visualized him naked before her while the whip in her hand cut into the sleek, shining black skin. He would beg her for mercy and she would be merciful. She stifled a low sound in her throat.

She returned to the carriage and ordered Napoleon to take her home. But there would be more trips into New

Orleans, she promised herself. Sara would not keep her a prisoner at Eden.

Napoleon drove through Rampart Street, on the edge of the city. Ava leaned forward with curiosity to inspect the rows of small, one-storied white cottages, where lived the quadroon girls who were mistresses to well-to-do white gentlemen—a tradition in Louisiana. Papa had told her all about them, with contempt. Papa had told her about many things because he suspected she already knew. Papa had loved her strangely, spoiled her outrageously, and left her destitute with his death.

When she returned to Eden, the house wore its afternoon quiet. Sara, on these hot days, capitulated and took a nap. But Vicky sat on the gallery with one of her perpetual books in hand.

"No nap?" Ava twitted, her mind racing.

"I like the breeze here," Vicky explained politely. Vicky was afraid of her, Ava decided with amusement. She was sure she could take Michael away from Vicky, if she really cared. But Sara would carry on and it wasn't worth it.

"It was dreadfully hot in New Orleans. Just unbelievable. I don't understand Michael's going in every day." She paused, a secretive smile on her face. "But of course, Michael has a special reason."

"His law practice," Vicky said quickly.

"I saw him this morning as we were coming into the city. He didn't see me, of course. He was going into one of those houses on Rampart Street." She smiled with sardonic humor. "I think a wife should know if her husband is keeping a mistress, don't you?"

Vicky gazed at her, stricken. Without another word Ava swept into the house.

Vicky sat stiffly in the rocker, the book open across her lap. Ava's words echoed through her mind. Michael with a mistress in New Orleans.

She had no will to leave the gallery. She sat there, with Sam at her feet, whimpering now and then for some demonstration of affection. How could she cope with this, loving Michael the way she did? How could she remain at Eden? Yet she knew she would.

The days began to fall into a pattern. An empty, frustrating pattern for Vicky, assaulted regularly by visions of Michael before a small white house on Rampart Street. She must do something with her time besides sit around and read. Ava rode or, despite Sara's objections, went into New Orleans. Vicky wished, desperately, that Betsy would come calling. She did not dare take the initiative.

Because she slept so poorly at night, Vicky found herself sleeping in the afternoons. Today she awoke with a start, hearing Socrates at the door, welcoming a caller.

No one ever called in the afternoon. Everyone knew Sara kept herself occupied with plantation affairs. Curious, Vicky left the bed, walked to the door, and opened it an inch.

"Please to come in de drawin' room, Miz King," Socrates was saying with dignity. "Ah tell Miz Sara yo' has come to call."

Vicky closed the door and crossed to the foot of the bed to reach for her dressing gown. Mrs. King. That would be the Judge's wife. Should she dress and go downstairs? Or would Mrs. Eden send for her if she wished to see her? She had no intention of pushing herself where she was not wanted.

She reached for one of the reviews she had brought up from the library and sat in a chair by the window. Her mother-in-law was probably mad as a hornet because she had been interrupted, but no Southern lady would admit to anything but delight at the presence of company.

Monique came up with a glass of lemonade and to remake Vicky's bed. Vicky heard the low hum of voices downstairs. No one was being sent to fetch her. She was simultaneously relieved and regretful.

Not until the family was seated at supper did Sara bring up the subject of her afternoon visitor, though she was obviously pleased at having received Mrs. King.

"Michael, you're terrible," she chided him with a brilliant smile as Seth brought in a huge tureen of ham-and-pea soup. "Why didn't you tell us about Judge King's invitation?

"What invitaton?" Bart pounced. "What's going on here?" His eyes swung from Sara to Michael. Even Ava stopped sulking to listen. "What's doing with Judge King and you?"

"He made me an offer," Michael said slowly. "To come into his law firm as his partner."

"Hey, Michael, that's a deal," his father said expansively. "I figured Vicky was making a conquest at the party." He bowed to her with good-humored mockery. "But seriously, he figures now that you're married, you're more responsible. I can't tell you how pleased I am, Michael."

"I told him I couldn't accept," Michael said carefully. His mother stared at him in disbelief. Ava seemed amused.

"Michael, what are you talking about?" Sara's voice was tense with shock. "Henry King is the finest attorney in this state. Nobody in their right mind would turn down that offer!"

"Henry knows he has to take somebody into the office," Bart said. "He's worked for thirty years to build up that practice, and not one of his five daughters married a man in law. He may look as good as ever, but since that stroke, he knows he isn't." Bart's face was bitter for a moment. "Now, Michael, you didn't turn it down just like that? You said you'd think about it?"

"I gave him a flat 'No,' " Michael said tiredly, "but of course I agreed to reconsider it, out of politeness."

"Don't waste too much time in telling him you're accepting," Bart boomed. "Any young lawyer in these parts would sell his mother for a partnership with the Judge."

"Not this one," Michael said firmly.

"Why not, Michael?" Sara was straining to remain calm.

"Because I loathe his approach to slavery." Suddenly Michael was passionate. "I disagree with his whole attitude. Some of the decisions he's made during his judge-ship—and believe me, I've read them all," he said grimly, "—make me sick. I could not, in good conscience, work with him."

"Damn it, Michael, you're beginning to sound like an abolitionist!" his father bellowed. "That's what comes of sending you up North to college! Let me tell you, the ab-olitionists don't know the first thing about slavery. The black bastards have a good thing going for them. They don't know the thousands of dollars those lazy Negroes owe us. Buying their food and clothes, giving them a place to live. And them so damn lazy they pick one-tenth the cotton they should. Steal our hogs right in front of our eyes. No, Judge King is right in what he has to say about keeping our Negroes in line!"

"Michael, look how kindly we treat our slaves," Sara reproached. The Edens did, but what about other owners? Vicky wondered somberly. "Then think about the children—and their parents—in the factories in En-gland and Scotland. Eight-year-olds working beside their parents fourteen hours a day, under horrible sanitary conditions. Orphans kept in workhouses, sent out on jobs to pay for their keep and not seeing a cent for themselves. Our slaves are better off, Michael." A vein throbbed in her throat. "Now, you tell the Judge you're proud and happy to accept that partnership."

"Judge King fought bitterly against the ruling to allow slaves and free Negroes to give testimony against whites in the law courts. It was passed in the Legislature despite his efforts," Michael pointed out.

"Lousiana was the only state in the South stupid enough to pass that law!" Bart exploded. "Taking a Ne-gro's word in court! Everybody knows how they lie!"

"It's an unjust practice, Papa," Michael said stubbornly. "It's wrong to deprive anyone of recourse to the courts. I can't bring myself to work with King."

"Now, Michael," Sara began impatiently, and Vicky interrupted.

"Michael must do what he thinks is right." Her eyes

defied her mother-in-law. Let Michael see that his wife stood behind him. "He owes that to himself!"

"My son's future is at stake!" Sara's voice shook with anger. "You will not interfere, Vicky."

"Mama, please," Michael reproached.

"Michael, I will not allow you to throw away this chance," Sara pursued. "You know the kind of fees the Judge commands. And we're going through a rough period. Michael, the income would be a help here at Eden." She took a deep breath. "Think about it. Coolly and intelligently. There is not an attorney your age in the state who wouldn't jump at this chance."

"No attorney who feels as I do about the institution of slavery," Michael said quietly, "could allow himself to work with Judge King. I know the Judge feels he's right," Michael acknowledged warily. "He doesn't see the change in the South in the last decade. Folks are thinking differently. They're coming to realize that slavery is a sin against God. We must think ahead to the time when slavery is abolished."

"The South cannot survive economically without slavery," Sara protested. "Nor can the slave survive without his master. How can you turn a slave loose to freedom?" Sara scoffed. "They wouldn't know how to feed or clothe themselves. Michael, they would be destroyed."

"Then it's up to us to teach them to cope with freedom," Michael said earnestly. "We have thousands of unused acres on this plantation. We could set some of them up as tenant farmers, renting them the land. We could bring in teachers to teach them to read and write—"

"Hear, hear," Ava drawled.

"Michael, you're talking like a damn fool," Bart interrupted. "If that's what you learned up at those fancy schools in New Jersey and Massachusetts, then we're crazy to have sent you! Look to the Bible and you'll see that slavery is accepted before God. Christ spoke of slaves, and told them to be obedient to their masters. And old patriarchs."

"Look at the Constitution of the United States," Michael shot back, but Sara's voice cut through his like a sharp-edged sword.

"I will not have this arguing at the supper table," she said imperiously. 'We will talk about this another time, Michael." Meaning, Vicky interpreted, when she was not around to add her brief comment.

Sara stood by a window in her bedroom, hearing Bart's voice droning away on the gallery. Didn't he know how nauseating he was?

Nancy came into the room with a pitcher of lemonade.

"Hit's gonna rain fo' sho' tonight, Missy," she said as thunder rumbled in the distance. "Dis heat wave's gonna break."

"I hope so, Nancy," Sara smiled automatically. She was distraught about Michael's reaction to the Judge's offer. Couldn't he understand what the extra money would do for Eden? The checks every month to Alex and Ava had been such a drain. Neither of them had ever learned to be practical. They spent money as though it were picked along with the cotton. "Nancy—" Suddenly she had made up her mind. "You go downstairs and tell Seth he's to drive me over to the Harrises'."

"Missy, when hit's gonna stoam?" Nancy protested.

"It'll go on like this for hours," Sara said brusquely. Suddenly it was urgent to talk to Joshua. "Tell him to bring the carriage out front. I'll be down directly."

"Yessum, but it don' seem right," Nancy complained, heading for the door. "Ah be waitin' up wit' dry clothes," she promised. "Fo yo' ketch yo' death o' cold."

Sara rearranged her hair and reached for a shawl to take along in the event the rain broke before she returned. There could be a tremendous drop in temperature after a summer storm.

Odalie was serving lemonade on the gallery as she reached the foyer.

"Odalie, you're looking peaked," Bart said. 'You go out and get to sleep before you come down with something, you hear?"

"Yessuh," she said softly. "Ah go to sleep."

Rare for Bart to be solicitous, Sara thought cynically. It must be all that talk of Michael's about the condition of the slaves. Odalie looked fine.

"I'm going over to talk to Joshua," she said briskly. "I may as well arrange to get his roofer over here as soon as possible. Jack's worried about at least half a dozen cabins."

"That's going to cost a pretty penny," Bart drawled, and she saw his eyes move slyly to Michael. "You're carrying on already about how broke we are."

"The roofs have to be fixed," she said with irritation. "This weather reminded me of it." She frowned as lightning darted across the sky.

"And it just can't wait until morning," he mocked, his eyes challenging hers.

"I'd like them to start to work tomorrow morning," she said coldly. "At least, on the two worst cabins. If the hands get sick, Bart, there'll be no work out of them." That he could understand. "Good night." She nodded impersonally to Michael and Vicky. Let Michael know how displeased she was with him.

Seth helped her into the carriage. She leaned back tiredly. Nobody would give her credit for it, she thought bitterly, but she worked harder than any hand about the plantation. What was the matter with Michael, being so difficult about this partnership? And how dare that girl interfere!

Joshua wouldn't mind her coming at this hour of the night. Her one real friend in this world, she thought with a surge of emotion. She could always turn to Joshua for advice.

How different it could have been for both of them if she had married Joshua. But Johsua had been married to Madeline, and Bart had come along to dazzle her with all that fencing-master splendor.

Truantly, passion welled in her. How many nights she lay in her bed and thought about Joshua! She sighed impatiently. What was the matter with her? She was forty-three years old. That part of her life was over.

Joshua would never touch a servant in the house or a worker in the fields. She found a sweet satisfaction in this knowledge. He had a towering contempt for Southern gentlemen who took their pleasure with the blacks. Not like Bart, she thought with recurrent fury.

All these years later she could feel the sting of humiliation she had suffered then, as Bart had paraded his string of black wenches through the house. What was wrong with her that he had gone to *them?* She had been too proud to fight with him, but remorselessly he had destroyed that passion she had felt for him, until she cared little about what went on behind the doors of his bedroom, because that was a room she never entered.

The carriage turned into the long roadway to the Harris house. The upper floor was dark where Madeline slept in that suite that was her whole world. On good days Patience took her by the hand and led her to the gallery off her rooms for some fresh air. On rainy days Patience knew how to sedate Madeline, because then she became overwrought about the little girls' getting wet.

Joshua and Betsy were sitting out, and Joshua rose to his feet as the carriage approached.

As soon as their greetings were over, Joshua, realizing her need to talk, took her to his study.

"The possibility of a storm upsets me, Joshua. Jack tells me at least six of the cabin roofs are in bad shape. I thought perhaps we could work out something whereby I could borrow your roofer for a month and you could use one of our hands in exchange."

"No reason why not, Sara," he said gently.

Such strength in him, she thought, along with that gentleness. Why couldn't Bart be like Joshua? She worried about the plantation if anything should happen to her. Would Michael and Alex be able to run the place? Michael would be mainly concerned about his law practice.

Sara and Joshua talked for a while over glasses of claret, Joshua knowing she had come to discuss more than the roofs in need of repair.

"I have a problem," she said finally, and told him about Michael's reaction to Judge King's offer.

"Sara, you must respect Michael's decision," Joshua said slowly.

Sara was startled. "Joshua, to lose an opportunity like this?" she protested.

"There are those who are upset at some of the Judge's decisions," Joshua reminded her. "He leans heavily against the colored. We all know that. And young folks today are growing more liberal. In just this past decade, there have been tremendous changes in thinking. You and I, Sara, know that slavery must go."

"In seventy-five years," she shot back. "We're not prepared for it now. They aren't prepared." She frowned, remembering Michael at the supper table. "How's Madeline? I feel guilty that I haven't been over to visit with her, but with the party I just couldn't manage." She spread her hands apologetically.

Madeline liked to have her come over and sit with her now and then. Nobody else came, and for that, Sara knew Joshua was grateful. There had been concern over Madeline's health since the second child's birth. All the time Madeline was carrying Betsy, she had been in complete seclusion.

It worried Joshua, she thought with compassion, that Betsy was different from the other young ladies. He thought about Madeline, and he worried. Sara thought his fears were groundless. Madeline had always been unstable. Not so Betsy.

"Michael's wife is lovely," Joshua said, bringing her back to the present. "Though we were all surprised that he married away from home."

"Joshua, I don't understand this marriage." Suddenly her voice was trembling. "A girl he knew only a few days." She battled a compulsion to confide completely in him. No, it would be disloyal to Michael. Determinedly she rose to her feet. Joshua watched her compassionately. "I'd best get home before the storm breaks, Joshua. I'll expect your roofer at Eden in the morning."

Vicky sat back in the rocker, not really hearing Bart

talk, finding a small pleasure in sitting beside Michael. Bart sent Jefferson, who had been sitting happily sucking at the mints Michael had given him earlier, to the kitchen to tell Juno to send out a plate of pralines.

"If the mosquitoes keep acting up this way," he complained, swatting at the small, singing insects, "we'll have to go inside."

Monique came out minutes later with the platter.

"Monique, when you get through with Young Missy tonight, you come down to my room," Bart ordered with ostentatious casualness. "Odalie's sick. I want you to come massage my back."

Monique's eyes were terrified. Vicky was conscious of Michael's sudden, uneasy attention.

"Yessuh," Monique whispered. "Me come."

"Michael," Bart said reproachfully, "you're neglecting your bride. All this time back home and you haven't taken her to New Orleans."

"Summer isn't the time to go into New Orleans," Michael reminded him sharply.

"There'll be a break in the heat. You take her in to see the city."

"Vicky has plenty of time to see New Orleans, Papa." Michael's face was stubbornly set.

They heard Sara returning. She went directly into the house, exhorting them not to linger too long outdoors when the lightning was flashing so persistently. In minutes Vicky, scratching at a string of small mosquito bites along one bare arm, said good night and retired to her room. As she closed the door she heard Michael come into the house.

Monique brought out a cool, fresh nightgown for her to wear, discarding the one she had worn for her nap. The girl seemed somber, unhappy. Was she afraid of Bart? He might yell, but he would never strike one of the servants. Sara was even against flogging of slaves in the fields, though Bart said it was a miracle Jack Lamartine managed the field hands without the whip. Vicky shuddered.

When she was, at last, in bed, the rain began to hit the house with a vengeance.

"Dat rain sho' come down," Monique said solemnly, arranging the netting over Vicky's bed. "But now hit won't be so hot."

Monique lingered as long as possible and then, with a look of desolation, left the room. Vicky lay in bed, her mind fighting sleep.

Suddenly restless, uncomfortable in the oppressive heat, she left the bed and crossed to the window. Monique had shut all the windows against the rain. It would be all right to open them from the bottom a little.

She lifted one and involuntarily paused because of the terrified voice that soared up to her in the stark night silence—Monique's voice, coming from the room below.

"Mist' Bart, please don't make me. Please don'!"

"Monique, do as I tell you!" Bart's voice was unnaturally husky. "Come on, girl. You just come here and rub me hard between the legs. Then rub this thing—like this—and in a minute it'll be shooting straight up to the sky. You just have to do it right, girl, and then it'll give you one hell of a good time."

Her face hot, Vicky shut the window and hurried across the room to the bed. That was why Monique was so frightened to go to Bart's room. The slaves knew. They all knew.

13 ～

In the deep recesses of her mind, drugged with sleep, Vicky realized that the storm which had ravaged the area earlier had broken out again. But not until a crash shattered one of the windows did she come fully awake. Instinctively she cried out, and stumbled toward the door.

"Vicky?" Michael was at the door, his voice taut with anxiety, but low so as not to awaken the others. "Are you all right?"

"I'm fine," she stammered, pulling the door wide. "Something crashed against the house."

Michael strode into the room, fumbled for the lamp, and lit it. The door slammed shut, and Vicky started.

"It was just the door," Michael soothed.

"Be careful of the glass," she exhorted as Michael walked toward the window. "It's all over the floor there."

Michael gingerly inspected the roof of the gallery, which extended directly beneath the bedroom windows.

"The magnolia at the side must have been hit." He squinted through a broken pane of glass. "A bough broke off and fell across the roof. We can't do anything about it until morning."

Thunder ricocheted about the sky. Vicky cowered as a garish streak of lightning darted into the room in the wake of the thunder.

"The storm's frightening you," Michael said sympathetically. "It's first cousin to a hurricane."

"I'm sorry I woke you," she whispered. Her face went hot as she realized she stood here in her nightdress with Michael. Suddenly she was remembering that night in his cabin aboard the *Mississippi Queen*. Disturbing emotions stirred within her.

"You didn't wake me, I couldn't sleep," he said. "You look beautiful with your hair loose that way." His voice was constrained. "You always look beautiful."

Again thunder ripped across the sky.

"Oh, Michael!" She shivered. Then all at once she was in his arms.

"It's all right," he soothed. "It's all right."

She lifted her face to his.

"I'm such a coward about thunderstorms." *Michael, love me. Please, love me.*

A low sound escaped him and then his mouth was on hers, his hands over her breasts. Her hands moved about his shoulders as he brought her toward him.

Wanton, she thought with joyous defiance. She was a wanton! But she was Michael's wife, in truth, and this was the way it was meant to be between them.

And then he was lifting her from the floor, carrying her to the bed, while lightning darted across the room and thunder echoed over the plantation.

"Oh! Oh, Michael, Michael!

They moved together to a shattering breath-absorbing climax. Oh, Michael, I love you, I love you!

She lay with a faint smile on her mouth, her eyes shut, until Michael lifted himself from her.

"Vicky, what can I say?" His voice was tortured as he hovered by the side of the bed. "After all my promises."

"Michael, please—"

"It won't ever happen again," he interrupted. "I drank too much tonight. Promise you won't leave Eden. I need you here. I won't let this happen again."

"I won't leave," she said softly. "I promise."

She lay motionless on the bed while Michael strode

from the room. She heard the door close gently behind him.

Liliane stood between them. He had come to her as he would go to a girl at Nina's. That was all she meant to him. Tears filled her eyes and spilled over. She leaned from the bed to retrieve her nightdress, hearing Michael move quietly about in his own room.

Vicky started at the familiar, cautious opening of her bedroom door. Monique peered in to see if she was awake.

"Come in, Monique," she said gently. With unfamiliar bitterness, she thought of last night. Monique barely fifteen, and Bart Eden had used her as though she were a whore. And what more was she to her husband? she taunted herself.

"Mawnin', Young Missy." In place of her usual vivacity, Monique wore a look of sullen evasiveness.

"Coffee smells so good." With pain Vicky inspected Monique's face.

Wordlessly Monique settled the tray across Vicky's lap, then crossed to the window to pull aside the draperies, revealing the morning's drabness.

"Is it still raining, Monique?"

"Hit's rainin'." Her voice was lifeless, her eyes avoiding Vicky's. "Me go bring de wash watuh."

When Vicky finally went downstairs, she encountered a discomforting air of depression about the house. In his room, the door open, Bart was yelling at Andrew for some minor mishap. In the library Sara was talking to Juno.

"Juno, I've told you the menus for the next four days," she was saying with strained patience. "If you don't remember, come check with me. Don't decide for yourself."

Vicky was startled to find Michael in the drawing room, hunched over the morning newspaper.

"Good morning." She forced a smile.

Michael looked up.

"Good morning, Vicky." Last night might never have happened. Only the tautness of his smile told her he remembered.

"The weather's so rotten I decided to work at home today." She remembered what Betsy had told her the night of the party. *He swore he'd never marry.* But last night had not been an act of marriage in Michael's eyes.

"Michael, may I talk to you a moment?"

"Is something wrong?"

"No," she reassured him. "It's just that I—I'm trying to find something useful to do with my time." Why was she stammering this way? "I know Betsy sews clothes for the babies at their plantation. Do you suppose I could do the same here? I'm not experienced, but I could learn—"

"That's fine, Vicky." Michael was relieved. "Would you like a sewing machine? They're being used around here quite a lot." He was happy she was not going to mention last night.

"I don't know how to run one," she said uncertainly.

"You can learn," he said with conviction. "If tomorrow clears up, you'll go into New Orleans with me. I'll ask Mr. Wasserman about the best place to buy a machine." He was remembering what his father said about his never taking her into the city. "Take Monique along with you, and the two of you can do some sight-seeing." He paused. "If I'm not all tied up around noon, I'll take you to a restaurant for dinner." Her eyes widened with astonishment. To have dinner in New Orleans with Michael!

She moved about the house for the rest of the day in a trance. Even Monique, when told about the impending trip to New Orleans, lost some of her covert sullenness.

At the supper table Michael reported that he was taking Vicky into New Orleans the next day if the rain cleared.

"What ever for?" Ava asked. "Everybody's running away from New Orleans this time of year."

"We have this break in the heat," Michael pointed out. "And I want to buy a sewing machine for Vicky, so she can spend some time making clothes for the babies in the quarters, the way Betsy does."

"There's no need for that," Sara said with annoyance. "I give the mothers plenty of calico and linsey-woolsey twice a year. They have time on Sundays after church to do their sewing."

"Mama," Michael said reprovingly, "Vicky will enjoy making the clothes and I'm sure they'll be welcomed." Always he was defensive with his mother. Why must he feel guilty because he disagreed with her?

"I haven't given Vicky a wedding present yet," said Michael. "We were waiting to see what she would like." He smiled at her now. But that was to make his mother, and his father, believe this was a real marriage.

"I'll love the sewing machine," Vicky said impetuously, then lowered her eyes lest Michael become aware of the depth of her feelings for him.

"They'll have to send a man out to show you how to operate it," Bart warned. "Damned complicated machines, from what I hear. But you're bright enough, Vicky." Maliciously his eyes moved to Sara for an instant. "You'll catch on."

Vicky woke early the next morning, fearful that something would interfere with the trip into New Orleans. When Monique pulled back the draperies, sunlight bathed the room. A delicious chill supplanted the enervating heat of the earlier part of the week.

Vicky talked over breakfast about the adventurous day ahead of them, realizing that Monique had never been away from Eden, and hoping the trip would make her less withdrawn.

Michael was waiting downstairs on the gallery for them. Colin had already been dispatched to bring the carriage. In moments Vicky was seated inside the carriage beside Michael and Monique was installed on the box with Colin.

On the river a pair of ships were racing. Vicky watched them until Colin took a turn away from the river. They were nearing the city now. Excitement welled in her. Would Michael let her and Monique walk about alone?

They were driving away from the houses now into the

noisy din of the business district, the horses' hooves clamoring noisily over the cobblestoned streets.

"My office is right ahead," Michael said with an undertone of pride in his voice. "Right next to Mr. Wasserman's shop."

Colin pulled up before a modest store, its windows discreetly draped. A sign out front indicated that here was the office of MICHAEL EDEN, ATTORNEY-AT-LAW.

Colin helped Monique down from the box, then held the carriage door for Michael and Vicky.

"Stay with Young Missy, Monique," Michael ordered, and turned uncertainly to Vicky. "Would you like to see my office before I take you into Mr. Wasserman's shop?"

"Please," Vicky's smile was bright. Of course she wanted to see Michael's office.

Michael took Vicky, trailed shyly by Monique, into his office, and introduced both to his very young, bespectacled clerk, David. This was where Michael worked. Vicky's eyes swept in all she could absorb. When she sat on the gallery at Eden, when Michael was in New Orleans, she would be able to envision him here at his desk, with David hovering near.

"Let's go next door to Mr. Wasserman. I'll leave you there awhile. You'll want to buy some yard goods," Michael reminded her.

"How much shall I buy?" she faltered.

"Tell Mr. Wasserman what you wish to do with it." He reached into his purse and brought forth bills. "Show him how much you have to spend."

As they entered the unexpectedly large, neatly arranged shop, where every inch of floor space was occupied with tables piled high with cloth, a slight, small man in his mid-fifties with intelligent eyes, well-cut features, and a gentle smile walked toward them. Mr. Wasserman.

"Never mind, Nathan." Mr. Wasserman brushed aside his clerk with quiet pleasure. He spoke in a faint accent. German? "These are my friends."

He welcomed them, obviously delighted to meet Vicky. Michael explained the purpose of their visit and asked Mr. Wasserman's advice about a machine.

"I think your best buy," he said expansively, "would be the Wilson and Wheeler's machine. Hunt's is about fifty dollars more, and you don't get better service."

"Where can we buy one, Sir?" Michael asked diffidently.

"I can pick one up for you and have it delivered to Eden within a few days," he said. "At whatever it costs me."

"Mr. Wasserman, we are here to do business," Michael objected.

"Michael, your grandfather signed the loan at the bank for me when I opened this shop twenty-two years ago. From his son I don't take a profit."

A few minutes later, Michael inspected his watch and excused himself. He was expecting a client. When Vicky was done with her shopping, she could take her packages to the carriage, where Colin would be sitting most of the day. Then, he suggested, she might wish to walk about the streets with Monique, keeping close enough so that she would not get lost.

"Come to the office around noon," he said. "We'll have dinner at a French restuarant not far from here. I'm sure you'll like it."

"Thank you, Michael." Her voice was unsteady with delight.

Mr. Wasserman led her about the shop, encouraging both her and Monique to feel the materials, knowing that the two of them were delighted with the display of satins, watered silks, velvets, crepes, and tulles, along with more utilitarian materials.

Then the business was transacted and the lengths of cloth—carefully cut, folded, and wrapped by Mr. Wasserman's clerk—were given to Monique to take out to the carriage.

"Monique, wait," Vicky said impulsively, her eyes on the display of ribbons that had attracted Monique's gaze. She extended a coin to the girl. "Buy something for yourself."

Monique gazed intently at the money, her eyes bewildered.

"It's for you, Monique. To buy something for yourself."

"Me buy?" With an air of disbelief she accepted the coin and turned it over in her hand. "Me spen' fo' me?"

"Please, Monique." She remembered the children on the Points, to whom she had given pennies, to be taken with no word of gratitude, though their eyes had been eloquent enough.

"Me nevuh hold no money befo'," Monique said with sudden delight. *"Mon Dieu! Merci, Missy!"* Eyes shining, she turned to the glass case that held the reels of ribbon, a riotous display of colors and widths.

"What would you like?" Mr. Wasserman asked with the same politeness he might have accorded New Orleans' wealthiest dowager.

Carefully Monique chose, then held up the coin questioningly. Yes, it was enough he assured her, though Vicky was certain he gave her a greater length than the coin could buy.

"Come back into the shop when you put the packages in the carriage," Vicky ordered anxiously when Mr. Wasserman had wrapped Monique's purchase and placed it atop the parcel wrapped for Vicky. "You don't want to get lost."

"Now you must have coffee with me," Mr. Wasserman said with an air of conspiracy. "This is the time of morning when I always have coffee."

"Thank you."

Mr. Wasserman led her to his apartment behind the store. Vicky stared at the unexpected splendor of the small sitting room, where a gold velvet sofa faced a pair of tapestry-covered chairs before a marble-faced fireplace. Tall French windows opened on a lush garden that hinted of much care.

"Georgette," he called crisply, and a white-turbaned black woman moved smilingly into view. "Coffee please, for Mrs. Eden and myself." He waved Vicky to the sofa and sat beside her. "How do you like Louisiana?" he inquired with warm interest.

"I haven't seen much of it," she said, laughing. "But

yes, I think it is the most beautiful place I have ever been."

"To me, when I came here in 1816 it was like moving into heaven," he said reminiscently. "I was thirteen, and I thought I was a man already." His eyes held a mixture of sadness and pleasure. "I had seen little that was beautiful in my life, though love we had," he said with pride. "We came to the United States—my mother, my father, my older brother and sister, and myself—in 1812.

"I came from a small village under Russian domination but governed by Germans," he said. "But it mattered not to us, because to be a Jew to Russian or German was not good. In Europe you had to be a Rothschild or a Moses Mendelssohn—a 'protected Jew'—to be safe. They told us the days of pogroms were over, but when eleven Jews were killed in our village and they said it was not a pogrom, it was an 'accident,' my father decided it was time to leave. It took us many months, but we made our way to New York."

"I remember how excited I was when my ship docked." Vicky's face was alight with recall. "I thought New York would be so wonderful. It was," she said with honesty. "For those who could afford to live in the fine houses and fancy hotels. But not where I lived with my aunt."

Mr. Wasserman nodded in comprehension.

"My father said to me, when Mama complained, 'Better we should be alive in New York than be dead in Europe.' Even when the five of us lived in one room and jobs were hard to find. Within two years my father had died and my older sister had married. My mother went to live with my sister, and my brother, Jacob, and I went to work for a distant relative in Louisville. But two years later Jacob decided we must come to New Orleans. For a long time we were peddlers, on foot first, then later with a wagon. Such beautiful country. It was a paradise." Suddenly his eyes were somber. "Except that it bothered me then, as now, that some folks should be owned by others. Georgette," he said with pride, "is not a slave. She is a free woman of color, who works for me."

"Michael is much disturbed about slavery," Vicky told

him, and saw by his expression that he was familiar with Michael's feelings on the subject.

"Michael is a lucky man," he said with a touch of gallantry, "to have found himself such a beautiful bride." If he had questions, he kept them carefully hidden. "This was my wife, here." He leaned forward to bring to Vicky a framed miniature. "And my daughter." A poignant pride in his eyes as he brought her the second miniature —a charming painting of a solemn-eyed little girl of about four. "I lost them both in the terrible epidemic we suffered in 1833." A tragedy he shared with Michael, who lost Liliane to yellow fever twenty years later.

"Mr. Wasserman," she said urgently. "You've known Michael and his family for many years. Tell me—tell me about Liliane."

His eyes widened with shock. He had not expected this.

"There's no one else I can ask," she pursued earnestly. "I'm sure Michael doesn't realize I even know. But please, tell me. What was she like?" Her voice was an agonized plea.

"Liliane was a lovely, sweet child. Michael feels a terrible guilt over her death." His voice was heavy with sadness. "Liliane tried to persuade Michael to give up his summer job in New Orleans because of the yellow fever and go back to Eden, which was near the Carter plantation. Michael was deeply involved in the law office where he was working—he couldn't bring himself to leave. So Liliane remained in town with her father, to be near Michael. She caught the fever. She died. Michael swore he would never marry."

"How sad," Vicky whispered. In truth he stood by his oath. She was not his wife. But someday, she promised herself, she would be. Michael must not waste his life in mourning. Liliane would not have wished that.

"But now Michael is no longer a boy. He's a man," Dr. Wasserman emphasized. "He has taken himself a bride. You must not let Liliane's death shadow your marriage."

Vicky smiled in gratitude.

"Thank you for telling me."

With Monique at her side, both of them intrigued by

the shops, by the hordes of people, the air of vitality everywhere, Vicky covered innumerable blocks of colorful New Orleans before she realized it was close to noon and time to hurry back to Michael's office. At irregular intervals Mr. Wasserman's exhortation filtered across her mind. *You must not let Liliane's death shadow your marriage.*

"Colin will take you to a grogshop," Michael explained to Monique when they arrived at the office.

Monique smiled. This was a great adventure. She hurried out into the street. Michael and Vicky heard her calling to Colin.

Michael took Vicky to a small, unpretentious French restaurant just around the corner from his office, where he was known and obviously well liked. A waiter seated them at a table in the low-ceilinged room, where the kitchen—on a slightly higher level—was in plain view, the chef with a pair of helpers moving about under ropes of garlic, red peppers, hanging game.

"It isn't fancy," said Michael, "but the food is fine and the atmosphere is pleasant, don't you think?" He seemed anxious that she be pleased.

"I'm fascinated," she said with a touch of her old exuberance.

A second waiter brought them a wide-mouthed bottle of claret and a basket with an enormous loaf of fresh-from-the-oven French bread.

"One sight you'll appreciate not seeing," Michael was saying, "is the slave auctions at both hotels. It is a sight more Louisianans than care to admit grow queasy at viewing."

Dinner would be a lengthy affair, Vicky realized as the waiter finally arrived with their soup—hearty, heavy, and followed by bouilli.

"It's the boiled meat from the soup," Michael explained. "Delicious with the sauce."

After the bouilli arrived a steaming platter of crawfish, to be followed by chicken with mushrooms in wine sauce and a salad of lettuce, shrimp, and dressing. All the while Michael talked about New Orleans, which he loved with a passion. Only now did she learn that the family kept a small house in the city.

"Papa used the house a lot before his stroke," Michael explained. "He would get restless at Eden, come into the city for a few days at a time. Mama comes to stay the night two or three times a year when she goes to the theater or the opera. I use it occasionally when the weather is bad. We have a pair of servants living there regularly." He gazed up with a smile as two boys arrived to clear away the table, preparatory to the serving of dessert and coffee.

"What a magnificent meal," Vicky said with a glow of approval. "I shan't eat another speck of food today."

It was past two o'clock, Vicky realized, when they finally removed themselves from the table and left the restaurant. Walking back toward the office, Michael suggested she might wish to walk a bit with Monique. In less than an hour, he promised, he would leave the office for the day and ride home with them in the carriage.

A day she would remember forever, Vicky thought with delicious extravagance. She had been to a fine New Orleans restaurant with her husband—for a while he had seemed truly her husband. And then, painfully, her exultation faded. Michael had married her, an inner voice taunted, to be free of those marriage-minded young ladies who threw themselves at his head. *I don't want to commit myself to any emotional entanglements. I know the life I want to lead.*

She must be careful, so very careful, not to let him know this new, consuming love for him that welled in her.

Bart was sitting on the gallery with his friend Charlie Griswold when the carriage deposited the returning party before the house. Politely Vicky acknowledged the introduction to Mr. Griswold, all the while aware of his covert inspection of Monique, who was scurrying around the side of the house to the kitchen entrance. She intercepted the look between the two men. They had talked about Monique. Mr. Griswold was impressed with her.

Vicky felt her face grow warm. These were matters that did not concern her. But her mind lashed back an instant retort. What happened at Eden—what happened in the South—did concern her. This was her home. Michael was her husband. She loathed the behavior that men like Bart Eden and Charlie Griswold assumed was their right.

Vicky went upstairs to her room while Michael lingered with his father and Griswold to discuss the first railroad bridge over the Mississippi, which had recently opened to connect Rock Island, Illinois, with Davenport, Iowa.

"The first locomotive to cross a river," Griswold was saying with relish.

Monique came up with a pitcher of cool water so Vicky could refresh herself before going downstairs to supper. The girl radiated a childlike happiness because of the gift of the ribbon. Vicky was touched. For now, Monique had washed from her mind that ugly hour in Bart's bedroom.

"You're not eating," Sara protested at supper.

"We had dinner at Madame Alphand's," Michael said. "You know what that is."

"I took Alex there once years ago," Bart recalled with amusement. "God, the boy never stopped tucking it away. Madame Alphand was ready to adopt him on the spot."

"Oh, I had a letter from Alex this morning," Sara said with an air of excitement. "He'll be home day after tomorrow." But her pleasure in the prospect of seeing her younger son was mixed with apprehension, Vicky thought. She was nervous about his being at Eden.

"Is he bringing Fred with him?" Michael asked.

"He said nothing about it," Sara reported. "If he were, I'm sure he would have said so."

"I suppose you'll be dragging him off to Baton Rouge," Bart drawled, but his eyes were wary.

"We'll talk about that when Alex arrives," said Sara, her eyes holding his ominously. A cold shiver zigzagged through Vicky.

She wished Alex were not coming to Eden day after

tomorrow; she wished he were never coming. All of a
sudden she was afraid. The parlor on Greene Street
seemed terribly real to her again.

14 ~

As Vicky left her room to head downstairs, she remembered that Alex would be arriving tomorrow. Another day
before she must face him, she realized with relief.

"Miss Sara ain't to home," Socrates was saying apologetically to Betsy in the foyer below.

"I didn't come to see Aunt Sara, Socrates," Betsy explained. "I thought Miss Vicky might be downstairs by
now."

"Coming, Betsy," Vicky called out, delighted at Betsy's
arrival.

"Papa says nobody goes calling in the morning," Betsy
said, "but I thought I'd come over and take you back with
me to Harris Acres, next door. Morning's the nicest time
of the day."

"That sounds fine." Vicky smiled with enthusiasm.

"Socrates, you tell Aunt Sara, when she returns, that
I've taken Miss Vicky over to our place. And don't be
expecting her for dinner."

The two young women left the house with an air of
happy conspiracy.

"I can't talk to most girls my age," Betsy said with
candor, "but I can talk to you."

The Harris plantation, "next door," was a twenty-minute drive away. Like Eden, the house was approached by a long, tree-lined driveway. A bevy of beagles romping about the grounds greeted them with exuberant barks.

"Cyrus is takir.g us directly to the stables," Betsy explained as the carriage veered away from the house.

Several slaves greeted them as Betsy led Vicky into the large room that was her animal infirmary. With admiration Vicky watched while Betsy applied salves, administered pills, changed bandages. Both young women were lavish with affection for the dogs, cats, birds, a lone horse, and a tame woodchuck. In England, Vicky recalled, there was a school where men could go to study to become animal doctors; but of course, she thought with a flicker of rebellion, they would never allow a girl to study there.

"Let's go up and visit with Mama for a few minutes," Betsy said when they were walking back to the house. "She likes company for a little bit, though nobody comes over, truly, except Aunt Sara. You won't mind if she says something strange?" Betsy's voice was faintly anxious.

"Certainly not," Vicky reassured her firmly.

The Harris house was furnished with none of the opulence of the Edens'—because Vicky guessed with compassion, Mrs. Harris had been incapable for so many years of performing the duties of the mistress of the house. Still, there was an air of solid comfort here that Vicky appreciated.

Together the two young women climbed the long marble staircase to the second floor. Betsy knocked lightly at the door at the head of the stairs. A round, gentle-faced black woman pulled the door wide.

"Patience, I've brought a friend to visit Mama." There was silent inquiry in her eyes.

"Yo' come rat inside, honey," Patience crooned. "She settin' at de window, watchin' de dawgs."

"Mama—" Betsy moved slowly into the room, approaching as she would a skittish colt. "Mama, I brought a friend to see you."

A small, slight, fair-haired woman turned around, her eyes a faded blue, an air of decaying prettiness about her.

"Betsy always calls me Mama," Madeline Harris said

with coquettish gaiety. "We're sisters, you know; but the girls call me Mama, so she likes to do that too." She frowned slightly. "Patience, when will the girls be home? They've been at the lake such a long time."

"Dey be home soon," Patience soothed. "Dey havin' a lotta fun down deah."

"Did you have a good breakfast this morning, Mama?"

"Oh, yes. I ate up everything. Patience was quite pleased with me." Now she turned her attention to Vicky. "Are you a new friend of my sister's?"

"Yes, I've—" she hesitated. "I've just come to live with the Edens."

"Betsy, do I know the Edens?" asked Madeline.

"You know Aunt Sara Eden," Betsy said gently. "She comes to visit with you."

"Oh, yes," Madeline said vaguely. "I remember." But she didn't.

By the time they were walking down the impressive marble staircase, the dinner table was being set. Joshua Harris emerged from a room off the hall and glanced up with a look of pleased surprise at Vicky's presence.

"I went over and swept her away, Papa," Betsy said with satisfaction. "She's staying for dinner."

"But of course," Joshua said. "It isn't often that Betsy approves of someone sufficiently to invite them for a meal."

Vicky glowed at the compliment. She liked Joshua Harris. She had been pleased that he sat beside her at the party. Sara Eden had great respect for him as a planter, she recalled. At intervals Bart made sarcastic remarks about how much she went to him for advice. "She doesn't rightly go to Joshua for advice," Bart had said last night on the gallery, "but to confirm what she's already decided."

They settled themselves at the dining table. Joshua, at the head, helped himself to redfish in creole sauce.

"How's Michael?" he asked.

"He's fine," Vicky reported. "He's still going into New Orleans every day." He would soon stop, except for once or twice a week, until autumn. The courts were closed during the summer, and there was the recurrent threat of epidemic.

"Is it true that he's taking on the Winthrop case?" Joshua asked curiously.

"I don't know anything about it," Vicky said quickly. "What is the Winthrop case?"

"Winthrop is an Englishman who came to Louisiana to take over his brother's plantation when the brother died about a year ago," Joshua explained. "He hired out some of his slaves. One ran away to report that the man who had rented him had given him fifty lashes for accidentally allowing a fork to go to the table with a speck of food remaining from an earlier meal." Joshua's eyes were angry. "Not only did he give the hand fifty lashes, he ordered him washed down with rum afterwards, which was probably more painful than the beating." He glanced from Vicky to Betsy with sudden apology. "I'm sorry; I shouldn't discuss this at the table."

"The slave can't go into the courts with the man, can he?" Vicky asked, absorbed in this hateful situation.

"No, the slave can't sue. Winthrop, the owner, is going into court. Ostensibly on the claim that his personal property was misused. Actually, to highlight the abominable habits of some of those who own or hire slaves. I heard a rumor in town yesterday that Michael was being approached to represent Winthrop."

"I must ask him," Vicky said with fervor. Yes! This was certainly the kind of case Michael relished.

"Strangers to the South think that all the land is owned by planters with hundreds of slaves each," Joshua said with dry humor. "They don't know that there are a piddling number of truly large plantations. We're a region predominantly of small, independent farmers, families who get out there and sweat under the sun alongside maybe four Negroes, often rented." His eyes settled speculatively on Vicky. "Are you set in your notions of slavery? Do you think we are all monsters?"

"I think the institution of slavery itself is an abomination," Vicky said with honesty. "The thought of anyone owning somebody else upsets me. But no," she said thoughtfully, "I don't think all slave owners are monsters."

"I agree with you on the evils of slavery," he said indulgently, "but slaves are born with a marvelous power of passive resistance, which tends to keep them from overworking." His eyes twinkled. "They work from 'dark to dark,' yes," he acknowledged, "with two hours out to rest during the day. But then, so do white farmers and the Northern factory workers. Still, the average plantation hand does about half the work of the average white farmhand in the North."

"Papa, that's not fair," Betsy contradicted hotly. "Bring your white farmhand to work under the Southern sun and his production is going to drop considerably."

"Granted," Joshua acknowledged, "but during the average cotton-picking season most of our hands pick about a hundred and fifty pounds a day. Some of them, knowing I'll give a cash bonus for real production, pick three hundred and fifty to five hundred pounds a day— when they want. And all those Northerners," he gibed, "think we're making ourselves a mint of money down here. If we're lucky, we do little above earning what it costs to keep the plantation up. If we didn't raise much of our own food, we'd be in serious trouble. Contrary to public opinion—and I think it's becoming increasingly obvious that public opinion is wrong—raising cotton is not a profitable venture today." Suddenly he was serious. "Business conditions in general are bad this year. And many of the planters are tied up with factors who overcharge unmercifully. But what can you do when money's tight? We're all land-poor here, Vicky. Our money tied up in plantations and slaves. Don't let anybody tell you differently." Then he forced himself to direct the conversation to more pleasant topics. "But how can we speak so seriously over Elvira's food? I'll bet you never tasted anything like this back in England," he teased. "If my memory serves me correctly, English food is apt to be bland and unexciting."

Vicky walked quickly down the corridor toward the

drawing room. Michael was home already; she could hear him talking with his father.

"What the hell keeps you running down to the city in this heat?" Bart asked. "Court closes the end of the month. Everything must be already scheduled till then."

"I have to go to trial with a new case," Michael said as Vicky walked into the room. His father and Ava were both sipping claret. Michael drank nothing since the night of the party, Vicky remembered. "I'm trying to get it squeezed into the calendar before summer recess."

"What's so urgent, Michael?" Sara asked from the doorway to the dining room.

"Jim Winthrop wants this case tried before he goes to England on business. He'll be away at least six months."

"Winthrop going to try to do business direct with the mills in England?" Bart asked with a smug grin. "I've been telling you for years, Sara, that's the only way to keep your head above water when you're raising cotton. Cut out the middleman. All that interest to the bastard factors."

"That would be the ideal way," Sara conceded with irritation. "Unfortunately, there are problems. What's this case about, Michael?"

"Winthrop rented out a slave," he began self-consciously. At a gesture of warning from his mother, he was silent as Nancy and the twins moved about the table serving the roast lamb. When they were gone, he briefed his parents on the Winthrop case. Ava listened with rare interest.

"Waste of good rum," Ava remarked.

"Winthrop is livid," Michael concluded. "He's going to court to sue for misuse of personal property."

"Come on," Bart objected. "Isn't that going a bit far?"

"Maybe he deserved the lashes," Ava suggested.

"For sending a fork to the table that had not been thoroughly washed?" asked Michael.

"Can't they settle out of court?" Sara inquired with distaste.

"The basic idea is to bring the suit into court," Michael said seriously. "To focus public attention on how some

folks are mistreating slaves. I know Jack would never
allow a slave to be flogged, but you've had other overseers," he reminded her, "who were not so fastidious."

"I fired them immediately!" Sara's eyes met his defensively, but Ava smiled. Ava remembered too, Vicky
thought. "I won't allow that kind of treatment at Eden."

"But some planters—some of them absentee owners—
don't know or care what goes on," Michael said passionately. "That has to be changed."

"Our knight on a white charger," Ava mocked, and
Michael frowned impatiently.

"You're not going to make friends with the local
judges," Bart warned, watching Michael speculatively.

"Who's the other man's attorney?" Sara asked.

Michael took a deep breath.

"Judge King."

Bart and Sara exchanged glances.

"Michael, for God's sake, turn down the case!" Bart
said bluntly. "You don't want to antagonize Henry."

"I'm accepting a case, Papa. Not carrying on a vendet-
ta with Judge King. I'm an attorney." His mouth was
stubbornly set.

"I don't care how well you plead the case against
Henry King, you'll lose," Sara said tightly.

"I'll try the case. It'll be duly reported in all the newspapers," Michael said with an effort at calmness. "I'll do
my best to win."

"You're behaving," Sara said, her face hot with color,
"like some Northern abolitionist. Michael, can't you see
how this will reflect on the family?"

"Surely no right-thinking person would approve of
giving fifty lashes for something so ridiculously small,"
Vicky interjected earnestly. "It's inhuman."

"Vicky, I have asked you before not to interfere between Michael and me." Sara's eyes flashed dangerously.

"I won't interfere," she said, her voice uneven, "if Michael asks me not to." Her eyes swung to his.

Michael was startled. "Mama," he said after a moment,
"Vicky is only supporting her husband." But Vicky knew
the effort this cost him.

Sara took a deep, shuddering breath. "I'm sorry," she said stiffly. "But as Michael's mother it would break my heart to see him wreck his future as a lawyer with this foolhardiness." She turned deliberately to Bart. "Bart, when did I tell you Alex's ship was scheduled to arrive? It's slipped my mind and I've misplaced his letter."

"The ship always arrives two hours late." Bart shrugged. "Seth will be there waiting when he comes in."

Sara Eden would never forgive her for this moment, Vicky thought unhappily—for having heard Michael defend her. And Alex was arriving tomorrow. Alex and his mother would have much to say to each other about her.

Vicky loved Michael. More than many a true wife loved her husband, she thought defiantly. No matter what the cost, she would support him in whatever he believed.

15 〰

"All right, Jefferson, go get my coffee and bring it out to the gallery," Bart ordered testily. "Andrew wheel me out now."

How the hell could he sleep this morning with Sara roaming about the house barking orders to everybody? He'd been awake since ten. It was as if Victoria and Albert were coming for a visit. Alex wouldn't notice if every room in the house were two weeks thick with dust and what the hell would he care that the draperies had been freshly changed in his honor?

"Andrew, go see if the papers have been brought up

yet," he said when he had been wheeled outside. "It's late enough, God knows."

"Yessuh," Andrew said with indulgence, knowing he was impatient to see Alex, though in forty-eight hours they would be at each other's throats.

"Andrew, forget about the papers," Bart yelled after him suddenly. Damn Sara with her efficiency. The papers would be coming up with Alex in the carriage. Five generations of Southerners behind her, and Sara didn't know yet that slaves were to be used to make their owners comfortable. Always complaining how the boys had been spoiled, never doing anything for themselves. Here he was, off a farm in Maryland, with not one slave to do his work for him, and he knew what all other Southerners knew. You owned slaves to make life easy for yourself. To the devil with the waste.

His mama had always said, "As long as there's a woman around, Bart won't want for anything." Where had he gone wrong? Marrying Sara, he thought bitterly. Sara put a lid on him.

His wife moved out onto the gallery, her face agitated. Bart inspected her dispassionately. Plenty of men would call Sara beautiful, even at her age.

"I don't know why Michael had to go into New Orleans today, and why Ava had to go also." She dropped into a rocker but without relaxing an inch. "They could have been here to greet Alex."

"It's almost time for dinner. I suppose you're going to say we have to wait for Alex," Bart grumbled.

Sara sighed with irritation.

"The ship must be extra-late today. But Alex ought to be riding up any minute. I told Juno to wait."

Jefferson came out of the gallery with a wide grin because he had not spilled any of the tall cup of coffee into the saucer.

"You go tell Juno," Sara said to Jefferson, "we'll wait for Mr. Alex just another few minutes; then I'll let her send in dinner."

"They're coming," Bart said suddenly. "I hear the carriage down below."

"Jefferson, tell Juno to start serving in five minutes," Sara ordered.

Her face aglow with anticipation, Sara rose to her feet. She used to look like that every time he came back from New Orleans, twenty-five years ago, Bart thought.

In a whirl of dust, the carriage rode up the driveway and swung about to come to a stop before the gallery. Sara hurried down the steps to greet her second-born.

"Oh, Alex, Alex!" She clung to him with the passion of a young bride, Bart thought with sardonic amusement: still upset every time Alex came home. Bart had told her three years ago the girl was gone for good—Alex would never see her again—but Sara still could not get Janine out of her mind.

"It was a good trip, Papa." Alex bolted up the stairs to shake his hand, his eyes opaque. Never knew what he was thinking these days, Bart reflected.

"We'll go right in to dinner," Sara said, holding the door wide so Alex could wheel his father into the house. Seth, cleaning the wall sconce near the bottom of the stairs, gazed up with a broad smile, then hurried down to greet Alex.

Bart spied Vicky at the head of the stairs, standing as if frozen.

"Come on down, Vicky," he called up briskly. "Alex has arrived." She wasn't going to relish meeting Alex again, he thought.

Obediently Vicky hurried down the stairs, a stiff little smile on her face.

"Hello, Alex," she said softly. Her eyes were somber; wary. They had met, Bart remembered, under sordid circumstances. Had to give the girl credit for one thing: she wasn't knuckling under to Sara.

"Hello." Alex's smile was inscrutable. He hadn't even bothered to call her by her name.

"Come on into the dining room," Sara urged them. "You're probably famished."

"Everything always tastes better at home, Mama," Alex said, his voice faintly accusing.

They went into the dining room and settled themselves

at the table. She always suspected the worst of Alex. She
would fall apart, Bart thought, if she knew about Michael.
Michael who could do no wrong. But he had kept that
from Sara, he reflected with grim satisfaction. Michael
should be grateful.

"I'll only be here a week," Alex said suddenly. That
shook up Sara. "I'm going up to Virginia to spend the
summer with Fred."

"If that's what you want," Sara said carefully. She was
heartsick at not having him home, but relieved that he
wouldn't be here. When was she going to get over this
craziness?

"You won't have to drag me all over the state, visiting
cousins," Alex teased, yet it was obvious that he hadn't
forgiven her for hustling him away from Eden every time
he came home.

"Is that why you're going up to Virginia?" Sara reproached with a brittle gaiety. "So you won't have to be
my escort when I go visiting?"

"Mama, you hate going visiting," Alex said with a faint
smile. "You worry every day you're away from Eden.
The cotton might not grow right without you there to
watch it."

"Alex, you know what a marvelous overseer Jack is,"
Sara said. "I don't have to worry one bit when I'm away.
And if something arises that Jack can't quite handle, all
he has to do is go over and talk with Joshua Harris." She
forced a smile. "What have you and Fred got planned for
the summer?"

Alex shrugged.

Sara was worried to death, Bart thought impatiently,
because Alex was going to be up there in Virginia on his
own. But she'd be more upset if he were here at Eden.

And the truth was that he never felt completely comfortable with Alex either. Not since he had wheeled himself into the stable that afternoon, to escape a sudden
downpour, and found Alex in the hay with Janine. Going
at it like he'd die if he couldn't. He'd been wild about the
girl. Bart felt himself in a cold sweat, remembering that
year.

"How do you like Louisiana?" Alex asked Vicky with deceptive politeness.

"I think it's the most beautiful place I've ever seen," Vicky said quietly. But she was as tense as hell, Bart thought. Alex was making her nervous. She'd be glad when he left for Virginia.

Bart sat alone on the gallery. The others had gone up to their rooms. Supper had been a strained affair, he thought grimly. Alex had a way of making every moment he was at Eden uncomfortable for everybody else. Maybe it had been a mistake to send him away to school in the first place. But Sara had done that for her own peace of mind, he thought with recurrent vindictiveness. It turned her stomach to look at Alex and remember. Her precious baby.

"Papa—" Alex's voice startled him. He turned his head swiftly to the doorway.

"I thought you'd gone up to bed."

"It's hot inside. I thought I'd try to cool off a little out here." Smiling his strange withdrawn smile, Alex crossed to a rocker and dropped into it with languid grace.

"Sure you want to go up there to Virginia, Alex?" Bart asked with sudden compassion. "You could spend the summer at home."

"Mama won't let me. Papa, you know that. She'll figure out a way to drag me away from here. Papa, why?" He leaned forward urgently. "Why is Mama so afraid for me to stay? Is it because she knows that Janine is somewhere nearby? Is she afraid I'll find her?"

"Alex, I told you a long time ago," Bart said carefully, "I sold Janine and her mama to a family up in North Carolina. A fine family, where she'll never have to do much of anything. Just be a lady's maid in a beautiful house."

"You know what I think?" Alex's voice trembled. "I think she's somewhere in New Orleans, and Mama knows it. I think Mama's scared to death I'll find her."

"You've got to stop thinking these crazy things. Alex.

You know that!" Suddenly his voice was uneven. "You put that girl out of your mind, once and for all."

Bart leaned back in his chair, willing himself to relax. He had planned to have Odalie come to his room tonight, but he had better wait till Alex left.

Why did Michael have to go chasing after him down to that whorehouse? Best thing in the world for Alex to have himself a fling with one of those bitches. They'd make him forget. They'd make a man out of him.

If Michael had not been so pious about rescuing Alex, Bart thought grimly, he wouldn't have got himself married. Damn that girl, she was going to back Michael up every inch of the way on this Winthrop business. That could kill the whole deal with Henry King.

A smile touched his mouth. Michael would bust a gut if he knew Sara had gone down to the Judge and asked him to give Michael over the summer to consider his offer. You had to give Sara credit. She wasn't afraid to fight for what she wanted.

Vicky walked along the river's edge, feeling a towering need to escape the tensions that pressed upon her within the house, seeing none of the beauty that had filled her with such pleasure upon her arrival.

Sam, trailing at her heels, shot off exuberantly after a rabbit.

"Sam, no!" she exhorted sternly. "Sam, come back here."

The quarry beyond reach, Sam trotted back to her. She bent to pick up a stick to toss it for him.

"Go get it, Sam," she coaxed, throwing it hard in the direction of the grove of pecans to their right.

Sam shot off to retrieve the stick while Vicky turned her attention to a steamer coming downstream. Suddenly she heard Alex saying, "Sam, what are you after?" And as Vicky swung about in confusion, Alex emerged from the trees to fondle Sam with the roughness he adored.

"Good morning," she said stiffly, poised to flee.

"Vicky, I want to talk to you," Alex said urgently.

"What about?"

"I want to apologize," he said miserably, "for writing Mama about you and Michael. About Nina's." He hesitated. "Did she say anything to you?"

"No," Vicky acknowledged. "But I knew."

"It was a rotten thing to do." His eyes were pained. "But I was so furious with Michael, I just sat down and wrote that stupid letter and mailed it right off. I could have killed myself afterwards. I haven't been able to look you straight in the eye since I came home."

"Why were you so furious with Michael? Because he married me?"

Alex appeared startled. "No. That's Michael's business. I was furious because he wouldn't try to talk to Mama about letting me stay in New York." He sighed. "Michael's the only one who has any influence with Mama."

"Alex, you know your mother wouldn't have allowed that," she protested gently. "Nothing Michael could have said would have helped."

"I was hoping they wouldn't let me back in school. I was hoping Mama would tell me to come home. Not just for the summer vacation. For good. But Mama won't ever let me come home."

"She expected you to be here for the summer," said Vicky, shaken by the anguish she felt in Alex. "She was shocked when you said you were only going to stay a week."

"Because in three days she would start with the damned visiting. Dragging me from one cousin to another, when she hates—as much as I—to be away from Eden. After I finish college, she'll find new ways to spirit me away. Do you know why, Vicky?"

"No," she said softly.

"Because she can't bear to look at me and know the truth!" A vein throbbed in his forehead. "Four years ago Papa brought a young slave out of the washing rooms and into the house as a maid. Janine." His voice deepened. "She was fourteen, the most beautiful thing I had ever seen. We found ways to escape from the house and meet in the stables. I loved her. It wasn't like Papa taking a slave into his bed. I loved Janine!" His voice trembled.

"And then one day Papa found us. He screamed at me. Called us every rotten name. And then he told me." Alex took a long, painful breath. "I can hear Papa's voice right now. 'My God, Alex, do you know what you've done? You've pleasured yourself with your own sister! Janine is my child. By Louise.'"

"Oh, Alex." A coldness rolled over Vicky.

"Three years ago this month Janine had a baby. Our baby. She suffered horribly. I was with her." His face was etched with grief. "The baby was a monster. Misshapen. A freak. Our incestuous, cursed child. Mercifully, he died. Right away Papa sold Janine and her mother. That's why Mama doesn't want me at Eden. She can't bear to look at me and remember."

"Alex, it isn't that at all," Vicky protested. "She loves you. She—" What could she say to Alex that he would believe? The curse of the South, come home to roost. How awful for Alex. How awful for his mother. She wasted no compassion on Bart.

"I believe that Papa sold Janine somewhere around here. He keeps telling me she's up in North Carolina, but I think—I *know*—she's somewhere in Louisiana. If I ever find her"—his voice was impassioned—"I'll take her away. Somehow I'll manage it!"

"That's why Michael feels so strongly against slavery," Vicky said softly.

Alex was startled.

"Michael doesn't know. All Papa ever told him was that I took Janine into the stables, and he found us there. That's all he knows. Don't tell him, Vicky. Please, don't tell him."

"I won't," she promised. Her eyes suddenly filled with tears. But Claudine Lamartine knew. This was part of what she had meant that morning they had sat together over tea in the Lamartines' sitting room. When she had talked about a curse on Eden.

16 ❧

Ava tapped restlessly with the toe of her shoe as she moved back and forth in her rocker. Alex sat on the steps, fondling Sam. Vicky apparently was absorbed in the conversation between Bart and Michael, Ava thought with exasperation. Would the two of them ever shut up?

"Papa, we've got to be realistic," Michael said. "This is building up into a real panic. It's going to get worse before it's better." His voice deepened with apprehension. "The banks are in bad shape."

Why was Sara so stupid, Ava wondered, about not selling slaves? She could have plenty of cash.

"You wouldn't have to worry about a panic," Bart said brusquely, "if you went in with Henry King."

"I'm not worried, Papa," Michael said with determined calm. "We'll manage to keep our heads above water."

"Your mother's worried," Bart said dryly. "She's sitting inside there with Jack trying to figure out how we're going to make it through the winter. If you picked up a few good cases with Henry—"

"I don't want to talk about Judge King," Michael interrupted quietly.

Ava rose with a frown.

"I'm going for a walk," she said to Vicky, and hurried down the steps.

She walked swiftly toward the river, her dress clinging in the humid heat of the night. How could Sara expect her

155

to keep on living here at Eden in this vacuum? But Sara kept herself so busy with plantation affairs she had no time to realize the emptiness of her life. Or did she?

Did Sara never suspect that she had taken her precious son to bed? And she could do it again, she thought with defiance. That would be one way to send Vicky running. But instinct warned her not to tangle with Sara. To her sister, Michael was sacred.

Were Jack and Sara just talking business there in the library? A couple of times a week the overseer came up, after the head count, to closet himself in the library with Sara, the door shut despite the heat. Were they talking that way, their voices filtering out to the gallery, just to reassure the rest of them? Was Jack talking about the price of molasses when his hand was beneath Sara's skirt?

Every time she tried to confront Jack, he ran like a terrified jackrabbit. She made him so passionate he didn't trust himself within six feet of her. He wasn't getting anything from his wife, if what Sara said was true. Maybe Sara wanted it to be true.

She walked more quickly, her mouth parted slightly, her breathing heavy as she visualized that strange horseback ride with Jack.

Following the river path, she paused to watch a paddleboat en route to port. The sounds of laughter and music on board were oddly arousing. She turned away and stalked swiftly into the woods. In the distance a pack of hounds howled. Some slaves, no doubt, sneaking out after the head count to hunt.

She walked in the direction of the quarters. A lamp glowed in one room of the Lamartines' small house. Cautiously, lest a dog be loose about the grounds, Ava approached the gate. For a moment she was disappointed; the windows of the lighted room were draped. No, there was a chink left carelessly open. Ava approached, an air of adventure spiraling within her. In the distance she heard a strange beat of a drum.

Standing at the window, Ava gazed into the bedroom, garishly adorned with wall hangings, paintings, statues of saints, a multitude of candles. A girandole lit the bed,

where an elderly black woman hovered over someone.
Without seeing the woman's face, Ava knew this was
Claudine Lamartine.

"You' drink dis' down, Missy, an' you' feel so good,"
the black woman promised, her voice almost mesmeriz-
ing. "Me fix jes' rat. Yo' feel so good in a li'l bit."

"Mama Daphne, it will not hurt me?" a plaintive voice
asked. "You are sure it will not hurt me?"

"Hit's jes' fine," the woman soothed. "Dat's de way—
drink hit all down."

The woman moved away so that Ava saw Claudine
stretched on the bed in her nightdress. That was Jack's
wife? she thought with contempt.

"Mama Daphne, nothing is happening," Claudine
complained. "I don't feel any different."

"Yo' will, honey," she soothed. "Jes' wait." She moved
out of the room, leaving the door ajar behind her. Ava,
bored with this, was about to turn away when Claudine
suddenly cried out.

"Mama Daphne, I feel so light. And hot! I'm burning
up!"

Then the door opened and a young girl walked inside.
No more than sixteen, Ava judged—tall, slim, black, and
beautiful. Ava's eyes clung compulsively to the window.

"Mama Daphne say ah come heah," the girl said in a
sing-song voice. "Come make yo' feel bettuh."

"I'm so hot," Claudine said fretfully. "I don't feel well
at all."

"Yo' jes' wait," the girl promised. "Ah make yo' feel
fine."

Mama Daphne walked to the bed with a peacock-
feather fan and waved it slowly. A pungent odor emerged
from the room. Incense, Ava guessed. The girl was leaning over Claudine, shucking away her nightdress. Claudine
lay naked on the bed, painfully thin, milk-white.

"I am ugly," Claudine moaned. "Once I was beautiful."

"Yo' a queen," the girl said, placing long, slender
hands on Claudine's young, adolescent breasts. "Fine
white queen," she soothed, massaging the tiny breasts.

Claudine began to move on the bed. When she spoke, her voice was husky. "Do you want to kiss me?"

Without a word the girl brought her mouth down to one breast. Did Claudine find this exciting? Or was it the drug the older slave had given to her that made her this way?

The girl opened her mouth to envelop one pink-brown nipple. Her hands moved rhythmically about Claudine's narrow pelvis. Claudine began to writhe.

"I feel so empty. So terribly empty," she complained. "Down there," she said with sudden urgency. "Down there!" But she didn't want Jack, Ava thought with unexpected excitement.

With one sweeping gesture, leaving her hands on Claudine's breasts, the girl brought her mouth down the moving slenderness to burrow between the taut thighs until Ava felt a heat within herself. For a moment she closed her eyes, remembering how it could be with Jack. Damn him!

She opened her eyes quickly at a sudden outcry from Claudine. The girl's mouth was filling her where she had been empty, one hand fondling the too-thin rump— probing now, until Claudine cried out again.

"Shh, Missy," Mama Daphne soothed. "Yo' don' wan' folks ahearin' yo' pleasure."

"Mama Daphne, I can't stand it! I can't stand it!"

She had heard about such things, Ava thought as she moved away from the window. In Europe there had been those who found their satisfaction in strange ways. But she had never loved a woman.

She walked back to the house along the river path, struggling to compose herself. Alex had gone to his room. Vicky and Michael sat on the gallery. From inside the house came the drone of voices as Sara and Jack continued their plantation conversation.

"Good night," Ava said tersely, crossing the gallery, and went up to her room.

Upstairs, she dismissed Odalie with impatience, wanting to be alone. She undressed, pulled on a flimsy nightdress and robe, and inspected herself in a mirror. Downstairs, Jack was leaving. She went to the claret bottle that Odalie had brought up earlier and poured herself a drink.

Standing at the window, she watched Jack walk along the path she herself had followed minutes ago. By now, the charade in the cottage was over.

Reluctant to go to bed, she poured herself a second glass of claret, drank it, and then decided to go downstairs and say good night to Sara.

Knowing the seductive picture she made, she walked slowly down the stairs. She was enough to stir even a man in a wheelchair, she thought with triumph.

"Ava!" Sara's voice stopped her short at the bottom of the stairs. "Where are you going like that?"

"Onto the gallery," she said sweetly.

"Go up to your room," Sara ordered furiously.

"Why?" Ava challenged. "Because of an old man in a wheelchair?"

But she laughed as she climbed the stairs again. If Sara got nervous enough, she'd sell a few slaves for her baby sister's return to Paris. But before she left, Ava thought, she'd find a way to send Vicky packing back to New York. Vicky would never be mistress of Eden.

17 ～

On a tyrannically hot morning exactly a week later, Alex waited on the gallery for Michael to join him so that they could ride together into New Orleans. Alex was leaving for Virginia. His father, awake early for this occasion, sat

hunched over the morning newspaper. Vicky sat in a
rocker beside him.

"I don't know why you insist on staying in the city all
day in weather like this," Sara said to Michael as they
walked out onto the gallery.

"Mama, I arrive at my office from home and I don't
stir outdoors until I leave to come home. David even
brings me my dinner."

Vicky's eyes clung to Michael's face. He seemed to be
telling the truth. No stops on Rampart Street, as Ava
said. Suddenly she understood. *Ava made that up about
Michael.*

"I hope the rest of the summer isn't as hot as this,"
Alex said with an enigmatic smile. He shook hands with
his father, then kissed his mother. Vicky saw Sara's hands
tighten for a moment at his shoulders. She desperately
wanted him to stay. Was Alex right? Was Janine somewhere in the area? But what life could there ever be for
them? she thought with sympathy. "Goodbye, Mama," he
said, a faint reproach in his voice that reached Sara.
Vicky saw her flinch. And then Alex was leaning down to
kiss her lightly on the cheek. "Goodbye, Vicky." There
was apology in his eyes, again, for having betrayed her to
his parents.

"Goodbye, Alex." She realized with surprise that she
was sorry to see him leave. They had not talked again on
a personal level, yet from those few poignant minutes
when Alex confided in her, she had felt that he was her
friend.

Late that same afternoon Ben Wasserman rode out to
Eden to deliver Vicky's sewing machine. Slaves were
summoned, amid much excitement, to carry the equipment from the wagon into the house and up the stairs to
Vicky's room. Even Bart joined Vicky and Sara in the
foyer as Mr. Wasserman superintended the move.

"A gentleman will arrive tomorrow morning to instruct
you in its operation," he promised Vicky. "I'm sure you
will have no trouble."

"Don't let any of the servants touch it," Bart warned.
"They wreck any decent piece of equipment. That's why

there's no slave labor used in the cotton mills. They're useless except on the land."

"Mr. Eden, I have customers," Ben said with an air of apology, "who allow their servants, when they've been properly trained, to sew on these machines, and they do remarkably well."

"We won't take any gamble," Sara said. "Only Vicky will use the machine." She was annoyed at the expenditure, Vicky thought guiltily. But Michael knew she would put the sewing machine to practical use. It would not be a waste of money.

"Mr. Wasserman, will you stay to have cake and lemonade with us?" Sara asked with perfunctory politeness.

"Thank you, Mrs. Eden, but I must return to the city," he said, remembering he had not been invited to the recent party. Why hadn't Michael insisted? Vicky wondered.

Later, though, when Michael came home, she decided she had better not ask. Something had obviously upset him. He was silent except when Sara questioned him on impersonal matters. Only as dessert and coffee were being served did he open up.

"Jim Winthrop's case is off the docket for six months," he reported unhappily. "The Judge used his influence to shift it to September, but Winthrop won't be back until the end of November or early December."

With the art of machine sewing speedily mastered, Vicky fell into a pattern of working each morning. First clothes for the infants, then for the older children. Monique was intrigued with her efforts, and when Sara left the house for the fields, Vicky secretly taught the girl to use the machine.

When Vicky ventured down to the slave quarters to distribute the garments they had made, Sara was furious, but the fact that Betsy performed these same tasks kept her silent.

Vicky walked about the quarters, pausing here and there to fondle a child, recurrently shocked at the living accommodations. One-room cabins served for four or

five slaves. This was where they slept, ate, lived their
hours away from the fields. Bart, unexpectedly defensive,
told her about other, less concerned plantations, where
these same cabins served for two families. On small
farms, he told her, a whole slave family would sleep on
rags in the kitchen. Worse even, she conceded, than Aunt
Mollie's two rooms at Five Points.

This morning she paused to talk with a young mother,
excused briefly from the fields to come to the quarters to
nurse her newborn. Impulsively she asked if she might
hold the infant before he was returned to the ten-year-
old girl who cared for the babies. Tenderness engulfed her
as she brought him against her shoulder, and she was surprised to find herself suddenly stifling a yawn.

"Ah sleepy all de time wit' mine too," the woman said
shyly, then darted off to return to work.

Vicky sat painfully still, the baby snug in her arms, her
mind computing. Two weeks past her time. She was pregnant. Michael's baby. Happiness suffused her.

Don't tell Michael yet. Be absolutely sure. Another two
weeks and there could be no mistake. *Michael's baby*. Liliane Carter had not given him a child. She would.

Vicky walked slowly back to the house, caught up in
the miracle of birth. She wanted to confide in Betsy, but
rejected the temptation. Nobody must know until she told
Michael.

On impulse she stopped off to visit with Claudine Lamartine, who seemed to derive an odd satisfaction from
the fact that Michael's wife bothered to call. Yet Claudine
had an uneasy reticence, as though she remembered her
earlier outburst, and regretted it. Vicky belonged to the
big house. Therefore, she was to be mistrusted.

Now the days dragged because she was so impatient to
impart her news to Michael. Constantly sleepy, it seemed,
she remained in bed later each morning. Betsy came over
to take her to Harris Acres five times within the next two
weeks. Joshua Harris, amused by the young women's enthusiasm for the sewing machine, ordered a like one for
Betsy.

Even though Michael was going into New Orleans only

twice a week in the enervating summer heat, Vicky saw little of him except in the evenings. He spent his days closeted in his room with his law books, or off on solitary walks. Sara worried about another outbreak of yellow fever, but the statistics this summer were no worse than those of the previous year.

And then, little more than two weeks after Alex left for Virginia, Vicky awoke with the sudden pain of stomach cramps. She lay in bed clenching her teeth at the sharp knotting in the pit of her stomach.

What was happening? Why did she hurt this way? The baby, she thought with panic. She was losing the baby. Or maybe she had not been pregnant at all. And then with a sudden wave of anguish she knew she was miscarrying.

She ought to call somebody, she thought, steeling herself against a fresh wave of pain. Where was Monique? As she made an effort to lift herself in bed, she suddenly cried out.

"Missy?" Monique darted anxiously into the room. She must have been waiting in the hall for a sign that Vicky was awake. "Missy?" She hovered over Vicky.

"Monique," she gasped, fighting against this newest pain. "Oh, Monique—" She felt a wetness at her thighs, sick as she knew the baby was flowing from her. "I'm losing the baby. I'm losing the baby."

In moments Sara, white-faced, was leaning over her, snapping out orders for Mama LaVerne to be brought immediately to the house, orders that somebody go for Dr. Ross. Vicky lay with eyes shut, tears streaming down her ashen face.

When, at last, Mama LaVerne and Dr. Ross were gone, she lay propped up, exhausted but resigned, sipping the lemonade Monique had brought her. "A couple of days in bed and you'll be right as rain," Dr. Ross had said cheerfully. But where once Michael's baby and hers had grown, there was nothing.

She started at the light knock on the door. Monique gazed at her inquiringly.

"Open the door, Monique," she said.

Michael walked in, his face taut, his eyes somber.

"Vicky—" He came to the bed. Monique silently left the room and closed the door behind her.

"Don't look like that, Michael," she protested. "I'm fine. I'm sorry about the baby." She tried to smile. "But Dr. Ross said we mustn't grieve. He said this was nature's way of getting rid of a bad seed."

"Vicky, you must not become pregnant again!" His voice trembled. "We must not let it happen again!"

"But Michael—"

"Vicky, there are things I can't talk to you about—" His voice broke off. He took a deep, shuddering breath. "There are ugly things that you don't know. You must not become pregnant again."

She gazed in anguish as he turned painfully away from her and strode from the room. This house so full of secrets! More than Liliane, she realized, stood between her and Michael.

Vicky fought against depression. Night after night she lay awake, silently mourning. Michael said nothing, but his eyes were moody, angry. The knowledge of her pregnancy and the miscarriage had unnerved him. But after that day nobody talked about the baby.

As time passed, Vicky had a strange sense of waiting— for what she could not imagine. At intervals Monique came to her in the morning with downcast eyes, and Vicky knew that the girl had been summoned again to the master's bedroom. How easy it was to recognize, now, the ugliness that lurked in the shadows of this house.

Didn't Sara guess? Didn't she care? Or was she too proud to allow herself to recognize her husband's strange relationships?

Sara was increasingly uneasy about the state of business. By August even Bart admitted the nation was in a financial crisis. Sara was further upset by the realization that the cotton crop would be considerably smaller than anticipated. Night after night Jack Lamartine sat with Sara in the library, in the cloying August heat, while they tried to arrive at the probable number of bales that would be brought in.

Late in August, a panic broke in Wall Street. The series of crashes in other communities had been reported in newspapers all over the country, but this one was felt throughout the nation. At Eden the family sat around the supper table, somberly discussing the news as carried in the *Picayune.*

"Michael, when you go into New Orleans this week," his mother said grimly, "check on what's doing with the railroad stocks. Many of the lines are failing. Find out where we stand with our stock."

"It doesn't make sense for the railroads to fail," Bart blustered. "They're going to be the backbone of the country!"

"Tell that to the ones that have declared bankruptcy," said Sara. "The last bad panic was back in 1837. Bart, you remember. It was caused by frenzied speculation, like now. Banks advanced heavily against the cotton crops even before the first seeds were planted."

"The panic of '37 was basically caused by President Jackson's Specie Circular in July of '36," Bart said caustically. "Which said that only gold and silver coins would be accepted in land payments."

"It was too much credit," Michael said, "from what I've read. And we're in the same situation again."

How bad were things? Vicky wondered. It was difficult for her to comprehend, considering the vast holdings of the Eden family in land and slaves. But Joshua Harris had said the plantation owners were "land-poor." Couldn't Sara sell some of the land if they were truly hurting financially? Michael said there were vast tracts that were idle—tracts that he envisioned, someday, sold off to former slaves, who could live in freedom.

"Thirty-seven was a rotten year," Bart was saying, "but it didn't hurt us too much."

"We survived," Sara said tartly, "because Papa was the most prosperous attorney operating in Louisiana. His fees carried the expenses of the plantation until he was brutally murdered. And then we had his insurance." She abandoned any pretense of eating.

Vicky understood the implications. Michael had been

practicing law for only two years. Did his mother expect him to carry the plantation in the face of this new panic? He wasn't an important attorney, like his grandfather. And suddenly she saw Sara's purpose: to remind Michael what he had lost by not going into Judge King's practice.

"Mr. Fleming suspected the crop might be poor this year," Michael said. "Of course, he doesn't truly know. He was judging by the almanac's weather predictions."

"The almanac was right," Bart said. The air at the table was charged now; he too had picked up Sara's message. "Michael, you did well getting as large a loan as you did."

"The way the fields look now, the crop won't even cover the advance," Sara warned, "much less carry us until the next one." She turned to Michael. "I wish you would talk to Judge King about going in with him."

"I've already turned him down."

"I've spoken to Henry King," Sara said slowly. "He's not going to consider anyone else until the fall." She smiled persuasively. "Michael, you can go to him and say you've thought about it, and you'll be happy to go in with him."

Michael stared at his mother in anger.

"I'm sorry," he said; "I can't go into Judge King's office. Not feeling the way I do about him."

"Please try to be practical, Michael. Next month the taxes on the property are due," Sara said. "The insurance will be due. The bills from the harness maker and the blacksmith are piling up. We have to put in food supplies for the hands. These are things that can't be ignored."

"I know you don't like selling slaves," Michael said warily, "but in the crisis we can manage with half a dozen hands less. Last week Ted Mitchell sold off fifty thousand dollars in hands." He saw his mother flinch. "You don't have to sell to just anyone—"

"I won't sell one slave," his mother interrupted with tight anger. "All we have is our slaves and the land. Without the slaves the land is useless. Start selling off slaves and we have nothing." She sighed. "Alex's allowance will have to be cut."

"I'll have some money coming in the first of the month," Michael said quietly. "Not much, but I'll bring it into the house."

Bart paused, a beef-laden fork in midair.

"You could go into New Orleans and see what can be done about unloading the railroad stock, Sara," he said uneasily.

"You couldn't give it away now," Sara said testily. "For all we know the railroad may already have failed."

"The house in the city is an unnecessary expense," Michael said. "We could sell it."

"We need the house," Sara contradicted. "It would cost you a fortune to stay at the hotel on nights when the weather is too bad to come home. Besides, this is no time to sell real estate. Nobody has cash. We'd have to give it away."

Nancy and Odalie came in to serve flaky peach cobbler and coffee. Vicky remembered that Michael had said his mother used the house servants with unusual efficiency. On many plantations, innumerable slaves with little to do wandered about the multiroomed mansions. Maids did little more than serve their masters or mistresses, considering themselves above menial household tasks.

When supper was over, Michael excused himself to go for a walk along the riverbank in the dwindling dusk. Vicky fought back an urge to run after him.

As Sara expected, business conditions became worse in September. More railroads failed, including the one into which Bart had bought. Stocks plunged downward. Hysteria mounted. And on October 13 the panic reached a climax. Citizens were starting runs on the banks. Specie payment was suspended indefinitely. It was the worst period in memory.

Jack Lamartine was in and out of the house constantly. The price of molasses, a staple among the slaves, was soaring. They were killing off more hogs than they could afford, Jack decreed, and he suggested encouraging the slaves to hunt for small game.

On a mid-October afternoon, hot as August, Vicky

abandoned her attempt to nap and opened the windows
wide. Sitting close to the window she looked over the
river, hoping for a breeze. It was difficult to realize that
the Edens were facing financial disaster in view of the fact
that their luxurious way of life continued unchanged as
far as Vicky could notice.

Vicky read the New York papers that Bart had sent to
Eden. Men were out of work in startling numbers. In
New York City alone it was expected that forty thousand
would be unemployed within the next six weeks. There
were demonstrations in the city, by people demanding
food and jobs. There was talk of developing an enormous
park in the center of the city, to provide jobs. Breadlines
and soup kitchens were already being set up.

"Bart?" Vicky heard Sara's voice on the side gallery.

"What do you want?" he asked in irritation. "I'm reading the newspapers."

"I want to talk to you about Michael." Her voice was
edged with desperation. "I spoke with Henry King again.
He's ailing. He can't wait any longer to bring an attorney
into his office. He wants a decision by the first of the
week."

"Look, Sara," Bart mocked, "since when did I ever
have any influence with Michael? He's your boy."

"Henry has two major cases pending. You know the
kind of fees he commands. He'll cut right down the middle with Michael. That'll handle the insurance right there.
We can't afford to let it lapse."

"You expect Michael to turn over every cent for plantation bills?"

"Michael would do just that," she said firmly. "Eden
will be his and Alex's one day. He's going to protect his
interests."

"Sometimes Michael can be as stubborn as you. You
won't get him to change his mind about Henry," Bart
warned. "We're mortgage-free, Sara. You could take on a
mortgage."

"No!"

"Then borrow from Joshua. He's been less hurt than anybody else around."

"I will not borrow one cent from Joshua!" Sara's voice was unfamiliarly strident.

"Why not?" Bart challenged. "You two are thick as thieves. You can give him a note on the plantation."

"I would borrow from Joshua without hesitation," she said flatly, "if Michael and Betsy were married. That would be different. That would be family."

"Make up your mind to one thing, Sara," Bart said testily. "Betsy is never going to marry. You know how she runs away from any man who looks at her twice. Michael and Alex are different—they're like brothers to her. She and Joshua never go out socially; it was only as a favor to you that they came to the party."

"I don't know why Betsy doesn't ever cultivate friends among the girls in the neighborhood," Sara said fretfully. "There are the Fitzgerald girls and the Butlers and the Martins—"

"Betsy has Vicky. That's all she wants. The others look at her as if they expect her to do something crazy at any moment because of Madeline."

"There's nothing wrong with Betsy. She's a bright, warm, sweet girl. To hint there could be something hereditary in Madeline's illness is outrageous," Sara said furiously. "Madeline cracked in the face of shattering tragedy."

"Madeline was peculiar before that," Bart said bluntly. "The way she refused to have black nurses for the girls. Bringing one white woman after another down to Harris Acres to care for them."

"Madeline isn't the first white woman to be afraid of Negroes," Sara pointed out. "That doesn't make her crazy. And she adores Patience, who's as black as the ace of spades."

"I still think your best bet is to borrow from Joshua," Bart said. "No use telling you to sell off some slaves."

"No, Bart. I won't sell any slaves. And I won't borrow from Joshua."

"What will you do, then, Sara?"

"I'm going to make Michael see his responsibility to the family. If my father could support the plantation from his attorney's fees, Michael can try."

"Sara, be practical," Bart exploded. "Your father was well established. Michael's just beginning."

Hastily Vicky retreated from the window and returned to the bed. Sara would not be happy until she bent Michael to her will. Couldn't she see what it would do to Michael, to make him go into the Judge's office?

All through supper Vicky waited tensely for Sara to open fire. She would do it gradually rather than make a direct attack, Vicky realized as Sara talked about the new decisions she had arrived at during the day.

"I don't relish writing this to Alex," she said slowly when the servants had left the dining room, "but he's going to have to leave college and come home. We don't have the money to send up there for the next semester. I'm writing him in the morning," she said tiredly.

"Alex won't mind too much." Bart callously voiced Vicky's thoughts.

"We're cutting off his education," Sara exclaimed. "Don't you realize the seriousness of that?" But more than cutting off his education, she feared bringing him back to Eden.

Michael's eyes were fastened on his plate. He knew this scene was being played for his benefit.

"Judge King is ailing again," his mother said finally. "With two big cases on his schedule." She took a deep breath and forced herself to gaze directly at Michael. "I spoke to him today, Michael. He's going to have to take somebody into his office right away. He can't cope. With his health the way it is, his wife tells me, he won't be able to resume his practice in full even when he's up and around."

"Mama, I told you," Michael said somberly, "I can't bring myself to go into the Judge's office."

"Michael, it's time to be realistic." Sara was fighting to remain calm. "Eden has been in the family for five generations! Someday it will belong to you and Alex. Both of you have responsibilities. Loyalties. I can't borrow another cent from the banks. You know that." But from the swift look Michael shot in his mother's direction, Vicky guessed he was thinking about Joshua Harris. "I refuse to weaken your inheritance by selling. That becomes a vicious habit. I want you to consider seriously your responsibilities. I want you to go into practice with Judge King. He's ready to be more than generous with you."

The atmosphere in the room was suddenly oppressive. Bart pretended interest in his dessert. Vicky was aghast. Trembling. How dare his mother push Michael against the wall this way!

"I'll have to think about it," Michael said miserably. "I'll give you a decision in forty-eight hours, Mama."

18

Vicky lay sleepless far into the night. In the stillness she could hear Michael prowling restlessly about his room. She prayed he would not knuckle under to his mother's demands. It was not as though the future of Eden depended on Michael's decision. There were alternatives.

At last, with the grayness of dawn touching the sky, Vicky fell asleep. But her decision had been made. She would not sit by and allow Michael to be railroaded into a job he would loathe. If Michael would not take action to help himself, then she would.

Immediately after breakfast Vicky left her room, ostensibly to go down to the quarters to deliver a pair of dresses she had finished for two newborns. But on her way back to the house, she stopped by the stables. For the first time since she had arrived at Eden, she was to issue an order to a slave other than Monique. She asked that someone bring out a carriage so that she could be driven to the Harris plantation.

In the carriage, with Seth on the box, she sat back with pounding heart, trying to frame words in her mind. Sara would be angry enough, Vicky thought guiltily, to kill her if she ever found out; but she must do this for Michael.

As the carriage turned into the roadway to Harris Acres, Vicky fought down a sudden panic. No, she would not turn coward.

Cyrus greeted her with a warm smile.

"Missy down in the stables," he reported.

"I'd like to see Mr. Harris first," Vicky said softly. "Is he home?"

"He in de study," Cyrus said doubtfully. Working on plantation matters, Cyrus meant. Not to be disturbed.

"Would you ask if I could talk to him for a few moments, Cyrus?" Vicky asked.

Cyrus walked down the hall to the study, then returned to the foyer, where Vicky waited.

"Mist' Joshua, he say yo' please come. Dis way."

As Vicky followed Cyrus into the airy study, Joshua rose from behind his paper-littered desk to walk toward her.

"It's always good to see you, Vicky," he said. But his eyes were bright with curiosity as he gestured her toward a pair of chairs that sat before a floor-to-ceiling window which opened onto a side gallery. The curtains were blowing gently in the morning breeze.

"I have no right to come to you this way," Vicky said honestly. "But for Michael I felt I had to, Mr. Harris."

His eyes inspected her keenly.

"To me the Edens are close as kin," he said gently. "If Michael's in trouble, I'll be proud to help."

"Mrs. Eden is trying to force him to go into Judge King's office. He hates everything the Judge stands for," Vicky said passionately. "And he's right! But his mother is pushing him against the wall because she's so short of money to run the plantation."

"I wondered if Sara might be having trouble. Why didn't she come to me?" he asked impatiently. "She never said a word." And then before Vicky could answer, he continued. "That damned pride of Sara's. It's ridiculous. If Sara needs money, of course I'll lend it to her."

"It'll mean Michael can remain his own man." Relief surged through Vicky. She had been right in coming. "He hasn't told her he would accept the Judge's offer, but I know Michael. He's gearing himself for it. He feels it's his responsibility to the family."

"That's nonsense," said Joshua. "I'll go to talk to Sara this afternoon. And don't worry, Vicky," he said. "Sara won't know you came to me." His eyes met hers with affection. "Betsy's out with the animals. Go visit with her." He was tacitly suggesting an explanation for her impetuous visit. "There'll be no need for Michael to force himself to go into Henry King's office. I can certainly help Sara out in this emergency."

With defiant gladness Vicky left the house to seek out her friend.

"Vicky, how nice! There's a new litter of kittens. You must see them. And you're staying for dinner," she added with mock sternness.

"I wouldn't dream of anything else," Vicky said. Then she hesitated. "Perhaps I'd better send Seth back to Eden. He may be wanted. I'll tell him to pick me up after dinner," she decided guiltily.

"Just send him home," said Betsy. "Cyrus and I will take you back this afternoon."

Sara leaned back in her chair behind the desk with a sigh. Jack sat across from her, totaling up figures on the sheet of paper in his hand.

"You're right, Sara," he agreed apprehensively. "Nothing wrong with the figures. That's rock bottom for winter supplies."

Sara frowned. Athena stood in the doorway.

"Juno say dinnuh be ready."

"All right, tell her she can serve in five minutes. Stay for dinner with us, Jack. I promise not to talk business at the table," she said with a sudden smile. Thank God for Jack. He was practical, like her. He didn't go to pieces in a crisis.

"Claudine's expecting me," he explained. He hesitated. "Look, Sara, you can hold up my salary for two or three months. We can manage."

"Thank you, Jack. I appreciate that." But she was angry that they were so pinched for money.

"Hell, the whole country's hurting," Jack said casually. "Why should we be different?" He rose briskly to his feet. "I think we'd do well to put in some winter vegetables. There's plenty of time right now."

"Whatever you think," Sara agreed.

Bart was in the dining room, a newspaper in his hands, when she walked in. He folded it and squeezed it beside him in the chair. He was in a rotten mood these days.

"Where's Vicky?" Although her daughter-in-law had been at Eden for almost six months, Sara's hostility toward her had not cooled. Rather, it had deepened. She saw a tough, stubborn streak underneath the fragile prettiness—normally a quality she would appreciate.

"Seth said he took her over the the Harrises' and she was staying for dinner," Bart reported. "She and Betsy are getting thick as thieves."

"Nobody else will bother with her," Sara reminded him. "Nobody comes calling." Recurrently this upset her. It was a reflection on the family.

"They know you have no time to entertain," Bart said. "And Vicky lopped off their most eligible bachelor. They don't feel kindly about that."

"I don't understand this marriage." Sara sighed. "I'll never understand it."

"I think Michael married her to buy himself some freedom," Bart said coolly. "To get you off his back." And then he abandoned this personal vein because the twins were coming into the room with platters of food, but he found malicious pleasure in seeing the consternation in

Sara's eyes. When they were alone again Bart asked, "Michael say anything to you about Henry King?"

"Not yet," she said with irritation.

"You write to Alex yet?"

"I'll do it this afternoon."

"Alex won't be upset," he said in a rare conciliatory gesture. "He hates school. It's not getting any easier for Southern boys up there anyway, with all the heated feelings against slavery. You ought to start teaching him plantation management," Bart went on. "Though I doubt he'll have much taste for it. But with Michael involved with the law, it's going to be up to Alex to share in the responsibility of running the place."

"Bart, I'm forty-three years old," Sara said tartly. "I'm not going to worry about training Alex at this point. But yes," she admitted, "he'll need something to occupy his time."

Sara was back at her desk, the afternoon naps eliminated with the departure of the summer heat, when she heard Joshua's voice in the foyer. With a surge of pleasure she walked out into the hall to call to him.

"Joshua, how good to see you." Her smile was brilliant. "Come into the library. Socrates, bring us some coffee and pralines." Joshua was a coffee drinker, even when the temperature hit 104.

She watched him approach her with long strides, a commandingly handsome man, though without the flamboyance that Bart had once possessed. Always in Joshua's presence she felt herself fully a woman.

"You're looking beautiful, Sara," Joshua said quietly.

"Joshua," she said, "You're so good for my morale." She laughed. "Come and sit down. How's Betsy?"

"Betsy's fine," he said with a faint smile. "Still playing the animal doctor. Instead of grandchildren I have a menagerie." He paused. "I worry about Betsy sometimes."

"I know you do," Sara said compassionately.

"I never know for sure what she's thinking. She lives in that private little world of her own. I'm grateful for Vicky." Sara stared at him in astonishment. "Vicky's brought her out of herself a little." He settled himself in a chair and leaned back with an air of relaxing.

For a few minutes they talked. "Sara, something's been bothering me for weeks. Conditions in the country are so bad. Not for me," he acknowledged conscientiously. "I've been remarkably fortunate. You know I have a fine deal with my factors—"

"I wish I had an arrangement," Sara admitted. "My interest rates are ridiculously high."

"And on top of everything else, the crops this year were so poor," Joshua continued. "How are you managing, Sara?"

Sara hesitated, color rising in her face.

"I—I'm managing, Joshua."

"The way I figure it, you're having a devil of a time," he shot back with rare impatience. "Sara, we've been close most of our lives." For a moment his eyes held hers, saying so much that she trembled. "Why can't you be honest with me? Don't I deserve that?"

"All right," she said unhappily. "I'm in a terrible bind. But I'm working things out. Alex is coming home from school—that's an expense I can't cope with now."

"You're cutting expenses, but the crop probably doesn't cover your advance—"

"No," Sara acknowledged tightly.

"You need money to carry you through the winter into the spring. And God knows what condition the banks will be in by spring." He leaned forward urgently. "Sara, I want to lend you twenty thousand to see you through, and don't talk to me about notes or any such nonsense. I'll have twenty thousand transferred to your account in your New Orleans bank tomorrow morning."

"Joshua, it may not be necessary," she hedged. "Michael might be in a position to—"

"Michael can't bring in the kind of money you need to take off the pressure," he said firmly. "He's a young lawyer just getting started. Even if he fell into some fancy fees, it would be a squeeze. Don't deny me the chance to help you, Sara." His eyes were saying what he would never dare put into words.

"Joshua, thank you," she said softly. "How would I ever survive without you?"

Sara was sincere in her thanks, but too honest with herself not to realize that in pulling her out of this crisis Joshua had freed Michael from the need to go into the Judge's offices.

"I'd better get back home." Harris rose to his feet with an air of regret. "You know me. I like to spend plenty of time out in the fields myself. I've never been able to find the likes of Jack. Overseers like him are hard to come by."

"You worry too much. Believe me, the slaves will survive if you allow yourself to take it easier."

"I have the guilt of five generations on my back, Sara." His eyes were unhappy. "Someday, we're going to have to pay dearly."

"You and Michael," Sara protested. "Both of you guilt-ridden. Everybody knows how well you take care of your slaves. As we try to do here at Eden." And they succeeded, she thought with pride. In the past twenty years not one slave had run away.

Sara walked with Joshua to the door. She frowned as she spied her daughter-in-law coming down the stairs.

"Good afternoon, Vicky." Joshua looked up at her with a smile.

"Good afternoon, Mr. Harris." How sweet she could sound when she wished.

"Thanks again, Joshua," Sara said softly. But Joshua wasn't looking at her, he was still gazing at Vicky. Then, self-consciously aware that Sara had spoken to him, he turned to her.

"What are friends for, Sara?" he reproached. "I'll take care of it first thing in the morning."

Joshua's carriage rattled off. Sara went into the house again. En route to the library she noticed Seth polishing the chandelier in the dining room. He was supposed to have that done this morning.

"Seth," she said with a sharpness that immediately made her feel guilty, "where were you this morning when you were supposed to do the chandelier? I sent Artemis looking all over for you."

"Ah took Young Missy ovuh to de Harris place," Seth explained, his dark eyes gently reproachful. "Den ah come rat back."

"Thank you, Seth. I didn't mean to scold."

Vicky was at the Harris plantation this morning. She always waited for Betsy to come over for her. *But this morning she had asked Seth to take her over.* Sara was recalling that odd exchange between Joshua and Vicky in the foyer. Vicky had gone to Joshua and told him she was in financial trouble. To prevent Michael from being pushed into Judge King's offices!

"Bart!" she called, striding furiously toward his room. "Bart!"

She pushed open his door, and he gazed up with surprise.

"What's eating you?"

"Joshua was just here." She closed the door behind her. "He came over to see if we were in financial difficulties."

"Sara, everybody is in financial difficulties, except for a few people like Joshua Harris." He leaned forward intently. "What did you tell him?"

"I admitted we were hard pressed."

"What did you work out with him?" She saw the glint of complacency in his eyes.

"Joshua insisted on a loan. He's transferring twenty thousand into our account in the morning."

"Fine," Bart approved. "You still bringing Alex home?"

"Naturally. We need that cash right here on the plantation. But do you know why Joshua came over to ask me if we needed help? Because Vicky went to him and told him so!" Her voice was hoarse with fury. "How dare she intrude in our private affairs!"

"Did Joshua tell you that?"

"Certainly not. Joshua wants me to think it was his own idea. But Vicky had Seth take her to Harris Acres this morning. She never goes there except when Betsy picks her up."

"So she's beginning to feel she's at home here. She took out a carriage. That's nothing to get excited about."

"Bart, I saw the look that passed between her and Joshua as he was leaving just now," she said bitterly. "I know Vicky went to him."

"Why the hell would she do that?" Bart asked. "Because she's afraid we won't eat?"

"She did it to keep Michael out of Henry King's office!"

Bart was startled. "If you want Michael in Henry King's office, you drive that girl away from Eden. I thought you would have her out of here by now!"

"Bart, she's Michael's wife. I can't throw her out of the house. But she's a bad influence. She's supporting him in his ridiculous convictions. Bart, I want to see Michael successfully launched as an attorney. He has the Eden name behind him, and my father's reputation. But if he talks outside the way he talks at home, he'll run himself into the ground. Nobody in Louisiana is going to hire an abolitionist attorney."

"Sara, you're too damn squeamish. I thought you'd take some action by now. I've let you have your head long enough," he continued, his voice smug. "I'm taking over. That girl's got to go."

"What are you going to do, Bart?" Sara was uneasy.

"Never mind asking questions. Just sit back and watch a master wait for the right moment. It'll come. And when it does, I'll send that little bitch tearing back to that whorehouse on Greene Street."

19

All through supper Vicky waited for Sara to tell Michael about the loan, but all she talked about was Jack's determined efforts to have the slaves plant their own gardens and catch their own game. Under Louisiana law every slave must be provided with meat daily.

Outside, the rain that had threatened in midafternoon began beating at the house in torrents. Servants were outside, closing the shutters against the near-hurricane force of the winds. There would be no sitting on the gallery tonight.

Not until they were in the drawing room, where Socrates had lit a fire, did Sara report Joshua's visit.

"We still must economize sharply," Sara finished. "I've written to Alex, telling him to return to Eden. But we'll be able to squeeze through until planting time again in the spring."

"By spring we should see an upturn in business conditions," Michael said seriously. How relieved he was! Vicky lowered her eyes lest she betray herself.

"Let's have some wine," Bart said expansively. "Michael, bring out the glasses."

They sat before the crackling fire and waited for Michael to serve them. He poured for everybody except himself. Vicky remembered his vow not to drink. Why was he so determined not to be with her again? She would allow pride to be pushed aside and accept him under any terms. Let him regard her as no better than a girl from Nina's, but let him come to her.

Ava watched Sara with covert speculation. She was thinking about that twenty thousand from Joshua Harris, Vicky guessed. She wanted to grab a handful of that money and hurry back to Paris.

"Vicky, do you play backgammon?" Michael asked unexpectedly.

"Yes." Her eyes lighted.

"Then we'll play."

Michael sought the board, the dice, and the pieces, then drew a small table close to the fireplace, oblivious of his mother's hostility.

"You play well," Michael said with surprised approval after a few moments.

"I used to play with my father when he was home. He was a backgammon champion at his school." Involuntarily she turned to look at Sara. Her mother-in-law would not believe that either.

Vicky tried diligently to concentrate on the game. It was difficult because of Michael's closeness. She was so glad that she had gone to Mr. Harris. Michael would not be pushed into Judge King's office.

When Socrates, unbidden, brought them hot chocolate because they were sitting up later than normal, Bart told him to send Andrew for Odalie.

"My back aches. It always gets me when there's a storm," he grumbled.

Vicky colored beneath the naked look he shot in her direction. All evening he had been surreptitiously staring at her in that way that made her faintly sick.

"When do you expect Alex home?" Michael asked while he put away the backgammon board.

"I imagine right away," Sara said with a flicker of humor. "He's not going to wait for a second invitation."

Andrew came into the library to wheel Bart into his room. He murmured something inaudible to the others— probably the message that Odalie was waiting for him.

The others walked up to their bedrooms. While Vicky prepared for bed, with Monique in attendance, she heard Ava go into Sara's room.

"You've got twenty thousand coming in from Joshua!"

Ava's voice could be heard throughout the house, Vicky thought. "Why can't you give me five thousand? You owe it to me, Sara! You've taken everything!"

"You have a home here, Ava. You'll always have a home at Eden. I can't give you five thousand. We need every cent to get through the winter."

For a few moments Ava hurled vituperations at Sara; then she slammed out of her room to return to her own. There was a noisy crash. Ava had thrown something against the wall. In the night her hysterical sobbing was painfully audible. Vicky turned over on her side, pulling the covers high about her shoulders. But she knew sleep would be slow in coming.

In the morning, Vicky felt too restless to sew. She left her room to sit on the gallery, intending to read. But the book remained shut. She leaned back in the rocker, trying to concentrate on the beautiful crispness of the morning, the fragrance of the autumn flowers. In the distance she saw Ava on horseback riding away from the stables for her morning canter.

Vicky started at the sound of the door opening. Jefferson was pushing Bart out onto the gallery. At this hour of the morning?

"Good morning," he said shortly, waving Jefferson away. Obediently Jefferson went back into the house.

"Good morning." Vicky tensed. Something about her father-in-law's eyes was putting her on the alert.

"Why the devil did you go to Joshua that way?" he demanded bluntly. "Sara's boiling."

"I don't know what you're talking about," she stammered, her eyes avoiding his.

"You know, Vicky," he said. "You went to Joshua and told him Sara was hurting financially."

"It was true." She forced her eyes to meet his. "Mrs. Eden kept telling us that."

"Damn, I know it was true! But you leave things like that to family! In time Sara would have come around to it."

"No, she wouldn't," said Vicky. "She was pushing Michael against the wall. She would have pushed him into the Judge's office, and he would hate it."

"Vicky, if you love Michael that much, get out of here," he said with disarming softness. "You're going to wreck his career."

"I don't believe that." But she was shaken.

"You're not being accepted, Vicky. You never will be. That's got to be obvious by now. A professional man in the Deep South might as well be dead if he doesn't marry well." He leaned forward with an air of earnestness. "I can talk to Sara about making a decent settlement on you so you can get started in something up North. Maybe a thousand dollars," he offered guardedly. "You'll find another man, a girl as pretty as you. A quiet divorce could be arranged."

"Mr. Eden, I have no intention of leaving." Vicky's voice trembled with rage. "I don't want your money. I'll never leave Eden unless Michael asks me to go." Her eyes defied Bart. He would never talk to Michael this way. "And I don't believe Michael is going to do that."

"Think about it, Vicky," he prodded.

"I won't think about it. I won't even discuss it with Michael." She saw him stiffen. The last thing he wanted her to do was discuss this with Michael! "And you won't tell him," she added with a surge of victory, "that I went to Mr. Harris."

A terse letter arrived from Alex to the effect that he would be arriving in New Orleans two days later. Sara was elated. Rugs were taken up to be beaten by a team of servants. Draperies were changed, furniture polished to a mirrorlike sheen.

"Good Lord, Sara," Bart protested over dinner, the day before Alex's arrival. "You'd think your lover was coming home instead of your son."

In the morning, an hour before Alex could possibly arrive, Sara was waiting on the gallery. Vicky, sewing upstairs in her room, could hear her scolding Sam for digging holes in the lawn. Bart would still be asleep.

When Vicky, caught up in the excitement of Alex's imminent arrival, was just at the point of abandoning sewing for the morning, she heard a carriage pull up before the house. Alex already? But when she hurried downstairs she found Sara talking with Betsy.

"Alex used to tie my pigtails together when Mr. Rogers wasn't watching," Betsy was saying reminiscently. "We used to fight like cats and dogs behind his back."

"I can't imagine you two battling," Sara said. "You looked so earnest, so sweet together, whenever I looked into the room when you were having your lessons."

"Oh, I hated Alex," Betsy said, laughing. "It was Michael I adored. He was the handsome prince from the fairy tales. I'm so glad he married someone as nice as Vicky."

Sara would not appreciate that comment, Vicky thought.

"Good morning," she said, forcing her tone to be pleasant. "Is this the welcoming committee?"

"I forgot Alex was coming in this morning," Betsy said quickly. But from the glow in her eyes Vicky suspected that, in the loneliness that surrounded Harris Acres, Betsy was eager to share the occasion. "I wanted to get some more salve from Mama LaVerne."

"Stay with us until Alex arrives," Sara encouraged. "He'll be happy to see you."

"Do you know," Betsy said with an air of disbelief, "I haven't seen Alex in three years? Except for a few minutes, that one time you stopped by the house on your way to Baton Rouge summer before last. I don't know if I'll even recognize him." Vicky saw sudden unease in her eyes.

"You and Alex were great friends," Sara chided. "There were just the two of you for years."

Bart joined them on the gallery moments before Seth pulled up before the house. Betsy remained shyly on the gallery as Sara rushed down the steps—Betsy, who was capable of such affection, Vicky thought, so fearful of opening up to others.

Arm in arm Sara and Alex mounted the stairs. He disengaged himself from his mother to kiss Vicky lightly on the cheek. She felt a pleasing closeness to him.

"Betsy?" Alex stared at her. "Betsy Harris! I don't believe it. You're all grown up."

"What did you expect? That I was just going to stand still?"

"I didn't expect you to grow up so damned pretty." He grinned. "We used to kill each other," he said to Vicky with a reminiscent glint in his eyes, "back when we were sharing a tutor. We were mortal enemies."

"Alex!" Bart's booming voice echoed across the foyer. "How are you, boy?" With a wide smile Jefferson pushed him toward the door.

"Papa, you're looking as handsome as ever," Alex teased, pulling the door wide. "You've got a harem here." His smile swept the ladies.

At Sara's insistence Betsy stayed for dinner, enjoying the surface gaiety. But Sara seriously questioned Alex about conditions up North, until Bart cut her off.

"He's a boy, Sara. What does he know about business conditions? All he saw was his college and the town of Princeton."

"Papa, no place in this country is not in trouble," Alex said soberly. "I saw it in New Jersey and I saw it in Virginia. I wasn't surprised too much, Mama, when you called me back." His eyes said he was glad to be home.

The pattern of life at Eden changed little with Alex's arrival. The family retired to the drawing room each evening after supper. Michael and Vicky played backgammon nightly. Alex went early to his room. Ava sat with the family and sulked.

Michael was disturbed by his lack of clients. Was Bart right? Vicky wondered. Was she responsible for this?

"Business is bad everywhere," Michael said self-consciously over supper, when his father questioned him.

"You don't find Henry short of clients," Sara said meaningfully.

"You ought to socialize more, Michael," Bart said casually. "We live such an isolated life out here. When was the last time you went out to supper down in New Orleans?"

"I want law cases, not supper invitations," Michael said sharply.

"Michael, don't be obtuse," Ava reproached. "Many a law case was picked up over a dining table." Her eyes moved appraisingly to Vicky. Vicky stiffened. Ava was saying that she was not an asset to Michael socially. His father had said this too, but Michael wouldn't want the kind of practice he'd acquire in that fashion.

"How do you like New Orleans, Vicky?" Alex asked, filling the awkward pause. "Seen much of it yet?"

"Michael took me to dinner once. I love New Orleans."

"The opera season's started," Michael said slowly. "We'll go one evening next week. We can stay over at the house in town."

"Oh, Michael, how lovely!" she said, a truant excitement in her because she and Michael would be alone in the town house. Perhaps, away from Eden, he might break through this wall he had erected between them.

With a vivid smile, Vicky turned to Sara and Bart. The comment froze on her lips. Michael's parents were furious that she and Michael were going into town.

20

Vicky hurried downstairs in the morning stillness, out of the house into the bright sunlight that lessened the morning chill. The grass was still damp beneath her feet. She walked with long strides, enjoying the sun on her face, full of joy because she and Michael would be going into New Orleans together.

This morning her destination was the stables. Monique had told her a new litter of kittens had been born the day before.

"How beautiful!" she exclaimed when she was shown the box where the new babies lay—tiny bundles of fur, blindly seeking their mother.

"Dey be real nice," her guide said complacently. Then, with a grin, he hurried away as he was sternly summoned to return to his labors.

Moments later Vicky started at the sound of voices just beyond. One of them was Alex's.

"Matthew, you remember Janine," he was saying. "Janine and her mama, Louise," he pushed. "My father sold them about three years ago—"

"Ah don' ratly recollec'," a male voice said uneasily. "Hones', Mist' Alex, ah don' recollec'."

"All right, Matthew," Alex said tiredly. "You don't recollect. But if you do, you come straight to me. You hear? It'll be just between the two of us."

"Yessuh," Matthew said nervously. "If ah recollec', ah come tell yo'."

Vicky sat motionless. Alex was leaving the stables. He had given up on Matthew. But he would ask others. Poor Alex.

Later, at the dinner table, she sat across from him and wished desperately that she could say something to assuage his unhappiness. Bart was unusually taciturn today, Sara silent. In an effort to break through the heaviness, Vicky talked compulsively about the prospective trip into New Orleans.

"I'm so excited about going to the opera," she said with a determined cheerfulness. "I've only been once in my life—" She stopped, remembering the last time she had mentioned attending the opera. Sara had not believed her.

"To folks in New Orleans," Alex said "the opera is a way of life. If they're poor, they'll go without a meal to

buy a seat. Mama and Papa and I don't bother much anymore, but Michael still makes a point of going to the opera
several times every season. You'll enjoy it."

The days dragged for Vicky. Like Alex she took to
wandering away from the house on long walks, waiting
impatiently for the trip into New Orleans. She was
plagued by inner tensions, lying sleepless night after night
conscious of Michael's presence in the next room. Conscious of herself as a woman.

She had known the arrangement when she married Michael. To him those two nights together were a blunder.
He had loved Liliane. Loved her so desperately he shut
his eyes to everyone else. Yet, once in a while, he looked
at her and something charged between them. The memory
of those two encounters. But he was determined to deny
them.

The morning of the day that Vicky was to meet Michael at the family town house, she awoke with an imme-
diate sense of joy. They would have supper at their house,
then go on to the theater to see *Les Huguenots,* the opera
by Meyerbeer that opened the New Orleans season each
year.

Monique arrived with Vicky's breakfast tray.

"Me pack fo' yo' now," she said while Vicky was still
eating breakfast.

"Monique," Vicky laughed tenderly, "we won't leave
until four." But she understood Monique's impatience.
She too wished it were time to climb into the carriage and
head for the city.

After breakfast she left the house and walked through
the pecan grove toward the Lamartines' cottage. She had
not visited with Claudine for two weeks, she thought
guiltily.

"Alex is back, I understand," said Claudine, "Is he
going to stay?"

"Yes." Vicky sat down on the small settee beside
Claudine, who beckoned to an elderly slave, garbed in a
colorful skirt and blouse, a flamboyantly green-and-orange

tignon covering her hair, and ordered her to bring them tea.

"I'm meeting Michael in New Orleans later," Vicky said. How wifelike she sounded. "He's taking me to the opera."

"I will go into the city next week," said Claudine. "Jack cares nothing for New Orleans, but I have met a charming Frenchwoman who moved there recently. She has a magnificent house and has invited me to stay overnight. Jack is annoyed that I am what he calls so frivolous when the country is in such a bad state. Even the opera attendance is off, he tells me. But I spend only the small money for my ticket. I will be Madame Coligny's guest at her house"—her tone became bitter—"though it shames me that I cannot return her hospitality. I cannot invite her here."

"If she enjoys your company, it doesn't matter," Vicky said. "I'm sure she's glad to have you."

Claudine stared hard at her.

"Vicky, are you happy at Eden?"

Vicky dropped her eyes in confusion.

"I love it here," she said quietly.

The servant, strikingly erect and graceful despite her age, brought them tea and small cakes. She regarded Vicky with a faint smile that was oddly disturbing.

"Mama Daphne is to be my maid and cook now," Claudine said with pleasure. "She has voodoo powers." Her eyes rested speculatively on Vicky. "But you do not believe in these things, do you? No one at the big house believes." Again she was putting Vicky on the side of the enemy.

"I know nothing about such things," Vicky said.

"Someday I will tell you," Claudine promised. "Someday you may wish her help."

When Vicky left the Lamartine cottage, she breathed a deep sigh of relief. She had felt such a coldness when she had looked into Mama Daphne's eyes. Claudine said Mama Daphne could foretell the future. What did Mama Daphne foresee in her life that she looked at her with such compassion and grief?

Vicky walked swiftly, taking the shortcut through the tall weeds beyond the clearing of the house, almost stumbling in her haste to leave the cottage behind her. Then all at once she froze, hearing voices a few feet beyond where she stood hidden by the weeds that rose a foot taller than she.

"Mama Daphne, you have to tell me," Alex wheedled. "The others are all afraid."

"Mist' Alex, don't ask," Mama Daphne pleaded. "Me be flogged if Mist' Bart t'ink me tell yo' dis."

"He won't know. I'm not going to hurt Janine. I just want to see her." His voice was desperate. "I know she's in New Orleans." Had someone told him or was he bluffing? "Mama Daphne, you were with me when the baby was born. Our baby. She's been through such terrible things. I want to see for myself that she's all right."

"A man named Lockwood," Mama Daphne said, her voice so low Vicky hardly heard. "Louise and Janine be sold to he in New Orleans. Joe Lockwood."

Vicky moved away with compulsive swiftness. *If I ever find her, I'll take her away. Somehow I'll manage it.* Alex had told her, and Vicky trembled as she remembered how Alex's face had looked.

She wondered if she should go to Michael and warn him; but she could never break her word to Alex. She had promised to tell Michael nothing. Yet where could Alex go with Janine? Where could they run?

She hurried back to the house trying to put the whispered dialogue behind her. Mama Daphne with Janine at the agonizing birth. Mama Daphne feeling a compulsion to reassure Alex that Janine was all right. How could Janine continue a slave and be all right? Vicky asked herself with a fresh awareness.

At the midday meal Alex was silent, distracted. Sara watched him anxiously while she talked about the new crop.

"Alex, you're not eating," Sara said distractedly.

"I'm not hungry," he said with veiled hostility.

"What time are you going into New Orleans?" Ava asked Vicky.

"Michael said I was to leave at four," she said uncomfortably.

"Napoleon will have to take you, or Titus," Sara said slowly. "We'll see when one of them is free."

Vicky stared at her with consternation. Michael had told her specifically to leave Eden at four.

"Send Titus," Bart drawled. "So he can sit up there on the box with that high-toned Monique. All she does around this house is stare at his handsome black face. Sara, I thought you prized yourself on keeping your Negroes busy."

Vicky tightened her mouth to keep back her rebellious thoughts.

"All right, Bart. Titus will drive Vicky into New Orleans," Sara said calmly, "since that seems so important to you."

Long before four Vicky was dressed and waiting on the gallery for Titus to pull up with the carriage. Monique, wearing a bright yellow-and-green tignon fashioned from a piece of madras given to her by Vicky, sat on the steps, clutching Vicky's portmanteau.

Inside Alex sat at the piano, playing over and over again a plaintive melody unfamiliar to her. She had not known until now that Alex even played.

"Alex, for God's sake, pick something else," Bart bellowed indoors. "That melody gives me the creeps.'

"Heah come de carriage," Monique announced exuberantly. Instantly she was on her feet, all smiles because Titus sat tall and handsome on the box.

Jefferson jumped down to open the door, helped her inside, then teasingly helped Monique, suddenly at a loss for words, up to her position beside Titus.

"Yo' drive caihful, Titus, yo' heah?" Jefferson said with mock sternness, as though he were Sara herself. "Don' git crazy 'cause yo' down in de city."

The carriage rolled away from the house. Vicky leaned back with an air of excitement. She was going into New Orleans, to the opera with Michael. To stay the night in the family town house. Her first night away from Eden in all these months.

The Eden town house on Chartres Street was two
stories high, dominated by galleries framed with delicate
ironwork and decorated with potted plants. From one of
the tall French windows that opened on a lower gallery
peered a rotund black woman in white apron and
matching turban. She disappeared instantly—hurrying to
the door, Vicky surmised, to welcome her.

The carriage rolled between the gates. The house was
astonishingly deep in proportion to its width, Vicky
noted. Titus pulled to a stop before a flight of wide,
graceful wooden stairs.

A door opened at the head of the stairs and the smiling
black woman bowed in extravagant welcome.

"Missy make long trip, be tired," she crooned sympathetically, her accent delighting Vicky as much as her
warmth. "Come into de drawin' room. Mist' Michael, him
read in de study. Me tell 'im yo' heah." ⁓   ⁓

Vicky was ushered into a huge, high-ceilinged, multiwindowed room comfortably furnished. The pungent
aroma of coffee filtered through the house.

"Emile!" the woman called imperiously as she left
Vicky seated on a small tapestry-covered sofa. "Go tell
Mist' Michael him lady be heah!"

As Vicky sat sipping strong, black coffee and nibbling
pralines, Michael belatedly came into the room.

"I see Caprice has taken good care of you," Michael
said. "Did you have a tiresome trip?"

"I enjoyed every minute of it," Vicky said ebulliently.
"I was so excited about coming into the city." For a poignant moment Vicky thought that Michael would reach
out to take her hand. But then he sat down beside her, a
fair distance between them, and called to Caprice to bring
coffee for him also.

Formal again, Michael talked to her about the opera
they were to see.

"When I was a child, Mama took me regularly to the
opera. It was always a great occasion. But then, with the
responsibility of running the plantation, she came less and
less into New Orleans. Mama is truly an astonishing
woman," he said with a touch of pride. "She runs Eden as

well as any man could do, yet you saw her at the party—
the perfect hostess."

Vicky suddenly remembered the night at Covent Garden with her father—seeing, in her mind, the elegantly
gowned, haughty woman in the box, who had cut them
dead. The same steel will.

When she had finished her coffee and pralines, Michael
cleared his throat self-consciously.

"Caprice will take you to your room." His formality
was painful to her. *Michael, remember.* "Caprice," he
called briskly. "Please show Miss Vicky to her room."

Vicky's room was large, multiwindowed to allow for
breezes against the summer heat, and elegantly furnished
in the French fashion. Monique was hanging away the
contents of Vicky's portmanteau.

"Missy dress fo' dinnuh now?" she asked.

"I'll rest awhile," said Vicky, all at once exhausted
from the excitement of being alone here with Michael
away from the tensions of Eden.

They left early for the opera because the drizzle that
fell during supper was threatening to become a downpour.
Michael seemed to find pleasure in Vicky's lively air of
anticipation.

Suddenly he leaned forward with an air of astonishment. "There's Alex!"

With a start Vicky followed Michael's gaze. Alex stood
in the rain, across from the bank, his face etched with
anguish in the spill of gaslight, his eyes fastened to an
upper window of a small house.

Michael made a motion to call to Titus, but Vicky put
a restraining hand on his arm.

"No," she insisted tightly. "Don't stop. Keep going.
Please, Michael."

Michael turned to her in bewilderment.

"Why, Vicky?"

"I can't tell you," she whispered, her face hot with
color. She knew Alex must be staring up at the house
where Janine lived. "But we can't do that to Alex. We
can't."

For a long moment Michael's eyes held hers; then he

withdrew his searching gaze and leaned back. They rode
in constrained silence for a block before Michael broke
the heavy silence between them.

"Vicky, does this have something to do with Janine?"
he asked unhappily. He paused. "Do you know about
Janine?"

She nodded.

"I promised Alex I would never talk about what he
told me."

"He's in New Orleans looking for her," Michael
guessed.

"I think so," Vicky conceded. Michael didn't know that
Janine was his half-sister. Only Alex could tell him that.
"Michael, what are you going to do?" she asked wor-
riedly.

"I have no right to try to run Alex's life for him," Michael said slowly.

Some of the joy of attending the opera was lost to
Vicky. She could not erase from her mind the memory of
Alex hoping for Janine to come to the window. Did she
know he was there?

After the performance Michael politely asked if she
would like to go somewhere for coffee or would she prefer
to go directly to the house.

"To the house, please." Michael too was disturbed by
the strange encounter with Alex. For all his matter-of-
fact decision not to intervene, he worried over his
brother.

In the carriage, Vicky was beset by doubts. Perhaps
she had been wrong to stop Michael the way she had, but
it was such a private moment.

"You're upset about Alex," Michael said when they
were in the house before a cozy fire in the drawing room.
Caprice and Emile, along with Colin, had retired to the
servant's quarters at the rear of the house. Monique was
in Vicky's room, waiting up for her. "You're sorry we
didn't stop?"

"No," Vicky said firmly. "But I'm afraid for him."

"Tomorrow night I'll talk with Alex," Michael decided.

"Gently," Vicky pleaded.

"I won't chop off his head." Michael hesitated, his eyes unhappy. "Vicky, I have to ask you. Are you happy at Eden? Do you regret coming to Louisiana?"

"I'm happy for every moment I've been at Eden," she declared.

"Vicky—" It was a tortured yet hopeful whisper. He reached for her hand and raised it to his mouth.

Then, while Vicky trembled, knowing his next move would be to bring her into his arms, a harsh knock at the front door splintered the silence.

"I'd better go," he said, oddly agitated. And yet, Vicky thought with anguish, he seemed relieved at this intrusion. "Emile and Caprice are already in bed."

Vicky sat on the sofa shaken with disappointment.

"Alex, you're soaking wet," she heard Michael say with solicitude. "Come in to the fire."

"Can I stay the night?" Alex asked. "I had Napoleon bring me in, but I sent him back. I told him to tell Mama I would sleep here. If it's all right—"

"Of course it's all right," Michael said. "Stand by the fire and dry out. I'll get you a shot of bourbon."

Vicky tried to smile as Alex's eyes met hers.

"Did you tell Michael?" he demanded.

"No," she whispered.

"Then I will."

Vicky sat silently on the sofa as Alex, in a strangled torrent of words, told him of the relationship of the Edens —father and younger son—to Janine. She saw Michael wince with shock.

"Papa told me he sold Janine to a family in North Carolina," Alex said. "He lied. He sold her and Louise to a Mr. Lockwood, who runs a bank here in town. He's a bachelor. Janine and her mother and one manservant run the house." His eyes met Michael's in some secret exchange. "I swore I'd take her away if I could find her."

"Alex, it's impossible," Michael said gently. "You can't buy Janine's freedom. And if you could, if you had the money and Lockwood would agree to sell her, where would you go? Alex," he said with painful finality,

"You're talking about a girl who is our half-sister. Yours and mine." Such anguish in him, Vicky thought. Alex's grief was his grief.

"Why did Papa lie to me?" Alex's voice soared in rage. "Why did he have to lie?"

"That's Papa's way." Michael suddenly seemed exhausted. "It was easier." He rose to his feet. "It's late. Let's all go to our rooms. I'll only be at my office in the morning. We'll all go home together at noon."

In Vicky's room, Monique waited to help her into bed. It had been arranged with Caprice that she would sleep on a pallet on the floor.

For Vicky, sleep was slow in coming. Long after she heard Monique's rhythmic breathing, she stared wide-eyed into the darkness, remembering the moment when Michael had taken her hand into his and brought it to his mouth.

21

Sharply at noon the next day, with last night's rain replaced by a glorious sunlight, Vicky and Alex settled themselves in the carriage for the return trip to Eden. Michael arrived, carrying a half-dozen leather-bound volumes.

"I want to read up before the trial." Michael indicated his stack of books with grim determination. "I don't want to miss out on a single point for Winthrop's case."

"Are you going to trial?" Vicky's face brightened. "I didn't know he had returned from England."

"He came back last week. I should have told you," he apologized. His voice was friendly, yet his eyes never met hers directly, Vicky realized with frustration.

"Will it be reported in the newspapers?" Vicky asked. "Fairly?"

Michael sighed.

"It's ridiculous to say we have freedom of the press in the South; not a word against slavery is ever permitted in Southern papers. But I'm going to fight as hard as I can to get unbiased coverage. The *Picayune* has been brutally frank on occasion, despite its subscribers' protests. I want to show all the South that in Louisiana a slave can give testimony in court against a white, and that a white man can lose when he's in the wrong."

"What makes you think the judge on the bench is going to consider him wrong?" Alex's eyes were bitter. "The worst drunken lout, if he's white, carries more weight than your most intelligent black. Michael, you know that."

"Alex, it's like I keep telling Mama and Papa. Times are changing. More and more Southerners are seeing the evils of slavery. Even though they won't come right out and say it."

"They're a handful compared with those in favor of slavery," Alex insisted. "We had this professor at college —he laid the whole thing out for us. After the Revolution, with its philosophy of inborn rights for all men, a lot of Americans freed their slaves. For generations Southerners with slaves felt guilty. And then, these last seven or eight years, there's been this strong crusade on the proslavery side to wash away that guilt. The Bible sanctions slavery, they claim," Alex said with contempt. "Slavery is justified. Even the founding fathers were on the side of slavery. They forced out of the Declaration of Independence, in committee, a resolution against slavery. Michael, that's hard to beat."

"I know the massive proslavery propaganda," said Michael. "They've managed to ease consciences in the South. But it won't endure, Alex. Slavery has got to go."

"And with it the Union," Alex warned.

"We're one country," Michael shot back. "For all our differences we must remain that way."

"Michael, about last night—" Alex was suddenly self-conscious. "I'm telling Mama I was at the casino."

Michael nodded gravely.

Alex returned to the newspaper he had been reading earlier, but Vicky sat back, going over in her mind what Michael had told her about the Winthrop slave, so badly treated by the man who had rented him.

Back at Eden, Vicky noted as they sat down to supper that Sara seemed worried—probably upset that Alex had gone to New Orleans.

"Did you have a pleasant trip?" she asked.

"Not bad." Alex pretended boredom. "How much gambling can you do at the casino with two dollars in your pocket? I watched," he said with amusement.

"Charlie Griswold dropped by this morning," Bart said casually, but his eyes were keenly watching Michael. "He tells me Winthrop's finally going to court with that stupid case."

Michael smiled faintly.

"Papa," he chided, "I'm his attorney. I'm trying the case for him." He paused. "Next week."

"Damn it, Michael, what's the matter with you?" Bart's voice soared in anger. "You want to ruin yourself as an attorney in New Orleans?"

"Michael, you're as good as dead if you take that case against Henry King," Sara said tightly. "You'll reek of abolitionist. Oh, *they* will call upon you," she conceded with distaste. "But what kind of legal future will you have?"

"Michael—" Vicky lifted her head defiantly. "May I come to court and see you?"

His eyes swung to hers with such gratitude that she trembled.

"I'd consider that an honor, Vicky."

Sara's mouth was a thin tight line of rage, this small exchange a personal affront to her. She turned to Alex, her hand unsteady as she lifted her fork to her mouth.

"Alex, I want you to start learning some of the book

work at Eden. It's time. Just an hour or two a day." Her voice was faintly strident. Sara hated her, Vicky thought defensively, because she was losing control of Michael.

Sara was at her desk when Joshua arrived at Eden. Socrates brought him into the library, then went off to instruct Juno to send in coffee and cake.

"I don't imagine you've heard the news, Sara," he said gravely, dropping into his favorite chair.

"What news, Joshua?" She leaned forward intently. "What's happened?"

"Henry King died this morning."

Suddenly cold, Sara gazed at him in shock.

"But he was recovering so nicely. He was back in his office on a full-time basis. Joshua, I can't believe it."

"I know. Everybody was stunned. The family sent a man over just now about the funeral on Friday morning. You'll want to go, of course?"

"Naturally, Joshua."

While Joshua talked sympathetically about the Judge's long legal career, Sara berated herself for not having pushed Michael into King's office. What a loss, she thought with frustration. He would have taken over the Judge's entire practice.

Bart was right, she taunted herself. She was losing Michael. Because of Vicky. Sometimes he looked at Vicky with the same tenderness he had accorded Liliane. It was a tragedy that Liliane had died so young, but it should not have meant the end of life for Michael. He could have married so well. There was hardly a girl in the state who would not have been proud to be his wife.

Nancy arrived with coffee and the English tea biscuits Joshua favored. Sara forced herself to concentrate on what Joshua was discussing.

"I never expected this to be such a rotten crop," Joshua was saying ruefully. "I don't think we picked one bale this whole month. Most years we have a full growth right into January."

"We've brought in nothing for the past three weeks," Sara reported. "Jack was terribly upset."

"Whose carriage came up a little while ago?" Bart interrupted from the hall. "Go see, Jefferson."

"Bart, Joshua is here," Sara called out. Why did he have to interest himself just now? Normally he never bothered to inquire about who came up to the house, unless he was expecting Charlie Griswold.

Jefferson pushed Bart into the library doorway, then, at a gesture from him, scampered away.

"The hardworking planter managing to take time off in the middle of the afternoon?" Bart gibed.

"I came over with bad news, Bart," Joshua explained. "Henry King died this morning."

"I'll be damned!" Bart swore softly. "When he was bragging about how well he was doing." His eyes narrowed. "Who'll be taking over his office?"

"He had nobody with him," Joshua pointed out. "I suppose the family will sell off his law books and let it go at that."

"Michael could have been in with Henry to take over," Sara said with frustration.

"Young folks have to make their own decisions, Sara," Joshua said gently.

"Michael has picked up some damn fancy ideas," Bart said bluntly. "He's going to remake the whole South."

Sara bit back a retort. "Joshua, I know it's early, but remember, we expect you and Betsy for Christmas dinner as usual."

"I look forward to that every year."

Sara sat back while Bart inveigled Joshua into one of his endless discussions on the current financial crisis, his voice growing louder as he refilled his glass from the bourbon bottle.

Sara's mind focused on Alex. She had been distraught when she discovered he had gone to the stables and ordered Napoleon to take him into the city. Napoleon, bless him, had returned directly to give her Alex's message, lest she be upset.

And Bart had seemed strange at supper when she told him Alex had gone into New Orleans. It was painful still for her to talk to Bart about Janine. Bart's child. He had insisted he had sold her to a planter in North Carolina, but he lied whenever it was convenient. She had to know if Alex had run to Janine last night.

Later, when she questioned Bart, he turned ugly, as he always did when confronted with something unpleasant.

"Damn you, Sara, are you going to spend the rest of your life persecuting me for one mistake?" he bellowed. "I told you I sold them to a man in North Carolina. You want a written statement from him?"

"I don't want Alex going to that girl, Bart." A vein throbbed in her throat. "She's his sister!"

"He knows." For once Bart was cowed. "He won't ever touch her again."

"Will you swear to me that she's in North Carolina?" Sara persisted.

"She's in North Carolina," he mumbled, and he reached to refill his glass.

The early-morning chill had disappeared by the time Ava left the stables with Venus. The sun was high and warm. She cantered across the fields in the direction of one of the shacks south of the pecan grove. Twenty feet short, she pulled tightly on the reins. Venus whinnied in reproach, but came to a halt.

The boy was there, as he had been for the past two mornings. He was replacing boards on one side of the shack. No more than sixteen, she estimated, but already close to six feet tall, with the kind of build she found fascinating. Wide of shoulders, narrow hips, a small tight rump.

She dismounted, tied Venus to a birch tree, and for a few moments stood watching, unobserved. He was stripped to the waist, his darkness intensified by a coat of sweat. Muscles rippled in his arms and back. The sound of his hammer had blocked out her approach.

Ava's eyes moved with the appreciation of a connoisseur down the powerful torso to trousers that were meant for a youth two sizes smaller. Her throat grew dry with excitement as her eyes lingered at his thighs.

She walked toward him. He glanced up, startled.

"What's your name, boy?" she asked with velvet softness.

"Bacchus, Missy," he stammered. He was frightened of her.

"What happened to the shack?" She smiled radiantly, knowing the impact she was having on him.

"Dat last stoahm got hit," Bacchus explained uneasily. "Mist' Jack, he says go fix."

"How old are you, Bacchus?" He had never had a woman. He was scared just being here alone with her.

"Fifteen," he said, looking at the ground.

"Bacchus, look at me!" she ordered imperiously.

"Yessum," he said, his voice low. Reluctantly he raised his eyes.

"Come here," she said, her eyes heated. "I'm not going to hurt you."

Silently he moved closer. Now there was no more than a foot between them. Ava pulled off a glove and reached with one hand to touch him, there where his trousers were too snug.

"Missy, don' do dat!" His eyes widened with shock. "Ah git in trouble."

"Pleasure, Bacchus," she crooned. Fifteen and never with a woman. She'd teach him. "Bacchus, come closer. Rub up against me."

"Ah dassn't," he stammered, and stepped back in alarm. "Dat's askin' fo' trouble—"

"Don't you turn me down!" Fury raged through Ava. She lifted the hand that held her riding crop and slapped him across his bare chest.

"Missy, no! No!"

"Ava!" Vicky's voice intruded with unfamiliar Strength. "Ava, put down that riding crop!"

"He molested me!" Ava screamed, with one hand tearing at the neckline of her dress. "You didn't see what he did to me!" She darted to Venus, mounted her, and galloped away.

She rode directly to the house, shouting to one of the gardeners to take the horse to the stables. They stared, alarmed, at her dishabille. Ava hurried into the house, her color high, eyes flashing.

"Sara!" she called loudly. "Sara!"

Nancy emerged from the library.

"Miss Sara be in de washin' room," she said. Her eyes fastened fearfully on Ava's ripped bodice.

"Bring her here immediately. I'll wait in the library."

Damn Vicky for butting in that way! He had wanted her; he had just needed some persuasion. In another two minutes he would have been on the floor of the shack with her.

She closed her eyes, visualizing how it might have been. She would have had him out of his mind in five minutes.

"Ava, what's happened?" Concern seeped through Sara's voice despite her air of calm. Nancy must have said she was in the library, upset and with her dress torn. "Cover yourself," she added sharply, turning fleetingly toward the open door.

"I was molested!" Ava took a deep breath. "I think he said his name was Bacchus. Tall, young, very black—"

"That's not true, Ava." Vicky hovered breathlessly in the doorway. She must have run every inch of the way. "I was on my way to the quarters. I saw what happened. You provoked him, Ava. And then you hit him with your riding crop when he didn't want to touch you."

"Ava, I thought you learned your lesson long ago!" Sara trembled with indignation.

"She's lying Sara. Do you believe her above your sister?" Ava's voice was edged with hysteria.

"I know you, Ava," Sara said with painful quietness. "How many times were you stopped from flogging a slave when you were no more than fifteen or sixteen?"

"That was different," she said with arrogance. "I was young and headstrong, and they were impudent."

"We know what they were," Sara said bluntly. "Now go to your room and change clothes." She hesitated. Uneasily her eyes swung to Vicky. "We won't talk about this any more."

Vicky nodded quietly.

"I'll find a way to pay you back for this," Ava said bitterly to Vicky, and swept from the library.

22

With the approach of Christmas, Vicky was busy sewing gifts to be sent to Aunt Mollie and her three little girls. Michael had already bought a magnificent collection of marbles for the two boys. He was unhappy that the Winston case was postponed until spring because of the change in defense attorney. In the interim he was reading everything that had been written against slavery for the past two hundred years, sometimes—to Vicky's disappointment—at the expense of their backgammon session.

When Christmas Day finally arrived, Vicky went downstairs to the chant of the servants, "Merry Christmas! Christmas gift!" For a little while, as the family went through the ritual of handing out small gifts to the servants, Vicky felt herself caught up in the holiday spirit, shyly expressing gratitude for the presents she received.

At two, Betsy and her father arrived to sit down to Christmas dinner with them. The guests, even though just neighbors, seemed to make Ava sparkle. None of the sullenness that she often brought to the table was in evidence, and Vicky realized with a start that Ava was out to charm Joshua Harris.

"We went to church services in the quarters this morning," Betsy said with pleasure, and Sara looked guilty because the Edens had not. "It was beautiful." Her eyes rested sympathetically on Alex, his unhappiness obvious on a day that was traditionally joyous.

Joshua, with flattering deference, was listening to Ava talk about Europe.

"People in Europe say this is a golden era for the Southern planters. Cotton prices are high and they're still buying from us."

"They're overlooking this past year's panic," Bart said grimly. "That didn't touch them."

"We're going to come out of it, Bart," Joshua said with confidence. "By spring money will ease up. Real estate will begin to move."

"Only the factors will make money," Bart said bitterly. "They exploit us outrageously."

"If it were not for the factors," Sara said brusquely, "we would have lost Eden years ago."

"Look what you pay for their favors," Bart said contemptuously. "Twelve percent for this year's loan, and you've never paid less than eight. On top of that, you pay a commission for selling cotton and for buying our supplies. And even that's not enough. I'd swear they're getting a rebate from the insurance and storage people."

"I made the best deal I could when I took over Eden," Sara said tightly. "If it were possible I would arrange better factoring terms, but we're not in a position to gamble."

"Joshua does better," said Bart.

"I've got a special deal," Joshua acknowledged uncomfortably. "Set up a long time ago."

"Papa, this is Christmas Day," Michael chided. "Don't let's talk business."

"Aunt Sara, will you come back with us to visit Mama?" Betsy asked eagerly.

"I never miss a Christmas visit with your mother," Sara said with unexpected gentleness. "Of course I'll come."

At regular intervals through dinner, as Socrates moved about the table serving sauterne and a fine Madeira, Vicky was conscious of the way Betsy's eyes strayed to Alex. He was no longer the exasperating boy with whom she had shared lessons. Vicky was disturbed. It would be beautiful if something were to develop between Alex and Betsy, but was it possible with Alex feeling the way he did about Janine?

"Joshua," Ava said with softness, while Socrates brought in the mammoth brandy-laced plum pudding, "how is Madeline these days?" She knew how Madeline was. Sara glared at her.

"Madeline's condition doesn't improve," Joshua said slowly. Suddenly Betsy lost the glow that had shone from her. "She's not well."

"Would it be all right if I dropped by to visit with her for a few minutes one afternoon?" Ava asked with persuasive sweetness.

"Madeline doesn't receive company, Ava," Joshua reminded her uncomfortably. "She just isn't up to it."

"Sara goes over now and then," Ava pointed out reproachfully. "She's going today. I think Madeline might enjoy a new face. I won't stay more than a few minutes. I'd like to take her a small present later this week. Some lovely perfumed soap I've brought back from Paris." She smiled ingratiatingly.

"If you'll understand if she doesn't receive you with her normal hospitality," Joshua capitulated awkwardly. "Sometimes she just sits for days, looking out the window and speaking to no one. Not even Betsy or me."

"I'll understand," Ava promised, but her eyes were brilliant with triumph.

"Socrates," Sara said with a sharpness she rarely used to the servants, "bring in the mince pies. Not everybody likes plum pudding."

After dinner, Sara went off to Harris Acres with Betsy and Joshua. As the others drifted from the drawing room, Vicky wheedled Alex into playing a game of backgammon. She hoped to improve his frame of mind.

"Alex, you're not concentrating," she reproached gently when they had played for a few minutes. But she had expected this. He had seemed restless, distraught, all through dinner. "You'll lose for sure."

Alex's smile was twisted.

"I'm a born loser."

"Mist' Alex—" Seth hovered uncertainly in the door-way, his eyes frightened. "Kin ah speak wit' yo' fo' a minute, Suh?"

"Excuse me, Vicky."

Suddenly uneasy, Vicky watched Seth whisper to Alex. She saw Alex turn pale.

"Where is he, Seth?" Alex demanded.

"In de kitchen, Suh." Seth was disturbed.

"I'll be back in a few moments, Vicky." Alex strode from the room.

Vicky left the backgammon table and walked to stand before the fireplace. Down the hall she could hear Bart arguing with Michael, enjoying the discussion. It was Christmas Day and Michael felt an obligation to cater to his father's whims. And then she heard a door close and Alex entered the drawing room.

He was white and trembling.

"Vicky, something has happened," he whispered, his eyes sick. "Louise sent for me. Janine is dying."

"Oh, Alex."

"I must go to her." His eyes focused on Vicky's face. "Will you come with me?"

"Of course. Just let me run upstairs for a cape." Her voice was husky with compassion.

"I'll be out front with the carriage. Please hurry."

Not until they were on the road to town did Vicky realize they had left without a word to Michael or his father.

"Janine asked for me," Alex explained. "There's no one in the house except the servants. Mr. Lockwood went to Baton Rouge until after New Year's."

"Alex, what happened?"

"She was pregnant. By Mr. Lockwood." His voice was strangled. "She didn't want to have the baby. She did something." He gestured his incomprehension. "She lost the baby, but she bled terribly. She's running a high fever. Vicky, let her live till we reach her. Let her live till then!" His voice broke, and Vicky reached for his hand. He clutched it convulsively.

They arrived within the city in record time and hurried through the empty streets. And then, mercifully, they were pulling up before the bank.

"This way," Alex said brusquely when he had helped her down from the carriage, and drew her with him toward a flight of wooden stairs that led to the second floor.

Alex knocked impatiently at the heavy oak door. A small woman with burnished skin and unexpectedly fine features opened it and drew Alex inside.

"Mist' Alex. Oh, Mist' Alex!" Tears spilled from her reddened eyes.

"Louise, where is she? Take me to her!" Alex ordered frantically.

Vicky followed Alex and Louise down the elegant hallway, past expensive wall hangings and crystal sconces.

"In heah, Mist' Alex," the woman said brokenly. "My baby. My baby."

The girl who lay under a silken counterpane was pale as death. Poignantly young. Beautiful. With a shock Vicky saw the resemblance to Alex and Michael.

"Janine!" Alex dropped to his knees beside the bed. "Janine—"

Her eyes fluttered wide. She managed a faint smile.

"Alex, yo' came. Ah knew yo' would."

"I've been here so many times, Janine," he said urgently. "Standing across the street, waiting for you to come to the window."

"Ah know," she whispered. "Ah saw yo' there. What else could theah evuh be fo' us, Alex? But Ah promised mahself Ah would nevuh carry his baby. Only ouh baby, Alex. Ouh po' punished baby." She lifted a slender golden hand to touch his face.

"Janine, I love you," Alex said passionately, and reached to pull her close. "I love you."

"Ah waited fo' yo' to come to me," she said with a sudden brilliant smile. "Ah waited." And then suddenly she lay limp against the pillow.

"Baby!" her mother shrieked. "My baby!"

"Alex—" Vicky walked to him and pulled him gently to his feet while Louise rocked Janine's body in her arms.

A manservant appeared in the doorway, his face etched with grief. Silently he handed a glass of brandy to Vicky.

"Alex, drink this," she commanded quietly. "Drink it."

Obediently he swallowed the spirits, fighting for control. His eyes never left the bed, where Louise mourned in wild abandon.

"Alex, you'd better come home." Michael's voice sounded at the door.

Vicky swung about in surprise. She had heard no one else enter the house.

"Not yet," Alex resisted.

"Seth told me. I followed right behind you," Michael explained. He turned to the manservant. "Where is Mr. Lockwood?"

"He be in Baton Rouge, Suh. Until aftuh New Yeah's Day."

"Alex, I'll arrange for the funeral," Michael said with a gentleness that brought tears to Vicky's eyes. "Go back to Eden with Vicky."

"I'm going to the funeral," Alex said defiantly.

"The three of us will go," Michael assured him. "Together."

23

Michael went directly to Newton Richards' Granite and Marble Yard the next morning, along with Alex, to arrange for Janine's tomb. Because of the city's moisture-saturated earth, burial was, of necessity, aboveground.

Alex, white-faced and somber, chose a marble structure that was a miniature of a fine Greek Revival house. The phrase to be etched below her name was MON PAUVRE AMOUR.

Alex found some satisfaction when Michael was able to arrange for burial in the fine St. Louis Cemetery. A young weeping willow would be placed by the grave. Services were scheduled for the following day. A telegram, over Alex's objection, went forth to Mr. Lockwood to inform him of Janine's death.

In a chill, dismal rain Vicky, Michael, and Alex joined Janine's mother before the tomb as Janine's body was carried to its final resting place. Louise wept bitterly throughout, but Alex was in tight control as he placed a bouquet of white roses before the tomb. Thank God Lockwood has not arrived, Michael thought with relief.

They spoke little on the drive back to Eden. Michael was visualizing his parents' expressions as he had told them of Janine's death. His father had been overtly shaken, though he had blustered about Janine's stupid action. His mother's eyes, to his astonishment, had filled with tears. For Janine or Alex? Or for both? Mama would worry no more about Alex and Janine. His half-sister.

Damn those Southern men, including Papa, who looked upon it as their right to take their pleasure where they willed. Poor Janine, so pretty, so bright. With two sons in the family, how could Papa have brought her into Mama's house!

A few mornings after the funeral, he sat in his office giving instructions to his clerk about a suit he was handling for, of all people, Charlie Griswold, when Jim Winthrop was announced.

"That's all for now, David," Michael said, dismissing his clerk.

"How are you, Michael?" Winthrop asked with his crisp British accent that reminded Michael of Vicky.

"Fine, sir," said Michael, "except that I'm having difficulty speeding up the trial."

"That's what I want to talk to you about." Winthrop cleared his throat, his eyes wary, and Michael snapped to attention. "I have decided to drop the case. You've earned your fee, of course," he added quickly.

"Why, for God's sake?" asked Michael.

"I've given it deep thought for the past several days. I feel it's in the best interest of all concerned."

"Mr. Winthrop, you were so determined to see this through to the finish. What's happened? We know we're in the right. And even if we lose we will have shown the state how savagely wrong slavery can be."

"Michael, I haven't changed my feelings about slavery. I'm not even upset about being called a dirty abolitionist," said Winthrop.

"We're not abolitionists," Michael corrected. "We're advocating a gradual, sensible process of emancipating the slaves."

"Michael, I don't like to do this, but common sense tells me I must." He was unhappy but firm. "I've had warnings that my man will be murdered if he tries to appear in court. Gilbert went through enough because of my stupidity at renting him out. I won't gamble with his life. Michael, I want you to institute whatever papers are necessary to free him. Immediately."

"That's a difficult situation," Michael began uneasily. "Years ago it was fairly simple, but the present laws complicate the matter. It could take a lot of time."

"If these men who threaten him have any idea of my plans, they'll murder him before I can carry them out," Winthrop said with painful calm.

"Sneak him out of New Orleans to Canada before anyone becomes aware of your intent."

"I've heard there are ways of spiriting a slave to the North. I'll give him papers proving I have set him free, and money enough to hold him till he finds work. Michael, can you arrange to get Gilbert to Canada for me?"

"If Gilbert gets to Canada, he won't need papers," Michael said, still reluctant to drop the case.

"I want this done, Michael. Can you arrange it for me?"

"I never have," Michael acknowledged. "But I have contacts that could take care of things."

"How long before you'll know for sure?"

"I'll know by this afternoon," Michael said with quiet conviction. "By three at the latest."

"I'll be here at three," Winthrop said resolutely, rising to his feet. "I don't want to gamble an unnecessary moment with Gilbert's life."

With Winthrop gone, Michael sat back in his chair, considering what must be done. He and Mr. Wasserman had never discussed the merchant's actual participation in helping slaves escape from Louisiana, yet there had been candid remarks, when they sat alone in his rooms behind the store.

Michael told David he was leaving the office briefly. He went next door to Mr. Wasserman's shop. The old man, sensing that this was more than a social call, insisted on their going back to his apartment for coffee.

"Georgette, coffee, please," he called gently, and prodded Michael into a chair. "How are you doing with the Winthrop case?"

"Mr. Winthrop's dropping it."

Mr. Wasserman leaned forward, his eyebrows raised in disbelief.

"Michael, how has this happened? What changed his mind?"

"Some fanatics here in town threatened to kill Gilbert if he testified in court," Michael said with heated frustration. "They meant it."

"And Winthrop's afraid for the man's life."

"That's it." Michael hesitated. "He wants to free him, spirit him up to Canada, where he'll be safe. Ben, what can I do to help?"

The old man thought for a few minutes. "Can Winthrop have his man here at five o'clock?"

"I'm sure he can." Michael's eyes were earnestly questioning.

"Georgette has a husband, Ebenezer—like her a free person of color. At regular intervals he delivers merchandise for me to my friend in Baton Rouge." His eyes twinkled. "Another peddler who prospered. At six this evening, when there is still daylight so there is no question of wrongdoing, Ebenezer, with Georgette to keep him company on the trip, will deliver two dozen bolts of yard goods to my friend. It will not be a particularly comfortable journey for Gilbert, but he will be safe in the dray beneath the material. In Baton Rouge, my friend will send Gilbert off on the next lap. In three weeks, God willing, he will be in Canada. A free man."

At precisely six o'clock Michael stood at the rear window of his private office, which looked out on the extension of Ben Wasserman's rooms and onto the alley that led to the rear doors of both Wasserman's quarters and his office. He stiffened as a carriage rolled slowly to a stop. A woman leaped down unaided and approached Wasserman's door.

Not a woman, Michael realized suddenly. Not with those shoulders. Gilbert, disguised as a woman. Mr. Winthrop was taking no chances with the rascals who were out for Gilbert's hide. Michael watched. Seconds later Ebenezer arrived with his dray. Georgette and Ben emerged from the door and the carriage departed. Ben held the door while Ebenezer lugged boxes from inside. Gilbert, after a furtive check of the alley, moved forward to join them. They were having difficulty, and Michael went to see what he could do, not realizing the start he would give the others until he was recognized.

"Let me help," he said quietly.

With the boxes loaded and Gilbert well concealed, Ebenezer and Georgette climbed up. The dray moved slowly down the dusk-brushed alley and around into the street. Ben smiled faintly as his eyes met Michael's.

Colin waited out in front of the office, as on any other afternoon, but today Michael didn't even try to read the paper as the carriage clattered along on the long ride home.

It was a shame Winthrop had to drop the case. Still, it was a satisfaction to know he had helped spirit Gilbert to freedom. He must tell Vicky; she would be pleased.

As night rolled in about the carriage and they moved into the rural quiet of farm country, Michael's mind fo-

cused on his wife. He looked forward, he realized with a
shock, to sitting across the table from her at supper every
night. To playing backgammon with her. Her support, so
earnest and sincere, fortified him. It had been exciting to
make love to her, he thought, and was immediately be-
sieged by guilt.

For a little while Vicky had carried their child. How
beautiful it could have been. Yet he had thanked God
that Vicky had lost their child. He and Alex. Cursed.

He reached for the paper, willing himself to read it.

Not until they had finished supper and were in the
drawing room did Michael broach the subject of the
Winthrop case.

"I lost a client today," he said as Vicky went for the
backgammon board.

"What ever on earth for?" Sara asked with astonishment.

"Winthrop's dropping the case against Jackson."

"Showing some sense at last," Bart said with satisfaction. "Though I know you hate losing a fee." His eyes
were triumphant as they sought his wife's. The only time
Mama and Papa were on friendly terms, Michael thought
wryly, was when they got together to side against him.

"Winthrop insists on paying the full fee," Michael said,
"even though we're not going to trial." Winthrop considered that Michael had fulfilled his obligations by making
the arrangements with Ben.

"I must say I'm glad," Sara said with relief. "I agree
that it was unconscionable of Jackson to beat a slave, but
there's no chance of winning the case in any Southern
court."

"He quit," Michael said bluntly, "under duress. They
threatened to kill his man."

"Michael, how awful!" Vicky's eyes flashed with indignation. "What kind of justice is that?"

"Winthrop isn't happy about it," Michael admitted.
"He just feels he can't gamble with Gilbert's life."

"There'll be another case," Vicky said impetuously.
"You'll see."

"Not like that one, I hope," Bart said tartly. "It casts a rotten light on the family for Michael to be pursuing that kind of action."

Was Vicky truly happy here? Was she lonesome?

Michael glanced at her and made a decision. "We'll go into New Orleans late in February. I'll take you to see the Mardi Gras parade."

"Michael, you know what's happened to the Mardi Gras these last years," said Sara sharply. "The newspapers have been campaigning for years to eliminate the Carnival. There are terrible fights between white men and boys and free Negroes. The whites," she said conscientiously, "are the worst of those from the Irish Channel, and they use Mardi Gras as an excuse to go on a rampage."

"You're forgetting last year," Michael said firmly. "I know none of us was there, but everybody in New Orleans talked for weeks about the magnificence of the parade put on by The Mystick Krewe of Comus. And it'll be equally good this year." Michael was astonished to realize how he was looking forward to this excursion with Vicky.

Earlier than usual his mother went up to her room. She was fighting the onset of a cold.

Minutes later his father yelled loudly for Jefferson, who usually sat cross-legged in the hallway waiting for the call.

"Jefferson, you go rustle up Andrew and tell him I'm tired. I'm ready to go to bed."

Michael and Vicky remained in the drawing room, their attention focused on the backgammon board. Tonight Michael felt a reluctance to go up to his solitary room. There was a tacit pact between them to play past their normal hour.

"Are you tired?" he asked when Vicky stifled a yawn.

"Not at all."

"Hot chocolate would be good about now," Michael decided. "Would you like some?"

"I'll go to the kitchen." Vicky pushed back her chair.

"Stay there," Michael ordered, feeling a stirring in him

that he struggled to ignore. "I'll go." He didn't want to sit here so close to Vicky, feeling this way.

He strode down the hall toward the kitchen, tensing at the sound of his father's voice, seeping from behind the heavy oak door of his room.

"What the devil's the matter with you, Monique?" he demanded hoarsely. "Come on, make some noise girl! Show me you're enjoying it."

Michael hurried past, a sickness in the pit of his stomach. Now it was Monique. What was the matter with Papa? Why couldn't he leave the servants alone?

At least, there would be no more children with Eden features and dark skin. For that, he thought bitterly, they must be grateful.

24

Vicky sat in a rocker on the gallery, Sam's silken head nuzzled beneath her hand. What a deliciously warm morning! This might have been May rather than late January. But she was restless, impatient for the weeks to speed past and to be in New Orleans with Michael. Michael looked at her in a way, too often, that made her churn with frustration. He loved her! It shone from him. What was this insurmountable wall between them?

Charlie Griswold's carriage was coming up the roadway. With Sam at her heels, she hurried down the steps away from the house. She liked none of Bart's personal friends—raucous, profane men who avoided Sara Eden's presence.

She walked swiftly through the pecan grove toward the quarters. The Lamartine cottage was just ahead.

Claudine greeted her with unexpected warmth.

"Mama Daphne," she called, her voice slightly shrill. "Bring tea and cakes." She turned again to Vicky with a smile. "I want to show you the gown I am making for myself. You must tell me if you think it is elegant enough for a fancy ball."

Claudine disappeared into another room and returned triumphantly bearing a gown of white satin, with yards of material in the skirt. It was sewn, Vicky thought, with exquisite skill.

"It's magnificent."

"I will wear a red ornament in my hair," Claudine said proudly. "And Madame Coligny, my friend whom I have told you about, is lending me a double string of pearls. Real pearls," she emphasized. "She is very rich. She is giving a private masquerade ball following the Mardi Gras parade."

"Oh, you're going to New Orleans for the Mardi Gras." Vicky's eyes lighted. "Michael and I are going too."

"Jack will stay at home," Claudine said dryly. "He does not enjoy socializing, and he is having difficulties with his Negro driver. Jack is annoyed because the man considers flogging necessary to maintain discipline among the slaves." Claudine paused, smiling automatically as Mama Daphne appeared with the tray. She did not continue until the slave had left her room. "The man's perfectly willing to accept the general rule that a slave is never to be flogged in anger, and never more than fifteen lashes. But Mrs. Eden and Jack flout what everybody in the South knows, that flogging is the only way to keep slaves in line."

"Fifteen lashes seems inhuman," Vicky protested. Any flogging, she thought privately, was inhuman.

"Oh, the slaves get off lightly," Claudine said with contempt. "They seldom go to jail, even for a crime that would send a white man up for years. Do you know what Jack gives out as punishment? He will force a buck who has picked trashy cotton to wash clothes or to wear a dress, to shame him. For something that is awful enough to deserve a back laid wide, he will throw a Negro into the plantation jail on holidays or Sundays. Do you know that on many plantations there are at least two or three whippings a week? I have heard of an old lady who runs a plantation by herself, and every Monday morning, religiously, she calls a dozen slaves into the house and personally flogs them."

Vicky shuddered and cast about for a different topic of conversation. "Claudine," she said on impulse, "I must bring Ava over to meet you. Ava lived for years in Paris. You two would have much to talk about."

Claudine's eyes lighted. She knew all about Ava. She must have been impatiently waiting for this meeting.

"I would like that," she said with barely contained excitement.

"Tomorrow morning," Vicky promised. As soon as possible, she excused herself.

Back at Eden, Vicky tried to think only of the Mardi Gras. At dinner she mentioned Claudine's plans, and Bart immediately began to reminisce about the first real parade in New Orleans on Fat Tuesday, 1838.

Sara heard nothing. Her eyes were stormy. Her mind was not with them, Vicky thought. But not until the evening did she reveal what disturbed her.

"Charlie Griswold was here today," she said to Michael, before supper. "He told your father that Jim Flournoy is buying the Richmond plantation." Michael raised an eyebrow. Mr Flournoy, Vicky recalled, was a client of Michael's. "He's having Bob Butler draw up the papers," Sara continued tightly.

Michael frowned fleetingly as he digested this.

"It's Flournoy's privilege to switch attorneys."

"Do you know why he switched attorneys? Because of your taking on the Winthrop case. Michael, I warned you.

Folks in Louisiana do not take to that kind of action. You're going to miss out on a lot of clients for talking so openly."

"At least old Charlie sends his friends, Michael," said Bart, but his eyes were wary.

"I think it's time we gave a ball," Sara said abruptly. "Something splashy. At the St. Charles Hotel."

"In these times?" Bart asked with malicious humor. "When we're one step from the poorhouse?"

"Michael must socialize with prospective clients," Sara said, fighting for calm. "More cases are acquired over a glass of wine than anywhere else."

"Mama, no balls," Michael objected. "They're not likely to bolster my practice. If folks ask me about the Winthrop case, they'll hear the truth: that I'm damned sorry Winthrop was frightened out of court."

"Michael, when are you going to learn?" Sara asked with exasperation. "Think what you wish; but damn it, have the good sense to be silent."

"I have been silent too long. We're heading for dangerous times. Not only is slavery morally wrong, it's costing the South too much in economic productivity. I read a book that came out a few months ago, by a man named Helper. He says that the Northern hay crop alone was worth more than all the cotton, rice, tobacco, and hemp produced in the fifteen slave states."

"We don't need all that hay," Bart slapped back. "With our warm climate our cattle and horses graze a large part of each year."

"Papa, you know yourself that only slaveholders in the most fertile districts of the South—and those exceptionally canny at management—are doing anything more than keeping their heads above water. The operation of slave plantations is not a profitable venture. To make even a slim margin of profit we have to raise a large part of the food supply for our hands." He turned to Sara. "Mama, you know that we're wearing out the soil, planting year after year the way we do."

"We've got plenty of land, Michael," Bart reproved. "Thousands of acres we never touch."

"No good for cotton," said Michael. "Therefore, it's never touched. And in addition to everything else slavery is responsible for the situation of the poor whites, because who is willing to pay a decent wage, that'll give a man his self-respect, when it's possible to buy a black man and keep him in bondage?"

"Hear, hear," his father drawled. "They'll be inviting you to speak at abolitionist meetings if you keep this up."

"Bart, be quiet," Sara ordered.

"I think slavery is wrong," Michael repeated with uneasy calm. "I think it's ruining the South economically. I intend to speak out whenever I have the occasion."

Sara shot a furious glance at Vicky, blaming her for Michael's defiance. Afraid of getting into an open fight with her son, she stood abruptly and left the room.

"Your mother's upset," Bart said to Michael with reproach. "Sara's used to having her own way. Folks respect Sara," he said with narrowed, contemplative eyes, "but they don't like her. She refuses to fit into their concept of the Southern lady. Not a woman who goes out to the fields to watch the slaves chop cotton. Not a woman who gets down on her hands and knees to feel the dirt run through her fingers, and talks to her overseer about what fertilizer is best. But not many folks win an argument with Sara Eden." His eyes held Vicky's. "Remember that."

A sudden chill closed in about Vicky. No matter how bitter he felt toward his wife, Bart and Sara stood together against her.

Shortly before Mardi Gras Day, Michael told Vicky they would have supper with Ben Wasserman after they watched the parade along Charles Street and spend the night in town.

On impulse he invited Alex—a quiet, morose figure about Eden—to go into New Orleans with them.

"I don't think so, Michael," said Alex, unable to wash the tragedy of Janine from his mind.

On Mardi Gras Day, Vicky awoke with an instant sense of expectancy. She threw aside the covers and hurried to the window. A glorious day. How awful if it had rained!

She and Michael waited until late afternoon to begin the trip into New Orleans. There would be, Michael predicted, many maskers out during the day; but the whole city would come alive at night.

By the time they arrived, people moved about in swarms, spilling into the city in carriageloads.

"So many people!" she marveled.

At the house they rested, waiting until dark for the real activities to begin. When they were just ready to leave, Alex appeared.

"Titus is putting away the carriage," Alex explained. He seemed in rare high spirits. "At the last moment I decided to come."

"Caprice and Emile have left for the evening with Monique," Michael said apologetically. "Vicky and I were invited out for supper—we didn't expect you to be coming in."

"Don't worry about me," Alex said quickly. "Juno prepared a supper basket. Titus and I will go to the parade and then I'll have supper here at the house. Titus will make coffee for me."

"You sure you wouldn't like to come along with Vicky and me? We're going over toward Lafayette Square."

"I'll have coffee first," Alex said after a brief hesitation. "Titus knows New Orleans well—he wants to take me around."

By the time Michael and Vicky left the house, half of New Orleans seemed to be crowded onto Charles Street. Michael slipped an arm about her lest they be separated.

"I'll betcha there's fifty thousand people here to see the parade," someone said with relish as they approached Lafayette Square to wait for the Mystick Krewe.

"It's nine o'clock," Michael said. "They ought to begin soon."

Then the crowd raised its voice at the sound of the bands. The glare of torchlights pierced the darkness.

"Here comes Comus!" somebody yelled jubilantly, and Vicky strained for a sight of the first float.

"The subject of the pageant is 'The Classic Pantheon,'" Michael explained with excitement. "I understand it's being presented in thirty-one parts."

On the first float, high on his royal seat, sat Comus, followed by Momus. After that came two-faced Janus in his Temple of the Four Seasons. Bacchus was drawn by leopards. Flora rode in a car of flowers, surrounded by gigantic butterflies. The pageant was endless, it seemed to Vicky, mesmerized by the splendor that rode before her. All about them white-clad Negroes with blazing flambeaux that lit the sky with a magical glow.

After the last float passed, Vicky and Michael pushed their way through the festive crowds in the direction of Ben Wasserman's shop, where he waited to share his late supper.

Georgette had set a festive table in his small dining room, and as soon as they were seated, she began to serve.

"Did you enjoy the parade?" Ben asked with a broad smile.

"It was marvelous," Vicky told him. "I've never seen anything like it."

Vicky was starting Georgette's jambalaya when Ben asked, "Michael, have you heard anything of Gilbert?"

"Only today," Michael said with quiet satisfaction. "Winthrop received word that Gilbert had arrived in Montreal."

Vicky saw Michael's smile and was grateful.

Over Georgette's superb rice pudding, rich with wine and spices and fruit, Ben confided that he was about to buy a house.

"We are haggling still, but I will buy. You will handle the legal matters for me, Michael?"

"With pleasure. Where is the house?"

"Next to a splendid house owned by Monsieur and Madame Coligny, who moved here only a few months ago." Vicky glanced up with surprise. Mme. Coligny? Claudine's Mme. Coligny? Probably not. In heavily French New Orleans the name was a common one. "Monsieur Coligny is a modest little man who represents a powerful New York factoring firm, among other things. His wife, I understand, is becoming a famous hostess." He glanced eagerly from Michael to Vicky. "Would you like to see the house? I must warn you, though, it is very modest in comparison with my neighbors'."

"I'd love to see it," Vicky said spontaneously.

The streets were still crowded when they left to go see Ben's prospective home. All around them were the sounds of laughter.

"Georgette and her husband, Ebenezer, will live in when I move." Vicky caught the closed look between Ben and Michael and understood that Ben's decision had a stronger basis than the wish for a comfortable new home. She had heard Bart's frequent snide remarks about the "nigger lovers" who helped runaway slaves escape to the North—slaves, Vicky guessed, who had been mistreated. She was proud of Michael.

"The house is right down here," Ben said, urging them down a narrow side street.

He paused before a plaster house painted a delicate peach. It was two-storied, faced with tall galleries of delicate ironwork with waist-high railings.

Vicky's eyes moved to the massive structure next door, four stories high and closed off from the street by a tall iron gate. Ben lit a candle and urged her inside.

This was the main floor, Vicky realized, the ceilings at least fifteen feet high. A half-dozen rooms led off from the side hall. They paused at the door of each room, admiring the spaciousness, the fine chandeliers, the marble mantels.

"Upstairs," Ben explained, "are rooms for Georgette and Ebenezer." Again that silent communication between Ben and Michael. Rooms for unexpected night visitors, Vicky interpreted.

Now Vicky and Michael followed Ben down the rear stairs into the moonlit courtyard. The charming sounds of revelry were remote.

Suddenly the stillness was shattered by a terrified scream, a child's scream.

"What is it?" Vicky whispered, cold with alarm. Her

eyes moved upward as the shriek was repeated with
anguished terror. For one unbelievable instant, in the spill
of moonlight, she saw the small black child, leaning back
against an open window on the top floor of the house next
door. There were hands at the child's shoulder. *Pushing.*
"Michael!" Her own hand reached out to Michael's arm.

But already the child was hurtling from the window to
the courtyard next door. *Four floors down.*

"Stay here!" Michael ordered, and dashed to the wall
that separated the two courtyards, scrambling over it with
an agility born of urgency.

"Mr. Wasserman, somebody pushed that child," Vicky
whispered. "I saw."

"A black child," Ben said grimly. "A slave."

"She's dead," Michael called to them from the other
side. "Let me knock at the windows here."

Vicky and Ben waited, but there was no response, and
Michael returned to the dividing wall and scaled it again.

"We'll have to go to the front of the house. Nobody
hears on this level."

"Michael, are you sure she's dead?"

"She's dead," Michael said gently. Pushed to her death.
She had not imagined those hands at the little girl's
shoulders. She had seen them.

Silently the three of them returned to the house and
hurried through it, locking doors behind them as they
moved to the street.

The iron fence next door was locked, but Vicky discovered a small entrance to one side through which they
could walk. At the main door richly carved with wreaths
of flowers and garlands in bas-relief, Michael hammered
with the knocker. Finally they heard footsteps and the
door swung wide. A tall, richly liveried mulatto butler
looked upon them inquiringly.

"Madame Coligny, please," Ben asked politely.

The butler frowned.

"Madame entertains a friend," he said loftily. His accent was that of a white Frenchman. "She does not wish
to be disturbed."

"You will please tell Madame Coligny that this is a

matter of urgency," Michael said firmly. "A child has fallen to her death from your top floor. Her body is lying in the courtyard. Tell her, please," Michael insisted, as the butler showed little concern.

"You will wait in the downstairs drawing room." The butler pointed to the double doors to the left. "I will tell Madame."

They walked into a room of astonishing opulence—high-ceilinged, with priceless furnishings, dramatic paintings, rich wall hangings.

"Folks have not been wrong in what they have said about the Coligny mansion," Mr. Wasserman said dryly. He was thinking of that poor dead child who lay in the courtyard.

A tall, slender, black-haired woman appeared in the doorway: somewhere in her thirties, Vicky judged.

"I am Jeanne Coligny," she introduced herself. "What is this that Dominique tells me? A child has fallen from my house?"

"A little girl, about eight," Michael said quietly.

The woman called to Dominique, speaking French too rapidly for Vicky to understand.

"Please, come with me to the courtyard," Mme. Coligny ordered—anxious, but in superb control.

They followed Mme. Coligny down a wide hallway.

"Dominique?" she called. "What do you see?"

"It is Ninette, Madame," he called up. His voice was impassive. "She is dead."

"Mon Dieu!" Suddenly Mme. Coligny swayed. Michael hurried to her side to steady her. "Please," she whispered. "Tell Dominique to bring me brandy."

Michael solicitously helped Jeanne Coligny into the drawing room. Slowly her color returned.

"She went to a window to watch the crowds in the street," Mme. Coligny whispered. "There is a fine view there, but she was warned to stay away from the windows." Vicky was about to speak, but instinct warned her to be silent.

"You had better notify the police," Michael said carefully.

Mme. Coligny's eyes flashed with sudden anger.

"Why should I call the police for a tragic accident such as this? It is a family matter."

"It is the custom in New Orleans," Michael said with an air of apology. "If you like, we will stop off at the police house and tell them to send over a man."

"Dominique will go," she said. "But first that poor child's body must be brought into the house." Again she spoke in rapid French to Dominique, then turned to them. "I am sorry that we must meet under such tragic circumstances, Monsieur."

"Permit me to introduce myself," Michael said with rare formality. "I am Michael Eden. This is my wife, Vicky. And Mr. Wasserman, who is considering the purchase of the house next door."

"Eden?" Mme. Coligny squinted in thought. "Then you know Claudine Lamartine. She is my guest."

"Yes, we know Madame Lamartine," Michael said politely.

"I must go to her," Jeanne Coligny said apologetically. "She will wonder what has happened." She paused. Then, trying to mask distaste, she said, "Dominique will go immediately to the police."

Vicky was trembling when they walked out into the pleasant night air. For a long time she would be haunted by the memory of that small figure hurtling into the courtyard.

"I'm sorry you had to see this, Vicky," Ben said with regret.

"Do you think Madame Coligny will send for the police?" Vicky asked. "Somebody did push the little girl from that window."

"She'll send for the police," Michael said. But his eyes were guarded.

"We ought to go to the police and tell them what we saw," Vicky said intensely.

"We saw a child falling from a window," Ben said with steely quietness. Vicky stared at him in disbelief.

"Mr. Wasserman, I saw hands push her!"

"The police will not believe you, Vicky," Ben said with

a rarely displayed bitterness. "And Madame Coligny does not want an investigation. The family is powerful. The police will do as she wishes."

"Do you mean the police will do nothing?" Vicky was indignant.

"I'll take you home," Michael said carefully. "Then I'll go over to the police house."

"Michael, you're wasting your time," Ben warned. "A slave child fell to her death. What does this mean to the New Orleans police?"

"I must go over there," Michael insisted. "After I take Vicky home."

They approached the Edens' house to see the drawing room lighted.

"Alex came directly home after the parade. He must be having his supper."

"You don't have to come up with me, Michael," Vicky told him with a shaky smile. "Go straight on over to the police."

"I won't be long," Michael promised.

He waited while Vicky hurried up the flight of stairs to the entrance. Vicky tried the door. It was open. After a brief wave of her hand to Michael, she walked inside, anxious to talk about the tragedy with Alex.

She walked toward the drawing room. No one was there, though all the candles in the elaborate chandelier had been lighted. She went into the hall and noticed that the door of the third bedroom was swung wide.

Hoping to talk to him, she hurried down the hall and was on the point of calling to him when she saw the shadowed tableau by the window. Titus was on his hands and knees, Alex hovering strangely above him. Suddenly she was ice cold as the figures grew less veiled by the darkness.

"Titus," Alex whispered hoarsely. Both were unconscious of Vicky's presence. "Tell me it's good! Tell me!"

Silently Vicky fled to the door and let herself out into the night. All these weeks when Alex had been so silent, either locked in his room or roaming about the woods,

had there been Titus? From Janine to Titus. Oh, Alex.
Poor Alex.

She knocked sharply at the door, struggling to wash
from her mind the strange coupling she had witnessed in
Alex's bedroom.

"Alex?" she called. She tried to make her voice sound
natural. "Alex."

And then she steeled herself to face Alex and Titus as
she heard footsteps down the hall. Either Alex or Titus
was coming to admit her.

25

Bart sat by the fire, drumming with one hand on the arm
of his wheelchair. Alex, as usual, had disappeared immediately after supper.

Ava, who had been reading a fashion magazine, tossed
it aside with a low sound of impatience and rose to her
feet.

"I'm going down to see Claudine," she announced.

"At this hour?" Sara asked with faint reproach.

"Claudine's alone," Ava said drily. "Jack's busy making the head count. I won't stay long."

Suddenly Ava was visiting constantly with Claudine, or
going down to New Orleans with her in one of the Eden
carriages. Vicky had done them both a favor, introducing
them that way.

"Vicky, would you like to go into New Orleans tomorrow?" Michael asked unexpectedly. "I thought we might
invite Ben over to the house for supper."

"Yes," Vicky agreed enthusiastically. "That would be lovely."

What was this business about going into New Orleans with Vicky again? Bart asked himself. They had gone in just last month for the Mardi Gras.

"Jefferson," he yelled loudly. "Go get Andrew. I want to go to bed."

Sara gazed at him in astonishment.

"So early?"

"Do you mind?" he asked sarcastically. "I want to get comfortable."

He waited in his room for Andrew.

"Get me into bed," he ordered when the boy appeared. "Jefferson, you go find Monique. Tell her I want her to come in here and rub my back. Odalie's getting a heavy hand." Already he was visualizing Monique on the bed with him. Damn it, when was she going to de-ice? "Scoot, Jefferson."

"Yessuh."

Andrew got him into bed, naked under the covers. He placed the bourbon bottle beside the bed and waited for dismissal. Bart's eyes glittered at the faint knock on the door.

"Come on in," he called, and Monique—scared and unhappy—came into the room. "All right, Andrew, go on," he said. "Jefferson, you wait outside at the door till I call."

Then he spoke to Monique. "Take off your dress," he said brusquely, "and come lie down beside me."

Wordlessly Monique pulled her dress over her head, laid it neatly on a chair, and walked to the bed. Carefully she lay down beside him.

"Play with it a little bit," he ordered. "Maybe something'll happen." If she touched him in just the right place, he'd get an erection. It didn't matter if he felt nothing. She ought to get excited. That was how he got his satisfaction.

"Yessuh." Her voice a whisper, her eyes downcast, she reached to stroke him with one slender hand.

"That's it," he said encouragingly after a few moments.

"Just keep it up that way." His eyes were watching. "There, you see," he drawled. "Doesn't that do something to you, Monique? Tell me." His voice was hoarse as he stared at her face.

"Yessuh," she lied.

"Monique," he said with deceptive softness, "I'll bet I know what'll drive you crazy. You bend over and you kiss that thing. You open your mouth and you take it right in. Damn it, don't look at me that way!" Suddenly he was furious. He reached for her with one powerful hand and brought her head down to him.

Why wasn't he feeling something? Time was he would have been so crazy he'd be yelling by now.

"All right," he said finally, "get up." He reached to pull her toward him. "Lift up." His voice was hoarse with synthetic excitement. In his mind he was remembering how it used to be. "That's the baby. Come on, now! Show some action!" His hands were at her shoulders as she went through the motions of passion—her eyes shut, her face glistening with perspiration, an odd cast to her skin.

"Don't you puke on me!" he yelled as she suddenly retched.

"Nossuh." Her eyes still shut, she spoke between clenched teeth. "Me don' do dat," she managed.

"All right," he said finally. "Tell Jefferson to go get a pitcher of hot water. I want you to wash me down."

Ava strode into the house, furious at being rejected again by Jack. She had timed herself perfectly, leaving the cottage a few minutes before Jack would be finished with the head count. She had met him there at the edge of the quarters, and he had deliberately pushed her away from him.

Didn't he understand about Claudine? Claudine hated having anything to do with a man. There was something odd about her and that Frenchwoman down in New Orleans. What was it like, doing things with another woman?

She spied Monique at the head of the stairs. She heard Vicky and Michael in the drawing room, playing their incessant backgammon.

"Monique," she called in sudden decision. "Wait there for me." She hurried up the stairs. Monique waited, curiously wistful. "Monique, I want you to come in and brush my hair. The way you do Miss Vicky's. You bring a special sheen to her hair that Odalie never seems to get in mine."

"Yessum." Monique waited for Ava to arrive at the second floor.

In her room, Ava took up a position in a chair by the fire, lighted earlier by Odalie so that the chill would be gone by the time she came up for the night. Monique went for the brush atop Ava's dresser, then returned to take her place beside the chair.

For a few moments Monique brushed Ava's hair, a painful submissiveness about her.

"Monique, would you like one of my old ball gowns?" Ava asked suddenly.

Startled, Monique gazed at her, nodding slowly.

"I have one that'll fit with some slight alterations." Ava rose to her feet, crossed to her closet, and reached inside. "This one." She brought down a white tulle over a slip of white glacé. "Take off your dress, Monique." A beautifully slender body, Ava thought, with those small, high breasts and that curvaceous rump. "Monique, take off your dress," she repeated with irritation.

"Yessum." Coloring, Monique pulled her dress over her head, then stood naked before Ava, her eyes downcast.

"Monique," Ava chided charmingly, "I believe you're embarrassed before me."

"Yessum," she acknowledged with discomfort.

"With a glorious body like that you should be proud," Ava said softly. "I'll bet every buck at Eden is after you."

"Me jes' fifteen," Monique said. But she looked at Titus and got itchy, Ava thought, and Bart messed around with her regularly.

"Men can be so rotten." Ava reached to touch Monique's taut nipples. The girl was feeling something, she thought with triumph. "Men don't know how to treat a woman," she improvised. "Monique, you go over to my bed and lie down for a few minutes." Monique was staring at her with consternation. "Then we'll try on the dress."

Monique walked to the bed, then hesitated.

"Lie down," Ava reiterated. What could Bart do with this girl that she couldn't?

Ava sat at the edge of the bed and lowered her parted mouth to one nipple. Her hand moved between the narrow thighs that stiffened in reproach. Was this the way Claudine and Jeanne Coligny made their covert love?

Vicky stood before the fire, enjoying the warmth on this cool evening. Usually Monique was waiting for her.

The door opened, startling her for a moment. An aura of desperation about her face, Monique moved slowly into the room. Bart again, Vicky thought furiously.

"Me sorry not iron yo' nightdress," she apologized, and took a deep, shuddering breath. "Me had a mind to, but Miss Ava brung me into her room." She lifted her eyes to Vicky's. All at once a coldness settled about Vicky. What was Monique trying to tell her? "Missy, kin me go back to de fields?" she pleaded. "Please, Missy?"

"Monique, what happened in Miss Ava's room? I want to know."

"Her use me," Monique whispered. "Lak her be a man. Her tech me. Her do dem t'ings to me."

"Monique, you stay here." Vicky's voice trembled. "I'll be right back."

Vicky hurried from her room to Ava's and knocked sharply.

"Come in," Ava called.

Vicky closed the door behind her, fighting panic. But what she had come here to say must be said.

"Ava, I know what you're doing to Monique. Leave her alone, or I'll tell your sister. And don't try to take this out on Monique, because it won't work!" Her eyes blazed.

Just in time she ducked to avoid being hit by the mirror Ava flung across the room.

26 ⟨

Vicky settled herself in the carriage and forced a smile onto her face. Alex pulled himself up beside her. Poor Monique, sitting there on the box with Titus, violated by Bart and Ava but with eyes only for him.

Michael was already at the house when they arrived. Alex waited only to see Vicky into the house, then ordered Titus to head for the casino.

"Me brung hot watuh fo' yo'," Monique said, waking Vicky from her nap. "Hit be all rat fo' anothuh few minutes effen yo' wanna lie in bed fo' a while," she added solicitously.

"I'll dress now," Vicky decided.

"Me gonna help Caprice," Monique reported. "Emile an' me serve."

Vicky was just emerging from her room when Ben was admitted to the foyer by Emile.

"Ben, I hope you're famished," Michael said, "because I gather Caprice is preparing a feast."

Michael enjoyed entertaining Ben, Vicky thought with pleasure as the two men talked earnestly, over the superb oyster soup, about the current Southern situation.

"We have to remember, above everything else," Ben said sternly, "that the Union must be preserved. In the Union is our strength."

"But try to tell that to most Southerners," Michael said with frustration. "They can't think beyond the minute. To

233

free the slaves gradually is our only chance, and I wonder if it's too late for that."

"The South is a land of poor illiterates," Ben said passionately, "and for that I blame the slave system."

"Blame the illiteracy on the lack of public schools," Michael said seriously. "The only Southern states making any real progress in that direction are Kentucky and North Carolina. On paper we have in Louisiana the most progressive public school system, but what does it mean when the laws are not carried out?"

"The planters in the South don't want to be taxed to pay for the education of the poor," said Ben. "And how many of the farmers themselves have any respect for education?"

"All the farmers know," Michael said unhappily, "is that they need their children to work the farms except for three months of the year, and those months the roads are bad for traveling."

"Don't forget those with pride," Ben said gently. "For a man to have to take an oath of poverty to send his children to a free school is unforgivable."

Vicky listened to all that was said. The undercurrents that were ripping the Union apart. The hints of a possible war if the Southern states should try to withdraw from the Union.

"This is only rumor," Ben said suddenly, "but I hear things about the Coligny house that disturb me."

"What kind of things, Ben?" Michael probed.

"It is said," Ben explained delicately, "that Madame Coligny does not treat her slaves well, that she personally flogs them even though she can easily send them to the whipping post in the Calaboose."

"She flogs them herself?" Vicky's voice was deep with shock.

"The rumors persist," he acknowledged. "They say, too, that she half-starves the staff.'"

"Mr. Wasserman, who says this?" Vicky asked.

"Madame Coligny entertains frequently. Some of her guests talk." Ben gestured eloquently. "Of course, rumors start that have no basis. Madame Coligny is an attractive woman, and there are those who are jealous. They may make up these things. But I remember the little girl, and I am concerned."

"What can be done?" Vicky looked from Ben to Michael.

"The police will do nothing," Michael said unhappily.

"In July I move into my house. Then I will be, perhaps, in a position to discover the truth. Folks talk about strange sounds in the night, muffled screams. I will know," Ben said with conviction, "if there is truth in these rumors. And somehow, Michael, we will bring this out into the open."

The torpid summer settled early about Louisiana this year. Vicky spent languid hours on the west gallery, which faced the river, reading the books about the Southern economy that Michael brought to her.

Today, though, Vicky was almost too hot to read. She looked up with a start as Bart wheeled himself through the tall, narrow door that led onto the gallery.

"Why don't you nap like Sara?" he demanded.

"I like to watch the river traffic." Vicky forced a smile.

"The heat doesn't stop Ava from running around. Going over there to the Harrises' all the time. Bothering poor Madeline."

"Betsy says her mother enjoys seeing Ava," Vicky reported conscientiously. "She always takes her some small present."

"You'd think with this weather she'd stop running into New Orleans all the time with Claudine. There's always a danger of fever. Anybody with any sense has left New Orleans for the summer."

"Claudine's friend Madame Coligny insists on staying in town."

"Who the devil is this fancy Madame Coligny?" Bart asked with curiosity. "Even Ava is impressed. I know her husband is involved in all kinds of businesses, but where do they come from?"

"Claudine says they lived in Paris for many years. He made a lot of money with his vineyards." Vicky had seen little of Claudine since she had introduced her to Ava. Claudine and Ava were often together, or both of them were down in New Orleans.

"We ought to return the hospitality the Colignys are extending to Ava," Bart said with a glint in his eyes. He had heard that Jeanne Coligny was a striking-looking woman. "I must tell Sara to invite them out to Eden." He stared narrowly at Vicky. "What's going on between you and Ava?"

"What do you mean?" Vicky started uneasily.

"Ava would like to bury a knife in your back," he said bluntly. "I see the way she looks at you sometimes."

"I'm sorry Ava doesn't like me," she hedged nervously.

"Ava's dangerous," Bart warned. "If you have the brains I think you have, you'll get as far away from Eden as you can."

"I can't do that." She tried to laugh, remembering the cold chill she often felt under Ava's eyes. "Michael wouldn't be happy away from here."

"Ava loathes you because you're so young and so damned pretty. But there's more now. I can't put my finger on it." His eyes searched hers. "Something's happened between you two that I don't know about. Damn this house!" he said with anger. "It's a breeding place for ugly secrets." All at once he leaned forward in his wheelchair, his attention drawn to someone coming through the pecan grove. Alex. "What goes on with Alex and Betsy?"

Vicky gazed at him in astonishment.

"Nothing," she stammered.

"There should be," he said truculently. "I see the way she looks at him. Why doesn't that boy wake up? You're thick as thieves with Betsy. Doesn't she talk to you about him?"

"No."

"You fix up something between Alex and Betsy," he prodded, "and Sara and I will be beholden to you."

"I don't think Alex is interested."

"You get a chance, you push that pair, Vicky. You hear? You'll be doing both of them a favor." He leaned back, considering the situation. One day Betsy would own

Harris Acres, one of the largest and most profitable plantations in the Lower South.

A carriage came rolling from the stables, circling around the house to the front. Bart moved his wheelchair to see who was leaving.

"Ava, of course," Bart said dryly. "She still thinks she's in Paris, the way she's always running off."

Ava glanced up at the box with annoyance. She had expected Titus to drive her over to Harris Acres. Instead, Seth was hopping down to open the carriage door for her.

She settled back, laying beside her the small flacon of perfume she was taking to Madeline. God, Titus was a beautiful animal! Always so proper, though, she thought with amusement. Never once had he looked sideways at her.

Titus was young. Twenty-two or twenty-three. That was when those black bucks were in their prime. She shifted restlessly, aware of a truant arousal in her. Her mind focused on Rudy. Months since she had been in bed with him. In bed with any man. She felt almost like a virgin again.

Joshua thought she was beautiful, Ava decided complacently. She could tell by the way he looked at her sometimes. Was it true that he never touched the black bitches? Maybe that was why he worked so hard at the plantation: so he'd be too tired to think about his empty bed.

And Madeline was getting to know her. She was like a little child, waiting for the present Ava brought each time. Even Joshua admitted that Madeline enjoyed her visits. But she hated that bitch who took care of Madeline—Patience, who looked at her with such distrust. Still, more times than not, when she stopped by to see Madeline, she managed to see Joshua.

The carriage turned into the private roadway that led up to the big house at Harris Acres. One of the richest plantations in the state, Ava remembered with satisfaction. Joshua was far wealthier than the Edens.

She would go upstairs to Madeline and talk awhile, and

then she'd stop by Joshua's study. This time of day he
would be at his desk. So conscientious about his duties.
Like Sara.

"How nice of you to come calling," Madeline greeted
her, eyes alight. She still could not remember her name,
Ava thought; but she knew Ava came bearing gifts. Her
gaze rested eagerly on the small package in Ava's hand.

"I found a flacon of perfume in my portmanteau, that I
brought back from Paris," Ava said. "I'd like you to have
it, Madeline."

"For me?" She reached avidly for the package Ava extended. "How lovely of you. Perfume from Paris! Wait
till I tell the girls about this." She hesitated, frowning.
"Patience, why are the girls not home yet? It seems to me
they have been gone a long time."

"Dey havin' a picnic, Missy," Patience soothed. "Dey
be along direc'ly."

"Tell me about Paris," Madeline ordered, unwrapping
the package and not hearing a word Ava told her about
the fantastic court of Napoleon III and Empress Eugénie.

After ten minutes, knowing that this was all the time
that Madeline could enjoy her presence, Ava rose to
leave, promising to come soon again.

"You don't have to have me shown downstairs, Patience," Ava said sweetly. "I'm going to stop by Mr. Harris' study for a moment."

She walked down the stairs with a secretive smile about
her mouth. "Do you have time to visit for a few minutes?" she called out gaily when she reached his study.

"For you, Ava, anytime," he said gallantly from behind
his desk.

"Joshua, I need to talk to someone, privately."

"Of course, Ava." Suddenly he was serious. Was he
worried that something was not right with Sara? Sometimes Ava was sure he was in love with her sister. "Let
me close the door." He crossed to the door, shut it, and
returned to sit beside her on the small settee, positioned
to catch any errant breeze from the river.

"I'm worried about Alex," she confided. "It's no secret

that he hated being away at school. Providentially for him, Sara had to bring him home. Yet he seems lost now." She leaned forward earnestly. "I think he's in love with Betsy."

Joshua gazed at her in shock.

"I've seen nothing to indicate that, Ava." But he wanted to believe it.

"You know there was some trouble before he went away to school," Ava said delicately, guessing Sara had confided in him. "That's all over, of course. He's young and handsome and it's natural that he should be in love."

"I see Betsy looking at him sometimes," Joshua conceded, "and I've thought that something was happening for her. But Betsy persists in saying she'll never marry." He sighed. "She's painfully shy. I thought she would be less so as she grew older, but it's worse. She refuses to meet any young men, to go out socially." He gestured his frustration.

"Joshua, if it meets with your approval, I'm going to try to bring them together." Seemingly on impulse, she dropped a hand on his arm. "I know what it is to be alone. To need love."

"I would be deeply happy to see something develop between Alex and Betsy," Joshua said seriously.

"Poor Joshua." She leaned toward him. "You're alone too. It's wrong to shut yourself away from life, Joshua. You're still a handsome man."

"I have my work, Ava. My family." He cleared his throat, pulling his eyes away from the milk-white cleavage displayed by her frock.

"Joshua, that's not enough," she murmured. "Joshua, look at me." She lifted her hands to pull his face toward her.

"Ava, this is crazy." His voice was a strangled whisper as she brought his hands to her breast.

She had not been wrong, she thought as his mouth clung to hers and his hands fondled her breasts. Suddenly she knew that in this unwary moment she could make him take her.

"Joshua, the door. Lock the door."

She lay back the length of the settee while Joshua clumsily locked the door and returned to stand beside her.

"You bitch," he whispered. "You overheated bitch."

She laughed softly as he dropped the weight of himself above her. It was going to be fine, she exulted. Just fine.

Ava leaned back against the settee, eyes triumphant as they watched Joshua rearranging his clothes. For the first time since she had set foot on American soil again, she felt almost happy. It had been almost the way it was with Rudy.

"Not in twenty years has this happened with me," Joshua said tightly, swinging about to face Ava. "It won't happen again."

"Joshua." She pretended to sulk as she rose from the sofa and walked to him. "Wasn't it good for you?"

"In a moment of weakness I allowed myself to be influenced by your beauty. But no more, Ava. Remember that."

If it were not for Madeline, she could marry Joshua. He was still quite distinguished-looking, and there was all that money. Only Madeline stood between them.

"Joshua, you could buy a small house in New Orleans. We could be together whenever we liked. Nobody would have to know."

"Ava, go back to Europe," Joshua said bluntly. "Perhaps your friends there play these games. At Harris Acres, we do not." He crossed to the door, unlocked it, and called loudly.

"Cyrus, please see Miss Ava to her carriage."

Laughing quietly to herself, Ava left the study. Joshua would change his mind.

27

Vicky was disappointed that Michael was spending so many evenings in New Orleans. She knew he was with Ben and Dean Foster, the prosecutor he was helping to unearth evidence against a white man—a small planter—accused of flogging a slave to death. The men were talking, too, about forming a Unionist group in New Orleans.

Two weeks earlier than scheduled Ben Wasserman moved into his new house. Michael reported this at the supper table on the first evening he had been home in a week.

"It's a small house," Michael said, "but Ben's working like a Trojan to make it beautiful."

"Pretentious little man," Bart said with dislike. "Giving himself airs."

"It's right next door to the Coligny mansion," Michael said, his eyes straying to Ava. "No competition for that one in elegance."

"You won't find a house anywhere in New Orleans to match the Colignys'," Ava said arrogantly.

"They're still there in the city, I hear." Michael appeared politely curious.

"Jeanne says it's too much to move with that huge staff of servants they have." Ava shrugged. "Her husband's been up in New York on business for weeks. He won't be back until September. There's just Jeanne and Suzette in the house."

"Suzette?" asked Vicky.

"The daughter," Ava explained. "Pretty little thing. She's about thirteen. It's a pity she's lame. And terribly shy."

"Oh, Vicky," said Michael, remembering. "We're invited to Ben's new house for supper tomorrow night. We can go in together. I'll work at home during the day."

"Michael, why do you persist in going into the city?" Sara asked worriedly. "You know this is fever weather. Every day new cases are reported."

"I stay away from crowds, Mama," Michael soothed. "And the Board of Health is working hard this summer, enforcing the quarantine law. By next year, they prophesy, there'll be less than a hundred deaths in the entire city."

"As long as there's one death, I don't like you down there," said Sara.

After supper, Vicky excused herself, pleading fatigue. "It's this heat," said Michael. "Are you sure you want to go into the city tomorrow?"

"I wouldn't miss it for anything," she said with startling intensity. A whole evening away from Eden. The carriage ride to and from New Orleans, alone with Michael.

Colin drove into the carriageway of the freshly painted small stucco house next to the Coligny mansion. As they walked up the stairs, Vicky recalled that Claudine was to have come into New Orleans this morning. Probably she was visiting next door.

Ben himself opened the heavy oak door, extending a hand in welcome.

"You are my first guests," he said with relish. "Come see my house now that it is furnished." His face lighted as he pointed out small treasures he had collected through the years: antique glassware, silver, a magnificent grandfather clock in miniature.

"The dining room is in here." He led them from the drawing room into the adjoining room, heretofore closed off by double doors.

"It's exquisite." Vicky's eyes swept the room with delight.

They settled themselves at the table, and Ebenezer began to serve.

"Georgette served her apprenticeship as a cook for a fine French lady," Ben explained with pleasure as Michael and Vicky exclaimed their appreciation of the *paté de fois gras,* the creamed filets of sole with oysters, shrimps, and smelts, the elegant *biscuit glacé*.

The table conversation was convivial, yet Vicky sensed a growing urgency in Ben to switch to more serious topics. Michael, too, noticed this.

"Ben, you've been in the house three nights. Have you heard anything?"

Ben hesitated. "There was a party last night. Someone carelessly left the draperies open in the dining room. Madame Coligny seems to be an excellent hostess. Her guests lingered at the table, drinking wine and eating walnuts, till the servants had to replace the tapers in the sconces. Each time," he said, "she left a sip of wine in her glass for the butler and he brought her a fresh glass. But it seemed to me that the servants are pathetically thin and cowed."

"You could see this through the window?" Michael asked softly.

Ben nodded.

"I could see. Later, Madame Coligny took her guests to the second-floor drawing rooms. The draperies were drawn tight. I could see nothing. But I could hear. There was the sound of a lash upon bare flesh. Smothered screams. I tell you, something horrible is going on in that house!"

"Unfortunately, it's legal to punish a slave with a whip," Michael said unhappily.

"This is worse, Michael." A vein throbbed in Ben's forehead. "In the middle of the night I hear dreadful weeping. Again, more muffled screams. And over and over again, the sound of the lash. Michael, how do we get the police to investigate that house?"

"We can't. If we complain to the authorities, they'll do nothing."

"Something must be done," Ben insisted.

"There's no way of getting in there, Ben, short of

burning them out. I'll talk to Dean Foster, but I doubt
that he'll be allowed to take any action."

"Come," Ben said briskly after a moment, "let us go
into the drawing room. I'll tell Georgette to bring more
coffee. And then I want to show Vicky my three volumes
of colored engravings by Audubon. You will excuse me
for a few minutes, please."

Ben ushered Vicky and Michael into the drawing room
and left them to call down the long, narrow hall to Georgette.

"I won't rest, Vicky," Michael said with sudden urgency, "until I discover what goes on in that house. Some
terrible evil almost close enough to touch."

"What can you do, Michael?"

"I'll try everything I can," Michael promised grimly.
Then he was silent because Georgette was approaching
them with fresh coffee.

"No wait for Mist' Ben," Georgette urged. "Drink
now." With a flourish she crossed to a cabinet to bring
out an ornate box that contained the inevitable pralines,
of which Ben was so enamored.

Vicky sat on the small golden velvet sofa beside Michael, feeling strangely happy.

"Michael!" Ben's voice came from the hall. "You'd
better come with me. I believe there's a fire next door."
Vicky saw the quick exchange between the two men.
"I've brought you the Audubon volumes, Vicky."

"Let me go with you!" She rose to her feet along with
Michael. "Please!" she pleaded, because Michael seemed
hesitant.

"You'll stay outside the house," Michael stipulated.
"Ben, we should notify the fire department."

"I've sent Ebenezer."

"The fire department is manned by volunteers," Michael told Vicky uneasily as they followed. "It may take
them a while to assemble."

By the time they were outside, smoke had begun to roll
from a rear window of the Coligny mansion. There was
the sound of excited voices. Women's voices. Claudine,
nearly hysterical, and Mme. Coligny, seemingly calm.

"Dominique, the paintings," Mme. Coligny ordered loudly. "Get the paintings out of the upstairs drawing rooms and into the street."

"Jeanne, we cannot stay here!" Claudine screamed. "We will be burnt to death!"

"The fire is in the kitchen," Ben called to the first volunteer firemen who were arriving with buckets.

"Vicky, stay here," Michael ordered sharply, and along with a cluster of volunteer firemen, he charged into the house with Ben.

Ben had started the fire, Vicky guessed. Michael had said, "There's no way of getting in there, Ben, short of burning them out."

Suddenly people were everywhere. A dozen or more charged into the house to help carry out the valuables as the firemen streamed into the house with buckets of water. On impulse Vicky joined a group of onlookers who suddenly decided to go inside to help.

Mme. Coligny stood at the top of the first flight of stairs, briskly ordering volunteers to carry out the wall hangings and fine pieces of furniture.

"Madame Coligny, are you sure the slaves are in no danger on the upper floors?" Ben was demanding with urgency. "The smoke is pouring upward at the rear of the house!"

"They are all right," she said sharply. Then she swung her head about in sudden fury as Michael charged past her, en route to the upper floors. "Mr. Eden, where are you going?"

"To the top floor," Michael called breathlessly over his shoulder without stopping his upward climb.

"You are to come down immediately!" she called after him. "Mr. Eden! How dare you disobey my orders!" But Michael was bolting the stairs two at a time.

Hordes of people jammed the foyer, impeding the transfer of valuables to the street. Claudine, white and tearful, pleaded with Jeanne Coligny to leave the house.

"Go on, Claudine, if you wish!" she said with agitation. "Mr. Eden!" she tried again. "I won't have my house invaded this way!"

Uneasily dodging a piece of statuary that was being carried out by passers-by, Vicky edged back into the lower-floor drawing room.

"Mademoiselle," a high young voice called out tremulously, and Vicky swerved about to face a pale young girl. Suzette, the lame daughter, Vicky surmised. "Mademoiselle, on the top floor," she whispered urgently. "Send someone to the top floor!"

Vicky's eyes met Suzette's. A chill shot through her. She understood what Suzette was trying to say.

"Right away," she promised. She darted back into the foyer and pushed her way through the horde toward the stairs.

"Where are you going?" Jeanne Coligny reached out a hand in outrage. Vicky vigorously brushed her aside. "Mademoiselle, where are you going?" But Vicky was already racing up the stairs.

"Michael!" she called, "Michael!"

Michael and Ben were struggling to open a door at the top of the stairs.

"The door's locked," Michael said with frustration.

"You must open it," Vicky insisted. "Suzette sent me up to tell you."

Michael and Ben exchanged a swift glance of apprehension.

"Stand back," Michael ordered.

He lunged at the door. It refused to budge. He lunged again, with increasing desperation, and then again. On the third try the lock gave way. Vicky followed Ben and Michael into the dark hall and down the hall into a room beyond. And then, as her eyes grew accustomed to the darkness, a wave of nausea rode over her.

"My God!" Ben's voice was outraged. "She's a monster."

An assortment of half-naked slaves of both sexes, wearing heavy spiked iron collars and irons on their feet, lay about the room, chained to spikes driven into the floor. The collars and manacles were cutting into the raw flesh of bodies wasted from malnutrition.

"It's all over," Michael said with infinite gentleness. "We're getting you out of here."

The three of them labored to free an elderly woman, whose body was covered with scars. Downstairs the firemen were calling out briskly.

"The fire's over! Just smoke now. You can bring everything back into the house in a little while."

Slowly, Ben and Michael carried the old woman, tortured for nobody knew how long, down the stairs. The people in the foyer gasped in shock.

"There are eight more like her upstairs," Michael said tersely. "Who'll help us bring them out?"

The air was filled with offers. Outside, the area was glutted with people, shaken that such sadistic treatment could have existed in the elegant house of the Colignys. One by one the slaves were carried down. As the last one was brought out, the iron gates were suddenly thrown closed and locked. Vicky spied the figure of Dominique locking the small entrance at the side.

"Where are the police?" someone demanded. "Why aren't the police here?"

The crowd took up the cry. "Where are the police?" But none appeared. The tortured slaves were revived, the crowd compassionately moving back so that they could be given water.

"Michael, why don't the police come?" Vicky asked with rising indignation. "They must have been notified."

"It's the way in the city," Michael said grimly. "The Colignys are influential people."

Quite suddenly, the crowd became threatening. They screamed at the closed windows. A riot seemed imminent. Ben and Michael exchanged apprehensive glances.

Before anyone could realize what was happening, the iron gates were swung wide. Dominique bolted out to scramble atop the carriage box.

"Giddap!" he ordered thunderously.

The carriage charged forward, forcing the bystanders back lest they be trampled. As the carriage lunged ahead, Vicky saw the white, frightened face of Claudine Lamartine. And beside her, Jeanne and young Suzette.

"Don't let her get away!" someone in the crowd yelled in rage. "Let's go after her!"

But the carriage rushed ahead, outdistancing the frenzied mob that tried to follow.

"Let's take that house apart!" One voice in the mob started a stampede.

Michael put an arm about Vicky, and he and Ben hurried her into the safety of the small house while the incensed mob rushed into the Coligny mansion.

From the windows of Ben's drawing room they watched as feather beds were thrown into the street; draperies were pulled down from the windows; paintings, armoires, bedsteads, silver, glass, china came sailing through the windows.

"Enough," Ben said tiredly at last, and drew his own draperies shut. Still, their voices infiltrated the house as Georgette, her face stern but triumphant, brought them fresh coffee and yet another box of pralines.

"It's all over," Ben said quietly. "Madame Coligny will never set foot in New Orleans again."

"Tomorrow all New Orleans will read about the Coligny house." Michael's eyes glowed. "Let them know the atrocities committed in a so-called civilized society because we allow slavery to exist."

28

Vicky and Michael leaned back in the carriage as it clattered noisily over the quiet streets. In a few minutes they would leave the humid heat of the city behind them, running from the painful excitement of the past three hours. The slaves rescued from the Coligny house were being nursed in the Calaboose, where they would be cared for until arrangements could be made for their future.

As long as she lived, Vicky thought, she would remember that horrifying moment when her eyes grew accustomed to the darkness in that room on the top floor of the Coligny house.

"Thank God for that fire," Michael said with deeply felt gratitude. "Thank God for Suzette Coligny."

"Thank God," Vicky said with tender conspiracy, "for Ben Wasserman's courage." She smiled as their eyes met.

"Tomorrow," Michael promised, "thousands of folks will hurry to the Calaboose to see those poor slaves. To see the instruments of torture Madame Coligny managed to acquire. I won't even tell you the terrible purposes of some of them. Vicky, how can they not see how desperately wrong slavery is, when something like this can happen within its framework?"

"This will help Dean Foster prosecute his case, won't it?"

"Definitely." Michael inspected her with solicitude

now. "We should have stayed in the city for the night. It's a long ride back to Eden when you're so tired."

"It'll be cooler there," Vicky reminded him. "Besides, your mother will be expecting us."

"There'll be harsh condemnation of Madame Coligny's actions in the newspapers," Michael acknowledged. "But no newspaper will dare to use this as an attack on slavery."

"Michael, anyone who reads about what happened will understand," Vicky said passionately.

"The lack of freedom of thought in the South is a depressing truth," Michael said. "I want to follow through what Ben and I have been discussing," he added earnestly. "This idea of a Unionist group in New Orleans. It alarms me to hear so much talk of secession."

Absorbed in all that Michael had to say, Vicky glanced out the carriage window with astonishment when Colin turned into the private roadway to Eden. She was almost sorry, despite their exhaustion, that they had arrived already.

Sara and Ava were sitting on the gallery. "It's just as well you didn't come home earlier," Ava said querulously. "It's as hot as an oven inside. We never have this kind of weather in Europe."

"It was quite an evening," Michael said slowly. Vicky saw his mother lean forward attentively. "You'll be reading about it in tomorrow's *Picayune*."

"What happened?" Ava's voice was electric.

Slowly, forcing himself to speak without passion, Michael reported what had happened. Sara and Ava listened silently, with shock.

"Claudine drove away with Madame Coligny and her daughter," Michael said uneasily. "I don't know if she was brought back here to Eden or not."

"We can't disturb Jack at this hour of the night," Sara decided carefully. "When he comes to the house in the morning, I'll discuss this with him." She shivered. "It makes me ill to think of those poor tortured souls."

"I always knew there was something odd about

Jeanne," Ava said attempting to appear horrified. "Always something secretive between her and Claudine."

"Mama, I'm not an abolitionist," Michael said quietly, "but this is enough to show you what's wrong about slavery. You have to understand the need for gradual emancipation."

"Because Ava's fine friend is a monster?" Sara was defensive. "Michael, don't be hysterical."

"If we did what's right we'd begin emancipation tomorrow. Mama, you're an intelligent woman; surely you can see that the South must clean house before some hotheads contrive to pull us out of the Union."

"That won't happen," Sara insisted.

"Let it happen." Bart's voice echoed sharply from the doorway. Automatically Michael moved forward to pull the door wide so that Andrew could push the wheelchair through the door.

"Papa, do you know what you just said?" Michael asked.

"I said, to the devil with the North. Let the South be independent."

"War, Papa?" Michael asked ominously.

"No!" Sara was pale. "No!"

"Bart doesn't have to worry," Ava said with silken sweetness. "He'll never have to go to war."

"I'm sick to death of hearing the South told how to run its business," Bart said irritably. "The sooner we make the break the better."

"There are many in this state who disagree with you, Papa," Michael said quietly. "A Unionist group is being formed in New Orleans."

"They'll be driven out of town, or lynched," Bart predicted.

"I'm working with them," Michael said.

"Michael, we'll be ostracized!" Sara was pale.

"We're not taking ads in the *Picayune* or the *Crescent*," Michael said gently. "We're simply meeting regularly in various homes to discuss the coming crisis."

"Not in our house!" Bart exploded. "I won't allow it!"

"That won't be necessary!" Vicky lashed at him. "Michael, you have an office in New Orleans. I'm sure we can borrow sufficient chairs to accommodate a meeting."

"Vicky, you're encouraging him in this!" Sara was indignant.

"Yes." Vicky lifted her head with pride. "Because Michael is right. He wants to preserve the Union. To keep peace in this country. I know about war. First my brother, then my father killed before their time because England told them to fight!" She swung about to Michael again. "Michael, let me help. Let me talk to those fine ladies in New Orleans who see only glory in war. Let me tell them what it was like in the Crimea. Let me tell them how it feels to be told that someone you love lies dead in battle!"

"That's enough!" Sara's voice rose perilously high. "Since the day you set foot in this house, you've pushed Michael away from us!"

"Mama, if you talk that way, we'll have to leave Eden," Michael said with soft reproach.

Sara's face tightened. Vicky saw the convulsive opening and closing of one hand. She was struggling for control. Alex was her baby, but Michael was her pride.

"I'm sorry, Vicky. I'm most upset about this whole situation." She pulled herself to her feet. "I think it's time I said good night."

Sara had apologized because she could not bear the prospect of Michael's leaving Eden. But for one exultant moment Vicky wished this would be a break. Yet even as she wished, Vicky knew there was some strange drama engulfing all of those who lived at Eden that must be acted out. Not until then would she and Michael be free.

The days following the fire at the Coligny house were uncomfortably tense at Eden. Michael was again often absent in the evenings, Ava left restless by the dramatic disappearance of Claudine. Jack had received no word of her. She had disappeared, with Jeanne Coligny and young Suzette, from the face of the earth.

Vicky moved about the house with constant awareness that, to Sara and Bart, she was an intruder. Bart talked openly of his approval of a breach with the North, not caring that Sara was plunged into agony at the thought of war.

It was a relief each time that Betsy came to carry Vicky off to the Harris plantation. Betsy was too conscious of Alex's presence at Eden to care to remain there long.

This afternoon Vicky lay in her bedroom, making the pretense of napping, wishing that there were more time to be with Michael.

The door opened a few inches. She spied Monique's face.

"Come in, Monique. I'm awake."

Monique came into the room. There was a new wisdom in her eyes these last weeks, Vicky thought with compassion, remembering the sadness in Monique's eyes when she looked at Titus.

"Missy Betsy, her heah," Monique reported. "Yo' feel lak comin' downstaihs?"

"Tell her I'll be right there," Vicky said.

With a sense of escape the two young women left the house, heading for the path that followed the river.

At the quarters they sought out Mama LaVerne in the plantation infirmary. Half a dozen cots were occupied by an assortment of ill female slaves. In one corner a girl no more than fifteen lay in advanced labor, attended by Mama Daphne.

"Yo' do lak me tell yo', gal," Mama Daphne said sternly. "Yo' swallow dis' heah, and in a li'l while yo' won't feel dat baby pushin' no more. Him pop out afo' yo' know it."

Perspiring from her efforts, the girl obediently accepted the medication between the fast-coming pains.

"She's so young," Vicky said compassionately as the girl writhed on the shaky cot.

"Him some big baby." Mama Daphne leaned over the girl. "Her small."

Suddenly the girl screamed—yet for all the pain, there was beauty on her face, and Vicky wished it were she lying there in labor.

"Dat drug help so her won' remembuh when de baby come," Mama Daphne explained. "Come on, gal," Mama Daphne urged her patiently. "Yo' kin push dat baby out effen yo' try hard 'nuf."

Vicky reached for a cloth, wet it in the bucket nearby, and washed the girl's face. Scream after scream ricocheted about the room, until with one superhuman effort, it seemed to Vicky, she expelled the baby while Mama Daphne crooned approval.

"Wait, me see what us got heah. A boy. Ain't it lak a boy to cause all dat trouble?"

"It's a beautiful baby," Vicky said.

"Her make lotsa babies," Mama LaVerne predicted. "Nex' time not so hard."

When the new mother was sleeping quietly, Betsy said with affection, "Mama LaVerne, Lightning has a stiffness in his foreleg that bothers me. Would you have more of that liniment you gave me last time?"

"Fo yo', Missy, me got," Mama LaVerne said with a toothless smile. "An' me got dis heah new powduh, fo' stoppin' bleedin' and cleanin' up after a bad cut," she boasted. "Wait, me go fetch."

Ava impatiently pushed her moist hair from her forehead, hurrying through the weeds in a frenzied effort not to lose sight of her quarry. She had seen him a moment ago. Where the devil had Titus disappeared?

Then she pushed her way through the sun-yellowed weeds until she stood in the small clearing where Titus leaned over the massive bough of a live oak.

"Titus!"

He turned around, his eyes meeting hers warily. Silently he put down the saw and straightened up, his black skin glistening with perspiration.

"Yo' wan' me to do somethin,' Missy?" he asked politely, but there was nothing servile in the way he stood before her.

"Come here, Titus." Her eyes were a challenge.

Silently he spanned the distance between them.

"Closer." Her nostrils dilated at the animal smell of

him. Why did he waste himself with Alex? Because of what Alex had done for him? She could take him away from Alex. She had made a bet with herself that she could. "Don't you like women?" she asked provocatively.

For a moment he was startled.

"Ah lak," he conceded, his eyes meeting hers unwaveringly. An arrogant bastard, she thought, but this oddly pleased her.

"I don't think you have anything down there," she said, and one hand shot out to touch him. She felt a surge of triumph at his instant reaction.

"Missy, yo' be askin' fo' trouble!" She set his teeth on edge, didn't she? He was dying, this minute, to push himself into her.

"I like trouble." With one swift movement she thrust her body against his. He groaned.

"Missy, trouble," he whispered uneasily.

"Pleasure," she promised. "Show me how good you are, Titus! Show me!"

The two young women left the slave quarters, taking the shortcut back home. They walked in companionable silence, both involved in the wonder of birth.

"You bitch!" The agonized voice seemed startlingly close. It was Alex.

Betsy's eyes widened in alarm. She swung uncertainly toward Vicky and they stood galvanized as Alex, unaware of their presence, hurled himself through the weeds, away from the tableau on the ground.

Ava lay on her back, eyes shut, mouth parted, skirts raised high, ignoring everything except the heated rhythm of the black body humped above hers. Titus.

Her face hot, Vicky clutched Betsy by the hand and pulled her away from the frenzied merging of black and white flesh. They heard, following them, the mingled cries of passion.

Vicky and Betsy moved with haste, silently, away from the pair on the ground until a sudden outcry—a cry of someone in pain—brought them to a halt.

"What was that?" Vicky whispered.

"Someone's hurt," Betsy said with fresh strength. Here she stood on firm ground. "The sound came from over there."

They pushed their way through the brush to a small shack. Betsy walked inside and cried out.

"What is it?" Vicky asked fearfully.

"Alex." Betsy fell to her knees before the prone, semiconscious figure on the dirt floor as Vicky followed her inside. "He's bleeding badly."

"We'll have to go for help." Vicky said in alarm. A sickening gush of blood spread down from his wrist, almost covering his hand.

"There's not time. He'll bleed to death. You'll have to help me," Betsy said. "Get a stick. A thin one. Fast." She was trying, vainly, to stop the spurt of blood by pressure.

Vicky stumbled outside, reached for the first stick she saw, and brought it to Betsy. Betsy was ripping off a segment of her petticoat.

"Betsy, what happened?"

"He slashed his wrist." She reached for the stick, then improvised a bandage. "We've got to stop the bleeding. This ought to do it for the moment."

"Bitch," Alex whispered under his breath. "Bitch!"

Betsy's eyes lifted fleetingly to Vicky's. Did she guess, Vicky thought, appalled, why Alex had tried to kill himself?

"The powder Mama LaVerne gave me," Betsy said, and reached into the small reticule she always carried with her. "Hold your hand here." She looked hard at Vicky. "You're not going to faint, are you?"

"No," Vicky promised, and reached to do as Betsy bade her.

She watched, pale and shaky, while Betsy followed Mama LaVerne's instructions, using the liniment as a liquid to form a paste with the powder.

"I can't leave the stick here," she explained. "Alex might develop gangrene. I'll let it stay just long enough for the paste to harden. When the bleeding stops, we'll go for help."

"No," Alex whispered. "Don't bring anybody else." He

forced his eyes open. "Let me stay here. Please, don't let anybody else know."

"Alex, you need help," Vicky said gently.

"Nobody else," he insisted, closing his eyes in weakness.

"We can bring Mama LaVerne to him," Betsy decided. "She'll know what to do."

"I'll go get her."

Vicky ran toward the quarters uneasily, skirting the area where Ava and Titus still lay coupled. She sought out Mama LaVerne and explained, in a whisper, what had happened.

"Me git some t'ings', Young Missy," Mama La Verne said calmly, and in moments, despite her age, she was moving with impressive speed along the path Vicky indicated.

Saying nothing to indicate there was anything unusual about Alex's need for attention, Mama LaVerne attended to the cut.

"Effen yo' not do lak dis, him be daid by now," Mama LaVerne said, praising Betsy. "Yo' make he take dis pill," she ordered. "Hit make him sleep." She saw Vicky's surprise. "Yo' cain't move he fo' a day or two. Dat wrist, him gotta heal first," she said gently.

"He wants to stay here," Betsy said softly. "Mama LaVerne, nobody is to know about this except the three of us. Mr. Alex wants it that way. Can you help us?"

Mama LaVerne nodded vigorously.

"Me come see he evuh fo', five houhs," she promised. "Couple days him kin go to de house." She frowned. "Dat shirt need be washed, but don't bothuh him today. Tomorrow me take to de quartuhs and wash. Hope dat blood come clean," she said doubtfully, rising to her feet. "Me bes' git back to de quartuhs now, but me come take caih lak me promise."

Betsy turned to Vicky.

"You'd better go on up to the house before anyone wonders where you are. Tell Cyrus to bring the carriage close to the shack near the quarters. He's to wait till I come."

"Will Alex be all right here alone?" Vicky asked anxiously while Betsy brought hay from a corner of the shack to place gently beneath his head.

"Mama LaVerne and I will care for him," Betsy said with confidence. "I can ride through the fields from our house to here. Nobody will notice." She frowned with sudden anxiety. "But what will they think at the house when Alex doesn't appear for supper?"

"Can I tell them you took Alex back with you to Harris Acres for a visit?" Vicky improvised. Sara would be delighted.

"Tell them that," Betsy agreed. "And pray that Papa doesn't come over here for the next two days, or Aunt Sara to Harris Acres."

Vicky returned to the house, pausing en route to instruct Cyrus.

Monique was in her room, hanging away dresses she had ironed earlier.

"Yo' git outta dat dress," Monique scolded. "Me lay out a fresh 'un."

"It was hot walking," Vicky said, apologizing for her appearance.

"Missy Betsy go home?" Monique asked curiously.

Vicky hesitated, but Cyrus was out of sight now.

"Yes," she said offhandedly. "She took Mr. Alex back to Harris Acres with her for a day or two." Monique brightened. Monique too knew that Betsy looked longingly at Alex.

Vicky lay back and tried to rest. In a little while she heard footsteps in the hall: Ava going to her room. The door slammed shut behind her. Vicky's face was hot as she envisioned Ava and Titus locked in passion. Not caring that Alex had discovered them. Not knowing that she and Betsy had stood just beyond the inadequate covering of weeds.

Behind the house she heard Juno singing one of the strange black melodies Vicky had come to love. In the afternoons the house servants were usually found taking it easy in the shade beneath the century-old live oak behind the house.

Alex would be hot. Thirsty. She would take him the

pitcher of lemonade that Monique had left in the room.
Nobody would see her leave the house.

She dressed swiftly and hurried from the house. Just
beyond the shack, in a clearing, she spied the carriage.
Cyrus was taking refuge from the sun beneath the trees.

Holding the frosty pitcher, Vicky approached the
shack.

"Betsy, remember Mr. Rogers?" Alex was saying
shakily. "Remember how angry he used to be when we
horsed around instead of listening to him?"

A smile on her mouth, Vicky pushed the door wide.

"It's me," she said quietly, "I've brought some cold
lemonade."

Walking back to the house by way of the shortcut, she
started at the sound of a horse close by. She glanced up,
nervous that Alex and Betsy might be found in the shack.
But the man on the horse had no eyes for her. He was
riding as fast as he could away from Eden.

Titus.

29

Vicky remained in her room until suppertime, steeling
herself to casually explain to Sara that Alex had gone
over to Betsy's for a day or two.

"Vicky, was Betsy over?" Sara asked curiously when
Vicky came down to the drawing room. "I thought I
heard her voice earlier."

"She was here for a while." Vicky forced a smile.

"Alex asked me to tell you he was going over to Harris Acres with her for a day or two."

Sara gazed at her with astonishment.

"Alex went to Harris Acres?"

"Betsy wanted to show him the new colt," Vicky lied. "She's determined to call him Alex."

Michael glanced at her. "So Alex went over to decide whether the colt was worthy of this honor?"

"He didn't have to stay a day or two for that," Sara said. "How strange that he didn't bother to tell me."

"You were napping," Vicky explained. "He didn't want to disturb you."

"Perhaps the change of scenery will be good for him." Sara smiled faintly. She had not been able to arrange a match between Betsy and Michael. All at once she had hopes for Betsy and Alex.

Ava walked into the room with an air of bravado.

"Alex's gone to Harris Acres with Betsy," Sara told her with an air of satisfaction. "He and Betsy seem to be renewing their old friendship."

"I wouldn't have called it that," Bart said dryly. "Alex was always teasing the life out of her when they were studying together."

"I may go over to talk to Joshua tomorrow," Sara said casually. "Alex can ride back with me."

"Stay away, Sara," Bart ordered bluntly. "Alex won't get into any trouble at Harris Acres. Leave him be."

Sara's eyes moved sharply past Bart. "What is it, Socrates?" she asked impatiently, then suddenly comprehended Socrates' distress at being forced to speak before them all. "Excuse me," she said and walked to the door.

"I'd like some wine," Ava announced imperiously.

"Coming, Princess," Bart drawled, and wheeled himself to the wine cabinet.

Vicky sat tensely on the edge of the settee.

"Vicky, did Alex say anything to you about taking Titus with him to Harris Acres?" Sara asked when she came back into the room.

"He didn't take Titus with him," Vicky said. "He went with Betsy in the carriage from Harris Acres."

"Socrates tells me that he had ordered Titus to wash all the glassware this afternoon. He didn't do it. Nor can Socrates find him now. He's looked everywhere."

"Damn it, you mean he's run away?" Bart demanded indignantly. "That bastard is worth fifteen hundred dollars! Michael, call together some neighbors and go after him!"

"I saw him early this afternoon," Vicky volunteered nervously. "Riding a horse along the river. That was hours ago."

"Why didn't you tell somebody?" Bart bellowed.

"I thought he was on an errand," Vicky stammered. Ava was relieved that Titus had taken off. She knew she had gone too far. "I didn't know he was running away."

"We don't know that he has," said Michael. "Have Socrates send somebody out to search for him."

"They've searched," Sara said with agitation. "If he took off hours ago, God knows where he is by now."

"The patrols may catch him if he's out after dark without a pass," said Michael. "They receive six dollars for every runaway they capture." There was scorn in his voice.

"We'll have to put ads in the newspapers," Sara decided. "It's so rare for a slave to run away in the Lower South. It's never happened before in all the years that I've been managing Eden."

"We'll get him back," Bart asserted. "Offer a stiff reward. Four hundred dollars."

"He may return on his own," Ava suggested. "A few days in the swamps and the plantation doesn't look so bad."

"Ava, we treat our slaves well." Sara's face was pained. "You know that."

"That's what you get for paying bonuses, Sara. I know you gave Titus cash for building those cabinets."

"It would have cost ten times as much if we had brought in a cabinetmaker," she flashed back.

"Those black bastards are only one step removed from savagery. You give them too loose a rein, Sara."

"This is the first runaway Mama's had," Michael protested.

"I want him back! That nigger's too smart for his breeches," Bart bristled. "And too damned good-looking. Some white woman with the hots will take him in and sneak him up North."

"Bart, how dare you talk like that in front of ladies!" Sara was white with anger.

"I apologize," Bart drawled. "The excitement of the situation made me careless."

Socrates hovered in the doorway again, his eyes troubled.

"All right, Socrates," Sara said briskly. "You can tell Juno to serve now."

Michael left his office ten minutes before noon to go to Ben's house to join him for dinner. Earlier Ben had sent his clerk in to say that Georgette was preparing pompano in her special fashion, which Michael found irresistible, and he would expect Michael at the table at noon.

Ben greeted him at the door to his house with affection.

"You are right on time. Georgette is this minute bringing your fish to the table. We will have it with a special wine I have just received from France."

Ebenezer came in when they had settled themselves at the table with the wine and two goblets from Ben's latest acquisition of Ravenscroft.

"Vicky admired my glassware when you were here for supper," Ben recalled with pride. "Tell her she must come to see my new goblets." He leaned forward with a confidential air. "Michael, I have word of Madame Coligny and her friend. Ebenezer was at the docks today."

"What did he hear?"

"At midnight, after the fire, the two women and the girl boarded a private boat that headed upriver. Most likely they are in New York by now, with Monsieur Coligny. They must have been told by him what happened here, because he has arranged, through his attorney, to dispose of all his holdings in Louisiana."

"I'll tell Jack," Michael promised. Jack had been upset at his wife's disappearance, but Michael could not believe that he was not happier alone.

"About our plans, Michael," Ben began, helping himself from the huge platter of pompano. "We will be able to have our first meeting early next week. Only a dozen, including ourselves," he said with honesty, "but we will grow."

Michael enjoyed Georgette's fine cooking. He was delighted with the progress he and Ben were making with their Unionist group. Yet he was constantly conscious of an inner restlessness. Even as he talked with Ben about the new group, he was aware of this sense of nagging frustration. Because of Vicky, he thought unhappily. It was torture living under the same roof with her, and never touching her. How insidiously he had come to love his wife!

After dinner he returned to his office, his afternoon's work planned. But sitting at his desk, he found it impossible to concentrate on the brief before him. Vicky's face intervened—passionate, earnest Vicky.

In a burst of impatience he stuffed the brief into a desk drawer and called to David.

"I'm going home early," he said. "This heat is getting to me. Close up early."

Michael walked to the stables, where he knew Colin had gone to have the horses shod.

"We're going home early," Michael explained.

"Dey bin ready for an hour, Suh," Colin said good-humoredly.

In the carriage, Michael unfolded the newspaper and willed himself to read. But his thoughts relentlessly traveled into the past. Liliane dying because of him. Vicky losing the baby, their baby. A pattern of retribution. And there was Alex and Janine.

Eden was wrapped in midafternoon stillness. The ladies, he remembered, would be taking their naps. A faint breeze came up from the river. He lowered himself into a rocker on the gallery, knowing it would be stifling indoors.

Socrates came to the door.

"Anothuh hot day, Suh," Socrates said sympathetically. "Hit musta been a scohchuh down in de city."

"It was," Michael conceded with a smile.

"Some claret, Suh, with ice?" Socrates offered. "Or ice tea?"

"Iced tea. I'll have it out here."

"You're home early," said Ava. "It must have been rotten in the city."

"It was," he said, uncomfortable as he always was alone with Ava.

"I'm glad you came home early," she said with an air of sudden decision. "Michael, when are you going to do something about Vicky and Alex?" she asked with deceptive calm.

"What are you talking about?" Michael recoiled from the implication in her eyes.

"Michael you can't be that blind," she said with a show of impatience. "The two of them carrying on practically in front of your eyes. Your mother suspects; that's why she keeps pushing Betsy at him."

"You're sick, Ava!" he lashed at her furiously.

"You don't want to see it, Michael, so I have to tell you. Vicky and Alex, Michael," she repeated slowly.

"You see filth in everything, Ava," Michael said with distaste. "I don't want you to say another word. Don't you ever breathe another word like that about Vicky to anyone, do you hear?" His voice shook with rage.

"You can't run away from the truth," Ava taunted. "It'll always be this way. We're not meant to be happy. Save yourself from more grief—send Vicky back to New York. Your father said it for us. An evil curse hangs over us, Michael. We can't escape it."

With a sigh of disgust, Michael strode down the steps and across the lawn, into the grove. I'll take a shortcut, he decided. It was a hot day for walking.

He started at the sound of voices from the shack in the midst of the weeds. Vicky and Betsy, he thought, busy with some injured animal. He moved eagerly toward the open door.

"Vicky—" and then his smile evaporated. He stopped dead in shock as he hovered in the doorway.

Alex lay prone on the ground, stripped to the waist. Vicky hovered above him. *Vicky and Alex.* He felt sick.

Vicky swung her head about, startled at his presence. Her eyes stricken.

"Excuse me—" He spun away from the shack, moving swiftly.

He walked without destination, knowing only that he must remove himself from that intimate view of his wife and his brother.

30

Her face ashen, Vicky rose awkwardly to her feet. Her instinct was to run after Michael, but Alex's hand closed in about her wrist.

"Vicky, wait. Vicky, please." His voice was an agonized whisper. "Don't tell Michael. I couldn't bear that."

"Alex, you know what he thinks," Vicky protested.

"Does it matter?" he challenged. "Do you care that he believes there's something between us?"

"Yes," she whispered with candor. "I care, Alex."

"Vicky, I can't bear to have the family know. They'll ask questions. They'll find out about—" He stumbled. "They'll find out the truth. For a while after Janine died, I lost my mind. I've told Betsy. She understands." His eyes were gentle. "But Mama won't. She always expects something awful of me. It's Michael who's perfect in her eyes. Michael can do no wrong." *Except to have married her.* "I couldn't stand to see her look at me again the way she looked at me after she found out about Janine and me." Alex pulled himself shakily into a sitting position. "I must go back to the house before she begins to wonder."

"Alex, no," Vicky said worriedly. "I told her you were at Harris Acres."

"Suppose she decides to go over? Vicky, I can't take that chance." He paused. They heard a horse close by. Alex's face lit up. "Betsy was with me until dawn," he said. "She stayed here putting cold cloths on my forehead until the fever broke. At the house, she said, they believed she was with the animals."

"I've brought you a custard," Betsy said gently, dropping to her knees beside Alex. "You're to eat every drop."

"Betsy, I must go home," Alex said urgently.

"You're too weak," she insisted. "And we'll talk no more until you've eaten this."

"Betsy, I can't stay," he began again, but she silenced him with a spoonful of custard.

"Betsy, does your father suspect anything?" Vicky asked worriedly.

"Papa went into New Orleans on business yesterday. He won't be home until supper tonight. If I tell him Alex was at the house, he won't ask questions. I've never lied to Papa before."

"Then I must go back to the house," Alex insisted. "Before your father returns."

"You can say that Alex was helping you with the animals," said Vicky, "and he accidentally cut himself. If he can make it, I think he's right. He ought to go back to Eden." Before they became entangled, she thought, in a maze of lies.

Betsy rose to her feet. "I'll go back to the house and bring the carriage. I'll take you home, Alex."

Betsy rode back to Harris Acres for a carriage. Vicky, trembling at the prospect of a confrontation with Michael, hurried back to the big house. How could she face him, knowing what he believed?

She paused as the house rose into view before her. Bart sat in his chair on the west gallery, hunched over a magazine. Jefferson was cross-legged on the floor, shelling pecans for him.

She walked upstairs and closed the door with a sense of reprieve. It was unfair of Alex to ask her to be silent.

Exhausted, she lay across her bed. She heard someone arriving and raised herself, listening. Alex was approaching the house with Betsy.

"Alex," his father called out brusquely, "what happened to your arm?"

"I had an accident," Alex said self-consciously. "It was nothing, really—"

Vicky closed her eyes and forced herself to try and sleep.

Late in the afternoon Monique came up with a pitcher of fresh water. There was a disconcerting resignation about the girl. Titus was gone, out of her life forever.

"Young Missy," Monique said gently after a few minutes, "Seth be settin' de table fo' suppuh. Almos' time yo' got downstaihs."

"That's right, Monique. I'll go right down."

Vicky's throat was tight, her hands wet with nervous perspiration as she walked down the corridor toward the drawing room. She could hear Sara talking to Alex about his accident.

"How could you have been so careless? That must have been a dreadfully deep cut."

"It was," Alex said. "If Betsy had not been so quick, I might have bled to death. Right away she sent Cyrus for Mama LaVerne."

"Betsy should have sent for the doctor," Bart said brusquely. "You know it's against the law for a slave to treat a white person."

"Bart, don't be absurd," Sara said. "Mama LaVerne has special skills. You see Alex is all right."

"Did you see the new colt, Alex?" Vicky struggled to sound serene. *Where was Michael?*

"Yes," Alex lied. "He's a marvelous animal."

"Oh, Vicky, I forgot to tell you," Bart said with sudden

recall. "Michael came home this afternoon to pack a few clothes. He had to go to Baton Rouge on business."

"Why didn't he tell me?" Sara asked with reproach. "Suddenly no one tells me anything."

"Michael came to my room to tell me because he knows I'm awake in the afternoon—just as he knows that the ladies of the house are napping."

"When will he be back?" Vicky asked.

"Three or four days," said Bart. "Something to do with a case he's handling."

Ava sauntered into the room in a resplendent gown, wearing some of the paste jewelry she said she'd had made up to replace what she had sold to remain in Europe. Bart lifted an eyebrow.

Vicky saw the fleeting visual clash between Ava and Alex as Sara told her about Alex's "accident." Ava was startled, unsure of herself. She took refuge in bravado.

"We've had some excitement at Eden," Ava drawled. "Alex almost bleeds to death and Titus runs away."

"When did that happen?" Alex fought for control.

"We discovered he was missing yesterday afternoon," Bart said. "That's what happens when you're too good to a slave."

"We've got advertisements in all the newspapers," Sara added. "But somehow, I doubt that we'll ever see him again."

"Fifteen hundred to write off," Bart grumbled. "In a bad year."

"How was Betsy's father?" Sara asked Alex. "I haven't seen him for almost a week."

"He was down in New Orleans," Alex explained after a pause. "He's due back today."

"Alex, you stayed at the house when Joshua was away?" Sara reproached.

"Her mother was there," Alex said defensively.

"Alex, you know her mother's condition," Sara was upset.

"Mama, the house was full of servants," Alex said patiently. "It was perfectly proper."

"I think I'll send Seth over to ask Joshua and Betsy

over for supper tomorrow evening," Sara decided. "It's been weeks since they've visited."

"That's a fine idea," Ava approved, and Sara stiffened. "Poor Joshua. It must be so lonely for him with Madeline in that condition. I don't know how he's borne it all these years."

Both Bart and Sara were pleased at the way Betsy and Alex seemed absorbed with each other the following evening. Sara was upset, though, by Ava's overt attentions to Joshua when they left the dining table and settled themselves in the drawing room.

Vicky felt an aching loss at Michael's absence. She sat with a set little smile on her face while Bart and Joshua discussed the first of the debates between the lawyer named Lincoln and Senator Douglas of Illinois, which had caused such a furor in the newspapers.

Vicky was relieved when Betsy and her father left for the evening and she could go to her room. For hours she sat by the window, gazing out into the night. Michael had left Eden because of her. What would happen when he returned? Would he order her to leave? Not if he knew the truth, she thought with agonizing certainty. But she could not tell him without betraying Alex.

In the morning, Vicky came downstairs to hear Sara sending Colin in to the town house.

"Colin should be there in case Michael returns from Baton Rouge early," Sara said, eyes resting curiously on Vicky. "You miss him," she said with quiet surprise.

"Yes," Vicky whispered.

Somehow, Vicky decided with rash determination, she would make Michael understand what had happened in that shack near the quarters. She must do this without violating Alex's confidence.

The hours dragged now as she waited for Colin to return from the city with Michael.

She made the pretense of napping, but at regular intervals she left the bed to stand by the window to watch for Michael's return. Earlier than usual, too restless to remain in her room, she dressed and went downstairs again, to sit on the gallery and wait.

Sam began to bark. Vicky rose eagerly to her feet. Someone was coming up the roadway.

"Is that Michael?" Sara came through the door with a glow of anticipation.

"Yes." Vicky was radiant. For the first time, she realized, her mother-in-law was sure she was in love with Michael.

The carriage pulled up before the house. Vicky darted down the steps as Colin leaped down from the box. But he was not opening the door.

"Mist' Michael, he back from Baton Rouge, but he say he stay in Noo Awleans fo' anothuh day or two," Colin explained politely, including Sara and Vicky in this message. "He say Emile bring him home when he ready."

"Thank you, Colin," Sara said, smiling to mask her disappointment. Without understanding, Vicky thought, she was apprehensive about Michael's absence.

Vicky left the gallery to walk toward the river. She started at the sound of footsteps behind her. Ava.

"Michael may never come back," Ava told her with a wise smile. Vicky stared at her. What was the matter with Ava? There was an odd exhilaration about her.

"Why shouldn't Michael come back?" Vicky whispered.

"The past is catching up with him," Ava said. "He remembers too much." Her eyes closed for a moment. When she opened them again, she smiled brilliantly. "He's been terrified since the moment I stepped off the ship from Europe. He can't forget what his father said to him when he caught Michael, fourteen to my twenty, in bed with me. You didn't know, did you? I was Michael's first lover. I taught him. And his father came in, while we lay there together, and screamed about our incestuous relationship. 'You'll pay!' he shrieked at Michael. 'Lying with your aunt!' He quoted Leviticus. Bart has a strange affection for the Bible at times. 'You'll be cursed all of your days,' he prophesied. And Michael believed him!"

Vicky swayed with shock. So much was clearer to her

now. She understood now the words that had seemed so inscrutable before. Liliane's dying, her losing the baby— the curse, Michael believed, that lay over him for incestuous acts with his aunt. As with Alex and Janine. But he had been a child. Ava had seduced him. Michael was not to blame.

"Do you still want to sleep with a man who was his aunt's lover?" Ava taunted.

Wordlessly Vicky spun about and ran toward the house.

Inside, she forced herself to seek out Sara.

"Mrs. Eden," she said, struggling to keep her voice even, "I'd like to go into New Orleans. May Seth drive me into the city?"

Sara inspected her gravely. For the first time since she had arrived at Eden, Vicky felt a closeness to her mother-in-law. Whatever was wrong between her and Michael, Vicky realized, his mother was anxious to see adjusted.

"Of course, Vicky. You go upstairs and get ready. I'll send Seth for the carriage."

"Thank you," Vicky said softly.

She was going to Michael. Somehow, she must make him understand he was wrong about her and Alex. She must make Michael trust her. If she could not, then she must leave Eden.

If she remained—and it was terrifying to think of being away from Michael—then she must convince him that he was not cursed, that he was free to love.

31 ❧

Dusk was embracing the city as the carriage arrived on Chartres Street. Vicky leaned forward impatiently. They were approaching the town house now. The chandelier in the dining room was lighted. Michael must be having his supper.

Seth drove in through the carriageway. Before he could leap down to open the door, she had opened it herself and was running up the stairs to the front entrance.

"Good evening, Young Missy," Emile greeted her, trying to conceal his surprise at her arrival. "Mist' Michael, him be at suppuh. Me tell Georgette to sen' in anothuh plate."

"Thank you, Emile," she said, managing a smile. Then she hurried down the hallway to the dining room.

Michael glanced up in astonishment.

She hovered uncertainly in the doorway. "Michael, I had to come."

"Sit down, Vicky. You haven't had supper, have you?"

"No," she said unsteadily. "Emile is going to tell Georgette."

"Oyster soup tonight. You know Georgette's oyster soup?"

"Everything Georgette prepares is marvelous." Must they go through all this small talk? But no, don't rush in with what she had to say to him—Michael was so un-

272

comfortable with her. "Was the trip to Baton Rouge worthwhile?"

"Yes." His face lighted. "I was following a lead for Dean Foster. You know the man on trial for flogging his slave to death?"

"Yes," Vicky said quickly.

"He had similar trouble in Baton Rouge. He was cleared, though many people were indignant. It should be an important point in the trial here."

"Were you able to get written affidavits?" she asked. "Something you can take into court?"

Michael smiled faintly. Some of his legal language had seeped through into her.

"I've come back with a file full of evidence on the Baton Rouge case. It should be dynamite."

Emile arrived with a plate of oyster soup, which Vicky ate without tasting it.

Not until Emile had served them their brandied peaches and coffee was Vicky able to muster the courage to try to talk to him.

"Michael, I have to explain—"

"You have nothing to explain," Michael interrupted.

"That's not true. You walked into a situation that appeared different from what it was. Alex—" She hesitated, groping for words. "Alex was in some—some difficulty. I can't tell you what, Michael, without betraying his confidence. He—it's all right now—but he'll have to tell you when he's ready." She hesitated again. "I feel very close to Alex, but only as his sister-in-law. Nothing more, Michael. Believe me. I was acting as Alex's friend."

"Vicky—" Michael leaned forward. "I should have known."

"Mist' Michael." Vicky started at the untimely interruption. Emile's voice was grave. "Andrew come down f'om Eden. Him wish to speak to yo'."

Michael was annoyed at the intrusion, but aware that Andrew's presence could not be ignored.

"Tell Andrew to come in," Michael ordered briskly. Fleetingly his eyes met Vicky's again, knowing she shared his concern.

Andrew hurried into the room with an air of apology.

"Mist' Bart say, please to come home rat away. Dey be some bad trouble at de Fremont plantation."

Michael pushed back his chair. "Andrew, what happened?"

"Ah not exackly sho', Suh," he said unhappily. "Ah think deah be an uprisin'."

"You'd better stay here, Vicky."

"Michael, no!" She stood up. "Please, let me go home with you."

"Vicky, there might be trouble."

"Michael, I want to be with you." She moved to stand beside him.

Michael hesitated, then turned again to Andrew.

"What's happening at Eden, Andrew?"

"No trouble at Eden, Suh," Andrew said with faint reproach, " 'ceptin' Mist' Bart, he got hisself all upset. Him and Mist' Alex brought out dey guns and dey be settin' out on de gallery. But nuthin's gonna happen at Eden. Dey's nevuh been trouble at Eden."

"Vicky, who brought you in tonight?" Michael asked.

"Seth."

"Andrew, tell Seth to stand by to follow us back to Eden. Tell him to stick close to us—is that clear?"

"Yessuh."

Within minutes they were in the carriage. There had been talk, from time to time, about uprisings in the South, yet they had seemed far removed. Ben had talked once about a woman who had been murdered by her own slaves; but who could look at the Eden slaves and even consider such an act?

"Michael—" Vicky turned to him worriedly when they had left the city and were driving as swiftly as the horses could manage through the fragrant night. "What do you suppose happened at the Fremont plantation?"

"I don't want to guess," Michael admitted uneasily. "Uprisings are what most Southern planters dread. But there won't be any trouble at Eden," he promised. "You don't have to worry about that."

"I know," Vicky said quickly.

"Nobody is afraid of their own Negroes. We worry about the neighbors' slaves. I wouldn't be afraid to stay alone at Eden if there were no other white person for forty miles around. At Eden I feel as safe as I would in the Tower of London."

"But something happened at the Fremont plantation," Vicky reminded him.

"I suspect that the relationship between the Fremonts and their slaves is not what it is between most Southern families and their Negroes," Michael said bluntly. "You've met the Fremonts. There've been no truly bad insurrections in the South since 1823. Year before last rumors were all over the South about plotted slave uprisings. Most of them were false. But because of those rumors a lot of innocent Negroes were killed. The fear of uprisings is what brought on the laws in most Southern states against teaching slaves to read and write. So they won't be able to understand the abolitionist literature."

Michael turned earnestly to talk about Dean Foster's case—talking, she suspected to allay her fears.

"Incidents like what happened tonight at the Fremont plantation," Michael acknowledged unhappily, "make it harder to bring a guilty white to justice."

Vicky felt an unfamiliar alarm as they turned off the road into the driveway that led up to the big house.

As they rolled to a halt, Vicky saw Bart, a shotgun across his lap, sitting in his wheelchair on the gallery beside Sara. Alex sat on the steps, a gun beside him, in somber conversation with Jack Lamartine.

"Did you see anything on the road?" Bart demanded as Michael ran up the steps.

"Not a sign of anything. What happened?"

"Sixteen black bastards plundered the Fremont house, that's what happened," Bart said harshly. "Their own field hands. Mr. Fremont is in Biloxi on business. They badly beat up Mary Fremont, violated the younger daughter, and escaped with all the silver, cash, and guns."

"Alex and I ought to join in the hunt for them," Michael said reluctantly.

"No," Sara objected. "As close as we are to the Fremont plantation, I want you here until the slaves are captured. You can't leave your father and three women alone here."

"There's been no real trouble in this area for years," Jack said somberly.

"I can't believe it!" Sara shuddered. "Mary beaten up that way. And that poor girl——"

"It could happen to any of us," Bart said brutally.

"No, Sir," Michael contradicted. "It happened to the Fremonts because of the way they treat their slaves. I've heard sorry tales about that."

"That's true enough," Jack said firmly. "Mary Fremont may not mean what she says, but she threatens her slaves something awful. And from time to time they have overseers who're too quick to use the whip."

"We spoil our slaves and they run away," Bart said bitterly. "Not a word yet on that damned Titus. God knows what kind of inflammatory talk he was circulating among the others. You never know what they're thinking —any of them. I wouldn't trust a one of them—not even little Jefferson—any further than I can throw a stick."

"Don't worry about Titus." Only now did the others realize Ava stood in the doorway. "He was arrogant. He figured he was too good to be a slave. He didn't bother with the others."

"We've got a four-hundred-dollar reward out for him," Bart shot back maliciously. "Somebody's going to turn him in."

"They won't," Ava said flatly. "You'll see."

Alex's eyes settled on the distant view, his face set. Ava smiled in amusement.

"Insurrections aren't new to the South, remember," Bart said with contempt. "Way back at the end of the last century there were those horrible massacres of the whites by the black slaves of Santo Domingo. Then five years later, right in Richmond, they discovered a slave plot to destroy the city. That's when Richmond set up a small standing army to protect the capital city. And then in 1822, in Charleston there was that Negro carpenter—he'd

won a fifteen-hundred-dollar lottery and bought his freedom—who organized a conspiracy to take over the city."

"Papa, that was never proved," Michael reminded him.

"Thank God, a slave reported it to his master," Bart
continued, disregarding Michael. "And thirty-five slaves
were hanged and thirty-four deported."

"On the flimsiest of evidence," Michael burst out. "It
was pure hysteria."

"You're going to tell me the Nat Turner Insurrection in
Virginia was hysteria?" Bart challenged. "That was just a
year after the trouble in Charleston. That Turner was
treated too damn well by his master, and what did he do?
Got together a band of slaves and went on a bloody rampage. Drunk on peach and apple brandy from their masters' cellars, they killed over sixty whites."

"And ever since then every time a slave looks cross-
eyed," Alex said dryly, "somebody yells insurrection."

Sara rose resolutely to her feet. "There's no need for
all of us to sit up through the night. Vicky, Ava, let's go
on upstairs and go to sleep. Nothing is going to happen at
Eden. We're perfectly safe."

"We'll stay here." Bart was enjoying the situation,
Vicky thought. He would find savage pleasure in shooting
down a slave. "If anybody shows up, they'll have a welcoming committee."

"Nancy's sleeping in my room," Sara said as she
walked with Vicky and Ava up the stairs. "She's got a
club beside her pallet, determined to protect me against
any invasion."

"Nothing's going to happen," Ava said, bored. "Those
slaves are probably miles away by now." She stifled a
yawn. "What's Jack doing here?" she asked curiously.

"I sent for him," Sara admitted. "I wanted him to be
sure he'd made a head count tonight."

"Has he had any word from Claudine?"

"Nothing," Sara said tightly.

But he knew, Vicky remembered, that Claudine had
gone off with Jeanne Coligny. Perhaps they would go up
to Claudine's beloved Quebec City. How strange, Vicky

thought, if Claudine and Jeanne went to a country where any slave could be absolutely sure of freedom.

Vicky allowed Monique, obviously frightened by the news of the nearby insurrection, to sleep on a pallet in her room. Perspiration dampened Vicky's forehead. Outside the netting a mosquito buzzed annoyingly. From the gallery, where a relieving breeze from the river could be felt, drifted up a quiet hum of voices.

Too restless to remain in bed, checking first to make sure Monique was sleeping soundly, Vicky arose, pulled on a dressing gown, and with infinite quietness left the room.

Michael glanced up questioningly as she pushed open the front door.

"Is it hot indoors?" he asked sympathetically.

"Rather," she admitted. "I couldn't sleep anyway."

"We're taking turns prowling the grounds with the dogs," Michael said. "Jack's off with them now."

"Vicky, go out to the kitchen and wake up somebody to make us a pot of coffee," Bart ordered. "If I have any more bourbon, I'll fall asleep right here."

"I'll go with you," Alex offered quickly, then hesitated, his eyes settling anxiously on Michael.

"Go on with her," said Michael. "Jack should be back anytime. I'll have to go out with the dogs."

Vicky sensed that Alex wanted to talk to her, and she busied herself with the coffee makings.

"Alex, it's all right with Michael and me," she told him with a reassuring smile. "I told him nothing," she added hastily, because Alex stared at her with alarm. "But he trusts me." He loved her, she thought with exultation.

"Vicky, I asked Betsy to marry me." Alex's voice was edged with desperation. "She turned me down. Not because of Titus. She made that clear. But she insisted she could never marry me. Why, Vicky? I know she loves me. She didn't deny that when I asked her."

"I don't know, Alex. Perhaps she wants a little time."

"Vicky, she said she could never marry me," Alex emphasized. "I have to know why. Will you talk to her? Vicky, please."

"All right, Alex," Vicky promised.

"Tomorrow?" He pinned her down.

"Tomorrow."

32

Although she slept only in snatches during the night, Vicky was wide awake when Monique came upstairs again to see if she was ready for her breakfast tray.

"Me bring yo' tray rat up," Monique said with a wisp of a smile. All the slaves were nervous because of what had happened at the Fremont's plantation, Vicky guessed.

She pulled herself up against the bolster, her mind darting back compulsively to those poignant moments in the dining room in the town house, when she had confronted Michael. If Andrew had not arrived when he did last night, would Michael have acknowledged his love for her?

A few minutes later, Monique elbowed her way through the door with tray in hand.

"De menfolks jes' went off to sleep. Dey been settin' on de gallery all night." Her voice betrayed her unease. "Andrew brung coffee fo' dem afo' dey went up to sleep. Nobody come to say nuthin' yet about dem bad slaves." She hesitated. "Missy, dey ketch Titus yet?"

"No, Monique," Vicky said gently. "I don't think they ever will." Monique was relieved.

As soon as she had eaten, Vicky rose and dressed. She had promised Alex she would talk to Betsy today. The sixteen slaves who had escaped would be in hiding in daylight, if they were not already many miles away. There was no reason why she could not go over to Harris Acres.

Vicky hesitated in the doorway to the library. Juno started at the sound of her voice.

"I thought I'd go over to visit with Betsy," Vicky said selfconsciously. "Since Michael is sleeping, would it be all right for Colin to take me over there?"

"This morning?" Sara frowned with reproach.

"It's important," Vicky said. "I promised Alex I'd talk to Betsy. They've had a little spat, and Alex is upset."

"I suppose it's all right in the day," Sara agreed, her eyes lighting at the tender insinuation. "Juno, send somebody out to the stables to tell Colin to bring the carriage over for Miss Vicky."

Vicky instructed Colin to take the shortcut through the fields, which would bring her directly to the stables.

Betsy was there as Vicky had expected.

"I was sure Aunt Sara wouldn't let you out of the house after what happened last night," she said. "I'm so glad you came."

Vicky stood by while Betsy applied salve to the rump of a docile lamb.

"Can we go outside somewhere and talk?" Vicky asked when Betsy had finished.

"All right."

They left the stables and walked toward the river path, away from the slaves pitching hay into the loft.

"Betsy," Vicky said softly. "Alex is terribly unhappy. He's in love with you. He wants to marry you."

Betsy's eyes were dark with anguish.

"Vicky, I told him I can never marry him. He's got to accept that."

"But Betsy, you love him," Vicky protested. She paused a moment. "He says you're willing to forget everything that's happened—"

"I can't forget what has happened to me," Betsy said with painful intensity. "Vicky, how can I marry when my mother is like she is? I don't dare marry. I don't dare have chidren. Can't Alex understand that?"

"Betsy, because your mother is—isn't well, it doesn't mean that you'll be that way too." Vicky's eyes held hers compellingly. "You can't stop living." She searched her mind for words to convince Betsy. "Your mother went through a terrible tragedy."

"Other women face tragedies," Betsy reminded her. "They don't crack. And she wasn't right even before my sisters drowned. I was too young to remember, but Papa admits that. I won't gamble, Vicky. Long ago I swore to that."

"You don't know that your mother's condition can be inherited, Betsy," Vicky reproached. "Talk to your doctor."

"I have talked to him." Betsy's face was pale. "He said there's no way of knowing if I would ever be that way too. She was like that when Papa first married her. My grandparents tried to pretend she was all right. And Papa tried to keep it from folks as long as he could—until she got so bad that there was no hiding it."

"Betsy, this seems so wrong." Her heart hurt for Betsy and Alex. "The doctor could be mistaken."

"I can't take that chance; I love Alex too much."

"Betsy, if another doctor—two doctors," she reinforced, "—assure you that your mother's illness can't be inherited, would you marry Alex?"

Betsy hesitated. "I don't know, Vicky. I just don't know. Anyway, in this parish can you find a doctor who would dare to contradict Dr. Mallard?"

Betsy returned to the stables, and Vicky slowly got back into the carriage.

"Colin—" She leaned from the window to talk to him. "Circle around, please, and go up to the Harris house."

There Cyrus told her that Joshua Harris was in the west fields.

"Hit's about twenty minutes drive thataway—" He pointed to a road that cut to the left of the house. "He be deah all mawnin'."

"Thank you, Cyrus." Vicky smiled at him and hurried

down from the gallery. "Colin, take me to the west fields."

Vicky was still astonished at the expanse of the very large plantations such as Eden and Harris Acres. What was it Michael had told her?—that a plantation was not too large to handle as long as no part of the working fields was more than an hour from the slave quarters.

Joshua was with his overseer, inspecting the first cotton of the season. He glanced up with astonishment as the carriage approached and he saw Vicky.

"May I talk to you for a few minutes, Mr. Harris?"

"Certainly, Vicky." He opened the carriage door and helped her down. His eyes were warm, yet she sensed the depth of his concern at her appearance here. He knew she had not come to the fields to pass the time of day.

In a silent pact they walked away from the slaves.

"Have you ever seen cotton being picked?" Joshua asked, giving her time to gear herself for what must be said.

"No, I haven't." She took a deep breath. "Mr. Harris, would you be pleased with Alex as a son-in-law?" she asked without forewarning.

He was startled.

"I would be delighted," he said with conviction.

"Alex asked Betsy to marry him," Vicky rushed on impetuously. "She turned him down, though she admits she's in love with him. Mr. Harris, she's afraid to marry Alex because—because of her mother's illness," she stammered. "She's terrified that someday she'll become ill too."

Joshua paled.

"That's why she's behaved the way she has so long?" he asked unsteadily. "So shy? So afraid to meet young men? My poor little girl." His voice deepened with anguish. "And I never once suspected—"

"Mr. Harris, your family doctor told her there's no way of telling if she'll be that way too. But he could be wrong," Vicky insisted with painful intensity. "If you could find other doctors who could convince Betsy that it won't happen that way—"

"I can do better than that," Joshua said with sudden strength. "Dr. Mallard doesn't know. Nobody outside of Harris Acres has ever known. Betsy is my child. She is not Madeline's child." He took a long, shuddering breath. "Madeline was unstable when we were married. Her parents hid that from me. She was so pretty, so sweet— and I took her heavy silences for shyness. Her parents hoped that marriage would straighten her out. It only made her worse. I hired a white nurse from up North to come and take care of Madeline after the two little girls were born. Anne was—she was special. A sweet Irish girl who was wonderful to Madeline and who adored the children. It was terribly lonely here for both of us; we were drawn together. Anne died when Betsy was born. Nobody outside of Harris Acres knew she was carrying a child. With Madeline's condition what it was, nobody came calling. It was easy to persuade Madeline that the new baby was hers. To the neighbors, Madeline had borne another daughter. I thought I was doing what was best for Betsy to pretend she was Madeline's child. I never realized what that might mean to her."

"Mr. Harris, will you tell Betsy? Will you let her know that she can marry Alex without fear?"

"We'll drive up to the house together," he said decisively. "I'll send to the stables for Betsy. Let her know the whole truth. Let her feel free to go to Alex." He smiled tenderly. "I think Sara will be pleased."

Ava smiled when Patience opened the door to Madeline's room. Patience detested her, she thought with amusement.

"I've come to call on Miss Madeline. How is she feeling today?"

"Lak always," Patience said warily. "She sets deah by de window waitin' fo' dem two little girls to come home."

"Madeline," said Ava. The room, as always, was heavy with the scent of lavender. "I've come calling again."

Madeline turned around eagerly. Once she must have been quite pretty, in a little-girl fashion that brought out Joshua's protective instinct.

"Have you brought me a present?" Madeline leaned forward with childlike anticipation.

"Madeline, darling. I always bring you a present," Ava reproached gently. "Two today."

"Patience, get us tea," Madeline ordered, her eyes fastened to the package Ava was withdrawing from her reticule.

Patience went into the next room, where a small kitchen had long ago been set up to care for Madeline's needs. Often Madeline slept much during the day and had to be served her meals when the others were in bed.

"I've brought you a fan from Spain," Ava said, taking the packet to Madeline and sitting in a tapestry-covered chair beside hers. "I hope you like it." Didn't Joshua realize how absurd it was to be faithful to a woman who could give him nothing?

Madeline impatiently tore away the wrappings of the package and opened it to pull forth the delicately painted fan.

"Oh, it's so pretty," she said delightedly. "I must show it to the girls." Her smile lost some of its luster. "I don't know why they haven't come home already."

"They'll be home soon," Ava soothed. She knew how to play this game. She had been playing it for weeks. "I saw them on the pond as I rode past."

For a moment she feared she had overplayed her hand. Madeline suddenly looked frightened and turned away to the window.

"They were having such a good time, Madeline," Ava said enthusiastically. "They'll tell you all about it when they come home." She waited anxiously. This was no time for Madeline to have one of her hysterical fits. *Not today.* "Will you let them play with the fan, Madeline?"

"Well, I might for a few minutes. They mustn't tear it," she said firmly. The possible return to reality was averted.

Patience brought the tea tray into the room and placed it upon a small table which she drew close to Madeline's rocker.

"I'll pour, Patience," Madeline said gaily. "I promise not to burn myself."

"Patience, would you mind bringing me honey instead of sugar?" Ava asked. "It's a habit I've just acquired."

"Yessum," Patience said unsmilingly. It was strange, thought Ava, how Patience distrusted her. It must be that she was jealous because Madeline liked her.

Ava waited until Patience had gone into the adjoining room for the honey, then leaned forward with a conspiratorial smile.

"I have another little present," she whispered, a hand moving swiftly into her reticule. "But it must be our secret. It's a special medicine Mama LaVerne gave me that will make you very happy. I take it all the time." She pulled forth the stopper from the tiny vial and poured its contents into Madeline's tea. "I had mine earlier. Now I feel happy, as if the whole world were just perfect."

"I don't know if I'll like it," Madeline said—doubtfully, yet wishing to please Ava.

"Here, let me take the first sip." Madeline lifted the dainty, hand-painted porcelain cup to her mouth. "It tastes delicious. And in a little while, you'll feel just wonderful." Not Mama LaVerne, but Mama Daphne had supplied her with the contents of the vial. Claudine had introduced her to the strange medicine. What a beautiful feeling they had experienced! Its effect was nothing like that of the opium or morphine she took occasionally for headaches. It was as if the whole world became more beautiful. Colors more intense. Music more exciting.

"It tastes good." Madeline was relieved that this was not an unpleasant potion.

"Drink it all down," Ava coaxed.

Patience returned with the honey, and Ava gaily asked about the cookies that Elvira usually sent up for them.

"Ah don' have none up heah," Patience said. "Ah brung pralines."

She headed toward the adjoining room. Ava wistfully pantomimed her disappointment.

"Patience, go downstairs and get them," Madeline insisted. "The ones with the walnuts on top."

"I'll stay with Missy," Ava said.

Reluctantly Patience left the room. Ava drained her teacup.

"Madeline, you haven't finished your tea," said Ava. This would work as she planned! "That's it. Drink it all down."

"See. Every drop." Triumphantly Madeline held out her teacup.

Now, Ava urged herself. Quickly. While Patience was gone.

"Madeline—" She rose to her feet and walked to the open French windows that led to the small upstairs gallery. "Madeline, I do believe I hear the girls! Madeline, I think the girls are coming home!"

"You hear them?" Madeline rose to her feet. "Oh, I feel so strange. So light—"

"Come over to the window and watch for the girls," Ava repeated. "They're coming, Madeline. See? There they are."

Unsure of her footing, Madeline moved to the window and stepped out onto the gallery.

"Where are they? I don't see them."

"Madeline, look hard," Ava ordered. "Lean over the railing a little and you'll see them. There they come with their nurse!"

"Where?" Her voice rose to a frenzy. "Where are they? Where are my little girls?"

"Down below, Madeline!" Ava insisted savagely. "Don't you see them? Bend over the railing!" With Mama Daphne's drug taking effect, Madeline had no sense of balance. Lean over now, Ava thought earnestly, before Patience returns.

"Madeline!" Joshua's agonized voice rose from below. "Oh, God, no!"

Her heart pounding, triumph an ugly glow in her eyes, Ava stepped back into the room, turning about to make the pretense of crying out for Patience. But Patience stood there. A kitchen knife was in her hand, upraised.

"Ah seen yo' put dat medicine in her tea," Patience said with cold rage. "Mama Daphne's medicine, what sen's folks outta dey minds!"

"It was something to make her feel better," Ava insisted, fighting off panic. Where was Joshua? Why wasn't he coming into the house? "I didn't know that she was going to hallucinate, that she was going out onto the gallery to look for the girls—"

"Yo' sen' her out deah! Mah po' li'l baby." Her eyes were filled with grief. "Yo' kill mah po' li'l baby."

"No! No!" Ava screamed as Patience lunged toward her with the kitchen knife. She felt the terrible pain in her breast. "No! No!"

It wasn't supposed to happen this way.

33

The air was humid, cloyingly sweet with the scent of late-summer blossoms. Vicky stood pale and shaken beside Joshua as he hovered over the lifeless body of his wife. The house servants who had heard his outcry gathered in a grief-stricken cluster about him, the massive black woman who had been the laundress at Harris Acres when Madeline came here as a bride wailing inconsolably.

"Dat po' li'l baby! How come she do dat? Mah po' li'l baby." She rocked back and forth, tears streaming down her face.

"Why was she left alone to do this?" Joshua stumbled to his feet, his grief seeking relief in anger. "Why wasn't Patience with her?"

"Mist' Eden, come quick!" A scared servant leaned over the railing of the narrow gallery above, over which moments ago Madeline's body had plummeted. "De lady from Eden. She bin kilt!"

"What's happening here?" Joshua was trying, dazedly, to assimilate the slave's message. "My God, what's happening?"

"Mr. Harris, we'd better go upstairs." Vicky reached out to him, her throat tight with alarm. *The lady from Eden.* It had to be Ava. "Please—" She could not bring herself to go alone into the house.

Joshua took a deep, shuddering breath, fighting to pull himself into control.

"Cyrus—" He laid a hand on Cyrus' quivering shoulders. "See that Missy is brought into the house. Take her to the small sitting room." Joshua was himself again.

Vicky followed at Joshua's heels as he charged up the steps and across the gallery into the house.

A terrified servant hovered at an open door. "Her daid, Mist' Joshua," she whispered. "Patience do it wit' a kitchen knife."

"Don't go in," Joshua said swiftly to Vicky. "Stay here."

Vicky stood stiffly just outside the door.

"My God!" Joshua gasped. "Ava!"

Vicky hurled herself into the room, then stopped, sickened by the sight of the blood that stained the front of Ava's dress.

"Mr. Harris, who did these things?" Vicky whispered.

"Ah kill her." The voice was contemptuous. Vicky's gaze swung around to settle on Patience, who stood against a wall, the knife at her feet. "She kill mah Missy. She put bad medicine in de tea, and den she tell Missy de li'l girls, dey come. 'Lean ovuh,' she say. An' she say it again—knowin' Missy not in huh rat mind—till Missy fall over dat railin'. Ah come back too late to stop, but Ah see!" Her voice was suddenly strong with rage. "Ah heah what she say, an' Ah see Missy fall." Suddenly Patience was wailing uncontrollably.

"Elizabeth, take care of her," Joshua ordered, and

turned with poignant helplessness to Vicky. "How can I tell Sara what has happened?"

"I'll tell her," Vicky promised with a strength she had not thought she possessed. "Please, let me return to Eden before—before Ava's body is brought home."

"I'll have to send for Betsy." Joshua fought for composure. "On a day that could have been so happy for her Betsy must hear this."

Vicky hurried to where Colin waited for her, his face anxious.

"Miss Ava is dead," she said quietly. "I must go home and tell the family." This was not real; it was a nightmare.

Vicky leaned back in the carriage, remembering what Claudine Lamartine had said those many months ago, when she had first arrived at Eden. *You do not know what goes on behind the walls of that beautiful house that sits so elegantly up there by the river. The curse that lies over it.*

"Socrates, where is Miss Sara?" Vicky asked breathlessly as she strode into the house.

"In de lib'ary, Young Missy."

At the door, Vicky paused.

"Mrs. Eden—"

Sara looked up from the books knowing instantly that something awful had happened.

"Vicky, what is it?" She rose from her chair.

"Ava." Haltingly, without sparing Ava, Vicky told her first of Madeline's death, then of Ava's. Not until she finished did she realize that Bart had wheeled himself into the doorway directly behind her.

"Good God, Sara, when will it end?" he said.

Sara stood, silent and ashen, behind the desk, leaning on its top for support.

"I never should have brought Ava home. None of this would have happened. Poor Joshua. How will I ever face him again?"

"Sara, you are not responsible for the whole world," Bart said impatiently.

"My fault," Sara insisted stubbornly. "Madeline would be alive if I had not brought Ava back from Paris. Ava would be alive." She shook her head in disbelief. "My little sister. Dead. I remember Ava at our wedding—the most beautiful young girl that ever lived."

"Ava was evil," Bart said bluntly. "From childhood she was bad. A bad seed, spoiled by your father. It's over, Sara," he said dryly. "You'll never have to worry again about Ava."

In front of the house a wagon pulled to a stop. Without being on the gallery, Vicky knew. Princess Ava Radzinski had come home for the last time.

Monique came into Vicky's bedroom and inspected her anxiously beneath the netting. Vicky turned around with a forced smile.

"I'm not sleeping, Monique."

"Hit's time to go downstaihs fo' suppuh," she said.

"All right, Monique. I'll get right up."

How strange to go downstairs for supper when tragedy hung over the house. Michael and Alex must have been told by now. They had still been asleep when Sara had sent her up to bed, belatedly stricken with an alarming trembling. Something in the tea that Monique brought to her had made her sleep. She shuddered. Something in Madeline's tea had sent her to her death.

In a haze of unreality Vicky allowed Monique to help her dress and went downstairs to the dining room. Bart's chair was already positioned at the table. One hand clutched a water tumbler half-filled with bourbon and ice. Sara stood before the cabinet that held her glassware, as though completely absorbed in appreciation. But her hands shook precariously.

"Have you told Michael and Alex?" Vicky asked.

"Two hours ago," Sara said. "Alex went directly to Harris Acres to be with Betsy." Sara's eyes were pained. Despite Madeline's state of mind, Betsy had been devoted to her. "Michael went into New Orleans with Ava's body. He's arranging for the funeral."

"It will have to be tomorrow because of the heat," said

Bart, deliberately callous. "There'll be no time to send for relatives."

"Artemis," Sara called sharply. "Tell Juno we're ready to sit down to supper if everything is prepared."

Sara and Vicky joined Bart at the table.

"Why the devil does Juno serve pork so damned much in the summer?" Bart complained as the roast was brought to the table.

"You were carrying on about being tired of chicken and lamb," Sara reminded him abstractedly. "There's probably more red snapper out in the kitchen if you want it."

"Never mind," he said testily. "I'll do with this."

Vicky wished desperately that Michael were home. She'd had no chance to speak with him alone since Andrew had arrived at the town house with word of the insurrection.

Poor Michael, again attending to funeral arrangements.

She glanced out the window. Rain before the night was over, judging from the way the sky looked right now. Tomorrow they would go into New Orleans for Ava's funeral. Would she be taken to the St. Louis Cemetery, where Janine was buried?

"They'll probably bury Madeline in the family plot near the house," Bart said calmly. "Harrises have been buried there for five generations. It's high enough there to put them into the ground."

Sara flinched.

"Have you heard anything about the Fremont slaves?" Deliberately she was rechanneling the conversation. "Have any of them been caught?"

Bart glanced up from his roast pork.

"I thought you knew. Charlie stopped by earlier. He said an even dozen of them were caught. Fremont's got them down in the New Orleans Calaboose for flogging. Said he didn't trust his overseer or driver with the whip—they might kill the lot of 'em before they go on trial. Caught 'em no more than eleven miles away."

Vicky and Sara remained at the table while Bart took himself a second helping of pie.

"You don't have to sit here with me," he said calmly. "Go on into the drawing room. It's cooler." He waved them away impatiently.

In the drawing room Sara stood before the oil painting of Ava that hung over the fireplace.

"I never dreamt it would end this way," she said with pain. "I never should have brought her back from Europe," she reiterated. "None of this would have happened."

"You had no way of knowing," Vicky said gently. Then suddenly both she and Sara were listening to sounds outside. "Somebody's coming. Perhaps it's Michael."

Vicky ran eagerly from the drawing room and down the hall toward the door. Socrates was already there. He pulled the door wide to admit Joshua, pale and drawn.

"Good evening, Socrates. Will you please ask Mrs. Eden if she will see me?"

"How is Betsy?" Vicky moved toward him as Socrates passed her en route to the drawing room.

"Mourning her mother. Madeline will always be her mother, though I've told her the truth."

"Joshua—" Sara appeared in the doorway. "Oh, Joshua, how can I face you?" Her voice broke. "They told me what Ava did—"

"Sara, you were not your sister's keeper," he said sternly. "I came here to talk to you about the funeral arrangements. I'd like us to be together at both burials." His eyes were infinitely tender as they rested on her. He knew, Vicky thought as tears filled her own eyes, that Sara desperately needed this support from him. "If you're burying Ava in the morning, then we'll lay Madeline to rest in the afternoon. You were Madeline's friend all these years," he said huskily. "Only you bothered to call on her."

Ava called, Vicky thought unhappily. Ava, with such an evil motive.

"Michael has gone into New Orleans to make the arrangements. Michael is my strength." Her eyes turned to Vicky with new recognition. "Michael and Vicky."

"I'll stay with you awhile," Joshua said. "Betsy is all right. Alex is with her."

"Come into the drawing room." Sara gazed about for one of the twins. "Athena, go out to the kitchen and tell Juno to send in cake and coffee."

They looked at each other with such intense longing, Sara and Joshua, that Vicky felt herself an intruder. Bart would linger forever in the dining room. Let her leave them alone in this painful moment.

"I'm going up to my room," Vicky said. "I didn't sleep much last night."

In the foyer she paused. Suddenly feeling a need for fresh air, she walked out onto the gallery and gazed up at the threatening sky. Clumps of black clouds obliterated the moon and stars: a storm on the way for sure. Let it not rain tomorrow, she prayed, remembering the chill drizzle when they had stood before the tomb where Janine had been laid to rest.

Sam trotted up the steps to thrust his silken head beneath her hand.

"Let's go for a walk, Sam," she said. No need to worry about the slaves who had escaped from the Fremont plantation. A dozen had been captured and the other four were far away.

She walked swiftly along the edge of the river, aware of the sharp drop in temperature. The Mississippi was rough tonight, devoid of traffic except for one small craft in a rush to arrive at the harbor. An occasional clap of thunder echoed around her as she and Sam walked away from the house.

Suddenly, without warning, a torrential downpour began, drenching her in moments.

"Sam, back to the house," she ordered breathlessly. "Come on!"

She arrived at the gallery wet to the skin. Sam took refuge behind the row of rockers, grunting his reproach when Vicky deserted him to go into the house.

She hurried upstairs to her room. Monique was there, determined to sleep in the room until every Fremont slave was captured.

"Missy, yo' all wet," she scolded. "Git outta dem clothes fo' yo' ketch yo' death."

Vicky was about to put on her nightdress when she heard Michael arriving downstairs. Trembling she allowed Monique to help her into another dress and dry shoes.

"Missy, yo' done kotch a cold," she reproached when Vicky sneezed. "How come yo' go out in de rain?"

"It wasn't raining when I went out."

"But it was nighttime."

"I won't go out again this late," Vicky promised. "Not until the runaways are caught."

She hurried downstairs to the drawing room, her face alight because she heard Michael's voice—her husband talking with an air of urgency.

"There's no doubt about it, Sir. Patience was provoked."

"How can you stand there and talk about the black bitch who killed your aunt as though she deserved our sympathy? Have you lost your senses?"

"I talked to Patience and I talked to Mama Daphne." Michael was forcing himself to speak without emotion. "Jack brought Mama Daphne to his cottage so I could question her. She admitted she gave Ava the drug. Something she's frequently used in voodoo rites. She had no idea what Ava meant to do with it. She and Claudine were in the habit of taking it with their tea. But Ava gave it to Mrs. Harris so that she could—" He paused with a look of apology for Joshua. "So she could persuade Mrs. Harris to lean too far over that railing. Papa, that was murder—no matter how much we try to tell ourselves anything else."

"Michael," Sara protested, "I know what an awful thing Ava did—I won't ever understand it—but how can you defend in court a slave who killed your aunt?"

"I have to defend her," Michael insisted. "But for Ava she would not be in jail."

"No court in the land will free her," Bart said with contempt.

"I have to try," Michael said stubbornly as Vicky tried

to smother a sneeze. "Mr. Harris, she's your slave. May I have your permission to defend her?"

"God help her, she'll need everything you can do for her," Joshua said slowly. "Yes, help Patience. She was devoted to Madeline."

Vicky tried, again, to smother a sneeze.

"You're catching a cold," said Michael. "Were you out in this rain?"

"I walked a bit along the river. With Sam," she added.

"Vicky, how could you?" His voice was sharp with alarm. "You know four of the Fremont slaves are still on the loose!"

"I'm sorry, Michael." Vicky smiled. "I didn't think."

"You're not to go out after dark again."

"Send Monique downstairs to fix you a cup of hot milk and rum," Sara ordered. "That'll give you a good night's rest. And you mustn't go into New Orleans tomorrow."

Vicky fell asleep with the knowledge that Monique hovered anxiously over her, feeling her forehead to make sure she was not running a fever. All this fuss over a slight cold. But Michael's genuine concern had filled her with pleasure.

She awoke many hours later with a guilty sense of having overslept. Monique stood by a window, gazing down below.

"Is the rain over?" Vicky asked, and Monique swung about with a smile.

"Hit stop in de middle o' de night," she reassured Vicky. "Sun's ashinin' and evuht'ing smells so good." She sniffed appreciatively. That lush morning-after-the-rain scent, Vicky thought. She was glad it would not be raining when Michael went with the family to lay Ava's body to rest.

"Me go git yo' breakfas'," Monique said. "Yo' don' move from dat bed."

"I feel fine," Vicky said. "Has the family left for New Orleans yet?"

"No, Missy, but dey be leavin' soon." Monique moved toward the door.

All at once the horror of yesterday was back with her. She saw Ava's inert body, blood-spattered, laying on the floor of Madeline's room. She heard Patience's voice. And here she lay in bed, removed from the grief that afflicted the family. For what comfort she might offer, she ought to be with Michael.

"I should dress and go with them." She made a move to throw aside the counterpane.

"Mist' Michael, him say no," Monique objected. "Him say, 'Monique, you keep Young Missy in bed all day.'"

"All right, Monique," Vicky capitulated with a faint smile.

She sat in bed, eating without tasting, listening to the sounds outside. Bart was on the gallery, scolding Sam and Hilda, who had chased after a squirrel.

"Sara!" he bellowed. "What the devil's taking you so long? Michael and Alex are waiting for you." Bart would not go to the cemetery either.

"We have plenty of time." Sara's strained voice rose up to Vicky's room. "Besides, we have to wait for Joshua and Betsy. I sent Socrates for them."

"They're coming now," Michael called.

Vicky's heart pounded at the sound of Michael's voice.

"Missy, eat," Monique said with mock ferocity. "Juno, her be mad iffen me bring back evuht'ing."

Vicky listened to the somber greetings as Joshua and Betsy arrived to join the family. Socrates was driving on the long trip to the cemetery. He had known Ava as a small girl.

"Andrew!" Bart called sharply as the others drove away. "Bring me a bourbon."

Vicky awoke from a three-hour nap with a start. She thrust aside the counterpane, lifted the netting, and darted to the window. Her eyes clung to the view below. Why were the servants running away from the house?

Vicky reached for her dressing gown and pulled it on as she rushed toward the door, which she fearfully cracked open.

"No! No!" Monique shrieked downstairs. "No!"

"Shut up!" Bart yelled at her. "Now get out of here, you black bastards! Before you all get killed!"

Unmindful of danger, Vicky flung the door wide and raced down the stairs and toward the library, from where the clatter came.

"Yo' put down dat gun," a strange deep voice ordered, "or Ah'll cut yo' heart out and shove it up yo' ass!"

"You don't threaten me!" Bart bellowed belligerently, and Vicky froze as two shots rang out. "Now you two, get the hell out of here," Bart ordered hoarsely, "or you'll get the same!"

Vicky ran breathlessly toward the door, arriving as another shot roared out. She hovered there as Bart, his eyes glazed in disbelief, struggled to rise in his wheelchair, then fell over at her feet.

"Missy," Monique whimpered, "dem two from de Fremont place."

Monique pointed to the two tall, swaggering, half-naked slaves who stood across the room. One of them had discovered the gun Alex had left in the desk drawer. He was holding it on Vicky.

34

Vicky pulled her eyes away from the barrel of the gun pointed at her, her mind frenziedly assessing the situation. The Eden slaves were running to the quarters for help.

"Are you from the Fremont plantation?" she asked, ice-cold with terror.

"Dat's rat." The younger one lifted his shoulders warily, his eyes moving nervously to his companion, who held the gun.

"Then you've been on the run for days," she said, as polite as she would have been to a guest taking refuge in a storm. *She mustn't let them know how frightened she was.* "You must be hungry." She turned to Monique, who watched her with consternation. "Monique, go out to the kitchen and bring in food for them." She forced a smile. Her eyes commanded Monique to follow her lead. "There must be half a pork roast out there, and a pecan pie. We hardly touched it at supper last night."

"Shad, you go wit' de gal," the massive black man with the gun ordered brusquely. He was intrigued by Vicky's casualness.

"Bring in the food, Monique," Vicky repeated carefully. She fought off faintness as her eyes unwarily dropped to the inert body of Bart Eden. Was he still alive? She turned to the slaves again. "You'll find the silver in the dining room." Now her eyes found the pair of bodies sprawled by the window, dead from Bart's bullets. "Shall I show you where?"

"Yeah," the gun-holder drawled. "Show us." The other prodded Monique with a slap. For an instant Monique's eyes flashed defiantly; then she swiftly lowered her lashes and walked from the room and down the hall toward the deserted kitchen.

Carefully Vicky skirted Bart's body. She could do nothing for him.

"The silver is in the sideboard in the dining room. You'll find a tablecloth there to wrap it in."

"Show me," he ordered brusquely.

Vicky walked ahead of him, as coolly as though she were conducting a guided tour.

"I'll lay out what you need for your meal." She made a move to the sideboard.

"Don' yo' staht nothin'," he warned, watching as she reached into the drawer. His eyes were bold with admiration as he settled himself with an air of bravado at the table. "Bring me some whiskey," he ordered with a wide smile that revealed several gaps in his teeth.

"There's bourbon right here," she said politely, still behaving as though he were a guest at Eden.

"Dat's good 'nough," he approved expansively.

Vicky reached into the cabinet to bring out a bottle of Bart's private stock. *Time. Play for time.* Gritting her teeth, she poured bourbon into two goblets. *Get them drunk. So drunk they would collapse at the table.* Where was Jack? *Why didn't he arrive with help?*

"Hey, Jesse, lookit dis!" The other slave stalked into the room with a broad grin, carrying a platter of roast pork in one hand, a carving knife in the other. Vicky suppressed a shudder as he brandished the knife mockingly at Monique.

"The bourbon is the best," Vicky said with pretended pride. "I'm sure you'll like it." Again, she fought against hysteria. "Monique put down the pecan pie."

"Jesse, we cain't stay heah." Shad was suddenly uneasy. "Eat fas' an' git out."

After killing her and Monique?

"Nobody heah but de ol' coot and dis gal. Ah seen dem leave a long time ago. Set down an' eat." He slammed his fist on the table. "Gimme a chunk o' dat roast pohk."

Vicky and Monique stood by while the two slaves ate voraciously. They slugged down the bourbon as though it were water. Without a word Vicky moved forward to refill their glasses. Once. Twice. Three times.

"Hey, Shad!" Jesse banged on the table with his fist as Shad collapsed from the liquor, his hand knocking the beautiful crystal goblet from which he had been drinking to the floor. "Shad, yo' dumb bastid!"

Jesse pushed back his chair and rose to his feet.

"Git out a tablecloth," he ordered Monique as he bent over the other slave. "Fill it up wit' de silvuh."

Monique's eyes swung, terrified, to Vicky.

"Do as he says, Monique." Vicky's voice was faintly unsteady.

"Ah'll git him up in a few minutes," Jesse decided. His eyes settled boldly on Vicky. "Ah guess yo' de prettiest li'l gal Ah ever did see." He strode toward her, his eyes overbright.

"Don' yo' tech Young Missy!" Monique lunged for his arm as he reached to pull Vicky to him. "Don' yo' put yo' hands on my Missy!"

"Monique!" Vicky screamed in anguish as he spun about and swatted her across the side of the head. With a whimper Monique collapsed, unconscious, to the floor.

Vicky reached out in panic for the girandole on the table, grasped it, and held it aloft before her.

"Don't you touch me!"

"Ain't dis 'un got spirit!" Jesse chortled, reaching to wrest the weapon from her hands.

They struggled, Vicky knowing she was helpless but fighting with frenzy. His hands were at her shoulders, ripping her dressing gown. His body, naked to the waist, dripped sweat.

"Take your hands off her!" Michael's voice. Miraculously, Michael's voice.

The slave released her and lunged for Michael. Vicky screamed. Where were the others? Why didn't someone come? He would kill Michael! In a minute he would kill him!

Vicky reached for the gun on the table and pointed it at the slave as he forced Michael back against the wall, his hands at Michael's throat. She couldn't miss him. Not this close.

The bullet was startlingly loud in her ears. She saw the slave stiffen in astonishment. He released his hold on Michael and swung around to face her with a terrible grimace. And then, as the gun fell from her fingers, he dropped to the floor.

"Oh, Michael, Michael!" she sobbed hysterically, conscious of Michael's arms around her. "I killed him! I killed him!"

"You saved my life, Vicky," said Michael. "Another minute and he would have choked the life from me."

"Michael!" It was Jack. "Is she all right?"

"She wasn't touched," Michael reassured him. "Look

to the girl." He pointed to Monique, unconscious on the floor.

Vicky lifted her face to Michael's.

"They're from the Fremont plantation," she whispered. "Both of them." She shivered. "Michael, I shot him."

"He'll live to hang," Jack prophesied, then dropped to his knees beside Monique.

"Is she all right?" Vicky asked anxiously.

"Just stunned. She's coming to already." Jack's eyes moved to Shad, slouched on his face at the table. "What about him?"

"He's drunk," Vicky said. "I kept serving him bourbon." She remembered her father-in-law on the library floor. "Michael, your father," she said urgently. "In the library."

While Jack poured a drink for Monique, Michael charged from the dining room down to the library. Vicky followed him.

"Papa—" With infinite tenderness Michael turned over his father. Bart's eyes gazed sightless at him. "He's dead."

"He took the two other slaves with him," Vicky said. "There, by the window."

Slowly Michael rose to his feet. "Papa died a hero. He would have liked that."

"Where are your mother and Alex?" They would come home from one burial to face another.

"They'll be home a little later. We met some folks in the city. They told us the Fremont slaves had been seen in the neighborhood last night. I was alarmed. I borrowed Ben's rig and hurried home."

"Let me go to Monique," Vicky said unsteadily.

"Vicky!" Michael cried out. For the first time in her life, Vicky collapsed in a faint.

Late-afternoon sunlight spilled over the facade of Eden as the family, along with Betsy and Joshua Harris, returned from burying Bart. Andrew, with infinite solemnity, maneuvered himself down from the box to open the door of the carriage as Sam and Hilda charged forward to welcome them.

"Down, Sam," Michael commanded, but he fondled Sam's head. "Down boy."

"You'll stay for supper," Sara said to Joshua and Betsy. Her face was strained and pale. "I told Juno to be prepared to serve early."

Vicky, with Michael's hand at her elbow, followed Sara down the hallway to the drawing room. Alex and Betsy, along with her father, joined them. Oddly, the house wore the aura of a festive evening. Juno, with Nancy and Odalie helping, had been cooking all day in preparation for the neighbors who would come to pay their respects. Bart Eden had died protecting his plantation.

"All right, Jefferson," Sara said gently as they walked into the room. "You can serve the claret now." His eyes were red from weeping, but his face lighted with a familiar grin when Michael handed him a peppermint.

Vicky turned away from the spot on the rug where Bart's body had lain. Despite Seth's labors, faint bloodstains remained. Don't think about that, she exhorted herself. Think of the days ahead. Everything would be all right for Alex and Betsy. And eventually, when the horror of these last days finally became a memory, Sara and Joshua would find themselves. But how could she convince Michael that no curse lay upon him? That they could live together without fear of imminent tragedy?

"Michael, what do you hear about the debates between that man Lincoln, from Illinois, and Senator Douglas?" Joshua asked, determined to lighten the somberness that pervaded the room.

For a few minutes the conversation was strongly political, until Seth came in to say that Juno was ready to serve. They moved into the dining room. Sara took her customary place at the foot of the table. Joshua sat at her right, with Betsy and Alex beside him. The head of the table remained conspicuously empty.

"Papa showed me a miniature of my mother," Betsy said with affection at a lull in table conversation. "She was so pretty."

"I think it was a mistake that Ava was never told about her real parents," Sara said slowly, "but Papa wanted it that way." A coldness closed in about Vicky. Her eyes darted to Michael, whose gaze fastened on his mother. His face was drained of color.

"Mama, what are you trying to say?" Michael's voice was uneven.

"I can say it now." Sara smiled sadly. "Ava was the child of distant cousins. Her parents died in a tornado in Alabama. Papa and Mama adopted her. She was only a few months old. Papa was a Congressman then—we lived in Washington. Nobody knew, when we returned to Louisiana, that Mama had not given birth to a late second child. Ava never knew."

Vicky's eyes swung to Michael. She saw the relief that washed over him. He was free. No incestuous-relationship had existed between him and Ava. The nightmare was over.

Vicky's hands were clammy. If Michael loved her, nothing stood between them now.

They were still at the table when the neighbors began to arrive. At first they spoke in low voices, acknowledging death. But then they began to partake of the feast prepared and drank Socrates' punch. There was a new serenity in the house, Vicky realized. The anger was gone. It was no longer the house about which Claudine Lamartine had spoken. *You do not know the ugliness of life at Eden, which strangers never see.* The ugliness had been drained away with pain and anguish. Ava and Bart were gone, but the Edens who were alive were free.

Vicky was exhausted, relieved, when the last of the guests had taken their leave, to be able to go to her room. Monique, recovered from her blow on the head, helped Vicky prepare for bed, then went to her pallet in the slave house. No longer did they need to fear runaway slaves.

Vicky lay restless beneath the netting—too tired, too tense for sleep, the awful events of the past days ricocheting in her mind. Poor Michael. What a trial this had been for him.

She started at the knock on her door. What now? she thought with fresh alarm. She reached for her dressing gown, pulling it about her as she darted to the door.

Michael stood before her. His eyes were so eloquent that she trembled.

"Were you asleep?"

"No," she said quickly.

"I couldn't stay alone in my room," he whispered. "It was too achingly empty without you."

"Oh, Michael! Michael!"

Michael was asleep. But even in sleep, she thought with exultation, he clung to her. Her husband. Truly her husband.

Folks talked of bad times coming for the South. Joshua Harris had talked about it tonight. Michael was unhappy at the possibility of a breach with the Union. He would not fight, he reiterated, unless Louisiana itself was invaded and it was necessary to defend his home. But no matter what hardship lay ahead, Vicky thought with certainty, she and Michael could see this through together. Nothing could destroy their union.